MABEL AND THE LITTLE GREEN MEN

Mysteries of Medicine Spring

Book One: Mabel Gets the Ax
Book Two: Mabel Goes to the Dogs
Book Three: Mabel and the Little Green Men

MABEL AND THE LITTLE GREEN MEN

By

Susan Kimmel Wright

DEDICATION

For my agent, Jim Hart, with fond appreciation for his kindness, dedication, and persistence, without which Mabel would not have made the transition from my laptop to the page.

ACKNOWLEDGMENTS

Heartfelt thanks go out to the following:

My patient and encouraging editor, Miralee Ferrell, whose insight has made each and every page better for my readers, and to the dedicated and hardworking team at Mountain Brook Ink.

Lynnette Bonner, who designs such beautiful and eye-catching covers.

My readers, whose love for Mabel and delight in her adventures make writing a joy. I can't adequately express how much I appreciate your kind comments and the many ways you've helped give Mabel and me a boost. Whether through purchasing, sharing, reading, recommending, reviewing and/or rating our books, you've blessed us, and Mabel and I thank you.

My dear family and friends, both human and animal, who unquestioningly support me every day through the good, bad, and ugly.

The ladies of the Second Saturday Christian Writers Group, with special thanks to Valerie Brendel, who has been an insightful and heroic beta reader even under tight time constraints and impending holidays.

Many thanks to my sister Cindy Kimmel, who is always "boots on the ground," spreading the word about this series.

Kika Wright, nonprofit administrator and antiracist educator, for providing a sensitivity review and suggestions as we begin to introduce some of the diverse members of the Medicine Spring community. Anything I may have gotten wrong is entirely my own fault!

As always, "I will give thanks to You, Lord my God, with all my heart, And I will glorify Your name forever." (Psalm 86:12 NASB) I have nothing in this world or the next but what comes through your goodness to me.

Chapter One

A GUST OF WIND ROCKED MABEL'S car as she rounded the bend, skirting an old stone arch bridge, no longer in service but preserved for its historic value. It stood spectral against the dark hemlocks and bare-trunked oaks and maples. To her left stretched fields of corn stubble and hay bales. She glanced at the dash clock and sighed. Already after eleven pm, and she still had another twenty miles to the outskirts of Medicine Spring, and another two from there to home.

The tri-county tourism meeting had run late, due to a long and bitter argument about paying for TV ads. That, and a chairman who didn't—in Mabel's opinion—use the gavel enough.

The historical society members were supposed to take turns attending the monthly tourism meetings, but Mabel suspected she'd be getting the assignment nearly every month. Some of the other members claimed conflicts, and the rest pled cataracts and poor night vision. Mabel, at fifty, was their token young member.

To begin with, she had only joined the society to get experience for the book she was writing—trying to write—for seniors on the joys and satisfactions of volunteering. In less than three months, she'd lost her long-time job as a low-level attorney, launched a new writing career funded by an inheritance from her late grandma—also named Mabel—and a fat settlement from the law firm for age discrimination. Plus, she had gotten herself involved in two murders…or was it six? She wasn't sure how to count them.

It was November now, and the few leaves still clinging to the trees whipped up and down like hands waving. It was dark out here in the countryside, away from the light pollution of the towns. A clear, star-pierced sky showed a near-full moon to good advantage—what Native Americans had called the beaver moon, in honor of the active critters who were getting ready for the coming winter.

Driving along the lonely stretch of road, lit only by the moon and Mabel's headlights, she realized she was getting sleepy. She rolled her window down a crack.

As she climbed the next hill, she gradually became aware of a humming sound. Was it her engine? Mabel's heart sank. The last thing she needed right now—with Grandma's rundown house to fix up, and no job—was car trouble. Let alone, way out here by herself.

At the top of the hill, she reluctantly pulled over. The tires lurched over the grassy verge and when she jerked to a stop, the car tilted to the right. At least, she hadn't rolled into a ditch. The fields fell away to either side now, a ghostly landscape of rolled hay bales wrapped in white plastic that gleamed in the moonlight. Dark stands of trees encircled the distance.

Please don't let this be car trouble. She turned off her engine, praying it would start again.

Still, the humming continued. Mabel patted her phone. It wasn't that either, but the bad news was she also had no signal up here, if she needed help.

Mabel rolled her window the rest of the way down and stuck her head out, looking for power lines. There were wires above her, but they were quiet. Her brain fixated on something else.

In the clear indigo sky, an array of lights sat in a curved formation like a boomerang. What was that constellation? Mabel never found anything but the Big and Little Dippers. Even Orion, which her sister Jen told her was also easy to find, always eluded her.

Or was it a plane? Might that explain the humming?

As she stared in fascination, she realized the lights seemed to have moved closer—much too close for a constellation. Maybe about the altitude of a private plane, with a pilot scanning for a safe landing place like those fields.

The lights now flashed red, white, and amber in a sort of rhythm. *Okay.* Stars definitely did not do that. In fact, she'd never seen a plane do that, either.

As she watched, one of the amber lights broke away and descended in an eye blink, to settle several yards above her car. The humming intensified and seemed to vibrate the car, and Mabel as well.

She jerked her head back inside and ran the window up, but it stopped halfway. The hairs on her arms rose.

The light bathed the car in a warm glow. *It's a drone,* she told herself. *It's just a drone…delivering somebody's order of foot powder. Or mapping the roads.*

Mabel fumbled to start her car, but nothing happened. Not so much as a click. It had completely died. Even the dashboard icons didn't flash on.

Surely, her battery wasn't dead. It couldn't be. She'd replaced it the week before her scheduled state inspection, a mere two months ago.

The humming continued. Mabel felt as if the sound and vibration were inside her body, and her brain seemed more and more detached from reality.

Dreaming. She must be dreaming. She was not out here in the middle of a cheap sci-fi B movie.

Was the car in park? Once she'd accidentally left the car in gear, and then freaked out when it wouldn't start. It had to be something simple.

Again and again, she tried the starter. *Nothing.*

Mabel stomped the brake, wiggled the steering wheel, and turned the key. And, just like that, the car started. As if not a thing was wrong with it.

Mabel threw her car into gear and hit the gas. The tires spun and squealed in the tall weeds and grass, and the car leapt forward, lurching over the bumps and back onto the pavement.

As Mabel tore down the road, the amber glow, which still hung over her, suddenly sharpened, and the car flooded with intense white light. Was she being abducted by aliens?

Mabel felt threatened. This wasn't something that typically happened to normal people. People who encountered weird lights in the sky tended to wind up on early morning talk shows, rambling about being beamed onto flying saucers and probed by little green men with bottomless black eyes.

The car skidded as Mabel took the next curve too fast. Heart pounding, she fought it back under control. Abruptly, the light shot away—straight into the sky.

The last time she'd looked, she had left the other lights behind her, still hanging in their precise array in the sky. Now, she wasn't going to take time to look back and see if they'd sped away, too. All she cared about was getting down off the lonely hills and into town, where the lights were the warm and friendly ones of lamps left on for latecomers, or TVs flickering in darkened family rooms.

Mabel pushed her car for the next ten miles, bucketing over potholes and abandoned railroad tracks, till she reached the commercial stretch outside Marklinton. The strip malls were still lit up, even though everything was closed at this hour, except for a combo gas station and convenience store.

Suddenly, she wanted desperately to stop. To go inside and use the restroom. To talk to another human being.

Mabel turned off and pulled as close to the building as she could. She wasn't going to get out and pump gas, even though her tank was down to a quarter. Somehow, she didn't want to stand out there, alone and exposed, in case…

In case…what? In case a spaceship came down from the sky and tried to abduct her? How ridiculous.

Never mind. She had enough in her tank to get home, it was late, and she was overtired and imagining things. She simply didn't want to waste time pumping gas. With her luck, it would be one of those slow pumps that took forever to produce one gallon, two gallons, three gallons, while her hand ached from holding down the trigger on the handle.

When she got out of the car, she realized she was wobbly. Mabel put a steadying hand on her car before hustling inside the station.

The garish lights smacked her in the eye, but they were good lights.

Mabel smiled at the young clerk, who seemed absorbed with his phone screen. He didn't bother to look up after the first glance, which she presumed had been merely to make sure he wasn't about to be robbed.

Mabel checked her phone. She'd charged it on the way to the meeting earlier, but now it was stone dead.

After a quick trip to the restroom, where the mirror showed a pasty-faced stranger with wild eyes, Mabel returned to the store. She took her time browsing the snack aisles, which ordinarily was one of her favorite road trip activities.

Tonight, her heart wasn't in it, though she finally selected a package of crème-filled snack cakes, a bag of red-hot potato fries, and a Coke for the caffeine jolt. When she brought them up to the register, the clerk took a moment to finish whatever he'd been reading on the screen. He set the phone down with an audible sigh.

"Good evening." Mabel smiled.

The young man—Tyler, according to his badge—grunted and picked up the snack cakes to scan.

"Must get boring here by yourself at night, huh?"

He shrugged one shoulder. Maybe he was mute. Poor fellow.

"Hey." Mabel chuckled a bit from embarrassment. "Did you ever notice anything in the sky around here at night…like something weird? I was up there." She gave a vague wave behind her. "And the strangest thing happened."

"Seven-fifty-six," he said, having recovered the power of speech.

"I'm sorry." Mabel dug out the money. "I, well…" Her voice trailed off as she realized he was looking at his phone again.

"Have a good evening." She rolled her eyes and headed back out into the night.

Chapter Two

DESPITE FALLING INTO BED SO LATE, Mabel woke early, with a crushing weight on her chest and a sense of paralysis. In a rush, she remembered the terrifying light that had surrounded her stalled car, and thrashed, trying to get up.

Barnacle was lying across her chest, she realized with a flood of relief. Sixty pounds of cattle dog mix was hard to shift from a sound sleep.

As he slid off and rolled onto his back next to her, she struggled to bring her breathing under control. Had she had a nightmare?

No. There on the nightstand, she saw the crumpled bag of red-hot pub fries. Not quite seven am, according to her alarm clock.

What had happened to her? What *was* that thing?

Her head pulsated. Gingerly, she felt it through the bed-head tangle. The first thing her fingers contacted was Koi, her tortoiseshell cat, who'd been sleeping across her forehead. The cat's weight and the vibration from her purring weren't helping, but even after Mabel removed Koi, her head still felt as if it were cracking from pressure.

Mabel groped around her nightstand until her fingers met her cell phone. She disconnected it from its charger and squinted at the screen. Not only fully charged, but still apparently operational. She remembered turning it on again last night with no problem once she'd gotten home. The battery had been low, but it shouldn't have shut off on her.

She swung her feet onto the icy floor. The poorly sealed old Victorian farmhouse she'd inherited from Grandma Mabel was going to be drafty and expensive to heat this winter, she thought with a sense of dread.

She loved the house, with all its many flaws. It reminded her of Grandma and had a character no pristine new box with its prefab components could ever hope to match.

Mabel pulled on a hooded sweatshirt and padded to the window. A faint, pearly glimmer showed between the trees and houses to the east.

Since she was out of bed, Barnacle assumed it was his potty time, and he frolicked around her feet. The fear and loneliness she'd felt last night still lingered. As she put Barnacle on his cable, she decided she would go out to breakfast.

Her writing still wasn't bringing a dime into the house, and she was already spending too much of Grandma's inheritance and the settlement she'd gotten from the law firm after they'd fired her. Yet, being with other humans this morning suddenly seemed like a necessary expense.

She rushed through her morning routine, anxious to get out of the shadowy old house. She shivered in the chill, wishing her ne'er-do-well handyman, Acey Davis, would finish up the work he still needed to do to bring her into compliance with the notices she'd received from the township. And maybe, finally, he could get to putting in some insulation and sealing the place up for the winter.

For a moment, her hand hovered over her phone. Her best friend Lisa, a kindergarten teacher, could be counted on for practical advice on anything from frozen pipes to UFOs, but she'd already be at work.

Briefly, she thought of calling her new boyfriend, private detective John Bigelow, and pouring everything out to him. She had texted when she finally got home last night, as he'd asked her to do—however late—to be sure she'd safely navigated those back roads. But she still didn't know what, if anything, she should say about what had happened to her up in the hills.

Was a possible UFO sighting something people in a relationship normally shared? Having lived most of her fifty years without romantic entanglements, Mabel wasn't sure. She sighed and tucked the phone into her hoodie pocket.

To Mabel's great relief, her car—like her cell phone—seemed fully recovered from the night before. The day was still gray and chilly when she arrived at The Coffee Cup Diner. A welcoming yellow light glowed through the steamed windows. Two pickup trucks and a pair of older cars occupied the back corner of the lot behind the building.

Unlike John, who believed in parking far from the entrance anywhere he went, hoping to squeeze in a bit more exercise, Mabel tried to park as near the door as possible, to save time and steps. Not to mention, this morning she simply didn't want to cross that empty, shadowy lot by herself.

The door swung open to a rush of warmth and the wonderful smells of coffee, bacon, and maple syrup. Men in camouflage and blaze orange crowded the two booths at the back, hats still squarely lodged on their heads. The hunting crowd, Mabel assumed.

No other customers seemed to be in evidence. Or so she thought, till she spied a couple of puffs of hair—one white and the other silver gray—just clearing the backs of one of the nearer booths.

"Good morning, Miss Birdie. Ms. Katherine Ann."

The two old ladies had been girlhood friends of Grandma Mabel's. Sometimes it gave Mabel a pang, not to see Grandma still part of the trio, but this morning she smiled at the sight of them. Though Miss Birdie adhered to many of the conventions she'd been raised with, Ms. Katherine Ann loved, as she said, to "shake things up a little." Though long widowed, she had become "Ms." in 1971 during a bout with women's liberation fever. As

Mabel walked up, she could see the two had been leaning across the table and whispering excitedly about something, but they sat up and smiled at Mabel.

"Good morning, Mabel." Miss Birdie scooted over. "Won't you join us?"

Usually, Mabel sat alone. She wasn't a morning person, and conversation before 10 am was simply too hard. Besides, clearly, she had interrupted something. But this morning, happy for company, she slid right in.

Miss Birdie was a spry little person, brown and wrinkled as a walnut, with sharp black eyes and wispy dandelion-fluff hair. She wore a magenta track suit and matching fanny pack, with sturdy, white, Velcroed walking shoes.

"What brings you out so early, child?"

Mabel hesitated. She wasn't ready to talk in the light of day about her otherworldly experience the night before. Maybe she never would be.

"Just woke up early, and after I let the dog out, I figured I might as well stay up."

The waitress appeared and took Mabel's order—scrambled eggs, turkey sausage, whole wheat toast, and home fries. Miss Birdie and Ms. Katherine Ann exchanged raised eyebrows.

"Are you sure you're feeling all right?" Ms. Katherine Ann asked Mabel. "Up so early and eating so light?"

Mabel blushed. Though she confessed to being "big-boned," Ms. Katherine Ann was, like Miss Birdie, a picture of geriatric health in her patterned teal and gray leggings, matching warm-up jacket and shiny metallic trainers. The old ladies powerwalked around the town square together early each morning and attended a Silver Sneakers workout class a couple of times a week. Though Ms. Katherine Ann enjoyed a frequent binge, Miss Birdie ate like a canary.

"I'm fine," Mabel mumbled. "Just trying to eat a little bit

healthier, like everybody else these days." In fact, she knew it was spending time with health-conscious John that made her want to do better, even though she still craved The Coffee Cup's signature Farmhand breakfast. She watched a groaning tray laden with eggs, pancakes, meat, and potatoes go by, headed for the hunters at the back.

"Please go ahead and eat." Mabel gestured at Ms. Katherine Ann's bowl of what looked like soggy bran flakes with blueberries, and Miss Birdie's whole grain toast and half a grapefruit.

"Thank you, Mabel. Perhaps we should if you don't mind." Miss Birdie spread her napkin over her lap.

Mabel stirred several French vanilla creamers into her coffee and added sugar. The reformation of her eating habits was a work in progress, and she felt it best done gradually.

Ms. Katherine Ann picked up her spoon, but then gave Miss Birdie a questioning look. She tipped her head in Mabel's direction. Miss Birdie responded with a small, quick nod.

Miss Birdie cleared her throat. "Katherine and I have been discussing the oddest thing."

Mabel sputtered on her coffee, coughed, and dabbed at her chin and the front of her hoodie. "Really?"

Ms. Katherine Ann glanced around. Several more people were arriving now, as the sky outside grew lighter. She leaned across the table in a confidential manner.

"Have you seen anything…unusual lately?" Ms. Katherine Ann rolled her eyes skyward.

"Umm…." What were they talking about? Surely, not the same thing that had appeared to Mabel. "Like what?"

"We saw…something last night," Miss Birdie said.

Mabel's heart began to pound in her ears. "What was that?"

"Well," Miss Birdie said, "Katherine and I had gone to the movies at the Galaxy. It was a silly thing—another remake of

Invasion of the Body Snatchers. We should have known it would be disappointing."

At this point, Ms. Katherine Ann chimed in on the movie review. For a moment, the two debated the film's low points and very few high points, while Mabel's food arrived, and she listened in confusion. "Two thumbs down?" she finally interjected. "Not recommended?"

Miss Birdie laughed. "We're sorry. We loved the 1956 version. We saw it with your grandmother, you know. We were afraid to walk home afterward. But no, not recommended.

"Anyway…" Miss Birdie paused. "Maybe the movie affected us more than we realized."

Ms. Katherine Ann plunked both hands down onto the table. "It was not the movie, and you know it."

"No. It wasn't." Miss Birdie shook her head. "What we saw was real. As we were driving home, some strange, colored lights appeared in the sky. Brighter and lower than a plane or anything we ever saw before. Brighter than anything that should have been there and flashing on and off in kind of a rhythm."

"We called the cops," Ms. Katherine Ann said. "They told us they'd gotten a few other calls."

"Really?" Mabel set her fork down, ignoring the tantalizing aromas rising from her Everyday Breakfast special. "Like what?"

"They didn't say. Rather like ours, I suppose." Miss Birdie shrugged and nibbled on her toast.

Mabel's mind raced, sputtered, stalled. She had tried to tell herself what happened to her was some fluky thing—the car merely had a hiccup. The lights were some explainable weather event. Maybe she'd started to nod off and had a waking dream. But here were two sensible, clearheaded old women calmly telling her the same thing had happened to them. Had happened to others.

Well…she'd never known Miss Birdie, at least, to be given

to flights of fancy. Mabel shoved her plate aside. "Did your car stall?"

Miss Birdie frowned. "No. We were stopped at the intersection of Walnut and Pike. After the lights went away, we sat and contemplated it all for a moment, and then Katherine drove on. Why do you ask?"

"It's…how did the lights leave? Did they fade out?"

"Oh, goodness no," Ms. Katherine Ann said. "They zoomed!" She made a zooming motion with her arm.

Miss Birdie laid a hand on Mabel's arm. "Are you sure you're all right, dear? You really don't look well."

Mabel speared a big forkful of scrambled eggs and home-fried potatoes and filled her mouth. Once she told the ladies about her experience, she knew they'd keep it confidential, if she asked them to. However, once she'd said it, she couldn't take it back. She'd be admitting to something that put her in the same category with kooks and conspiracy theorists.

The two dear, old faces watched her with obvious concern.

Washing down her bite of food with a sip of coffee, Mabel made up her mind. Miss Birdie and Ms. Katherine Ann wouldn't judge her. They'd already admitted to having had pretty much the same experience she'd had.

"I'm okay. Just trying to process what you're telling me. You see…I, uh, had a similar experience last night."

The two listened intently as Mabel told her story, leaving out her panic and sense of being somehow threatened. Both nodded encouragement and touched her arm from time to time, as if in solidarity with what she was saying.

"Good grief, Mabel," said Ms. Katherine Ann at last. "That must have been terrifying for you up there all by yourself. At least, Birdie and I had each other, and we were right here in town, but it still shook us up."

She leaned closer, peering into Mabel's eyes. "You

might've been beamed up in their ship and never knew it. Those aliens can stop clocks, so you lose all track of time, and then they wipe your memories."

"Katherine." Miss Birdie glared at her friend.

"She might've been probed," Ms. Katherine Ann hissed.

Mabel frowned. Her car and cell phone had gone dead, so maybe… No. She definitely did *not* get probed.

"This isn't the first time something like this has happened in Medicine Spring," Miss Birdie said. "I'm actually rather glad we didn't miss this one."

Chapter Three

THE DINER NOISES CONTINUED AROUND THEM as Mabel stared at Miss Birdie. There had been a previous UFO event here and she had never heard of it? "There was? What was that all about?"

"It was back in 1958," Ms. Katherine Ann said. "The Russians had sent up Sputnik just the year before."

"Do you know what Sputnik is?" Miss Birdie asked.

"Uh, sure. It was a satellite, right?"

"The first one," Miss Birdie told her. "Everybody was afraid the Russians were going to win the space race."

"It was a very space-conscious time," Ms. Katherine Ann said. "So, when this happened, it actually made the national news."

"What did?"

"The UFO crash. Oh, it was a big deal." Ms. Katherine Ann waved both arms wide, nearly knocking over Miss Birdie's water glass.

"Outside town, back in Miller's Woods," Miss Birdie added. "People up that way reported seeing a fireball headed right for town. Some people thought Sputnik was either crashing or that the Russians had sent it to destroy us."

She and Ms. Katherine Ann cackled, remembering. "Naturally," Miss Birdie said dryly, "Medicine Spring would be a prime target for the Russian space program."

"Sputnik already burned up on its way back to earth, months earlier—for sure, it wasn't that. So many people started calling the police, the lines were jammed. We were on a party line in those days," Ms. Katherine Ann said. "Do you remember those?"

Mabel shook her head.

"Three or more houses all on the same line. If your neighbor was talking, you'd pick up the phone and hear their whole conversation."

"Unless you were too polite to listen in," Miss Birdie added, with a big wink.

"Of course, if somebody was yakking, you couldn't call out, either. Remember Estelle Porter, Birdie? Even if you made noise and clicked the receiver, she'd keep right on about her goiter or the weather or whatever else had her undies in a twist."

The two laughed again.

"People called the police?" Mabel didn't want to be rude, but the old friends kept losing the main thread of the conversation.

"Especially after people on that side of the ridge saw the thing go down in the woods." Miss Birdie laid her crumpled napkin on her plate. "We didn't have 911 then, of course, so folks called the fire department too. They thought maybe a small plane had crashed and set the woods on fire."

"The cops did go out." Ms. Katherine Ann leaned back, settling into the account. "And the fire department. Most people with even a grain of curiosity or general nosiness went right after them."

"Did you go?" Mabel looked from one to the other. "Did either of you see anything?"

Ms. Katherine Ann shook her head. "I was the youngest of us, but like an idiot, I got married right out of high school. Birdie and your grandma called me, but my husband worked nights and I was home with a colicky baby." She looked regretful to Mabel, as if remembering the excitement of that long ago night, and her own frustration.

"Wait. Grandma Mabel saw all this?" How could she have never told Mabel?

Miss Birdie shrugged. "There wasn't much for us to see. By the time we got there, the police had closed off the road a good piece back. We saw the glow through the treetops, but that's about it."

"What did they find?"

"Doubt we'll ever know, baby. For days afterward, the police kept everybody away. Couple of the local boys tried to sneak in by the back way, through the woods, but they got hauled into the police station. Said they got questioned by federal agents of some kind."

"Seriously?"

"Now, have I ever lied to you, Miss Mabel?"

"No, ma'am. It's…wow."

"Wow," Ms. Katherine Ann agreed.

"They finally opened it up, right? I mean you can't keep private property locked up forever."

"Took about what?" Miss Birdie looked over at Ms. Katherine. "Two weeks?"

"Ten days at least."

"Government men in black cars came and they took everything away in Army trucks."

"Men in black? Are we talking like Roswell? Area 51?"

Both women nodded. "Yep." Ms. Katherine Ann folded her arms.

"How did I never know this? Did you go back and look around after it opened up again?"

"Oh, sure. Not much to see, and all we ever heard was rumors." Ms. Katherine Ann sighed.

"What were the rumors?"

"Would you like a box for that?"

Mabel jumped. She hadn't even noticed the waitress. How long had she been standing there?

"Um. Sure, thanks." She'd been so caught up in the story, she'd actually forgotten to eat.

"People said it was a flying saucer." Miss Birdie unzipped her fanny pack and pulled out some bills. She waited a moment till the waitress returned with Mabel's take-out box and the checks and left again.

"There were bodies," Ms. Katherine Ann hissed.

"What?" Mabel clamped a hand over her mouth. She hadn't intended that to come out quite so loud.

"I don't recall exactly." Miss Birdie frowned. "Somebody claimed either he saw something, or he had a relative in the Army who helped carry them out. Little green men, they were saying."

"I heard one was still alive, but it kind of shriveled up, like, when they tried to treat it," Ms. Katherine Ann added. "They have it in a jar someplace in West Virginia."

"Where is this crash site?"

Both ladies talked at once, trying to explain to Mabel, but their directions were full of reference points which meant nothing to her—old barns with Mail Pouch signs that were "faded now," and "the place where Betty's oldest granddaughter lives."

Finally, Miss Birdie drew a map on an unused napkin. "There's a marker back in there. Once in a while, somebody will claim he found a fragment or such, but I don't believe it."

"Guy who owns the property has a little…what he calls a museum," Ms. Katherine Ann said.

Both ladies snickered. "More like a gift shop in his garage. He wants people to pay to go look at a patch of ordinary Pennsylvania woods." Miss Birdie shook her head.

Mabel felt a pang of discouragement but supposed it might still be worth going to check the place out. Something was drawing her to it now that she knew of its existence.

At that moment, her phone rang. It was *Hot Blooded*—John's ringtone.

She felt her face go warm, but the old women smiled. Before she could protest, Miss Birdie had scooped up Mabel's check and shook her head when Mabel tried to grab it back.

"My treat, sugar. Never had a child or grandchild, and I feel like you're my own. Go on and talk to your man now. We'll chat again soon."

Chapter Four

When Mabel got home from breakfast, a familiar small, purple, older-model sedan was sitting at her curb. She frowned in puzzlement. Seventy-something Nanette was as close to a good friend as Mabel had in the local historical society, but she'd never come to the house. This sudden, unannounced appearance struck Mabel as peculiar—even suspicious, given the historical society headquarters was right up there at the corner, a mere long block from Mabel's place at the dead end.

Approach with caution, a little voice told her.

Nanette's car door opened. "Good morning, Mabel—I was about to call you. Sorry to drop in like this."

Mabel managed a leery smile. "Hi. Is something wrong?"

Nanette put her hand on the car as she stepped up over the grassy incline onto the overgrown flagstones running parallel between the street and Mabel's porch. "Oh, goodness, no. How are you this morning?"

"Fine, thanks. Can I help you with something?"

Nanette's tight smile broadened. "I'm so glad you asked."

"Would you like to come in?"

Nanette darted a glance at the living room window, where Barnacle had appeared, barking what might have been either a "welcome home," or an intruder alert. "No, thank you. I can only stay a moment, but I have a wee favor to ask."

Mabel stepped closer, alarm bells starting to clang in her brain as Nanette opened her rear car door. This could be anything from a litter of kittens in need of a foster mother to a huge box of historical society calendars she'd be responsible for selling at ten dollars a pop.

Nanette called, "Could you possibly pull the door out a bit more?" as she struggled to maneuver something out of the rear seat. "I think it's hitting that little slope below the sidewalk."

Mabel tugged at the door. She raised an eyebrow as a political sign emerged into view. *Preserve Historic Thompson Privy—VOTE LeRoy Casselman, Supervisor.*

Nanette thrust the sign into Mabel's hand. "Thank you. I'm sure Cora will be most grateful."

Mabel stared at the placard she was holding. She didn't recall having agreed to do anything, but if it was a simple matter of erecting a political sign in her yard at the dead end of the block, how bad could it be? Still, the inner alarm bells continued to clang. If the domineering society president was behind this request, trouble was sure to follow.

"Huh?"

"LeRoy is Cora's nephew. She's requested support from all of us to help with the campaign."

Mabel's heart dropped. She knew nothing about this guy, except for his relationship to Cora, and that, in her judgment, was not a recommendation. "What's this historic privy? What makes an old outhouse qualify as historic, anyway?"

"It's one of LeRoy's campaign planks. Cora figured as a matter of policy, anyone affiliated with the society would certainly applaud historic preservation efforts."

"But…"

"The privy is one of the oldest structures within Medicine Spring limits, and the lone surviving building from the Thompson farm."

At Mabel's blank look, Nanette added, "Thompson was Medicine Spring's first white settler. He became a close friend of the chief of the local Native American tribe, who taught him about the healing properties of our namesake spring. The privy dates to at least the very early 1800s—it has a stone foundation."

Mabel's brow furrowed. "I don't—"

"LeRoy's opponent is Cletus Pettigrew—the incumbent on the board. He has been pushing to have the privy torn down. It sits on Medicine Spring Municipal Park property now, and Cletus and his supporters on the board are advocating replacing it with a dog park."

"I see."

Nanette closed the rear car door and then fished around in the front passenger area. "Here is a list of LeRoy's positions on the various issues confronting Medicine Spring voters." Despite their isolation, she cast a glance at the Sauer mansion on the corner, where the society was headquartered, and dropped her voice. "No one can tell you how to vote, but it would be better if you went ahead and put the sign up. Your house sits on a dead-end next to Willow Creek Park. Who's going to see it, after all? Except Cora, naturally, when she pulls into the Sauer driveway."

Point taken.

"Okay. That seems harmless enough."

"God bless you, Mabel. Thank you!"

"No problem." If Nanette's gratitude seemed a bit excessive, Mabel didn't dwell on it. As the little purple car turned around in her driveway, Mabel stuck the sign in the dirt beside her porch steps, then headed into the house.

She navigated Barnacle's enthusiastic wiggles and jumps and plopped her big purse on the kitchen table. Koi didn't come to greet her. At last, she found the cat in the living room, primly sitting on the back of the couch, tail tucked around her feet as she stared out the window toward the street corner where the historical society headquarters sat.

Must be a squirrel or a bird out there, Mabel thought. She petted Koi's silken head and peered around the cat.

She'd just turned around when she heard the unmistakable rattle of Acey Davis's approaching truck. Koi streaked past

Mabel and underneath the Hoosier cupboard.

"You were trying to warn me, weren't you?"

This was odd…Mabel hadn't expected Acey today. Oh, well. She needed to talk to him anyway about starting the winterizing before bad weather set in.

She headed out the kitchen door, pulling on her light parka as she went, but strangely, there was no sign of Acey. Typically, he pulled right into the side driveway.

Mabel trudged around to the front, where she saw the back end of his truck, parked at the curb in the same spot Nanette had occupied moments before. Her scrawny handyman was pacing and sputtering in front of LeRoy's campaign sign and throwing his hands in the air.

She wasn't sure what had flipped his switch, but Mabel took a cautious, silent step backward, hoping to fade away before he saw her. She wasn't that lucky.

Acey's glare caught Mabel before her back foot hit the ground, and he stormed up, mouth running. "What's the meaning of this here, little lady?" He flung a hand in the direction of the newly planted campaign sign.

Mabel's brow creased. "Umm…"

"Lee Roy"—Acey dragged out the name and spat—"didn't even grow up in Medicine Spring. He's what they call a carpetbagger."

Acey shot Mabel a look clearly designed to remind her she hadn't grown up here either.

"But…"

Acey turned on his heel and stalked back to his truck, pulled another sign out of the back, and marched up to Mabel. He planted the sign in front of her. It read, *Stick With Pettigrew—Our Native Son, Eight Years Experience, He Knows Medicine Spring!*

Mabel's jaw flapped. The lack of an apostrophe, while distracting, wasn't worth quibbling about, given her larger problem here. "I…"

Acey thrust the sign at her. He steamed back to the truck and returned with two more signs, took his stand in front of her, and displayed them:

Tear Down the Eyesore Outhouse—We Need A Dog Park! Dogs For Pettigrew

LeRoy Casselman Is A Crook & We All Know It!

"Oh, now, wait a minute. You can't—"

Acey dropped the signs with a clatter and folded his arms. "You with the town or the crook?"

Pain pulsed behind Mabel's left eye. She eased the third sign onto the grass. "Acey, please…"

He glowered.

"Look. Here's my problem. LeRoy is Cora's nephew—she asked me to put that up. I can't take it down." Mabel cast an eye at the historical society building in case Cora might have arrived when she wasn't watching. She gave Acey a pleading look. "She'll kill me."

He scratched his stubbly chin. "Waall…"

"Please, Acey. It's not like anybody's even going to see that sign way down here. Except Cora."

"I'm gonna see it."

"Acey…"

"Oh, all right." He waved a hand. "Don't blow a gasket. You move that piece of trash down by the park fence and let me get these here put up in front, and we'll call it square."

Mabel squirmed. *As if Cora isn't going to notice that.* "I can't do that. She'll kill me, and they'll never find the body. Let me work something out this evening—I promise you'll like it. But just one sign, okay? This one." She waved the "Eight Years Experience" placard.

After a pregnant pause, he said, "I'll be back tomorrow." It sounded more like a threat than a promise, but Mabel managed a smile and an obsequious thank you.

She was getting ready to ask about winterizing, when Acey cleared his throat. "One more thing, little lady. Got to let you know the town hired me to put up the Christmas lights along Main Street. It's gonna take me a while."

Everything took Acey "a while." At this rate, snow would still be blowing in around her windows in February. "How many hours a week can you spare me for doing some winterizing before the bad weather hits?"

He stared blankly. "None. Those lights are a darn big job, y'know."

With a heroic effort, Mabel resisted yelling at him. "Holiday lights are nice and all that, but my animals and I are going to freeze if you don't do the winterizing you promised."

"Don't you worry, little lady. We'll get the home ranch all fixed up snug before you can whistle *Auld Lang Syne.*"

Mabel gritted her teeth. "I expect you here at least five hours a week till it's done. In fact, that might give you plenty of time to finish by next week. I can't wait till New Year's—you promised."

"Well, when you start payin' me what I'm gonna get from the township, I might be more inclined."

For all his obstinacy, Mabel knew she was Acey's steadiest customer. He couldn't afford to have her run off to Bartles Grove or someplace else for another handyman.

"I mean it. You got your sign. I want my storm windows."

Fuming under his breath, Acey stomped off. Still, his lack of a comeback made her pretty sure he planned on complying. More or less.

Exhausted, Mabel watched his truck turn the corner before realizing he hadn't picked up the other two signs she'd refused to take. With a growl, she tossed them all onto the porch. She could deal with them later.

Once in the kitchen, she grabbed her phone and plopped

down at the table. Barnacle squirmed with delight, ramming his nose at her leg for attention. Absently, she petted him while dialing Lisa. Suddenly, the urge to return to the ridge and look for clues to what on earth…but perhaps not *of* this earth…she'd seen the night before seized her. Unless Lisa had to stay late for some reason, she'd be done by three, and they'd still have a couple hours' daylight left.

She'd leave a voicemail. Lisa, she knew, would always be up for a road trip.

That taken care of, Mabel called Nanette. "Okay, what's the deal with Cletus Pettigrew?" she asked without preamble.

"I don't understand."

Mabel explained the scene Acey had created mere moments earlier. "What's up with that? Now, I'm caught in the middle, and I don't know what to do."

"Oh, dear, I should have thought." Nanette's sigh carried across town. "Of course. Acey and Cletus are cousins. I'm so sorry to have put you in this position. Let me think about this."

Mabel's mind balked at the idea of Acey's having a relative in public office. "I'm surprised. I guess I shouldn't pigeonhole the entire family tree, but…"

"No, Mabel, you're quite correct. Pettigrews are everywhere, and every one of them is rather…unique. Naturally, they have a substantial voting bloc in every election."

Mabel's head started to pound, as the pain behind her left eye moved on to occupy the rest of her skull.

Her phone vibrated in her hand as Lisa's name popped up. "Oh, excuse me—I have to take this other call. Please think about what I ought to do. How can I possibly support two candidates?"

About whom I know nothing positive.

Chapter Five

Mabel's car traveled the Ridge Road again, this time from the opposite direction and in welcome daylight. Better still, she wasn't alone. Barnacle's hot breath steamed her shoulder. And Lisa, to her relief, not only hadn't made fun of her but was excited to revisit the scene of Mabel's encounter.

"You're so lucky. You're always the one who finds the bodies and gets visited by UFOs." Lisa sighed.

Mabel shot her friend a sidelong glance. Lisa might well be describing someone a bit off balance. "Seriously?"

"Sure. Somebody's got to be the one. I'm not jealous or anything, but I can't help wondering why it's always you."

"Yeah. Me too," Mabel muttered.

"I don't know that I've ever been up this way. It's kind of desolate, isn't it?"

"Try it late at night. Then let your car stall out and your phone die on you."

Lisa glowed. "With an eerie alien craft hovering in the sky." She shivered and hugged herself.

"I never said it was an alien craft. It wasn't cool in real life, either—it seemed to be chasing me."

Lisa made a sad face. "Oh, I guess you're right. Your car might have quit again, or the flying saucer could have beamed you up." Lisa gave another shiver, but she still looked more excited than horrified.

"Lisa. I never said it was a flying saucer."

"Okay, okay." Lisa patted Mabel's shoulder. "How much farther?"

"It should be right over this next hill and around the bend.

Not too long before you get to the old stone bridge."

Lisa nodded absently, and Mabel realized Lisa likely had no idea where the old bridge stood. She took the next curve, hugging the shoulder, with Barnacle standing on the seat dribbling drool on her neck. "Down." She shoved at him uselessly.

As they cleared the top of the hill, the fields spread below them, acres of white-plastic-wrapped haybales like so many giant marshmallows with the dark woods encircling.

Lisa sat up again. "Is this it? I'll bet those looked ghostly in the moonlight."

"Right down there." Mabel tipped her head, then coasted partway onto the grassy shoulder, stopping across from what she remembered to be the spot the car had stalled.

She hesitated to turn off the engine. "Is your cell working?"

Lisa checked. "No problem. Only a couple bars, but yeah."

Mabel's seemed to be okay too. "All right. Ready to investigate?"

Lisa already had her door open, and Barnacle was squirming and whining. Mabel fumbled with the leash clip. "Hold still."

By the time Mabel and Barnacle were out of the car, Lisa was standing in the road, looking around her. "Over there?"

"Yeah, but watch where you step."

"You know me better than to think I'd mess up any clues."

"I do, but they may be kind of subtle, and I don't know what we're looking for exactly."

As Lisa crossed the road, Barnacle towed Mabel forward, seemingly intent on a smell perceptible to him alone. She waited as the dog reached his target, performed his thorough nasal CSI, then peed on whatever it was. Mabel waited till the dog stepped away, and then she checked in case there might be an alien candy wrapper—*Mars bar, maybe?*—or something similar dropped in the grass.

Coyote scat. She wrinkled her nose.

Lisa studied the ground across the road. Mabel saw what had to be her own tracks lurching off into the grass and weeds, leaving a definite path.

"This was you?"

Mabel nodded, pulling Barnacle back.

"Looks like you burned rubber on the way out."

"You would have too."

Lisa's eyes roved over the field. "Point to where it first appeared. Should we scout around for anything in the field or the woods?"

Mabel pointed. "We can, but I doubt we'll find anything."

Lisa shrugged. "We don't know till we look—something may have fallen. Or it might have clipped trees or even come down and landed after you left."

She was right. Mabel nodded. "Let's go then. But we better be quick before it starts getting dark."

At Lisa's suggestion, they split and walked to the left and right, passing through the field in successive paths till they could meet in the middle. The woods were already growing dark, so although they scanned the edge of the trees, they didn't venture farther in, despite urging from Barnacle.

As she walked the field, Mabel couldn't help glancing at the cloud-smudged sky. Nothing appeared, but still she looked and listened for the strange humming that had accompanied her sighting.

Barnacle was excited, snuffling everything as usual, but his reaction didn't seem any different from his usual browsing for smells. His biggest reaction had been with the coyote droppings. Somehow, she'd half-expected his ruff to bristle at some point, when he caught the scent of little green men or felt residual electromagnetic waves or radiation.

When they walked up the last row, Lisa approached from the opposite direction. "Nothing," she said.

"Me neither. I don't know whether to be disappointed or relieved. My phone had a glitch. Wouldn't be the first time. The car…" Mabel shrugged. Even on a normal day, her car's workings were a mystery to her.

Lisa frowned in apparent thought. "Look, Mabel. I know you. If you say you saw something—and all that stuff happened with your car and cell phone, then it did. Maybe there's a natural explanation. We merely need to keep investigating till we find out what it is."

Mabel didn't reply. How could they possibly investigate any further?

"You ready to head home?" Lisa gestured at the car.

"Okay. The wind's picking up anyway, and it'll be dark soon. Let me sleep on it, and I'll let you know if I can come up with anything."

As Mabel drove Lisa home, she told her about the 1958 UFO incident Miss Birdie and Ms. Katherine Ann had described.

"No kidding? And there's a museum here in Medicine Spring?"

Mabel waggled her head back and forth. "Well…"

"We should definitely get over there." Lisa messed with her phone. "Maybe the guy who runs it knows more about what you and the old ladies saw."

"Maybe…" Mabel failed to keep the doubtful note out of her voice.

Lisa tossed her phone into her purse. "No internet. Until we can figure out a time to visit the museum, there are a couple of TV shows you could watch for background."

Mabel raised an eyebrow. She was used to Lisa's true crime obsession, but she hadn't known her to watch paranormal shows. In fact, Lisa had scoffed at Mabel's previous research via the *Ghost Diggers* reality series. "Really?"

"Of course. For the most part, they're docuseries that cover historic sighting reports. Plus, the famous government Blue Book investigation, naturally."

"Naturally." Mabel made a mental note to look up the Blue Book, which she had always thought dealt with used car pricing.

Lisa rattled off a couple show names for Mabel to check out. "I'll give you a call this evening, and we can talk and decide when we want to go visit the museum."

"Sure. I guess so."

"It can't be Sunday—if the museum's even open then. We'll need to check their hours." Lisa frowned and looked off across the fields. "We're having dinner and spending the day with Tim's family."

"That's nice," Mabel ventured. "They're local?"

"Closer to Wilkie. I don't think they like me."

"Oh, come on. I don't believe that for a minute." Lisa's fiancé, Tim, was crazy about her. In Mabel's opinion, Lisa had done wonders in bringing the shy woodworker out of his shell. "Any parent would be thrilled to snag you for a daughter-in-law."

Lisa hunched one shoulder in a shrug.

"Of course, they like you. When they get to know you, they'll love you as much as Tim does."

Mabel worked on calming Lisa's jitters as a fifty-year-old first-time bride on the rest of the drive back to Medicine Spring under darkening skies. But as she reassured Lisa, and even got her to laugh, Mabel had to squelch her own growing uneasiness.

Mabel was also a fifty-year-old first-time maid-of-honor, and it had just occurred to her that she was probably expected to put together a bridal shower. This was one more challenge outside her skill set—and all at the same time as she was trying to deal with a floundering writing career, a UFO sighting, and the dark underbelly of Medicine Spring politics.

Chapter Six

Mabel found both shows Lisa had recommended in her cable provider's archives. After feeding her anxious dog and cat, she settled into her favorite spot on the saggy couch with a couple of leftover pizza slices and the TV remote.

At first, Barnacle pawed at her knee, begging for a share of pizza. Finally, with a dramatic sigh, he gave up and plopped himself down on the floor, resting his weight against her dangling left leg, and began a thorough after-dinner grooming session. Koi, who was allowed on the couch, paraded past the dog, small pink nose in the air, and leapt up next to Mabel.

Dark Visitors seemed to adhere to a format of video clip or reenactment with voiceover, supplemented by witness interviews, followed by analysis from the *DV* team. That show appeared to have ended its run a few years back. The second program, *Are Empty Eyes Watching?*, looked like a *Dark Visitors* spin-off. With a quick scan of the credits, Mabel confirmed the lead investigator, Leif Steele, had previously been the designated "hot young guy" on the *DV* team.

Now headlining a show of his own, Steele was also listed as executive producer. Mabel shook her head. He didn't strike her as overly bright. She wondered how a guy like him had become such a success. Maybe forty at this point, he continued to cultivate a younger look with chaotic dark hair and trademark forelock, a steely—Mabel would have said squinty—gaze, trendy five o'clock shadow, and muscles straining at too-small tees or open-neck shirts—always in black.

She snorted, causing both animals to look at her with concern.

Steele's newer show interspersed studies of UFO reports with "Steele On Location" episodes, where he did his own field investigations of active sites prone to recurrent UFO events. Like *Dark Visitors*, each episode ended with a post-mortem, where Steele brought in special guests to review and debate the evidence with him.

Mabel quickly found she lacked the patience to watch entire episodes of either series. Mostly, she watched the grainy video clips and witness interviews, only dipping into the discussion portions of the shows for occasional amusement. She was forced to admit her encounter had much in common with a multitude of other sightings, though the physical effects she'd experienced stood out.

She eventually noticed one guest analyst popping up with increasing frequency. Curious, Mabel stopped fast-forwarding and hit the play button. According to the chyron, the handsome, silver-templed sixty-something, sleeves of his white dress shirt casually rolled, was Prof. Arthur Frost—Emeritus, Charles Harding Univ.

A local. Mabel sat forward, dislodging Barnacle from his lounging position against her dangling leg. He groaned and toppled dramatically the rest of the way to the floor.

The discussion in this episode centered around 1980s reports of mystery lights, which had allegedly appeared in the skies over a farming community in the Midwest. Frost, whose academic discipline had been mechanical engineering, dismissed the witnesses as uneducated rubes and mocked their rustic speech. "Them lights," he drawled, "they wasn't of this world." Leif Steele, who'd been advocating for the authenticity of the account up to that point, sniggered.

Mabel scowled. She didn't appreciate their patronizing attitudes. She hit "stop" and searched for another episode, but soon realized how predictable Frost's performances were. He was there as a professional debunker, snorting at any and all reported sightings. Whether civilian or military, Frost dismissed them as either naive misidentifications or unconvincing hoaxes. He offered his own "rational explanation" of the event, then made fun of the witnesses.

At first, Mabel cringed at the vision of Frost and Steele attacking her own sighting report, but then scowled. Given the chance, she'd love to face off with these bozos.

She yawned and glanced at her phone. Already near midnight, and she should go to bed. But she'd discovered an episode with an intriguing blurb that was different from the rest.

Barnacle whined. "Okay. Quick potty break and then, this one last episode."

Mabel's legs didn't want to unfold from her position on the couch. Wincing at the cramps in her thigh, she put her foot down, but then found she couldn't straighten. Hunched over like the ancient Keeper of the Bridge of Death in *Monty Python & the Holy Grail*, she hobbled to the back door behind the dog. She nearly tripped over Koi, who'd decided to slalom between Mabel's feet on the way.

Mabel stumbled and caught the doorknob. "Out you go."

While Barnacle pottied, Mabel grabbed snacks for both animals and a bag of chips for herself and checked her messages. A text from John reminded her she'd promised to go for a walk tomorrow. She groaned. Another, from a candidate for state treasurer, made her grumble under her breath as she deleted it. It reminded her of the heated local campaign for supervisor, which she'd unwittingly gotten herself in the middle of. She'd have to deal with that problem tomorrow.

Back on the couch, Mabel clicked on one last episode of *Are Empty Eyes Watching?* Rather than one more typical report of a possible spacecraft sighting, this installment featured a purported alien abduction. Uneasily, Mabel shifted in her seat, remembering

Ms. Katherine Ann's suggestion she had been "probed."

Ridiculous. Mabel stuffed a potato chip in her mouth and focused on the crunch.

Barnacle laid his big paw on her knee. She ignored it—or tried to. But when Koi started licking salt and crumbs from her fingers, Mabel gave up and broke a small chip in two, splitting it between her animals. "There you go. That's all you're getting."

She wiped her fingers and resumed the show.

In order to follow the discussion, Mabel had to go back to the alleged abductee's report, which launched the episode. Stanley Koslowski was a normal-enough looking middle-aged guy with receding hair and a paunch. He described his terror at being surrounded by a bright light from the sky when his car stalled, and waking up hours later, still in his car, but with mysterious marks on his body and no memory of the lost time.

Mabel's mind began ticking off similarities—the stalled car, the bright light. But just as quickly, her brain grabbed at the differences. She had no lost time and—definitely—no weird marks on her body. She realized she was holding her breath, and she forced herself to release it and breathe normally.

The discussion portion of the program was much livelier than any of the previous episodes. For one thing, Leif Steele had more than one commentator with him. Arthur Frost was back, but so was Koslowski, the supposed abductee.

At first, Steele talked about something he called the "Hynek classifications," calling Koslowski's experience a "close encounter of the sixth kind." Mabel's eyes widened. She got up again and dug through her collection of old DVDs in the box beside the TV. The familiar movie, *Close Encounters of the Third Kind,* emerged from the depths, minus its clamshell. Was this "close encounters" business a real thing?

Having already gotten a sample of Arthur Frost's opinions, Mabel was pretty sure where he stood on that issue. She expected fireworks, and they weren't long in coming.

"Oh, please." Frost affected a yawn. "More like a close encounter of the financially advantageous kind. This man, as you know, operates a slack-jawed yokel trap, which he has the audacity to call a museum. Two words: publicity stunt."

"How dare you?" Koslowski quivered with apparent rage. "I know what happened to me. You, sir, do not."

A smile flickered at the corner of Frost's mouth. "I understood you to say you'd lost all memory of this time period. Now you claim to 'know what happened' to you. Both claims cannot be true."

Koslowski half rose, but Leif Steele gently reseated him. "You're twisting what I said. I was physically injured in that encounter." Koslowski's voice shook.

"Yes, Stanley." Leif Steele soothed his guest. "As I recall, you have independent verification of those injuries?"

"Injuries—posh."

Koslowski focused his attention on Steele and ignored Frost. "You know I do. I was examined at the urgent care, and I have photos."

"The urgent care at your local Big Danny's Food & Drug." Frost examined a fingernail. "Not the Mayo Clinic."

"I wasn't getting a liver transplant," Koslowski huffed. "I only needed someone to check the marks on my side."

"No. Not a liver transplant, by any stretch of the imagination. A few tiny marks, which the 'urgent care'"—Mabel heard the quotation marks—"couldn't possibly verify weren't self-inflicted."

Koslowski launched from his seat with an inarticulate roar and threw himself at Frost. Leif Steele made a half-hearted grab at the abductee before letting some guy in a headset, who ran in from off-screen, pull his guests apart.

Koslowski jerked himself free and stood panting, his face

twisted with fury. "I refuse to sit here and subject myself to this slander. I'm leaving."

Frost straightened his collar, which Koslowski had disarranged. "Please do. You are a fraud and a shameless opportunist."

The credits began to roll as Steele came toward the camera, holding up two books. "That is all the time we have. I'd like to thank my two guests for today's stimulating discussion. If you would like to explore the fascinating—and controversial—topic of alien abduction, please consider picking up, *My Lost Hours,* by Stanley Koslowski, and *It's Never Little Green Men*, by Dr. Arthur Frost."

Thank goodness, a park bench.

"Can we take a break?" Mabel wheezed.

"Of course." John took Barnacle's leash and joined her on the bench, which faced Lake Margaret.

Mabel surreptitiously checked the fitness tracker John had given her for her birthday. Three quarters of a mile? They'd only gone three quarters of a mile?

Barnacle, like John, was in a transport of joy over walking around the lake on a crisp November day. While the dog nosed through the fallen leaves, John took Mabel's hand.

"Beautiful, isn't it?"

Mabel looked out over a sparkling, glasslike sheet of water that reflected the dark green serrations of hemlock and skeletal shapes of mostly bare oak and maple branches. "It really is." She tried to keep the surprise out of her voice.

In fact, between struggling to keep up with John and Barnacle, and mentally rehearsing how to broach the topic of her alien encounter, she had scarcely noticed nature's grandeur till now. She stretched her legs and wiggled her toes. Her new hiking boots looked almost as outdoorsy cute on her as they did on the mannequin at the Eddie Bauer store, but they were starting to give her a blister. At least, her pink plaid flannel shirt and gray puffy down vest and new dark wash jeans weren't giving her any issues except a serious case of alluring outdoors woman.

John seemed to think so, too. His arm went around her, and he gave her a slow kiss.

Mabel's arms wound their own way around his neck without any direction from her. Every time she was with John, she still felt as if she were living in a dream. Only a few weeks ago, she'd been facing her fiftieth birthday and the loss of her job. She'd never even had a ridiculous middle school boyfriend she could reminisce and laugh about. Now, she had John, who was everything she could ever have hoped for. He was smart and kind and funny, and he seemed to care about her.

After a moment, he untangled himself, seemingly reluctantly, from her arms.

"Hey, Mabel, I—"

"Listen, John—"

"I'm sorry," he said. "Go ahead. You first."

Darn it. Now that it was time to speak, she was having second thoughts. "No, you…."

"It was nothing important. Go on."

"You'll think I'm crazy."

He laughed. "Never. Well, at least not any crazier than we both already know you to be."

"I'm serious, John. Something happened to me Tuesday night, and even I'm kind of wondering if I imagined it."

John's face sobered. "What?"

"It was late, and I was wiped out, so maybe, oh…I don't know. But okay, here it is."

She proceeded to tell him all about her experience. The late, lonely drive. The hum. Pulling over. The lights in the sky, and how one seemed to engulf her car. The way her car refused to start afterward.

John's attention was flattering. He listened without asking any questions, focusing intently while she tried to explain how the thing appeared and sounded—and how she'd felt.

He didn't laugh. When she finally finished, he remained silent for a moment.

"That's incredible," he said at last.

"'Incredible' like 'wow?'—or 'incredible' like 'I don't believe any of it?' Aren't you going to ask me any questions?"

"Well, sure. About a bazillion of them. I'm just trying to digest it all." He shook his head. "Of course, I meant 'wow.' You're amazingly lucky."

"Huh?"

"I've always wondered what it would be like to see a UFO."

"You don't think I was seeing things?"

"Well, you saw *something*, right? We don't know what, but it's sure intriguing. A UFO isn't necessarily an alien spacecraft— it's simply an unidentified flying object."

"Right. I guess so. It just sounds so cheesy—like a fifties B movie. I feel like I should be practical about it, and say it was probably a weather balloon or something."

John snorted. "A weather balloon? I don't think so. I agree you should be reasonable and look for simple explanations. Look though. What you saw defies an easy explanation. It was scary and didn't seem to follow the normal rules we all expect. So shouldn't we also keep our minds open to the possibility that what you saw was…something more?"

"Extraterrestrial?"

"Why not? Even the US government is starting to admit there are things out there we don't understand. They're finally releasing reports from the military that go back decades."

"I wasn't going to suggest aliens."

John shrugged. "What you saw doesn't make sense. So maybe there's intelligence behind it." He grinned. "Intelligence not of this earth."

"Okay. Now I feel like I *am* in a B movie." Mabel stared. "And you've crawled out of a pod somewhere to come take me away."

He wiggled his eyebrows at her. "I'd surely love to take you away—but not to Mars."

Mabel allowed herself a little inner squeal—John wanted to carry her away. Reluctantly, she shook off her warm and fuzzy fantasies. "Do you think I should report it?"

"Yeah. I think I would. Just for the record. Look at it this way. What if aliens are visiting earth, and everybody who sees them pretends they haven't? We'll never get a handle on what's happening unless people are open and honest about it. Once we get a hundred reports, maybe that will mean something and even bring about some serious research. A hundred experiences and zero reports are another matter. How would the average person ever know anything? How will any research come about?"

Mabel sighed deeply. "To the police? I don't think I can face Lieutenant Sizemore one more time. Especially not with this."

"Would it help if I came with you?"

"Maybe." Mabel thought about Miss Birdie and Ms. Katherine Ann. Those two old ladies knew what they'd seen, and they hadn't hesitated to report it. When you hit ninety, perhaps you no longer cared what people thought. Maybe you could just speak your mind.

Mabel, on the other hand, had never had much trouble speaking her mind. In fact, that had been the source of much trouble in her life, including the loss of her job. This was embarrassing though.

"You could also just call it in, you know. I imagine Lt. Sizemore won't ever enter into it."

Mabel hesitated.

"Want to do that now? I'll buy you a nice dinner afterward. What do you think? Or we could go see a movie and neck in the back row. I hear the Galaxy's playing *Invasion of the Body Snatchers*."

John was right about reporting her experience to the police. She had gotten a soft-voiced female clerk who took down the information and informed Mabel she was their fifth caller. "Of course, there's nothing we can do at this point," the clerk said. "However, it's still important to know what was being reported about Tuesday night. You never know what might develop."

Mabel was relieved when it was over, and the clerk had even thanked her for coming forward. "You'd be surprised how timid people are about reporting something like this," she had said.

Because she had done her duty, Mabel got to collect on John's offer of dinner and a movie. She felt as if she was making up for her lost teenage dating opportunities by going out for burgers, onion rings, and shakes…even if John's burger had originated in a soybean field.

The movie was every bit as bad as Miss Birdie and Ms. Katherine Ann had warned her. At least the part Mabel actually watched was incredibly hokey and overacted.

The highlight of the movie was, as John had told her, necking in the back row. At least until one of the young employees shone his flashlight on them.

"Okay, kids," he said, as Mabel scrambled to rearrange her hair.

"Oh, hey, Professor Bigelow."

"Hi, Gavin." John grinned, and the boy grinned back.

"Sorry to interrupt you, man. Part of my job."

"No problem. I promise not to let it affect your grade."

The kid laughed. "Right. Hey, enjoy the movie. Or whatever."

John winked. "You can turn off that flashlight now."

"Oh, right."

Mabel, mortified, slumped in her seat as the usher walked away.

"I'm sorry." John kissed her palm. "I can't help myself. You make me feel like I'm fifteen."

Mabel melted. After all, John didn't seem the least bit embarrassed.

"Come here, you. I promise to behave," he said. "I wouldn't want to get us kicked out before we find out if our hero defeats the pod people."

With a sigh, Mabel settled into the crook of John's arm, laying her head on his manly-smelling shoulder. She didn't care what happened between the hero and the pod people…at least, not unless they were real. Not unless she'd witnessed their arrival Tuesday night.

Chapter Seven

SATURDAY MORNING AT FIVE MINUTES TILL ten, Mabel and Lisa waited in the gravel lot in front of a low concrete block building bearing a printed banner reading, "UFO Museum." It sat next to a narrow story-and-a-half house sided with coarse reddish shingles.

Mabel squinted at the hand-lettered notice on the museum door. "Open at ten." A wind gust penetrated Mabel's jacket hood and she gathered it tighter around her neck.

Lisa turned her back to the wintry blast with a shiver. "I hope this place is heated."

"Guess we were due for a cold snap." Mabel turned slowly to look around at the barren fields across the road and encroaching leafless trees behind the building.

Lisa followed her gaze. She nodded toward the trees. "Is that Miller's Woods?"

"According to Miss Birdie. This all used to be Miller's farm, but he and his family are long gone. That little house across the parking lot was a tenant place. From what I understand, a guy who grew up over there ended up buying it along with the woods and opening the UFO museum."

Lisa's eyes lit with interest. "I wonder how old he is. If he grew up here, he might have seen the fifties UFO crash."

"I think he did, though he was probably little. That could be why he created the museum."

The click of a lock made them turn. A hand flipped the cardboard sign in the single, small front window from "Closed" to "Open."

"I can't believe I never knew about this," Lisa said. "I've

lived here for years now."

"I suppose a UFO museum isn't field trip material for your kindergarteners."

Lisa grinned. "I'm sure I'd be getting some calls from parents when that permission slip showed up in the book bags."

Mabel tugged open the door and led the way inside, then froze and stared. Lisa had to step around her.

"Oh, my." Lisa's eyes traveled to the green, five-foot, inflatable alien dangling from the low ceiling.

A sales table sat front and center, surrounded by racks of tees, sweatshirts, ballcaps, books, postcards, toys, and what might be described as collectibles. A big stand-up sign read: No more than two teenagers at a time permitted in the building.

"Hello, ladies." A male voice filtered through the clutter.

Mabel tore her eyes away from the alien hanging from the ceiling and scanned the room. A pudgy middle-aged man disentangled himself from what appeared to be a string of flying saucer-shaped lights. "Hang on a sec. Didn't realize anybody was out there when I opened up, and I was about to start hanging these."

He came forward, multicolored spaceships jangling around his neck like so many Mardi Gras beads. "Please step over here for tickets."

Mabel decided flattery would be a good idea. "You look very familiar. Are you—?"

"I am." The man extended his hand, looking pleased. "Stanley Koslowski, at your service." He gestured at a book display at one end of the table.

"*My Lost Hours*," Lisa read and picked up the display copy. When she turned it over and started reading the back cover, her eyes widened.

"I've seen you on TV." Mabel still marveled that the owner of her local UFO museum was the alleged alien abductee she'd seen brawling on Leif Steele's nationally televised program.

Koslowski beamed, then swiftly sobered. "I've suffered through a nightmare I'd wish on no one. But it *has* given me a unique opportunity to share that experience with the world."

Or at least that portion of the world which watches paranormal documentaries.

Mabel stifled that uncharitable thought and dug out her credit card. Ten dollars a person seemed steep for admission to what—as far as she could see—was a particularly junky gift shop.

As if reading her thoughts, while processing the card Koslowski dug out a couple of museum brochures and nodded toward the back, where black floor-to-ceiling curtains crossed the width of the room. "You go through there to the right—besides the crash stuff, you'll find an exhibit about my abduction. Take all the time you want. Any questions, ask me."

When Mabel turned around, she found Lisa off in a corner, checking prices on flying saucer lamps and nightlights. "These are kind of cool."

"Later." Mabel shoved Lisa's ticket at her. "Remember the mission."

Lisa grinned. "Of course. But I have to at least get a tee-shirt."

A handwritten notice, pinned at the slit in the curtains, read: Potentially Frightening Images. Children under 12 must be accompanied by an adult.

"Cool!" Lisa grinned.

The museum, Mabel soon realized, occupied almost as much space as the gift shop. As they entered through the curtains, they immediately confronted an immense gray papier mache alien, who nearly brushed the nine or ten-foot ceiling, bathed in a pool of reddish light.

His almond eyes gleamed red, and the figure's location— coupled with the moment it took for one's vision to adjust to the dim lighting—seemed calculated to give visitors a shock. He might have been terrifying, were it not for the huge hole in one leg—at about the level of a well-placed kick from a rowdy eight-year-old.

"Pfft." Lisa scowled at the alien. "Cheap theatrics. Everyone knows grays are small—like three feet or so."

"Assuming they exist."

"Of course."

"And assuming Stanley Koslowski didn't get abducted and see ten-foot gray aliens in actuality. Because if he did, he'd be the expert here."

Lisa rolled her eyes.

As they ventured farther into the room, Mabel snuck a backward peek, then leaned closer to Lisa. "Have you seen him on those TV shows you recommended?"

"Stanley? No, I'm not a regular viewer."

"He was on the *Empty Eyes* one, talking about his abduction experience."

Lisa rolled her eyes. "Isn't Leif Steele a narcissistic dummy? He's got some good content, but I can't stand his constant posing."

Mabel hesitated, hearing Grandma Mabel's voice in her head. *If you can't say something nice, don't say anything at all.* This advice, of course, eliminated a lot of interesting conversation, but Mabel found Grandma about as hard to ignore from the beyond as she had been in real life.

"Let's say I don't plan to join the fan club. What I wanted to say was that on the abduction episode, Steele also had a debunker who tore into Koslowski. I admit it was hard to swallow all that beaming-up business and getting probed and all, but this guy was really mean about it."

"Arthur Frost? Steele has him on a lot. I guess the audience must enjoy watching him on the attack."

"That's him. I don't get people's attraction to brawls—or why somebody like him would stoop to engage in them. Looks like he's got a reputable academic background. He's a scientist, for goodness' sake."

Lisa rubbed her right thumb and fingers together. "Professors don't get rich."

"Grandma always said when she saw what some people did for their money, she was happy to be poor."

Lisa smiled and patted Mabel's arm. "Your grandma was a wise woman."

"I guess we go counterclockwise here." Mabel stepped up to the first exhibit, which featured laminated, yellowed newspaper articles mounted on a fold-out display board.

Lisa peered closer. "These are hard to read."

"Well, they are over a half-century old at this point."

"I realize that, but if he's going to keep the lights this dim, he should blow these up. And print them on white paper."

Mabel stopped herself before pointing out that it didn't help that she and Lisa were both headed into bifocal territory. "Agreed. Can you read them?"

"If I squint."

Mabel scanned the articles, which pretty well tracked what Miss Birdie and Ms. Katherine Ann had told her. There were a few witness names she hadn't heard before, though, so she pulled out her little notebook and scribbled those down.

While Lisa continued reading, Mabel drifted to the next display, which focused on the days and weeks after the crash. Like the old ladies had told her, a few local boys had been called in for questioning about their unauthorized snooping around the outskirts of the crash site. Several residents had reported identical black cars with government plates showing up in town for weeks afterward, along with mysterious "men in black," who a waitress from the now long-defunct Black Cat Diner said, "weren't chatty" and didn't tip. "They left their sunglasses on the whole time they were eating," she related.

Lingering reports of strange, randomly appearing lights in the sky had continued to trickle in for a few weeks. Eventually, those stories dried up, along with rumors of government vehicles and silent strangers in town.

"Hey, Lisa."

"Huh?"

"I'm sorry. Were you still reading about the UFO crash?"

"Nope—about to move on."

"Okay, I'm guessing you'll want to read about all the weird stuff that happened right after the crash. It's bonkers. Listen to this. Supposedly, the night this UFO came down, a fleet of Army trucks and Jeeps showed up and cordoned off the whole area. They hacked a road back into the woods and swarmed around, cleaning up every trace of evidence and loading it onto their vehicles. More than one person claimed they actually saw this."

Lisa raised her eyebrows. "Like who?"

"Fair question. A couple of witnesses were kids who snuck in to see if they could find souvenirs or whatever. At least one guy came forward a few years later—anonymously—and said he'd been one of the soldiers who was detailed that night. He confirmed this happened—the Army did move in and clean up the scene."

"This person remains anonymous, however."

"Of course. He wouldn't want to be labeled a kook—or get in trouble with the military."

"You'd think the government could track him down anyway. Big Brother, you know. Anybody leaking government secrets would be locked up in a minute."

"Maybe. Let's assume for the moment though that the reports are legit. Here's the crazy part. This guy—or maybe one of the teenage—the reporter didn't specify which witness told him this—said there were survivors."

"Survivors…"

Mabel nodded.

"Little green men."

"Or gray, more likely."

"That's nuts."

"Look over here." Mabel pointed to a full-page article that had been cut from what looked like the magazine section of a Pittsburgh paper dated 1961. A sketch artist had rendered the scene as reported by witnesses. The drawing showed men in uniform loading a small, wizened body with an oversized head onto a stretcher. Other soldiers in the background were putting bags into the back of a truck.

"Are those supposed to be body bags?"

Mabel nodded. "This article doesn't say what the government did with the bodies, but Miss Birdie and Ms. Katherine Ann told me at least one of the aliens was still alive when they recovered him. He supposedly died when they tried to treat his injuries. They said the body's still in a jar somewhere."

"Good grief. And you believe this?"

"Of course not. I said it was the crazy part." Mabel scowled. She couldn't believe Lisa would think Mabel was buying into something out of a pulp sci-fi magazine. "But no matter how the rumor mill twisted the story, doesn't it seem pretty clear *something* strange happened that night? There were too many witnesses for it all to have come out of nowhere."

Lisa nodded slowly. "You saw something. Those people saw something. We just don't know what."

Had Mabel learned anything worthwhile? She sighed. *Not much.* "Do you want to look at Koslowski's abduction exhibit?"

"No. I'm just going to browse through this section on the aftermath. Meet you over at the display case."

Mabel had no interest in the abduction stuff either. She'd only come here in the first place for information about sightings.

As long as she herself hadn't been beamed up, she didn't want to waste her time wandering too far afield.

Casting an eye toward the front curtains, she decided she'd better at least skim Koslowski's pet display. In case he asked what she thought about it.

That done, she headed for the glass cases containing various artifacts. A few small fragments of metal bore tags indicating "possible space metal," though they could have been anything at all.

Mabel peered at a group of plaster casts purporting to have been taken from giant three-toed prints found in the dirt back in the woods. A tag read, "Possible Alien Footprints." Mabel snorted. *Possible Turkey Footprints.* She'd seen enough of those in the park behind her house, and knew they spread and looked much larger when the earth was damp or muddy.

Mabel didn't spend a lot of time on precious relics like a flashlight carried by one of the boys on their covert mission to spy on the crash scene. She was nearly at the end of the wall, having looked at color photographs of now-elderly witnesses and fuzzy black-and-whites of the reputed fireball lighting up the woods, when Lisa caught up to her.

"Let's get out of here. My brain can't take any more."

"Agreed. It's not that I doubt something unexplained happened that night. It's—"

"This guy's only out for a buck," Lisa concluded Mabel's sentence.

"That's kind of what Miss Birdie and Ms. Katherine Ann warned me about. This place is fun for a bit, but let's go take a look at the woods now."

"And check out the gift shop."

"You know you're supporting this guy's bogus museum."

Lisa shrugged. "So, sue me. I want a tee-shirt. Or a hoodie."

Mabel sighed. "Okay. Me too."

Chapter Eight

MABEL AND LISA HAD TROUBLE EXTRICATING themselves from the so-called UFO museum without buying a copy of *My Lost Hours*. Koslowski went so far as to pull up an online listing where a signed copy of the book was being offered for $1,000. "Buy it here for $18.99, and I'll sign it for you. Each of you," he amended. "You can each have your own personalized copy for a fraction of what it would cost for one book online."

"No, thank you. Not right now." Mabel hoped to give the impression she'd be making that purchase later on.

Koslowski seemed somewhat placated by their clothing purchases and Lisa's alien salt-and-pepper set. As he bagged their souvenirs, he gave them directions to the crash site. "All you have to do is follow the green blazes on the trees, the path's pretty clear. There's a sign to show right about where the ship came down. Came close to plowing into the back part of the Pleasant Union Cemetery."

He leaned in as if imparting a secret. "You might want to stop in there too, while you're out this way. Folks say there's an alien grave in there—that once the government was done experimenting with those alien bodies, they brought 'em back and buried them right there."

"No kidding?" Mabel picked up her shopping bag, which featured a cartoon image of a flying saucer beaming up a cow.

Koslowski nodded firmly. "It's only a little bitty, flat marker, kind of overgrown now, but you'll find it behind the Trombino mausoleum. "Can't miss it. At least, you can't miss the mausoleum."

"Is the grave marked? I mean does it say, 'Here lie alien

flying saucer crew members?'" Mabel lifted an eyebrow.

He stared at her. "Now, you know they're never going to put that out there in public, carved in stone. It's just initials. A.G.— alien grave."

"Alien grave…" Lisa's lips twitched.

"Okay, thanks." Mabel made a hasty grab for the door.

"Wait. I forgot to put these in your bags." Koslowski handed them a couple of slick flyers. "Don't forget to sign the guest book there by the door."

A few snowflakes swirled in the air when they escaped outside at last. "Let's put our bags in the car before we walk back there," Lisa said. "It's freezing. I'm half tempted to put on my new sweatshirt, except I don't want to take off my coat to do it."

"We'll be warmer when we start walking," Mabel predicted.

The path into the woods was well marked, as Koslowski had told them. Their feet squished through damp leaves, leaving prints in the small patches of wet snow that had accumulated in spots.

"That must be it." Lisa shoved bushes aside to see around Mabel.

"Yep." The clearing ahead had obviously been emptied of brush by somebody whacking at it with some sort of implement. It was also apparent that something had long ago plowed a path through the woods, because the trees in a swath leading up to the clearing were noticeably skinnier and younger than those on either side of it.

"I'm surprised you can really tell, after all these years." Lisa looked down along the band of smaller trees and blew snowflakes off her nose.

Mabel tilted her head. "It's been over sixty years. Those trees don't even look sixty years old."

"Maybe the ground was irradiated or something, and it stunted their growth."

"Or maybe the scene isn't exactly untouched. Maybe

somebody—say, somebody who owns the property and is very invested in making money off the UFO crash, not to name any names—has had some incentive to do some pruning over the years." Now that she studied the trees, Mabel could well imagine they had been topped a time or two.

Lisa kicked at the ground. "Guess there's not much hope of our turning up any pieces of flying saucer or alien fingernails at this point."

Mabel shook her head. "Not after several decades, a bunch of official investigators, curiosity seekers, and a ton of fallen leaves."

"It's kind of a letdown. I don't know what I was expecting, but there's nothing here."

Mabel shivered. "No point in hanging around. We can always come back if we want a better look."

"For ten dollars."

"It's a rip-off, but I need to sit down and run the car heater for a bit." For the sake of the investigation, Mabel took a few photos with her phone before stuffing it—and her stiff, red fingers—into her jacket pockets.

She couldn't sit right in the museum parking lot, where Koslowski could spy on them. Mabel drove down the road a few hundred feet and pulled in behind the 1862 Pleasant Union Church. The congregation had merged with another years ago, and regular services were no longer held in the old building, which was now used only for "Old Home Week" and the occasional wedding.

A low stone wall set the graves off from the churchyard. Burials still took place here from time to time. Mabel had occasionally noticed a black canopy over one of the plots as she drove by or seen digging equipment at work, but interments appeared few and far between these days.

The snow had stopped by the time Mabel and Lisa got out,

and the sun was trying to peer through the clouds. A wrought-iron arch marked the cemetery entrance.

"All these graves are from the nineteenth century." Lisa ran her fingers over a weeping willow engraved on one of the headstones.

"I'll bet this is the oldest section, since it's closest to the church. Whenever I've seen a burial taking place these days, it's been down closer to the road." Mabel pointed. "Or maybe that's because I couldn't see what was going on up here from my car."

"No, I think you're right. They'd have started right here and then filled up the available space as they went along."

"Koslowski said the back end of the cemetery, which is most likely where they were burying people in the fifties. I guess we head to where it butts up against Miller's Woods." Mabel wended her way through the rows of tombstones, pausing now and then to study an inscription.

"I'd love to come back here on a nicer day and look around," Lisa said. "A lot of these family names are familiar. I have kids in my kindergarten class who I bet are related."

Mabel drew in her breath. "Look."

She and Lisa both gazed upward at a monument topped with a life-size, weeping angel. The solitary name engraved on the memorial was SAUER.

"It must be where Walter Sauer, Sr. and Jr. are buried." Lisa walked around the low iron fence enclosing the pillar. "I'm surprised there aren't any first names carved on there. I'd think Margarethe and the rest of them would have been buried here too."

That was a question for another day, Mabel decided, anxious to put distance between herself and the victims of Medicine Spring's notorious double murder. Recently, she'd almost died herself in the Sauer ax murder house, which now housed the historical society. "At least now we know we're up to the 1930s."

"Well," Lisa said a moment later, "there's the tree line, and we're still only up to the early forties."

"He did say the area was overgrown. I'm guessing if they did bury a bunch of alien remains and didn't want to advertise it, they might have done their digging back there in the trees and brush."

Lisa pointed. "The Trombino mausoleum was our landmark, remember? The alien grave must be right behind it, not too far into the scrub."

"I'm sure other people visit this grave all the time. It can't be too well hidden, under the circumstances." Mabel picked up a sturdy branch and broke off the twigs. As she followed a narrow path into the woods, she scratched at the leaf litter with her stick, hoping to hit a grave marker.

"That must be it right there. Sort of crowded by brush, but somebody has the marker cleared off," Mabel said.

"Gosh, it sure is." Lisa snapped a picture of the flat, five-inch-by-five-inch concrete slab, engraved with an A.G.

"Don't you wish you knew who was down there?" Mabel tapped her lip in thought. "Wouldn't there be cemetery records of some kind?"

"I'd think so. We could ask. I'm betting we wouldn't be the first."

"The church has been closed for ages. I'll have to ask around or look online to see who to contact."

While Lisa studied the cryptic marker, Mabel pushed farther into the trees. Before long, she came up against a six-foot chain-link fence. "No Trespassing" signs hung at intervals, interspersed with others that read, "Medicine Spring UFO Museum Property" or "Do Not Enter."

The fence was certainly more recent than 1958. Mabel suspected it would've been easy for a military truck to have driven back in here through the crash area to make a quiet, out-of-the-way burial. Especially if the woods were still closed to the public. Even if the site had been reopened by that point, the furor couldn't have lasted more than a few months after the event.

"Mabel."

She jumped at the touch on the shoulder of her jacket.

"Sorry." Lisa giggled. "Are you about done? You want to get lunch somewhere?"

"Sure. Let's go."

Back in the car, they drove toward the highway ramp, where a commercial strip included several fast-food restaurants. They pulled up to the closest eatery and hustled inside to place their orders.

It was after one o'clock, and Mabel was ravenous from tramping around in the cold. She ordered an extra-size meal, something she rarely did anymore, confident she'd burned enough calories to justify replenishing her strength.

They selected a table by the windows, and while they waited for a fresh batch of fries to come out of the fryer, Lisa opened her museum bag to admire her new hoodie. As she pulled it out, one of the glossy flyers Koslowski had pressed on them fluttered to the floor.

Mabel bent to retrieve it from under the table. "Oh, wow, look at this."

She held the paper so they could both read at the same time.

"Medicine Spring UFO Days," Lisa read. "Look at all this stuff. Special appearances, lectures, book-signings, a festival in the old armory…"

"I wonder what prompted this event. I don't remember ever hearing about this before. It's not a milestone anniversary of the crash."

Lisa turned the paper over. "I wouldn't be surprised if they're hoping to start some annual event to cash in on the 1958 incident. Looks like the immediate inspiration came from your idol, Leif Steele."

Mabel grabbed the flyer. "You're kidding me."

"Number eleven," someone called out. Mabel looked up to see their order sitting on the counter.

"Hang on." The flyer would have to wait. Hot fries never did.

By the time she returned with their tray of food, Lisa was studying her phone. "I looked up Steele's website. Here's the scoop."

Mabel sorted out their orders, then started into her fries while Lisa waited for hers to cool. Of course, Mabel burned the roof of her mouth with her first bite and had to gulp her soft drink.

"He's doing a *Steele on Location* episode right here," Lisa said. "It's going to be an expanded two-hour program, and he and his crew will be coming to investigate the '58 crash. He says with the recent declassification of all those military records concerning UFO encounters, he thought a deep dive on our local incident was long overdue."

"Wow. At the risk of sounding like an *Empty Eyes* fan, that's pretty big stuff."

"It's as big as they come, for this town." Lisa removed the lid from her salad and poured on some dressing. "People will go loco."

"I wonder if he got wind of the recent incidents. Maybe that's another reason he's doing this right now." Mabel waved a fry to cool it before dipping it in ketchup. "No, wait. The latest sightings are too recent. All this other stuff had to have been in the works for a while."

"What do you want to bet Stanley Koslowski and his UFO museum are going to be right in the middle of everything?"

Chapter Nine

"HEY, JOHN?" MABEL PERCHED ON A barstool next to John's kitchen counter as he added a garnish of herbs, lemon zest, and homemade croutons to two bowls of butternut squash, kale, and white bean soup.

He grinned. "Don't worry. You'll like the bread, anyway. Would you mind pulling it out now?"

She slid down and grabbed a mitt. "I wasn't going to cast aspersions on your soup. I had a question, but I guess if the food's ready, we can talk over dinner."

"Here or at the table?"

Mabel always felt insecure, perched on a high stool—and it was awkward getting up and down. "Table."

When they were finally ready to eat, Mabel started with a thick, warm slice of bread spread with melting butter. John had been right—she could be happy having bread for dinner.

But that bowl of squash and bean soup sat there at the corner of her eye. Having finished her first slice of bread, Mabel pulled the bowl closer. Maybe she should get another slice of bread to help buffer the soup.

John looked up. "I won't be hurt if you don't like it."

She wanted to like it though. It would be awful to have John go through all that work and have her bowl of soup go to waste. Mabel eased her spoon underneath a crouton, getting a bit of the orange mixture along with it.

She took a bite and felt her whole body relax. "This isn't bad."

John laughed out loud. "Highest praise. There's more where that came from, so don't be shy."

Mabel grimaced. "You know what I meant. It's…different. But nice."

He laid a hand over hers. "Thanks for being a good sport and trying it."

"Hey, I plan on doing more than trying it. Really. It *is* good." Mabel sawed off another thick slice of bread and buttered it. If she could avoid the worst of the kale, and balance the soup and bread, she thought it might grow on her.

"Anyway," she said, "what I wanted to ask you about earlier is a crazy story Lisa and I heard today."

"About?"

"Well, when Lisa and I were at the UFO museum outside town, that guy who runs it—he claims to have been abducted by aliens—told us there's a grave in the cemetery next door, where the government buried bodies after the '58 crash."

John grinned and dabbed at his lips. "Ah, yes, the alien grave. To tell the truth, I'm surprised you didn't hear about it before this."

She set down her spoon. "Tell me everything."

"You used to stay with your grandma in the summer, didn't you?"

Mabel nodded.

"Didn't the other kids ever talk about it? It's the juiciest bit of childhood lore in Medicine Spring. At least, it used to be. I'm betting it still is."

Mabel cast her mind back to those long-ago summers…fishing for minnows in the creek, catching fireflies, camping in somebody's back yard, exploring a dusty attic or two… "Maybe it was more of a guy thing?"

Then, a flash came to her. "Oh, wait. They used to talk about a haunted grave where weird stuff happened after dark. I never went—they always said they'd take me, but never did. I think everybody was too scared. But I thought that was in Mount Joy cemetery."

"No, I'm sure that was the same story—twisted around into a haunted grave. Did they say it was Mount Joy?"

"No. That was just the only cemetery I knew about."

"That alien grave was the object of many a dare. A few guys did go out there and try to spend the night, and a few claimed they did it. Of course, they couldn't prove it. I know a lot of guys—myself included—ended up running."

"Why? What happened?"

John laughed out loud. "Nothing. At least, in my case. Found out later a bunch of guys snuck around to scare us by sending up a white balloon. It rose up behind the graves, wavered a bit, and then hit a twig or something and made a big pop.

"When we could breathe again afterward, we all knew what happened. It was such a clumsy trick it wouldn't have fooled any of us for a second if we hadn't already scared ourselves half to death before we ever got there."

"So the story you heard was that it was an alien grave?"

He nodded. "More soup?"

Mabel looked down at her bowl in surprise. At some point she'd picked up her spoon again and finished her squash soup, kale and all.

"Um, no, thanks. That was plenty for me. It was delicious though."

"Good work, Mabel." He started clearing. "I'll get out the dessert, if you're ready, or we can wait."

"Let's wait. I want to hear about the alien grave."

"It's just rumors. Anything I heard came from kids aged eight to eighteen. So, allowances for that."

"And…?"

He straightened from loading the dishwasher and shrugged. "The older kids said it was where the Army buried the crew from that flying saucer that crashed. No survivors."

"I heard there was at least one. But he died too when they tried to treat him."

"Well, that's all I know. Some of the kids said the same thing you heard—that it was haunted."

"Did they say *how* it was haunted?"

John had put the leftovers in his fridge, and he waited till he'd finished rinsing out the soup pot. He wiped his hands on a towel hanging on the oven door. "Compasses spinning wildly? Sudden headaches? Stopped wristwatches?"

"Really?"

"No. I was joking. More your typical graveyard haunting— ghostly wailing, filmy apparitions. All the stuff you'd expect. Not electromagnetic spikes or leaching radiation."

"Darn."

John grinned again and gave her a hug. "Sorry, babe."

Mabel sighed. "I didn't really expect evidence of something from outer space being buried there. I do have to wonder what truly happened in '58, though—and what I saw the other night. Nothing seems to bring me any closer to an answer."

"You might try talking to your older friends. Some of them go back to when the rumors first started."

"That's a good idea. Or maybe I'll be able to find a burial record that tells me who's in that grave."

Mabel's headlights picked out the political signs before she was halfway down her block. Acey had been here—and, obviously impatient, posted his own signs for his cousin's campaign.

Even though Barnacle was raising a fuss inside, Mabel stomped around to the front of the house and pulled up the offending signs. It would have been bad enough to have dueling campaign signs in her yard for both candidates, but two-thirds of Pettigrew's signage was outright slanderous.

Nanette still hadn't gotten back to her with suggestions, but since Acey had now resorted to self-help, Mabel deemed this an emergency. She had to do something right away, even if it turned out to be no more than a stopgap.

She paused and considered her options. Giving a firm nod, she moved the least offensive Pettigrew sign to the front corner of her yard, facing the street. She hoped Acey would consider that location the prime spot—and prayed Cora didn't have binoculars. The other two she returned to her porch. Later, she'd have to remember to move them all the way inside, out of Acey's reach.

Then Mabel marched over and yanked LeRoy Casselman's sign from the ground and stuck it on the floor behind her driver's seat. As she drove toward the Sauer house on the corner, she resolved to call Nanette again.

She glanced at her dash clock. It was still plenty early. Once she'd gotten LeRoy's sign replanted—and let Barnacle out—she would call Nanette and ask for a ruling on the campaign signs. While she was at it, she'd also ask what Nanette knew about the alleged alien grave.

Nanette would have been a young child in 1958, but the reported spaceship crash would surely have been one of the most dramatic and memorable events of her life.

Mabel was happy to see only a security light burning at the Sauer house. She had noticed a tendency, as darkness fell earlier, for the historical society diehards to head home earlier than usual.

Picking a spot halfway between her house and the Sauer property, Mabel toted LeRoy's sign over and attempted to jam the wire legs into the ground. This proved more difficult than she'd expected.

The earth couldn't be frozen yet. Still, one of the legs refused to sink into the ground.

She tried another nearby spot. Then another.

Finally, both legs sank to a secure depth, and Mabel stood back to admire her work. She smiled a little, pleased with her cleverness.

The Casselman sign stood perpendicular to the street. If Cora looked this way, she'd see her nephew's sign on full display. Cletus Pettigrew's sign, being turned to face the street, wouldn't be legible unless you stood right in front of it.

Anyone approaching the house should only notice the Casselman sign.

This arrangement should take care of Cora, but what would happen the next time Acey drove down the street? Mabel groaned. What she would give for an early warning system.

By the time she opened the kitchen door, Barnacle threw himself at her, nearly bowling her over. "Hold on, guy. Here, go out and do your business, and I'll get you some dinner."

Koi, perched atop the Hoosier cupboard, watched like an impassive gargoyle.

Mabel looked up as she began filling food dishes. "What's the daily report?"

Koi blinked down at her.

"Okay, I'll go first. I've had quite a day in the ufology and political realms, but I didn't get a bit of writing done. I see you and Barnacle made no progress with the decluttering while I was out."

As Mabel set down the dishes, Koi unfolded herself and made a graceful leap to the Hoosier pull-out shelf, dislodging a flurry of papers before lighting next to her food. Mabel grumbled as she gathered them, feeling all the more irritated at her own failure to use a better filing system.

Out in the yard, Barnacle gave a sharp bark. "Coming."

She was still bringing the dog inside when her phone rang.

Mabel caught it on the fourth ring.

"Mabel? This is Nanette."

"I'm so glad you called. I was about to call you."

After a slight pause, Nanette said, "It was about the election."

"Oh, good. Did you have a suggestion for dealing with the signs? Because I worked something out for now, but I expect a big blow-up with Acey the next time he comes around."

Another pause. "I'm so sorry. No, I haven't come up with a thing. This is a problem for King Solomon."

Mabel counted to ten, telling herself Nanette was her friend. "Well, I hope you have a phone number for him, because I've sure got nothing."

"Who?"

"King Solomon."

"No, I'm afraid I don't." Nanette gave an awkward laugh. "Actually, I've another favor to ask—on Cora's behalf."

Mabel felt her jaw clench. It occurred to her that Nanette held up Cora's name as a shield when she delivered bad news.

"Here's the thing. With the election approaching in a couple weeks, LeRoy is in need of canvassers to go door to door for his campaign."

"Oh, no. No canvassing."

"Now, it's very simple," Nanette said in a soothing voice. "You will get a list of ten voters—or so—who live on the same couple blocks. Just knock on the door and if they answer, you give them LeRoy's information sheet and offer to tell them about his positions."

Mabel attempted to point out she didn't know squat about LeRoy's positions, but Nanette blithely continued. Maybe her hearing was going.

"In a lot of cases, you won't get an answer at the door, so in that event you just leave your information and move on."

Mabel chewed her lip. Politics was a slippery slope. She should never have accepted that first sign to begin with. Though if she hadn't, it would be Cora, as well as Acey, stalking her.

"Mabel?"

"Sorry. I don't know about canvassing. I'm so busy with my writing and working on my grandmother's house…"

Nanette tutted. "It truly takes an hour or less. In most cases."

Mabel reflected. People's reluctance to interact with door-to-door solicitors might work in her favor here. Goodness knew Mabel tried never to answer the door to somebody she didn't know. And she still needed more volunteer experience for her planned book on volunteering for seniors. She'd never considered being a political volunteer, but this might make an interesting section.

"Well…"

"Oh, good. Cora will be so pleased. We'll look for you down at campaign headquarters—that's next to Trout's secondhand store—Monday at, say, nine? Does that work for you?"

"Would ten be all right?"

"Of course. I'll look for you then."

"Wait a minute. I'm sorry. I had a kind of odd question I wanted to ask you. About local history?"

"I'll be happy to help, if I can."

"Thanks. I know this may sound strange, but I remember your giving a talk about local cemeteries?"

"Yes, of course."

"So, I was over at Pleasant Union Cemetery today, and someone told me the most unbelievable story about one of the graves."

Nanette remained silent, so Mabel cleared her throat and continued. "There's a stone way in the back—one of those flat little squares sunk into the ground like a corner marker. The initials say, 'A.G.'"

She thought she heard breathing, so she guessed Nanette was still on the line. Mabel gave a self-conscious giggle. "Somebody told me—well, to tell the truth, it was that guy at the UFO museum next door—that it was some kind of alien grave. Do you know anything about that? I understand there are a lot of local stories about the 1958 incident, and about that grave. Since I didn't grow up here, I figured you might be able to fill me in."

"I'm sorry I can't help you there. I do have to be going now, anyway. Thank you for volunteering for the campaign."

"Have…?" Mabel's voice trailed off as she stared at the phone. Nanette had already hung up.

Chapter Ten

THERE WAS SOMETHING TO BE SAID for getting out and about early, Mabel thought with satisfaction. With any luck, she'd be done canvassing before Acey Davis was even out of bed.

She'd arrived at LeRoy Casselman HQ a couple minutes after ten am. For a mercy, Cora hadn't been there—just a sea of gray-haired volunteers stuffing envelopes. Nanette had lit up at the sight of her and hustled to tow her over to a table in the corner, where she handed Mabel a list of names and addresses and repeated her instructions with additional caveats in the event things didn't go as planned. "Return your list here when you're done, and any signs you weren't able to give away."

Nanette hadn't previously mentioned any signs. Oh, well, Mabel thought, as she stuffed them into her rear seat, she could always bring them all back again.

At least, Nanette had seemed friendly and natural again this morning. The way she'd clammed up and ended their conversation Saturday evening had left Mabel wondering if she'd stepped into some sensitive topic she knew nothing about. The last thing Mabel wanted was to upset or hurt Nanette—though she couldn't think of anything she'd said that might have been offensive.

Mabel had been assigned both sides of a two-block area to canvass. She was familiar with this neighborhood. It was where she'd found Koi as a scrawny half-grown kitten trapped in an empty house several years ago, while staying with Grandma.

She smiled, remembering Pete, the man who'd lived in the house next door. She wouldn't mind running into him or his wife Viola again—unless they turned out to be rabid Cletus Pettigrew voters.

Leaving the signs in her car, Mabel started walking down the block. As Nanette had suggested, the route went quickly, as nobody was answering her ring. At one house, she was sure she saw a curtain move, but it might have been a cat or dog.

The flyer was printed on cardstock and designed to hang over the doorknob. Before she knew it, she'd finished one side of the street, leaving a trail of decorated doorknobs behind her, and was starting back the other way.

She'd noticed the formerly unoccupied house when she'd passed going the other way. It had changed dramatically since her last visit. The Victorian had been painted a color that hesitated between lilac and gray, the gingerbread trim a sunny yellow. Windows once boarded shut were now sparkling glass with white curtains. She wondered if the absentee owners had returned home.

Though she heard a radio, and perhaps an electric drill, coming from the rear, no one responded to the doorbell. Possibly, someone was working in the back yard and never even heard it…which was fine with Mabel. She left her flyer with a sense of glee and moved on to Pete's house next door.

This time, there was no avoiding a conversation, because the man himself was lounging in an Adirondack chair on the front porch. He straightened up and peered at her as she came up the walk.

"Hi, Pete. I don't know if you remember me."

The man, in about his mid-seventies, came to the porch railing, still squinting at her as he raked a hand through his shaggy brown and gray mop. His face brightened. "Mabel Browne—long time, no see. Didn't recognize you at first—a wee bit heavier, y'know. And a bit more gray hair, like all of us."

Mabel scowled. "It's just my coat. Everybody looks heavier in winter clothes." She studied Pete's flannel shirt and sweatpants. "Speaking of which, what brings you out here? This isn't porch-sitting weather."

Pete stole a furtive glance behind him. "Viola's on a cleaning fit. I needed a break. What brings you about?"

Mabel suppressed a sigh. "I'm handing out campaign flyers for town supervisor. Are you planning on voting?" Some instinct for self-preservation made her reluctant to mention the candidate's name before she knew where Pete stood.

"I dunno." He grimaced. "Cletus's head's only good for holding up his hat. And LeRoy's a dang fool."

Mabel felt herself relax. It seemed she and Pete were on the same wavelength. "Never mind the flyer. Hey, what's going on next door? Did the Gundersens move back in?"

"No, they finally sold the place. Have a seat."

Mabel eyed the available Adirondack chair, unsure whether she'd be able to extricate her bottom again. Holding her breath, she eased onto the edge of the seat.

Pete nodded at the neighboring house. "Younger couple, name of Welton, bought it last year. Been working on turning it into a B&B."

"A B&B in Medicine Spring? I wonder if they'll get any business, especially this time of year."

"You'd be surprised," he said darkly. "Don't think anyone's here yet, but they say they're booked up for the next month. Got guests arriving tomorrow for sure."

"What's the big occasion? Hunting season?"

"You gotta be kidding. Whole town's gone UFO crazy." Pete shook his head.

Mabel stared. "Huh?"

"It's not enough all the crazies think they're seeing flying saucers. Now, they say a film crew's coming to do a big documentary thing on the '58 crash." Pete's voice shook. "Supposed to be bankrolling a whole new investigation. Even gonna dig into the alien grave, I heard." He glared. "Let the little green guys rest in peace, I say…if any of them are really in there."

Mabel narrowed her eyes. *Crazies think they're seeing flying saucers? What does that make me?*

"Well," she said, "I suppose all the attention will be good for the community. More visitors and so on."

Pete glowered. "If you want my opinion, it's asking for trouble. Digging up the past never turns out good."

Pete's degree of agitation puzzled her. "Well," Mabel repeated, ready to mention the great historic and archaeological discoveries that had come of digging into the past.

"You're as likely to run into things you wish you hadn't. If you ask me."

"I'm sure it'll all be okay in the end," Mabel soothed. "But I guess it might be more activity next door than you're used to, for a little while."

"Pete!" A strident female voice came from somewhere in the house.

He heaved a sigh. "Guess my break's over."

Mabel gave him a sympathetic smile and got stiffly to her feet. "Vote for…somebody."

Mabel had finished canvassing, and it wasn't quite eleven. She admired the sun glinting through the bare tree branches as she unlocked her car, feeling all was right with the world. Maybe she'd head home and write up some notes on political activism for her volunteer book, while everything was still fresh in her head.

First, of course, she needed to drop these signs at campaign HQ. Mabel shook off a vague prickling of guilt that she hadn't even tried to foist any of them onto the people on her route. After all, she hadn't volunteered for this job, she'd been shanghaied.

There had been an open box of doughnuts on the table

nearest the door, Mabel recalled. She hoped there were still some left.

But as she began to make the turn onto Main Street, a chilling sight met her eye. Mabel abruptly jerked the wheel the other direction, hearing brakes squeal behind her. She waved a little apology and stayed on Market, which angled away to the north.

That had been a close call. Half a block from LeRoy Casselman's headquarters, Acey Davis had been standing in an open truck bed, stringing lights and enormous red Christmas bells between the lampposts.

She pulled into a spot along the curb on Market. A bag covered the parking meter. Mabel recalled the supervisors had passed a resolution making parking free in the downtown area during the holiday shopping season.

She'd been incredibly lucky to avoid bumping into Acey while she was out canvassing. She sure didn't want to have to wave at him now, as she walked into the campaign office.

Mabel chewed at her lip, unsure how to occupy herself till Acey moved out of sight. She had no idea how long that might be, but she hoped not very. She guessed she could browse the shops along here. Not being much of a shopper, she hadn't spent a lot of time on Market Street since moving to Medicine Spring.

When she got out of her car, Mabel realized she was but a few steps from the Reader's Retreat Bookshop. She brightened. Lisa had mentioned the bookstore, and Mabel had been wanting to check it out.

The dark-green clapboard façade with its green-striped awning over the window made a welcoming frame for the assortment of new and used books on display. The UFO Days flyer occupied a spot in the corner by the door, next to a poster that advertised an upcoming UFO Days book-signing event.

An old-fashioned bell over the door announced Mabel's

arrival. A small, scruffy dog she hadn't noticed from outside—because it had been napping in the window behind the posters—stretched and yawned.

"Well, hi, there." She stretched a hand for a sniff, figuring a shop dog should be friendly.

The gray-muzzled Yorkie sniffed and growled in a disinterested way, then plopped back down and shut its eyes. Mabel lifted her eyebrows.

"Welcome to Readers' Retreat. That's our watchdog, Tabasco. He thinks he's hot stuff."

Mabel turned to face a woman roughly her age and a couple of inches taller than Mabel's own five-nine. She noticed the stranger's hair first—an explosion of tight, crinkly, near-black curls highlighted by dark honey-gold strands, suggesting glints of sunshine in shadowed creek water. Her beaming face, with its halo of gold-streaked hair brushing her shoulders and framing her face five inches all around, reminded Mabel of the icon of a particularly powerful angel.

"Omigosh, Mabel." The woman grinned and extended her hand to shake. Mabel couldn't help staring. The woman's startling, light gray eyes were so familiar, but…

The woman scrunched her into a ferocious hug. "It is Mabel, isn't it? Remember me? It's Nita. Shanita Bedford. I'd know you anywhere."

Mabel recovered her senses. "Nita. I haven't seen you in…" She paused to calculate.

"Over thirty-five years," Nita supplied. "How've you been? What brings you here? You don't live here, do you?"

"I do now. I moved into my Grandma Mabel's house a bit over six months ago. I'm doing good. How about you?"

"I didn't realize you planned to stay on after your grandma passed. Grapevine said you were just here settling the estate." Nita hugged her again. "I was so sorry about your grandma—she was a nice lady. A good customer too." She glanced toward the back, where a register sat surrounded by more bookshelves. "Kenny, can you cover me for a bit?"

Even as the dark, slender young man was nodding, Nita covered her mouth. "Oh, sorry. I never even asked. Are you in a hurry? Can you sit for a bit? I'm dying to talk to you."

As had always happened to her around Nita, Mabel felt herself being swept along. "Sure."

She followed Nita toward a door in the back, while her brain raced to catch up. Mabel had played with Nita every summer for years, during visits to Grandma's. But that Nita—while she'd had the same exuberant personality—had been lean and supple and strong. She'd worn her hair pulled back and dressed in tee-shirts and jeans. That Nita had climbed trees and swam like a fish. She'd belted a softball like the boys and could leave Mabel in the dust when they rode bikes.

This Nita was gorgeous. At some point, when Mabel hadn't been looking, she'd also grown several inches and developed a full figure. She was still wearing jeans—though now form-fitting and complemented by a splashy, purple-and-gold argyle V-neck, a stack of thin gold necklaces, and purple suede shoes with gold-metallic high heels. Her generous curves rolled hypnotically with her purposeful stride.

Once inside the office, Nita kicked off the heels, dropping her height back into Mabel's own range. "These things kill my feet. I've been trying to wear them a few hours at a time to break 'em in, but I might have to give it up. I hope not." She held one up and turned it this way and that as she studied it with apparent regret.

"You'll get used to them," Mabel predicted. No mere shoe would ever defeat Shanita Bedford.

She looked around at the comfy, cozy room—the cluttered desk, lush green plants overflowing the bookcases under the window next to an overstuffed chair with a floor lamp at its other side. A gray tabby lay curled in the chair. "Do you manage this place?"

Nita laughed and lifted the cat off the chair, motioning Mabel to sit. "Worse. I own it."

"Wow. That's great—you're your own boss."

Nita lighted on the desk chair, a big old-fashioned oak creation with what looked like leather upholstery. She slapped the arm. "I bought this from the courthouse when they remodeled. Should say I stole it. People don't appreciate vintage quality."

Nita sighed and leaned back facing Mabel, and the cat leapt into her lap. "It might sound like I've got it made, but anybody who owns a small business has a million headaches you don't even want to know about. Independent bookshops aren't the hottest market segment nowadays."

"Still…" Mabel looked around her with some wistfulness. "This is such an embracing place."

Nita grinned. "I'm glad you think so—I love it. The man who owned it before me created something special. I like to think I made it even 'specialer.'"

She studied Mabel for a moment. "So, I saw how you solved our famous ax murders—well done, girl. I told anybody who'd listen to me that I knew you when. Sometime when we have time for a real sit-down, I want to hear all the details, okay? But tell me. Did you ever become a Perry Mason type lawyer like you used to talk about?"

Mabel shifted in her chair. "I was a lawyer for a while, but it wasn't me. I'm a writer now."

"Now it's my turn to say 'wow.'" Nita beamed. "Books? Let's give you a signing. Get the old team back together."

"Um, not yet. I'm still working on a couple things." Mabel hoped Nita wouldn't push it any further than that, since "working" was a slight exaggeration these days.

"Remember your old friend when they come out, okay?" Another sigh. "I'd love to have a nice, normal signing, once the space dust clears."

Mabel's ears perked up. "Space dust?"

"Oh, girl. That whole 'let's cash in on the 1958 flying saucer episode' fever. It's giving me a headache." She rubbed her forehead.

"Should be good for your business though, right?"

Nita threw herself back, arms outflung. "That's what I don't know, and it's keeping me up nights. I thought so at first. Could've found out more. Could've gone a little slower. But did I? No, ma'am. Not Shanita Bedford. Went in whole hog. Invited three authors—*three*."

"Well, isn't that what they say? 'Go big or go home?' 'Fortune favors the bold?'"

"You saw who I signed up, didn't you?"

"Um, I…"

Nita rested both elbows on the desk and dropped her head into her hands with a moan. The gray cat, having been squished, leapt to the floor with a single backward dirty look and onto Mabel's lap. "Leif Steele. Arthur Frost. Stanley Koslowski."

"Oh, no." Mabel grimaced.

Nita looked up and wailed. "See. You know—I didn't. Why didn't I take a minute to look into these guys? I had no idea I was gonna be hosting World War III."

"I'm sure it'll be okay," Mabel soothed. "In the end, they all want to sell books. I'm sure they'll behave like professionals."

"Unless they decide to 'perform' for the customers. At least two of these guys are known for being mortal enemies—that's probably exactly what their fans will be expecting."

"Oh, dear. Maybe forget the signing and do pay per view?"

"Very funny. Ha-ha."

"Look." Mabel suspected she'd regret it, but somehow found herself speaking before she could stop herself. "Do you need some help for the night of the signing? When is it again?"

Nita perked up. "Are you serious? I'd love having another bouncer on the premises. Just kidding," she added hastily. "You're the best. Here we haven't seen each other in forever, and you step right in and save my life."

"We always said, 'One for all and all for one,' right?" Mabel said heartily, despite the sinking feeling in her stomach.

Nita hopped to her now-bare feet and squeezed Mabel in another hug. "I'm so glad you're back in my life. If we survive this thing, we'll have to get together for some real girl talk. We got a lot of years to cover."

If. What had Mabel gotten herself into now?

Chapter Eleven

MABEL PEERED AROUND THE CORNER OF Market and Main Street. Acey's truck was no longer parked by LeRoy Casselman's campaign office. Swoops of garland and holiday lights now hung all along this side of the block, punctuated by massive, red, faux bells.

As both the opposite side of the block and all the next block remained undecorated, she assumed Acey had merely gone off on one of his many daily breaks. This job would never get done—which meant her house might not get winterized till the robins returned in the spring.

In any event, the coast appeared as clear as it was going to get. Juggling her armload of signs, Mabel scuttled toward the campaign office doors. She'd almost made it, when the familiar rattle and crash of Acey's returning truck sent her scrambling for the narrow alley next to the building.

Panting, she did her best to flatten herself against the brick wall behind a row of smelly trash cans. She eased the stack of campaign signs to the ground, keeping an eye on the mouth of the alley.

To her horror, the pickup shuddered to a stop across the street, right across from her hiding place. *Blast.*

Mabel watched as Acey slid out of the cab and ambled toward the truck bed, which was heaped with Medicine Spring's traditional holiday decorations. She chewed her lip. Once Acey started stringing up the lights, his back would be facing her—but scant feet away.

Did she dare pick her moment and make a dash for it?

No. The man was like some feral creature with heightened

senses. He'd catch a glimpse of her out of the corner of his eye—or hear her shoes scratching on the sidewalk. For all she knew, he'd point his sharp nose in the air and catch her scent.

How long would it take him to finish the other side of the block? Goodness knew.

Mabel scanned the surrounding walls, envisioning herself scaling toward the roof like an action-movie heroine.

Then her eye caught a battered metal door in the near wall. Was this the side entrance to campaign headquarters?

Mabel shot another glance across the street. Acey was fumbling with a strand of lights—and tangling them all the worse, as far as she could see.

Keeping an eye on him, she edged nearer the door. There was no knob or handle, and the lock was set flush in the plate. Mabel pushed, but of course, the door didn't move.

She tapped.

Acey continued yanking at the wires and stomping his feet. He seemed to be muttering something, as well—a bit like Rumpelstiltskin, throwing a tantrum when the miller's daughter outwitted him.

She knocked louder.

To her relief, the door opened to reveal the round, surprised face of Rosalyn Andrianakis, a fellow historical society volunteer and—it appeared—fellow campaign conscriptee. In most cases, Mabel tried to avoid Rosalyn, who was on a perpetual campaign of her own, to find a wife for her son.

But as Mabel tumbled through the door, she couldn't have been happier to see Rosalyn. What she'd always heard was true. Politics did make strange bedfellows.

"Mabel Browne, what on earth?"

"Thanks, Rosalyn. I don't have time to explain right now, but I finished canvassing, and I need to drop off my extra signs."

"Looks like you didn't have much luck. But no need to sneak

around—Cora's not here."

Rosalyn gestured at the signs leaning against the wall. "It's a heated contest. People don't want to publicly commit themselves."

Thinking of Acey, Mabel sighed and nodded. "Well, here's my list, all marked off. I did try to leave a window sign at the bookstore, but the owner said they can't afford to take sides."

Rosalyn folded her arms and shook her head. "People have had their houses egged and toilet papered. I never thought I'd see this level of violence and political unrest in Medicine Spring."

Mabel craned her neck but only glimpsed the corner of one front window from back here—and, sadly, the empty box from the campaign-office doughnuts sitting in the waste can. "If you don't mind, I'd still like to use the rear door?"

"Of course."

Mabel slipped back into the alley and the door latched behind her. To her great relief, Acey was preoccupied with a stubborn hook arrangement when she reached the street.

She sighed as she slid inside her car and shut the door. This election couldn't be over soon enough.

Before she could start the engine, her phone pinged with a text from John.

What are you up to?

The lunch bell in Mabel's stomach was ringing loud and clear.

Done canvassing. Headed for Coffee Cup.

The phone pinged again.

Meet you there in 10.

Mabel smiled. Done canvassing, had avoided a political brawl with Acey Davis, and now she had a lunch date.

She arrived at the diner ahead of John, and the lunch rush had already died down. By the time he came in, she was waving from a back booth.

He grinned, and her heart flipped.

When he'd kissed Mabel and slid into the booth opposite her, she raised her brows. "Not working this afternoon?"

He shook his head. "That sometimes happens when your jobs are all part-time."

John's PI license had been suspended a while back when he'd made a tough call in protecting a client. While waiting for the licensing board to rule on lifting his suspension, he'd been working as a substitute teacher and lecturing at the community college.

Mabel eyed the yellow-covered workbook he'd set at the end of the table. "*Ethics in Law Enforcement,*" she read upside down. "Is that what you're teaching this semester?" She had no recollection of hearing that.

John made a wry face. "Unfortunately, no. I got a tip—I might be required to take this ethics course before I can get my license back. I know this stuff backward and forward already, but I figured I'd get a jump on it, anyway. Been carrying this in case I have a few free minutes."

"Sorry I asked."

He lifted one shoulder in a shrug. "Like I've said before, if I had it to do over again, I think I'd do the same. I knew the risk and took a chance. If I hadn't, and it cost a life, I'd blame myself forever."

That was John. He didn't stew over past mistakes the way Mabel did. She cleared her throat. "Do you know what you want for lunch?"

He glanced at the menu despite the fact he could, in all likelihood, recite it from memory. "Grilled chicken sandwich, lettuce, tomato, hold the brioche. Sub honey mustard for the mayo. Side of cottage cheese and a fruit cup."

Mabel wrestled with her conscience. John never shamed her eating habits but spending time with him had made her more aware of their effect on her health. She combed the menu, searching for something healthy, filling, and delicious.

This was a challenge. Nowadays, it was hard to find any foods that some article didn't claim were a nutritional time bomb.

"Have you tried their veggie soup? They make it here, and it's good."

She liked soup. With thick slices of bread dripping with butter.

The waitress was approaching. Mabel gestured for John to order first. While he did, she thought fast. The articles stressed protein, she recalled. And fruits and vegetables. Not to mention fiber.

"For you, miss?"

"Um, buckwheat pancakes, please. A short stack." She stole a glance at John, to see if he noticed her restraint. "Fruit topping. Turkey sausage. A glass of milk."

"Whipped cream on your pancakes?"

Mabel's head started to nod automatically. She had never understood how something so light and frothy could possibly be bad for you. No, she had to draw the line somewhere. She shook her head.

As the waitress closed her pad, Mabel added, "And two scrambled eggs." *More protein.*

As the waitress departed, John smiled at her. "How'd the canvassing go? Was it exciting to be a political activist?"

"Very funny. But you know what? It was a lot more exciting than I expected, at least at the end." Mabel described her cat-and-mouse game with Acey.

John snorted. "I wish I could have seen that."

"It took years off my life."

"You mentioned stopping at the bookstore. I can't believe you hadn't been in there before. What did you think of it?"

"I can't say I saw much of it. Mostly sat in back, talking to

Shanita."

"What did you think of Nita, then?"

"It was great running into her. Since I moved here, I've been so busy with the estate and the house and—"

"The murders."

"Well, yeah. I was going to say my writing. I didn't even realize Nita was still in town."

"You know, it didn't occur to me you knew her before."

"Yeah, I offered to help with her book-signing. She was my best friend in Medicine Spring when I used to visit my grandma in the summers. We traded sleepovers and, I'm sure, drove Grandma Mabel up a wall." Mabel tilted her head. "I didn't know *you* knew her."

"Come on." John laughed. "Everybody knows Shanita. She's a force on the Chamber of Commerce nowadays, but my gosh, I've known her my whole life. She was a grade behind me in a pretty tiny school district. She went off to a great college and had a big corporate job for a while. Traveled all over the country. Then one day, she got fed up and moved back."

"Huh." Mabel stared into her coffee for a moment, feeling a pang that she'd missed so much of Nita's life. They should have stayed in better touch.

John rolled his mug in his hands. "Came home for the holidays and never left."

Mabel grinned. "Did she take over the family Christmas tree farm?"

John frowned. "What Christmas tree farm?"

"Or was she here to foreclose on the toy store, but ended up falling in love with the cute owner?"

"Huh?"

"Common tropes. I guess men don't watch made-for-TV holiday romance movies."

"I can't speak for my millions of brothers, but I don't. And nope. She didn't walk out of her old life into a romance, if that's what you mean. She just came home and stayed."

"Did she get married, though?"

"Yes, she got married. But that's Nita's story to tell." John moved his cup out of the way as the waitress approached. "What are you doing this afternoon? Writing?"

Mabel stopped herself mid-sigh. "Yeah. I need to write up my notes about my canvassing experience."

She leaned back to allow the waitress to set down their food. It all looked and smelled good, especially the pancakes covered in a gooey, sweetened mixture of strawberries, blueberries, and cherries. It did look a bit naked without a smidge of whipped cream, but darn it, she was eating healthy now.

"Hey, John. Are you doing anything this evening?"

"Nothing I can't move around." He grinned. "Are you asking me out?"

Mabel felt her face redden. "No. I mean…would you maybe want to go out to the cemetery with me tonight?"

"Cemetery?"

She busied herself with cutting her pancakes into bite-size pieces, as if assisting a toddler. "Pleasant Union," she said without looking up. "I, uh, wondered if there was anything unusual to see at night."

John's grin broadened. "I wouldn't miss that for the world. Hopefully, we'll see a ghost and you'll jump into my manly arms for protection."

She knew her face was flaming now, and she focused on cutting her pancakes into smaller pieces. "Is ten too late? Or maybe it has to be the witching hour?"

Chapter Twelve

THE TIRES ON JOHN'S VINTAGE MUSCLE car—a half-painted work in progress—crunched on the gravel as they pulled into the deserted Pleasant Union church parking lot. Mabel and John had compromised on eleven pm, but Barnacle had gotten into the garbage, and it took Mabel an extra ten minutes to clean up the mess. Especially after Koi had taken off with an empty tuna packet, leaping to the top of the cabinets, which meant Mabel had to climb on a chair to retrieve it from her unhappy cat.

A single pole light lit the parking lot, casting inky shadows across the crushed stone and dirt. Mabel looked up at the old, wood-frame church, with its tall, skinny windows of plain glass, whose pointed frames echoed the peak of its Gothic spire. The time-worn building seemed to loom over them, disapproving if not outright threatening, like something out of Edgar Allan Poe.

Now they were here, she was having second thoughts. The woods were forbidding. It was bad enough, knowing wild animals prowled around in the dark, but if anything unearthly were to happen, she was afraid she'd disgrace herself. Or worse, get sucked up into outer space by an aggrieved alien, out to avenge his fallen comrades.

John was already holding her door. She struggled a bit and then launched herself out of the low seat. He caught her arm and steadied her. "Ready?"

Her gaze flickered from the old church to the cemetery and the black row of trees beyond. The weird, humped shapes of the nearer gravestones looked for all the world like a flock of ghost sheep. Now, as the clouds shifted in their journey across the sky, an eerie wash of moonlight bathed the church façade, painting it a dull, gleaming color like unpolished pewter.

"Okay." She cleared her throat. "Let's go."

To her relief, John went first. A few steps would carry them beyond the soft glow from the pole light and the remains of the full moon. Mabel kept a finger on her flashlight button as they navigated the dozing gravestones.

Suddenly, John threw out his right arm. Mabel blundered into it with an audible *oof.*

He pulled her sideways, into the shadow of the imposing Sauer monument, and nodded toward the edge of the woods. A light flickered between the trees.

Mabel struggled to breathe—partly because of the unreasoning fear shoving at her lungs, and in part because she'd already had the air knocked out of her. *John's right here. It's okay.*

Still her eyes flitted to the car—so close and yet so out of reach, as she imagined trying to run and dodge around tombstones. Shamelessly, she clutched John's arm like a coward.

Trixie Belden wouldn't be cowering. Nancy Drew would already be crouched down, slipping from the shadow of one stone to the next, trying to get a look at where that light was coming from.

The mental pep talk wasn't working.

"Look," John whispered into her hair.

Mabel ventured a peek around his shoulder. The flicker had resolved itself into the steady, approaching beam of a flashlight. A shape that might have been a man came behind, holding it.

Must be a curiosity seeker. Like us.

The figure stepped into the moonlight, a few paces from the Trombino mausoleum.

"Pete?" Mabel stared as he jumped, his flashlight beam skittering over the headstones and skeletal trees. Something glanced off the stones of the crypt with a metallic clang.

Gasping, Pete clutched his chest with his flashlight hand. In the other, he held a garden hoe and long-handled pruner.

"Sorry for scaring you." Mabel hoped she hadn't given him a heart attack.

"That's…okay. I…was…just startled."

John remained silent, eyes on Pete.

Mabel gestured. "This is my friend, John. John, this is Pete." Should she ask Pete what the tools were for?

As she tried to frame a question, he began sputtering. "How do. Surprised to run into anybody way out here at this hour. Never heard you drive up or nothing."

Instinctively, Mabel's glance drifted to the deserted parking lot. Pete lived miles from the cemetery, and he was lugging big tools.

"We didn't notice your car either."

"Oh. Ha." He shifted his feet. "I'm parked there behind the church. Figured some of the local young vandals might be about. Don't want to get my truck keyed."

Might as well take the bull by the horns. "Um, what brings you out tonight?"

Pete's breath came in puffs that were visible in the moonlight. He lifted his chin. "I…felt kind of sorry for the little alien guys. What with the film crew coming in with their ground-penetrating radar and diggers and all. Figured I'd go clean up around the grave a bit. Show some respect, y'know."

At almost midnight.

"That's very public-spirited of you," John said dryly.

"What brings you folks out this evening?" Pete tucked his flashlight under his arm while he shifted the tools to his other hand.

"We—I wanted to have a look at the grave at night." Mabel knew she must sound like a childish thrill-seeker.

"Mabel didn't grow up here." John smiled. "She never had

the experience of scaring herself half to death out here, just for the fun of it, like we locals did."

Pete laughed, but his eyes darted like an animal looking for an escape route. "Well...nice running into you, Mabel." He ducked his chin at John. "Nice meeting you. Guess I better get home now, before Viola comes looking."

With that, he scuttled off. Mabel watched till he'd crossed the moonlit parking area and disappeared behind the church. A moment later, engine sounds announced his departure.

A dark pickup truck rounded the building corner and headed toward the road. Gravel spurted as he pulled out.

Mabel stared after him and shivered as a wind gust reminded her she was cold. "That was weird."

"It was. Coming out here late at night with tools. Hiding his truck from the road."

"And acting jumpy. That's not typical Pete." Mabel had stuffed her flashlight in her coat pocket, and she pulled it out again.

"I saw him earlier today, when I was canvassing, and he had a real bee in his bonnet about the UFO festival they're doing. Especially the film crew coming in, like he mentioned."

"UFO festival? What was that about radar and diggers?"

"Nita's book signing is part of it. Let's wait till we're done here, and I can finish explaining about the film crew."

"Okay. Let's go satisfy your curiosity and experience the wonders of the alien grave at night."

They turned their flashlights back on, and John parted the bushes for Mabel. "There's a path, as I'm sure you and Lisa noticed earlier, but not too well kept, particularly for night explorations."

"It's odd Pete didn't widen it out a bit, as long as he was trimming."

"It is. But if he's not happy about the film crew, maybe he doesn't want to go out of his way to make it easier for them."

"That doesn't make sense either, since he's ostensibly out here 'cleaning up.'" Mabel stopped short of the A.G. marker. "Huh. Would you look at that."

"Whatever he was doing back here, it sure wasn't cleaning up the grave."

Wild brambles, which the locals referred to as shin-scratchers, still rambled over the burial place, and a sizeable, leafless sapling had taken root less than a foot from the marker. Mabel caught the slim trunk in her hand. "It would've been easy to lop that off."

John shone his light deeper into the woods. "That's where he was working. Look."

Mabel frowned. A rough path had been hacked into the brush. Her flashlight cast a yellow beam on the roughly cleared ground, which showed signs of recent disturbance. "That must've been where he was using his hoe."

"So it appears." John kicked at the loosened earth. "'Curiouser and curiouser,' as Alice said."

"I like Pete. He helped me out once."

John nodded. "Not saying he's doing anything shady, but I have to wonder what he's been up to."

Mabel blew out a gusty breath. "Me too. Guess there's not much we can do but wait and see." But she couldn't help fretting about Pete and his furtive digging.

"Speaking of waiting, do you want to shut off the lights and hang out a while, to see if the aliens rise tonight?"

She shook her head. "If they haven't been scared away by all this activity, I'd be surprised. I'm cold. But I might try again some quieter night."

"Good call. Let's stop at the all-night place up by the interchange. I'll buy you a hot cocoa."

Mabel brightened. There wasn't a lot chocolate couldn't fix.

Chapter Thirteen

THE NEXT DAY, MABEL STRUGGLED TO focus on her writing. Ever since her close encounter, her floundering career had gone straight into the ditch. In fact, UFOs had turned out to be almost as distracting as murder, which had, until recently, tended to be her usual problem.

Barnacle lay with his chin on her foot and looked up with mournful eyes. She wasn't sure if this was sympathy for the wreckage of her new calling before it ever got off the ground, or depression over her preoccupation with UFOs, which was sidetracking Mabel from his walk schedule.

"I'm sorry, okay? I promise we'll go as soon as I get these notes organized."

The dog sighed and flopped on his side, back to her.

"Hurtful, Barnacle."

Nevertheless, Mabel realized he had a point. With one eye on the time, she turned her chair away from Barnacle's dramatic display of victimization.

Maybe she should start with a title for this section. That might help her find her focus. So far, she'd strained to find anything at all affirmative about her foray into politics.

Think positive, Mabel.

So, what was positive about wrangling two opposing candidates, both of whom she was supposed to be supporting? Or hiding behind trashcans in alleyways? For that matter, what was exciting about trying to canvass voters who went out of their way to avoid you?

Maybe her personal experience wasn't typical. Wasn't that what the weight-loss ads always said—"Your results may vary?"

Okay, she would write from the perspective of a campaign volunteer who was supporting one single candidate. That seemed like a good start.

The morning flew by. Or, at least, what was left of it, since she hadn't gotten out of bed and started till close to 10:30.

Mabel checked the time with a sense of relief. She could legitimately take a lunch break now, and she knew where she was going. A month ago, the Medicine Spring Volunteer Fire Department had begun hosting a food truck in their parking lot three days a week, and today was a food truck day. She'd take Barnacle along, which would kill two birds with one stone.

As she bundled herself up and got a leash on her squirming dog, she pondered what she might have for lunch. Several different trucks came to the MSVFD on a rotating schedule, but all were good, and a nice change from scrounging through her leftovers.

The day was brilliantly sunny, but brisk, and Mabel felt in high spirits after actually working this morning. Barnacle seemed to share her good mood, stopping to sniff every bush along the route. When he stopped to potty on the front lawn of the Sauer mansion, she tried to pull him away. It would be just her luck if Cora were there and happened to look out.

Somehow, she got the reluctant dog moving again. At least he waited to do his business under the hedge at the end of the property, the corner where Carteret Street ended. With a new spring in his step, Barnacle turned and followed his nose in the direction of the fire department.

Taco day. Mabel smiled when she saw the Taco Fiesta truck with its splashy paint job featuring a green cactus with a red flower and beaming yellow sun. Barnacle tugged her toward the aroma of beef and chicken.

Several people had gotten there ahead of her, and the line stretched along the side of the firehall. As she waited, trying to restrain Barnacle from sniffing the man in front of them, she read the event announcements posted on the glass-covered corkboard.

Bartle County UFO Society

Mabel had never heard of this organization but surmised it might be a good place to learn more about what had happened to her the other night. She checked the date and time and was startled to see they met monthly, and it looked like tonight was the night.

Struggling not to drop her phone while hanging onto Barnacle, she texted Lisa and John, hoping at least one of them would be willing to go with her. By the time she got up to the taco window, she still hadn't heard from Lisa, but John had promised to come.

Ravenous at this point, Mabel ordered one beef and two chicken tacos with a side of rice, black beans, guacamole, tortilla chips, and a fruit punch-flavored Jarritos soda pop.

"We better double-bag," the young man told her.

Contemplating the walk home with all that food plus an excited dog, Mabel had to agree. She hoped her lunch survived the trip.

That evening, Mabel was waiting for her ride to the UFO meeting. Lisa had declared herself eager to attend, and John had promised to pick her up too.

When Mabel fed her hungry animals, both sniffed their dishes and then looked up at her, as if asking whether this was going to be it. Koi meowed soundlessly, something she tended to do when she found the gravity of Mabel's shortcomings too great to express in audible cat language.

"Come on, guys. Give me a break. I didn't mind sharing a bite of my lunch with you, but you can't expect chicken and beef at every meal."

Barnacle had already stuck his face in his dish and was

swallowing gulps of food with no discernible pause to chew. Koi simply walked off. Mabel could almost hear the mournful soundtrack the moment required.

Having finished his dinner and licked out the bowl, Barnacle ambled over to the cat's dish. Mabel swooped in and lifted it to the top of the cabinets—well above the dog's reach, but an easy leap for Koi, once she'd finished pouting.

Hearing John's car in the driveway, she grabbed her coat and bag, and set the alarm. "Be good," she told the animals sternly, but without hope.

As they drove to Lisa's apartment, Mabel had to calm an attack of butterflies in her stomach, which could have rivalled the great annual monarch migration. She had seen a UFO herself—and Miss Birdie and Ms. Katherine Ann were normal enough. Still, Mabel couldn't help fearing these UFO groupies might be a bunch of paranormal fanatics and conspiracy theorists, seeing Martians and government cover-ups behind every cell phone tower.

"Hey." Lisa crawled into John's back seat. "This'll be fun. Whatever it is, we'll either learn something or at least be entertained, right?"

"Right," Mabel said, but the butterflies kept batting at her ribs, trying to escape and continue their migration to Mexico.

John had already told her that he believed in UFOs. Plus, he believed her. Lisa admitted to some interest in the topic, and she also believed Mabel.

But so far, Mabel hadn't told her family or other friends about her sighting. Maybe she didn't want to find out what they really believed or how they'd look at her when they found out. In fact, though she was sure Lisa would never make fun of her, Mabel didn't even know what Lisa believed.

As far as she knew, Lisa felt the same way Mabel had felt a week ago. UFOs were interesting—"fun." Unexplained, but likely explainable as natural phenomena, hoaxes, classified US government experiments…or the product of someone's overactive imagination.

John reached across and took her hand in his big, warm one. He slid her a sideways smile but didn't say anything. It seemed he could sense her agitation.

There were more cars in the parking lot than Mabel had expected.

"Some of these must be firefighters," John said, as if reading her thoughts. "Like the ones parked over there toward the back."

The night was chilly, under a clear, star-pierced sky. Mabel scanned the heavens, but tonight, nothing seemed out of place.

They entered through a windowed hallway, following a long display case that contained plaques, a few old helmets and badges, photos, and newspaper clippings. "Oh, look!"

The light in the passageway was pretty dim, so Mabel leaned in to scan a familiar photocopied article and surrounding photos. "This is about the Miller's Woods UFO crash," she said. "The fire department responded. I'll bet it was one of the most interesting things in the history of the department."

"I should think so." John leaned over her shoulder, distracting her with his warm bulk and the scent of his aftershave. "You don't get those calls every week."

"Hey," Lisa said. "I think they might be starting."

About thirty attendees milled around the brightly lit firehall. People were beginning to claim chairs at some of the tables, and many stared at Mabel and her friends.

Mabel hated to be conspicuous. She was glad to find an open table off to the side, but they'd barely slid into their seats when a fortyish woman with messy beige hair and a bunchy wool skirt and yellow cardigan plopped down next to her.

"Hi." The newcomer offered Mabel a hand. "I'm Jackie. Welcome to the group. Are you all just curious, or…?"

"Um…"

Jackie shoved her blue-framed glasses back up her nose and glanced toward the front. "Oops. Looks like we're about to start. I'll introduce you all later. But real quick, the guy fiddling with the mic is the president, Larry Prater. That's his wife Dani. He's a walking library of UAP knowledge. He teaches physics at the State U campus in Wilkie, so he's scientific in the way he looks at phenomena. But he thinks ufology is important to study. I'm not sure about her. She's quiet most of the time."

Jackie gestured toward the opposite back corner. "Those are the kooks. Avoid them."

Another gesture, this time toward the front tables. "The group on our right are true believers. All pretty solid, fact-based types. But they lean toward wanting sightings to be extraterrestrial. Now, the group on the left don't necessarily disbelieve in extraterrestrial UAPs, but I'd call them 'interested skeptics.' They'll refuse to believe any sightings are the work of aliens, until proven otherwise."

"Good evening, all." Prater looked toward Mabel's group. "And welcome to our visitors. For those new to the group, a few general observations. First of all, UFOs. There's no such thing as 'not believing in UFOs.' Why? Because a UFO simply refers to something unidentified in the sky.

"The term we use now is UAP, which stands for unidentified aerial—or sometimes anomalous—phenomena, depending on whether it's something airborne. No one can deny the existence of flying objects or other anomalies which can't be readily identified. Right?"

Mabel caught herself nodding.

"Now, extraterrestrial or alien-created spacecraft are a different matter. Not every UAP is potentially extraterrestrial in origin or created by alien intelligence. In fact, we believe five percent or fewer UAPs fall into that category."

"Wow." Mabel covered her mouth.

Prater grinned at her. "Not very many, huh?"

There was restless movement in the true believers' group and murmuring among what Jackie had referred to as the kook fringe.

"Tonight, we have a lot to cover. Besides our scheduled presentation, we need to talk about the exciting upcoming UFO festival and the arrival of Leif Steele's film crew, which will be investigating our '58 crash. So, let's get started, shall we?

"As I mentioned, potential extraterrestrial UAPs comprise no more than five percent of all reported incidents. An even smaller—much smaller—category encompasses alien abduction. We're all familiar with the movie *Close Encounters of the Third Kind*. That's not a fictional category. It's one of the classifications created by prominent UAP scientist, J. Allen Hynek, and applies to sightings of alien occupants.

"Encounters of the Fourth Kind are the rarest of the rare. Most of us here know Stanley Koslowski." Prater gestured and gave him a smile. "If not from this group, then perhaps his appearances on the *Country Morning* television show."

"I was on that show," Mabel whispered to Jackie.

Lisa jiggled her arm. "It's the museum guy."

"As you may know, Stanley has evidence of at least one Encounter of the Fourth Kind. Tonight, he'll tell us a bit about his recent hypnotic regression therapy, which he says has helped him recover memories of two additional abductions. Stanley?"

"Junk science!"

Heads turned toward the doorway, where a silver-templed man stood sneering.

Mabel recognized Arthur Frost's chiseled features, despite a new and quite masculine stubble of facial hair he hadn't been sporting in the old *Empty Eyes* episodes. He'd also traded his white dress shirt for fashionably shabby jeans and a quarter-zip navy sweater. Although he was now years older, the overall effect was more youthful.

A scruffy, bearded man launched to his feet, as if to tackle the naysayer.

Mabel ducked instinctively, expecting a brawl. Jackie half rose in her chair. Fortunately, someone next to the bearded man grabbed him by the tail of his long, black coat and pulled him down into his seat.

Koslowski's face reddened. He looked toward Prater for support, visibly trembling with apparent rage.

Prater appeared unperturbed as he waved the heckler into the room. "Have a seat, Arthur. If you have something to contribute to the program, we'll be happy to hear you following Stanley's presentation."

"Frost has no open mind whatsoever," Jackie whispered. "He actually sat in the *Country Morning* audience when Stanley was on, and when they called for questions, all he did was bait him."

Mabel scowled. She hated bullies.

Frost strolled across the room to a seat directly in line with Stanley.

"Oooh," Lisa said. "Now this is getting interesting."

Chapter Fourteen

As the UFO meeting continued, many in the room stole uneasy glances at the disruptive debunker, as if waiting for a volcano to erupt.

"Okay, Stanley," Prater said. "We're looking forward to what you can tell us. Perhaps, first, you could provide a bit of background on your initial abduction for our visitors?"

Mabel stole a look at John, whose face wore a quizzical expression. He seemed to be stuck on the alien abduction concept. As she was.

Lisa appeared to be struggling to control a smirk.

But as Stanley told his story, it didn't seem very funny to Mabel. In fact, it was chilling. Two years before, he said, he'd been driving at night on a lonely road, returning from a meeting outside Wilkie, when he came to a railroad crossing.

As he was crossing the tracks, his car stalled out, leaving him a sitting duck for any passing trains. Frantic, he'd tried to restart his engine, but it was dead.

Knowing a freight train was due around midnight, he got out and tried to push his car off the tracks. The vehicle rocked a bit but remained caught on the tracks. If he couldn't get it going, he could only hope the train would be able to stop in time.

Koslowski had been so desperately focused on his car he didn't notice right away that the area around him had been growing brighter. Startled, he'd glanced up to see what looked like a descending broad-brimmed garden hat made of shiny metal and rimmed in blue and white lights.

A golden beam shone down from the center, illuminating everything with a midday glow. Shielding his eyes against the intense light, he made out what looked like a wide window in the brim of the hat, with the silhouettes of three humanoid figures inside.

Mabel stifled a gasp. She wouldn't have thought to compare "her" UFO to a garden hat, but the description was pretty apt. Apart from the window and humanoid figures, Stanley's description was disturbingly familiar. Maybe his had been closer to the ground, so he'd been able to observe more.

"As they drew nearer, the tallest figure made eye contact with me. Or what would have been eye contact if the thing had eyes. What werelooking back were huge, black, almond-shaped holes in a gray face. Once we locked gazes, I felt he was speaking to me—not with words, but through mental telepathy. Still, my mind received them as words, probably because that's what the human brain is wired for."

Another snort came from Arthur Frost, followed by a stern glare from Prater.

Koslowski cleared his throat and asked for water, which Prater's wife handed him.

"Thank you. I don't recall much of what he told me—it was something about our destruction of the planet, and the need to be better stewards. Then, he said, 'Come.'"

This time Mabel gasped aloud, and John squeezed her hand.

The realization was beginning to sink in that Mabel might have come close to being abducted like Stanley Koslowski. Was that why the spaceship had approached her?

Of course not, Mabel. Get hold of yourself.

Koslowski gave Mabel a sad smile. She hoped he thought her outburst had been due to sympathy—not fellowship.

"That's the last thing I remembered until I regained consciousness sometime later, naked on the ground beside my car. I had strange marks on several areas of my skin, about the size of a teaspoon. I presume those are where the aliens had taken skin scrapings for analysis."

Mabel cringed, partly in revulsion and pity, and partly in embarrassment on Koslowski's behalf, that he seemed to believe such a wild tale.

"The light was gone, and so were the ship and three aliens. My car was no longer sitting on the tracks, and when I turned the key, it started right up. I was shocked when I looked at the dashboard. I felt I'd been unconscious for a matter of minutes, but the clock showed I had been gone two hours."

Frost shifted in his seat. He must have made some movement to speak because Prater told him to hold his remarks.

"Anyway, a couple nights after that, the dreams started. I was on a cold metal table, with intense white light all around me. Gray aliens surrounded me, staring down as the tall one conducted horrible experiments on my body, inserting wires into my ears, and—"

Mabel shuddered.

"I asked you to save your questions, Professor Frost. I'm sure we all respect your reputation, but you will get a turn like everyone else."

The second portion of Koslowski's presentation related to his hypnosis sessions with a psychologist who had worked with other reported alien abductees. Koslowski claimed the sessions brought his repressed memories of the abduction out of his subconscious and into his conscious mind. Subsequent sessions brought out similar memories of other, later abductions.

Koslowski called for questions.

"Did you wake up naked beside the road after those, too?"

Mabel jerked her head around. This catcall had not come from Arthur Frost.

"I woke up in my own bed, in my pajamas, with zero memory of any abduction, aliens, or even strange lights. Apparently, these other abductions occurred at night, in my sleep."

"Now that the aliens have your address—" the second, unidentified male voice said with an audible laugh.

"That will be enough," Prater snapped. "As Hynek once said, 'Ridicule is not a part of the scientific method, and the public should not be taught that it is.' There is significant evidence for the legitimacy of the phenomenon of alien abduction. Stanley is far from the first. If we are to have any value as a UAP organization, we have an obligation to consider the evidence fairly and reasonably—and with no preconceptions. Stanley is a colleague. I expect we will all treat him as such."

"I can show you my scars," Koslowski offered.

"No, thank you." Frost laughed.

To Mabel's surprise, Lisa raised her hand. "Did the later abductions leave any marks on your body which you couldn't explain? At least, until after you did the hypnotic regression?"

Koslowski shook his head. "No. And that's another reason I didn't suspect it had happened until the hypnosis."

Other questions followed, most interested and respectful. The unidentified catcaller maintained a tactful silence under Prater's steely eye.

The debunker, Arthur Frost, raised a languid hand.

Koslowski's jaw tightened. "Frost."

Frost spoke around a grin. "You do realize the pseudo-science of recovered memories has been pretty thoroughly disproven at this point."

"I don't believe that to be true," Koslowski said through clenched teeth. "There's plenty of evidence that recovered memories are perfectly valid."

"Let me read you a statement from the American Medical Association. Would you agree that is an authoritative source?"

"I would agree it is one source. Hardly the sole source. And I am familiar with that statement. In any event, it does not say recovered memories are invalid—simply that the validity cannot be determined. Other credible authorities are convinced otherwise."

Frost's grin broadened. "'Credible.'" He made air quotes. "We've had this discussion before but let's look at your first alleged abduction experience. Leaving aside the 'recovered'"—more air quotes—"memories of that event, let's consider the elements that you were able to recall initially, shall we?"

Koslowski sputtered. "That evidence has been thoroughly investigated by this group. By scientists. By MUFON. I don't think anyone here cares to spend all night rehashing what's well established."

"Mutual UFO Network," Jackie whispered in response to Mabel's quizzical look.

Frost looked around. "Anybody want to talk about what this so-called 'evidence' is? Because if you all think extraterrestrial visitations are an actual, provable, scientific phenomenon, then it should stand up to critical thinking."

Koslowski glowered. "It has and does. Perhaps you saw my case on the History Channel. Or that mine was the focal study case at a conference at the University of Pittsburgh last year."

"For one thing, I don't recall the Pitt forum endorsing your…tale. And TV producers in search of a sensational story for the credulous?" Frost snorted. "People who aren't aware of your little problem." He made a hand gesture, suggesting tipping a glass.

"Liar!" Koslowski roared, lunging at Frost.

Prater reached for Koslowski's arm at the same time John sprang to his feet and blocked Frost's answering lunge. "We're done." Prater said. "This ends the program portion of our meeting."

Frost straightened his tie and his chair screeched as he shoved it aside. "I simply find it morally objectionable for someone to get paid to speak and write about a fabricated episode which gullible people wish were true."

Prater restrained Koslowski and watched Frost go. Once the door had closed and the receding footsteps faded away, he released his grip. Koslowski returned to his seat.

Prater cleared his throat. "Apologies to our visitors. Moving on, I have a couple of interesting news items to share." He reached into a messenger bag on the floor, pulled out a stack of papers, and set them on the lectern.

Despite several hands in the air, it appeared Prater didn't want to deal with any more questions or commentary. Hands drifted back downward, accompanied by a certain amount of mumbling.

"Now, moving along, I wanted to make you all aware we've received a number of recent UAP reports from down in Guthrie County. As you know, they're super rural down there and don't have a local group to investigate.

"They're claiming to have seen unexplained lights— typically one large and intense amber light plus several smaller lights variously reported as white, blue, red, orange, green. Some report electrical disturbances, stalled automobiles, and even attacks on animals. We may be planning a field investigation in the next week or so. Stay tuned."

"Hey!" Mabel blurted. "That's where my thing happened."

Jackie turned to look at her, and Mabel clapped a hand over her mouth.

To Mabel's relief, no one at the other tables seemed to have heard her eruption. Prater continued with his report. "Interestingly, we're also hearing some word of mouth about some additional sightings right in and around Medicine Spring in the last day or two. Anyone here have more info on that?"

Jackie raised her hand. "Similar to the light patterns you described from Guthrie County. Simply lights in the sky, from what I've heard. No other associated phenomena."

"Odd." Prater rubbed his chin. "Of course, people see unexplained lights in the sky all the time. Though they don't usually come in clusters. If you hear more, try to follow up. Doubt they're anything important, but you never know."

A hand went up at the table Jackie had identified as the kook fringe. "Word is the *Empty Eyes* crew's supposed to start rolling in tomorrow. Are we going to talk about the UFO Days festival?"

"I think we should. Of course, nobody saw fit to contact us in advance, but I'd like to see us set up a booth to hand out accurate information about UAPs—and membership forms in case anybody's interested. Looks like table space is fifty dollars. How much do we have in the treasury, Hank?"

"About that."

"Everybody okay with paying for a space?"

No hands went up, so Mabel assumed that meant nobody was opposed—or at least, nobody with the energy to argue about it.

"Sherri, would you see about getting us signed up for the festival space in the armory?"

Someone near the front, presumably Sherri, nodded.

"We can chat amongst ourselves afterward here, but if there's no other business, this meeting is closed."

As chairs scraped and chatter erupted, Jackie grabbed Mabel's arm. "You saw something?"

"Well…" The last thing Mabel wanted to do was get into any of that right now. She looked around, but sadly, saw no sign of a refreshment table.

"It's okay. Most of us here have had sightings."

Mabel glanced toward the kook fringe, who now seemed to be arguing among themselves. She shrugged. "Maybe. Probably nothing."

"Lights?"

"Yeah. Lights."

"Down in Guthrie, you said?"

"That direction. Up on the ridge."

"Look. If you're not comfortable talking about it right now, that's okay. But if you decide you'd like to share, here's my number." Jackie rooted around in the depths of a voluminous, obviously handmade patchwork bag. "I promise it won't go any further, if you don't want it to. I'll be happy to discuss my experience too."

After throwing most of the contents onto the table—a matching handmade wallet and bulging tissue holder, a bag of cough drops, tablet computer, pens, small spiral notebook, crumpled paper, and a five-inch stuffed Martian—she located a business card. A loose cough drop had unwrapped and stuck itself to the card, but Jackie pried it loose with no apparent embarrassment.

She handed the card to Mabel, who grasped it by the least sticky corner and read the script, which appeared inside a shooting star on a background of other stars and planets.

Jacquelin Masefield

Science Fiction & Fantasy Writer

Contact information followed.

"You're a writer." Mabel stated the obvious. "So am I."

Lisa tapped her shoulder. "I'm going to stop in the restroom. I'll meet you by the door."

The hint was blatant. John was still waiting patiently, but Lisa had an early school day tomorrow.

"Look. I came with my friends, and I need to get going, but maybe I'll give you a call." *Maybe, but not likely.*

Jackie seemed to sense Mabel was slipping away from her. "Hey, look. You're a writer? Why don't you come to our writers' group over at the library in Bartles Grove? I'll put the info on the back of my card."

After some more fiddling around, trying to come up with a pen that was up to the job, Jackie returned her business card to Mabel. "Do you have a card?"

"Not on me." *Or anywhere else.*

"Okay. Just tell me, and I'll write it down."

Short of the awkward "no," Mabel was stuck. At least Jackie seemed normal enough. Hopefully, she wouldn't become a pest and force Mabel to change her number and move out of town.

Mabel dictated the number. Jackie pushed up her sleeve and wrote it on her arm. After exchanging pleasantries, Mabel watched her phone number walk out of the room.

Chapter Fifteen

THE MORNING AFTER THE UFO GROUP meeting Mabel woke shortly after six am from a terrifying dream of being abducted by aliens, to the sound of Barnacle's whining and frantic scratching at the bedroom door.

Ordinarily, Mabel wouldn't have appreciated the dog's early potty call. But given she'd woken in her own bed, without any spacemen hovering over her with scalpels, she could only go limp with relief.

Mabel opened one eye. "I'm coming." The room was dark, and she had to fumble for her slippers. The moment she opened the bedroom door, Barnacle charged down the steps—and the moment she opened the outside door, she realized she'd made a huge mistake.

Before she could get him clipped to his run-out cable, the dog blasted across the yard. This wasn't a potty call.

Almost at once, the stench of skunk filled the air. "Barnacle!" she shrieked.

Luckily—or unluckily—he came racing back, and she barely managed to snag his collar before he could bring the smell inside. Trying to hold her breath, she hooked him to the cable. She hoped the skunk had left. Hopefully, it wasn't able to spray again so soon after the first blast.

Backing through the door, she shoved at him with her slippered foot. "Stay," she ordered, shutting him outside and herself inside.

She gagged at the stench that had wafted through the open door while she'd been struggling with Barnacle. These slippers would have to be burned...or at least, triple bagged and tossed.

The dog clean-up took hours, between online research, gathering and mixing home remedies, and lugging everything out to the back yard, including bucket after bucket of water, not to mention the actual scrubbing and rinsing. It was freezing outside too. "You might have had the decency to do this in August instead of November."

When she'd run through all her concoctions and washed and rinsed the dog three times, Mabel conceded defeat. Barnacle was hanging his head in apparent embarrassment and misery, shivering, with his tail between his legs—and he still reeked.

The worst of the stink had dissipated somewhat, mixed as it was with lavender-scented dish liquid and tomato juice. But she still couldn't conceive of living with this smell.

As soon as she brought him indoors, Mabel shoved the unhappy dog into the basement. "I'm sorry, bud, but this is your fault. I'm going to have to leave you in there till I can get you to a groomer for a professional treatment."

The old towels she'd used went straight into a trash bag, along with her slippers and pjs. She set the bag outside and went upstairs for a scalding shower and shampoo. Koi, still peacefully draped across Mabel's pillow, opened one incurious eye and closed it again. The cat didn't seem bothered by her smell, which Mabel received as good news. Maybe her aroma wasn't so bad.

By eight o'clock, Mabel was drinking coffee and trying to ignore Barnacle's mournful howls and scratching at the basement door, as she combed online listings for grooming shops that professed themselves willing and capable of de-skunking dogs. They were few and far between, but she finally got an online booking for a horrifying price at a place beyond Bartles Grove for later that afternoon.

She considered her half box of frosted cereal for a few

seconds, then decided she deserved a diner breakfast after what she'd been through. "Back soon," she promised over Barnacle's yowls. Koi, tail tucked neatly around her front feet, didn't even look up from her bowl of kibble.

The odor of skunk still lingered when Mabel stepped out into the foggy back yard. Holding her breath, she lugged the heavy trash bag to the covered metal can beside the wreckage of her shed, which Acey had recently demolished when his truck brakes failed. Then, she hustled inside her car for the short trip into town.

Mabel was surprised when she had to wait to make her left turn at the corner of Carteret and Pike. It had been a while since she'd been out and about during morning rush hour. She glanced at her dash clock. Lisa would already be at work by now.

She thought of calling or texting John but didn't want to appear pushy. Besides, maybe she should try her aroma on the other diner patrons before exposing John to it. She couldn't notice it on herself anymore but suspected she might have burned out her sense of smell.

She was about to pass Ash Street when she realized the typically quiet residential street was clogged with vehicles, including trucks and trailers, some of which bore the familiar "Explore" network logo and one with a larger-than-life headshot of Leif Steele. It appeared the *Empty Eyes* investigative team had arrived.

Unable to resist rubbernecking, Mabel pulled into a spot on Main Street and walked back.

Despite the early hour, a crowd had gathered outside the new bed-and-breakfast next to Pete's house. Mabel recognized a few *Empty Eyes* groupies from last night's meeting. Several held familiar cream-colored go cups with "The Coffee Cup" in brown script. Almost everyone was holding a cell phone, shooting pictures or video.

Pete stood on his covered porch in a red-plaid flannel

bathrobe, staring at the chaos with gloom written across his face. Mabel recalled his strange behavior in the cemetery the night before. Clearly, Pete was deeply disturbed by everything about this proposed investigation. And clearly—at least in Mabel's eyes—his agitation amounted to more than simple, even admirable, respect for the remains of the flying saucer crew. It even went beyond the annoyance of having this…traveling circus setting up right at his doorstep.

She worked her way through the crowd, collecting a few dirty looks from people who seemed to think she wanted to jump ahead of them for a better view. "Good morning," she called, and Pete looked over.

Pete had always been friendly and welcoming when she stopped by. This time, though, his expression closed.

Ignoring the snub, Mabel climbed the porch steps and gave him a big smile. "This is unbelievable. Doesn't even seem like Medicine Spring, does it?"

He shook his head, and, leaning on the railing, glanced over at the B&B. "Viola took a couple headache pills and went back to bed with earplugs in. And it's not even lunch time, Day One."

"I know it's a big house, but how can they hold the film crew, on-air people, investigators, and the—you know—tourists?"

"They can't. This is mainly gonna be the big cheese and such. From what I understand, everybody else will be heading out to Scooter's Motel."

"I guess it wouldn't be *so* bad, if not for the fans and such." Mabel made a sympathetic face at Pete. "At least when the TV personalities leave, or go inside and shut the doors, maybe everybody else will leave too."

He shook his head. "People were camped out there all night long. They had lawn chairs and sleeping bags, and one outfit set up and was ready to cook on a hibachi thing. Viola had to call the cops to get the firebugs to disperse. They said they couldn't do anything about people on a public sidewalk."

"A few people at night maybe, if they weren't disturbing the peace or anything. Surely, they aren't allowed to block the street during the day."

Pete tossed a nod toward the far end of the block, where a cruiser was parked. Two officers lounged against the car, apparently just watching the show.

Looking in that direction, Mabel spotted two other, familiar figures. Miss Birdie and Ms. Katherine Ann stood at the edge of the crowd, both doing bicep curls with their hand weights as they took in the excitement. Mabel waved, but they didn't seem to see her. Their attention was riveted on the milling crowd.

"Any idea how long these folks plan to be in town?"

"None whatsoever, 'cept it's got to be expensive to put up all these people, even over at Scooter's—which isn't the best, I hate to say—not to mention all the paychecks. Plus, I expect they got rentals on a lot of their equipment."

Mabel patted his hand. "That's the spirit. Look on the bright side. How long can they possibly afford to waste here?" Chaos erupted in the street as the crowd surged toward the B&B with a great deal of shoving. Mabel craned to see what had generated so much excitement.

Arthur Frost had come out onto the B&B porch, coffee mug in hand, his nearly chin-length silver-threaded hair swept back and appearing damp from a shower. Today, he wore a variation on his costume from the night before—slim jeans paired with a charcoal, quarter-zip sweater.

As a roughly equal volume of questions, cheers, and boos went up from the shoving mass of people, Frost raised a hand. "Thank you, all. I'm only attempting to enjoy my morning coffee, so no need to become agitated." The hand made a shooing motion. "As you were."

Mabel snorted. He could've had his coffee inside if he didn't want to interact with people. "He's enjoying this."

"Oh, for sure." Pete made a show of checking a nonexistent wristwatch. "Must be ego-feeding time."

"Whoa." Mabel ducked instinctively as a raw egg, thrown from somewhere in the crowd, flew toward the arrogant debunker. The egg missed by yards, smashing against the back of some guy's Mothman hoodie. The red-faced victim spun around and launched himself through the crowd in search of the perpetrator.

The angry young man grabbed the jacket collar of a sixtyish man, who was yelling at Frost about his having humiliated him on national television during an episode of a haunted house reality show.

A few stool pigeons in the crowd hissed and pointed at another scruffy, middle-aged, bearded guy in a black coat, slinking toward the back of the crowd. He was carrying an egg in one hand, and the carton quite obviously protruded from his coat pocket. Mabel startled. She recognized him from the UFO meeting, when he'd made a move to tackle the debunker. He was even wearing the same coat—she recognized the rip on the right sleeve.

The guy in the yolk-spattered hoodie let go of the guy he'd been holding onto and with a roar, charged after the egg man.

"Mr. Frost." A thirtyish man, brandishing a voice recorder, pushed through the crowd and advanced on the house despite Frost's rebuff. Mabel recognized the newshound as a reporter for the *Bartle County Shopper* newspaper, whose photo appeared above a weekly column, though his name escaped her. His bristly dirty-blond hair and trademark wire-rim glasses were unmistakable.

Renny Martin…that's it.

"May I have a moment of your time, Mr. Frost?"

Frost sneered. "It's *Dr.* Frost or *Professor* Frost."

"Then, may I please have a moment of your time, Dr. Frost?"

"No, you may not. You must have a hearing impairment because I've already stated that I wish to quietly enjoy my coffee…such as it is."

Frost leaned picturesquely against a porch column as people snapped photos. If he had been hoping the eager-beaver reporter would continue to beg for an interview, he was out of luck.

The entire crowd, including Renny Martin, turned at once, like spilled iron filings drawn to a magnet, as a low, dark-green sports car turned the corner. His preening interrupted, Frost pushed off from the pillar and headed inside. His posture was nonchalant, but Mabel had caught the scowl on his face.

"Dang fools are gonna get themselves run over." Pete watched the surging crowd and shook his head.

"Look at that car." Mabel knew less than nothing about cars, but she recognized this one was something special.

"Classic Jaguar. Must be the big cheese, whatshisname."

Mabel looked from the car back to Pete. "Leif Steele?"

"Yep. That's him."

Chapter Sixteen

IN SECONDS, STEELE'S CLASSIC CAR WAS covered in screaming, babbling, stammering fans. He laid on the horn till Mabel's ears rang, and a couple of burly types converged on the car and began peeling people away.

The blare of the horn also finally seemed to arouse the two police officers, who pushed their way through the clog of rabid fans. One raised a bullhorn. "Everybody out of the street. Back on the sidewalk. No shoving or you'll be required to disperse."

One of Steele's security detail had to physically remove a thirtyish, magenta-streaked bleach-blonde who was sobbing, either in despair or inexpressible joy, as she was dragged away from the car. "He signed my shirt," she sobbed. "Look. He signed my shirt."

Okay. Joy, then. Mabel shrugged.

Now, the cops were pulling another woman away from the blonde. It seemed she'd tried to rip the shirt right off the blonde's back.

Pete wiped his nose. "You remember the Beatles, Mabel?"

Mabel frowned. "I'm familiar with the Beatles. I certainly don't 'remember' them."

"That's the way teenage girls used to screech when they saw Ringo Starr."

Mabel watched as Steele headed for the B&B porch, surrounded by his security team and police escort. Despite the cold, the intrepid UFO investigator was wearing an unzipped black motorcycle jacket over a black tee-shirt. He kept his handsome profile angled downward till he got to the porch steps, where he paused, turned, and raised one hand to wave to his appreciative fans.

Arthur Frost had stepped back outside. He watched Steele's approach with apparent amusement. As Steele stepped onto the porch, Frost, grinning, leaned in and spoke into his ear.

Steele, appearing momentarily disconcerted, looked sharply at the debunker, before pulling himself together and turning back to thank his supporters for coming out. He gestured at Frost with one hand. "I'm sure this man needs no introduction. Dr. Arthur Frost will be joining our investigation here in Medicine Spring in hopes of debunking the 1958 crash reports."

More boos rose from the assembled throng. It seemed, though Frost was a celebrity of sorts, his chosen role as a spoiler hadn't endeared him to the flying saucer crowd.

As Mabel watched the small drama unfold, Pete turned to her. "I believe the wind shifted there. I just got a whiff of skunk."

As Mabel made her way back to her car, she marveled at the number of people milling around Ash Street and even beyond. Since the law firm fired her months ago, she had experienced a lot of financial stress and self-doubt but had to admit she'd enjoyed not having to get dressed up and go to work every weekday morning.

Now, here were all these folks who also seemed free to wander about on a Wednesday morning, and many were much too young to be ordinary retirees. Surely, they couldn't all be unemployed—not in a town the size of Medicine Spring.

Mabel peered at license plates. Sure enough, there were several out-of-state plates parked right on this block. Of course, those weren't all that uncommon in the Tri-State area of western Pennsylvania, but one plate was from Kentucky—definitely not a neighboring state.

"Hey, Mabel." She turned at the shout and saw Jackie from

the UFO group, crossing the street in her direction.

"Hi." Mabel waited till Jackie had navigated the unusually heavy traffic, which included a battered, repurposed school bus, belching blue smoke and emblazoned with a drooping side banner that read, "UFO Search Team."

The sci-fi writer was wrapped in what appeared to be a handmade granny-square coat that flapped around the ankles of her Army-surplus, olive drab rainboots. "What brings you out here?" Jackie lifted one ear flap of her trapper hat, presumably so she'd be able to converse without saying, "Huh?" every couple minutes.

Mabel explained about getting skunked…probably unnecessarily, since Jackie had approached and then moved a couple casual paces back already. "When I saw all the activity over on Ash, I had to go rubberneck."

Jackie's cheeks were rosy from the morning chill, and she looked younger than she had under the fluorescent lights. "It's a lot of excitement for Medicine Spring, but I plan to wait and see what they turn up before I get too carried away. I want proof."

Mabel tilted her head. Jackie was less starstruck and more levelheaded than she'd expected. "What kind of proof?"

Jackie seemed to think. "Maybe underground imaging an objective third-party expert can analyze. Maybe historical images or documents that can be authenticated, for instance."

"Isn't that what Dr. Frost is here for? To subject whatever evidence Steele produces to a high level of scrutiny?"

"In theory." Jackie glanced over her shoulder and then leaned back into the skunk zone. "Frost is supposed to be objective, but anybody can see one hand washes the other. It's a rare Leif Steele special investigation that Frost doesn't end up 'amazed' by the 'incredible evidence.' And maybe it is…but the pattern makes you wonder."

"Well, I guess at least the film crew should get access to

places and things none of the rest of us ever would. Technology is light years better today than it was in '58."

Jackie nodded. "True. It's going to make fascinating viewing, no matter what Steele's conclusions are. Even people who think Leif Steele's a joke—and they are legion—will have to tune in, right? He's correct that this incident was ripe for a deep dive, and people are going to be interested."

Jackie resettled her blue-framed glasses and lowered her voice. "If you ask me, I think he's been holding this one in his hip pocket for a while, just waiting for when he needed it most."

Mabel frowned. "What does that mean?"

"When his ratings needed a huge boost."

"And they do?"

"Yeah, he's been slipping for a while. Shows with bigger budgets have been doing whole seasons investigating high-profile/restricted-access places like Skinwalker Ranch. Or you'll have younger investigators that draw a wider audience. Stuff like that." Again, Jackie cast a look around, as if Leif Steele himself were going to come charging up and confront her.

"So this is his big do-or-die?"

"Well…maybe not quite that bad. But yeah. He needs hype, and he needs to produce."

After removing a neon green slip of paper from beneath her windshield wiper, Mabel unlocked her car and slid inside. The flyer invited the recipient to enjoy a half-price Little Green Man daquiri during happy hour at the Continental Lounge. Mabel rolled her eyes and stuffed it in her litter bag. The hype Steele needed to generate for this special investigation stunt of his seemed to be going gangbusters—at least, here in Medicine Spring.

As she waited for a break in traffic, Mabel noticed someone standing at a distance, hunched in a navy winter parka and watching the craziness in front of the B&B. *Nanette?* Mabel shook her head. Of all people. It appeared UFO fever was getting to everybody.

Main Street was—if possible—even busier than Ash Street, where Leif Steele was drawing crowds. Here was Acey, on a ladder this time, struggling to attach a UFO Days banner to a light pole. It seemed UFOs took precedence over Christmas lights, as well as Mabel's storm windows. There was enough wind so that every time Acey attempted to hang the banner, it either flipped over or blew out of his hand.

Acey hadn't even mentioned this other side job to her. Her home winterization seemed more distant by the day. Mabel was tempted to blast her horn at him but managed to control that unworthy impulse. Maybe she should go ahead and buy some of that shrink-type plastic people used to cover their windows, then try to use a blow dryer and do it herself.

Mabel reached The Coffee Cup but reluctantly crawled on by. People were standing in line out the door. She couldn't remember a single time that had ever happened, even on Sunday after church, ordinarily the diner's busiest time.

She had to stomp the brake to avoid a couple of giggling, darting teenagers. Why weren't they in school? Was everybody playing hooky today?

Mabel was still hungry, and since she was running the heater, she thought she could smell skunk.

She checked the time. It was still hours till Barnacle's grooming appointment. If she grabbed something quick to eat, she had time to take another shower, wash her hair again, and burn her clothes…theoretically. Drive-through breakfast was probably a better idea, anyway. She should get home soon to feed her bad boy, still waiting in the cellar.

Feeling resigned, she turned at the next corner and headed out of town, toward the fast-food cluster by the mall. She could always eat takeout in her car.

On her way to breakfast, Mabel passed Scooter's. The old one-level strip motel must have dated back at least to the sixties and could have used a fresh coat of turquoise paint. It was the sort of place that makes you decide to keep driving and look for someplace better, even if you're exhausted, and it's after ten at night. Their lot was full though—possibly for the first time since it was built—and she saw a couple of what looked like equipment trucks.

Mabel turned in at the first drive-through that advertised breakfast on their sign and ordered pancakes, sausage patties, eggs, and a biscuit with coffee. Then a pang of conscience assailed her when she thought of John, and she added an orange juice.

When she'd picked up her order, she parked facing the row of stores and businesses and arranged her food on the dashboard and her lap. Maple syrup had been a mistake, she soon realized. Napkins and hand sanitizer were not equal to the job.

There sat the Continental Lounge at the far end of the strip. Next to it, Gianni's Italian Restaurant. When the door opened and someone carried pizza to his car, Mabel smelled the fennel in the sausage, and her mouth watered. She hadn't realized you could get pizza this early. She considered calling in an order to take home with her, but then sternly reminded herself she was still eating breakfast.

Party Time…the special occasion store made her cringe. It reminded her that as Lisa's maid of honor, she was responsible for planning a bridal shower—and soon. She didn't even know a lot of Lisa's friends—a college roommate, other teachers, people from her church. She supposed Job One would be procuring a list of phone numbers and email addresses from Lisa…and then, praying someone else on the friend list was good at planning things.

As she ruminated over where and how to make a bridal shower happen, the doors next to Party Time opened, and chattering young women began trickling out. Most wore open coats over what looked like slim-fitting yoga gear and carried rolled-up mats.

When a familiar—and fuller—figure emerged, Mabel did a doubletake. She hadn't seen Shanita in decades, and now, she seemed to be everywhere.

Mabel pushed the button to roll down her window, then realized she'd need to turn on the engine again. After shuffling her food to the passenger seat, she opened her door. "Nita."

Nita turned her head and brightened. Giving a quick wave, she looked both ways and trotted over to Mabel's car. Her scarlet swing coat whirled around her, opening and closing over snug black yoga pants and scoop-neck tee.

Nita looked like a million bucks. Mabel wondered what it would feel like to have her confidence.

"Hey, Mabel. I'd ask if you wanted to go for breakfast, but I see you already got yours."

Darn. Mabel sighed. "I shouldn't, anyway. My dog Barnacle got skunked this morning, and I kind of did too."

"Well, I don't notice anything. I usually pick up a bite to take back to the shop on yoga mornings, but I'd rather eat with you."

"Well, if you want to grab something and join me, that would be great."

"Give me a sec to dump my gear in my car and go get my food—be right back." Nita thumped the roof of Mabel's car.

By the time her friend returned, Mabel had moved her food from the passenger seat and spread a few napkins over the tiny sticky spot left after she'd wiped up a few drops of escaped syrup. Nita hopped in and opened a bag containing a breakfast sandwich, hashbrowns, a yogurt parfait, and hot tea.

"How's it going with the book event?"

Nita unwrapped her sandwich. "Okay, at least with what I can control. What worries me is what I *can't.*"

"Are you taking any…precautions?"

Nita held up a finger as she took a big bite of her sandwich, chewed, and swallowed. "Hard to know what kind of precautions to take. I mean for all I know, they'll have a big old brawl. I know I don't want any of my other stock anywhere near where they're signing."

"Can you put their tables in different areas of the store? Maybe if they're not right next to each other, the warring factions won't end up mixing."

Nita paused with a hashbrown patty halfway to her mouth and gave Mabel a disbelieving look. "Mabel. You have seen my store. Where you think I'm going to put three separate tables? Not to mention the food. I always have some punch or something like that to drink. Cheese and veggie trays, cookies. You know. Everybody's gonna stop and check out the food. And there is no way, earthly or otherwise, I can set up three food tables."

"I see the problem, but—"

"His security team called me last night."

"Whose? Leif Steele?"

"Yup. Who else? They wanted to know where the exits were. Had I hired any private security for the evening? Did I make any arrangements for crowd control? I'm afraid I'm either going to end up getting sued or lose my insurance over this."

"Well, wait a minute. There must be things we can do. You mentioned crowd control. Why don't you post someone at the door and only let in so many people at a time? Set up rope dividers to keep the lines under control? You must be able to rent those somewhere around here."

Shanita was nodding as she ate. "Not a bad idea. Maybe pick up a couple extra fire extinguishers."

Mabel's eyes widened. "I wouldn't think anybody's going to torch the place."

"Don't be too sure. Anyway, I was thinking we could use 'em to separate the folks who get out of control."

Chapter Seventeen

IT HAD BEEN A LONG, STRESSFUL day by the time she and Barnacle returned home from the groomer. The dog hung over her shoulder as she drove, grinning and drooling with happiness.

Mabel sniffed. She couldn't smell skunk anymore—on either of them. She wasn't sure if the improved air quality was due to all the scrubbing, or if her nose had finally surrendered and adapted to the skunk bouquet.

Barnacle's professional treatment should be effective, for what she'd paid. Thanks to him, she'd now spent what she'd set aside for unplanned repairs to her aging car.

The sun was already down, and only the afterglow still lingered over the horizon as she approached the house. As her headlights hit the side driveway, she groaned. A car already sat blocking her.

Who in the world?

Mabel pulled to the curb and clipped Barnacle's leash to his collar. She stepped out to see a figure emerge from the shadows of her front porch.

"There you are at last." Linnea came down the steps, as welcome a sight as a swarm of murder hornets.

Barnacle growled and lunged, then subsided into happy whining and more lunging and jumping. Mabel shortened the leash, leaned back, and held on.

"Hi, Linnea. Was there something you needed?"

"There *was.* But since I'm here, I also need to ask, what is the meaning of this?" She flashed an intense LED penlight beam first to the front of Mabel's house, where all three of Cletus Pettigrew's campaign signs stood in formation. Then her spotlight swept to the brush at the far corner where Mabel's property ended at the Willow Creek Park boundary. She squinted. Through the tangle of vines and branches, Mabel could make out a few legible words on LeRoy Casselman's sign.

Terrific. Could this day get any worse? Mabel gritted her teeth.

"Acey Davis. He must've stopped by. He's Pettigrew's cousin." Hanging onto Barnacle with one hand, she wrestled to pull the offensive signs out of the ground.

She snuck a peek but as expected saw no evidence her handyman had done a lick of work while he was here. Mabel threw the signs onto the porch with more violence than strictly required for the job.

"Look, I need to get my dog inside and feed my pets. You're welcome to come in for a moment."

A look of distaste crossed Linnea's face. "No, thank you. What about the other sign?"

Mabel looked around. Other sign? There wasn't another sign.

Linnea cleared her throat and pointed. "LeRoy's sign. Really, Mabel. Were you planning to leave it in the weeds?"

Good grief. Give me a break.

Dragging her whining, excited dog behind her, Mabel stomped over to the property line and yanked at the sign until she'd gotten it free of the earth and untangled from the bushes. She almost lost her balance and landed on her backside, but after a moment's flailing, stomped back to Linnea and jammed the wire supports into the ground.

"There."

"Sorry to say this, but I'm forced to question your support for our candidate."

No kidding.

Linnea's eyes narrowed. "As you know, election day is fast

approaching, and we have no time to drag our feet. I've come to ask you to join our phone bank at campaign headquarters this weekend."

Mabel felt her eyes widen in horror. "But…"

"Cora asked me personally to make sure all hands were on deck. We're going to be working four-hour shifts Saturday and Sunday, but of course, you are more than welcome to do a double." She shoved a schedule at Mabel. "Now, which slot or slots do you prefer?"

"Oh, Linnea, I'm sorry, but I didn't know. I, uh, have plans to visit my parents this weekend. They're extremely elderly, and I can't disappoint them." Mabel's plans had been made the instant she heard the words "phone bank."

"You won't be tied up for the entire weekend, will you? Can't you spare just four hours?"

Mabel wavered. Her parents lived right on the other side of Bartles Grove, and there was no way she was staying overnight—not in view of the book-signing she'd offered to help with. But she wasn't phone banking, and she wasn't going to lie.

Slowly, she shook her head. "I've made other commitments for my weekend. I'm sorry, but there's no way I can help."

Linnea moved closer and placed a hand on Mabel's shoulder. Her eyes met Mabel's with a look worthy of a heartrending plea for one of Mabel's kidneys. "Do it for the privy."

"I'm sorry," Mabel repeated, turning firmly toward her back door, tugging at Barnacle, who was running his nose intently over Linnea's woolen pantleg. "I can't. Not even for the outhouse."

Her parting image of Linnea was an expression mixed of equal parts disbelief at being turned down and general disgust with Mabel. Mabel smiled. In the end, it had been a satisfying exchange.

Except now, she had to arrange a previously unplanned visit

with her parents. She'd be glad to see them, of course, except that she'd been avoiding going home for the past few weeks due to her mother's unrelenting pressure to get Grandma Mabel's clutter out of the house. As if Mabel weren't already stressed enough.

Koi met them at the kitchen door, fixing Mabel with a judgmental eye. She might as well have demanded, "Where have you been all this time, young lady?"

"Sorry," Mabel repeated. She was less than half joking whenever she told people Koi ran things around here.

Dumping her coat and purse on the kitchen table, she began filling food dishes for the animals. What a day this had been.

While her animals gobbled their dinner, and Mabel's leftovers heated in the microwave, she called to let Mom know she planned to visit. Then, she went upstairs to change into leggings and a sweatshirt, her usual cold-weather sleep attire. She was sliding her feet into her slippers with a sense of relief when her phone began playing John's ringtone.

"Hey, Mabel. What have you been up to?"

"I don't even know where to begin. It's been quite a day."

"You want to go to a movie?"

Mabel had never dreamed she'd turn down a date with John, but the thought of leaving the house again tonight felt like having to scale the side of a building. "You know what? I'd love to, but I'm wiped out."

"That's okay. To be honest, I don't even know what's playing right now. Mostly, just wanted to talk. Have you heard the scuttlebutt in town?"

"If you mean the UFO festival, I've heard all kinds of scuttlebutt. Which scuttlebutt are you talking about?"

"Not about the festival, it's all these new sightings."

"New sightings? What?"

"Apparently, the past couple nights, all sorts of people have started reporting more strange lights in the sky. In fact, one of my students at the community college up in Bartles Grove told me he saw them, and he's pretty solid."

Mabel retrieved her dinner from the microwave and plopped herself down at the table. "Like what? Tell me."

"Well, he was walking to his car at the student parking lot by my building after class yesterday. It was still pretty early, but the sun had gone down. He'd gotten his keys out when, as he says, a brilliant light flashed overhead. It was intense, but it happened so fast he never even got a chance to look up."

This didn't sound anything at all like Mabel's experience. "Shooting star? I've seen a couple of those before."

"Yeah, I have too. But they were way high in the sky—and not really all that bright. Not what he described."

Mabel chewed her lip. "Advertising maybe? You know those searchlights they put up sometimes?"

"Again, usually much farther away and dimmer. Plus, he waited and watched to see if it reappeared, and it didn't. You know how those searchlights keep cycling around."

"It does sound kind of weird, but that's not what I saw. Or even what Miss Birdie and Ms. Katherine Ann said they saw. Those were all arrays of colored lights and they hovered. They did a bit more than streak overhead."

John laughed. "You haven't heard the half of it yet. Everybody seems to know somebody who's seen mysterious lights in the sky—talking only the past couple days, mind you. Josh—my student—only saw that quick flash he couldn't explain. But a few people describe seeing some sort of shape in the light. Like a ship of some kind. Others swear they heard unearthly sounds."

"Who's saying this?" Mabel realized she was forgetting to eat and shoveled a rapidly-cooling spoonful of reheated chili into her mouth.

"To be honest, I suspect it's like that Gossip game, where one whispers to the next, and after a while, the story bears no resemblance to where it started out. You've got to allow for folks with vivid imaginations in the mix."

"But who? Did anybody else you or I know say they've seen something?"

"No. They only said someone *they* knew claims to have seen the lights. Or a friend of a friend says they overheard something at the grocery store or in line at the post office."

Mabel shook her head to clear it and sighed. "I'm guessing it's all part of the general hysteria. I wish that stupid Leif Steele film crew had never decided to zero in on Medicine Spring. It sounded fun at first, but now people are acting plain foolish. Half of them are starstruck, half of them are moonstruck, and half of them—like me—wish everybody would go on home and settle down."

"That's three halves."

"You know what I mean. There are people seeing green men with antennas on their heads in their own back yards, and the rest are mooning over all these B-list celebrities who've decided to grace our town with their presence. I'll bet a bunch of the UFO crowd is hoping they'll get to be interviewed on camera."

"Like the guy with the museum."

"Right. Unless he and that horrible debunker manage to kill each other first. And, sure, all this national attention sounds exciting, but the more I hear, the more I feel like it's not worth it. Even if we get more visitors, are we sure this is the kind of attention we want? We could end up a laughingstock."

"Come on, Mabel. Our downtown's been half dead for years. Now, every business in town's doing a brisk business in tee-shirts, junky souvenirs, and UFO-themed food. You can hardly get a seat in The Coffee Cup anymore."

"I, myself, *prefer* being able to find a seat at The Coffee Cup. And a place to park. Anyway, how long are these lookie-loos going to stick around after filming is over? One TV special won't salvage our economy."

"Cletus Pettigrew says it will. He wants to start producing brochures promoting Medicine Spring as a UFO destination and make the festival an annual thing."

Mabel massaged her head. "I'm going to speculate LeRoy Casselman's agin it."

"Of course. He wants to cash in on Medicine Spring's smalltown charm—reclaim the gardens on the Jubilee Johnson property, restore the privy—"

"And draw tourists to our charming ax murder house," Mabel couldn't resist adding.

John snorted. "Which candidate are you supporting again?"

"It's complicated. But I think even the business owners are going to have to think about the larger consequences of this influx of single-interest visitors, not to mention what the film crew is up to. Apparently, they roll right in and get carte blanche? Stunts like drones and LIDAR scans…"

"LIDAR?"

"You've got to get with the lingo. Light detection and ranging—you use it, or at least I think—to do modeling of ground elevations. Can you imagine the reports police will be getting once they're flying drones over Medicine Spring?"

"I'd rather not," John said. "How long till somebody decides we're under attack and tries to shoot one down?"

"That's my point. Tensions within the UFO 'community' and maybe even the TV squad, from what I've seen, are bonkers. I think it could get dangerous."

"It shouldn't have to be this way. Like the guy in charge of the meeting we went to was saying, we should be studying all this evidence scientifically."

"Exactly. Not feeding into a panic—or ridiculing and fighting with people who disagree with us." Mabel pushed away her now-cold chili. She got up to search the freezer for the remains of that carton of orange-pineapple ice cream she'd been rationing out, because it was so hard to find.

Mabel moved a frost-covered half bag of green beans. "Nita's worrying about security and crowd control for her book-signing. Can you even imagine?"

"Afraid so, after what I've been seeing."

"I volunteered to help out—but I'm starting to think I ought to wear a helmet and flak jacket."

John was silent for a moment. Mabel dug out the somewhat crumpled box of ice cream and a spoon. "You there?"

"I don't like the sound of that. You didn't mention it was that bad. Do you think I should come too?"

"Glad you mentioned that. To be honest, I was going to ask you. Lisa too."

"What exactly is the problem? Those two who were practically brawling at the meeting?"

"Not to mention their fans. You remember Jackie, the one who was telling us about the different factions in the local UFO group. So, they can't get along under normal circumstances. Now, you're going to put them all in a tiny space, where their gurus are there specifically to promote their respective theories, and expect them to keep to their own kind and not talk trash?"

John whistled. "I wouldn't."

"No, and now Nita wishes she hadn't. She didn't know when she set up the big signing event, and now, it's too late."

"I hope there's a cop or two around."

"Me too. Nita and I were also talking about a few other things we can do to try to keep a lid on it though."

John yawned. "Let's plan to get together with her ahead of time and get a battle plan in place. Since we didn't go anywhere tonight, you want to try to get breakfast tomorrow?"

"If we can wrangle a seat at The Coffee Cup."

"We'll go early—with the hunters."

Mabel groaned inwardly. At least breakfast was a powerful incentive.

Chapter Eighteen

While she got ready to meet John for breakfast, Mabel turned on the *Country Morning* TV show. She was rarely up and ready to face the chipper faces of the AM hosts before her coffee, but today she felt she needed that extra help getting her eyes open.

As she was feeding her animals their breakfast and waiting for her coffee to finish brewing, the weatherman pointed out low pressure systems and talked about the chance of a few snowflakes later in the day. Mabel listened with half an ear.

She ran upstairs to put on a little makeup, something she felt was a public service when she was going to be out and about, especially with John. She pulled out her favorite slim jeans and was grieved to see a new snag on the left knee. Was it tiny enough to go unnoticed? She hoped so.

When Mabel came downstairs again, the weather was over, and the program had gone back to the morning team. She was about to dash into the kitchen to pour some coffee when she heard Bee Novak mention "our very special guest, Leif Steele."

Mabel scrambled to grab her mug and get back to the living room, narrowly missing falling over Barnacle on her way back. The segment had already started by the time she settled on the couch with her coffee and a quick glance at the time on her phone. She had ten minutes.

Leif Steele looked as if a giant hand had plucked him off the *Empty Eyes* show with its mystery/adventure/paranormal vibe and dropped him into a kitschy farmhouse living room, complete with a fake window behind the couch offering a view of rolling autumn fields. He lounged in one of the overstuffed chairs, legs crossed with a booted foot resting on the opposite knee. His gray-flecked dark hair was a bit more tousled than usual, suggesting he'd just rolled out of bed, too cool to overthink his appearance. Steele wore one of his show's signature graphic tees—black, of course, and a size too small, so that his muscles were fighting to escape.

Bee was giggling as she interviewed him, obviously more than a bit starstruck. At least to Mabel's knowledge, the biggest name ever to appear on *Country Morning* previously had been a state senator. Mabel had appeared on the show herself not long ago, and Bee had certainly not simpered over her this way.

"So, Mr. Steele—"

"Please. Call me Leif." Steele smiled, displaying a mouthful of spectacular dental work.

"Leif." Another little giggle. "This is such an honor. Would you mind telling our viewers what made you decide to come to Bartle County for this special investigation—and then, what do you have in mind for us?"

"Glad to, Bee. Over the years, teams have investigated so many famous UFO incidents in this country, or UAP—that's unidentified anomalous phenomena—as we now call them. Roswell, of course. Hopkinsville, Kentucky. The Lubbock Lights. I could go on, of course."

"Of course," Bee and her co-host—the similarly starry-eyed Doug Constantino—chorused.

"Yet some equally credible incidents have never gotten the attention they really deserve. I find the '58 Miller's Woods crash to be one of the most fascinating, as well as one of the least known. We aim to change that.

"My team and I intend to ferret out the truth of what happened that night, using the most advanced modern technology available—ground-penetrating radar, LIDAR, aerial photography, EMF meters, radiation detectors…"

Steele paused and beamed at Bee. "I'll be happy to explain

all that to your viewers in a moment, of course." Mabel was forced to admire how he'd managed to make it appear that any clarification was strictly for the audience, and that Bee and Doug were already conversant with all the latest tech.

"Before we go there—one more item I find particularly intriguing about Medicine Spring—or the Miller's Woods event, as I like to call it—is the anecdotal evidence that crew members were recovered from this crash, and at least one of them was removed from the wreckage alive."

Steele paused for a gasp from Bee Novak. Like Mabel, she appeared previously unfamiliar with the details of the event, perhaps because she had first moved from Texas a couple of years ago to take this job. Though Mabel wouldn't have been surprised if the gasp had been calculated to add excitement to the interview.

"A unique aspect of this account," Leif continued, "is the persistent rumor that alien remains were interred right here in Bartle County, in the vicinity of the original crash site. We are proposing, if our investigation shows the existence of such remains, to disinter those remains—with permission, of course— for DNA analysis. The exhumation will occur, I hope, on live TV. Obviously, all of this is groundbreaking scientific work, as well as must-see TV viewing."

Koi, who'd been curled on Mabel's lap, looked at her with something like disbelief. "Ridiculous, right?" Mabel asked. "And live TV, yet. That's pretty much asking for disaster. Three words come to mind—Al Capone's vault."

Doug Constantino leaned forward. Mabel suspected he'd been feeling like the third wheel thus far in this interview. "Say, Leif, I'm guessing you must've heard you came here to Bartle County at an opportune time."

Steele smiled and raised an inquiring eyebrow.

"According to police, there's been a rash of UFO sighting reports in and around Medicine Spring in the last couple weeks."

Mabel jerked in her seat, spewing coffee onto Koi, who'd returned to napping. As she mopped at her arm with a wad of tissues and inspected her top for coffee spray, the cat gave her a dirty look and licked herself vigorously. "Sorry," Mabel mouthed.

Mabel prayed fervently that the police wouldn't release the names of people who'd reported encounters.

"Why, yes, that's been brought to our attention. We're hoping to get in touch with those individuals for firsthand interviews, if possible."

No. No, no, no, no.

Steele looked into the camera. "If any of you are watching right now, we'd love to hear from you." He glanced off-screen. "Could we get that contact number up for your viewers?"

The show went to commercial shortly thereafter, and Mabel realized she needed to get down to The Coffee Cup, even though Doug Constantino had promised they'd "be right back for more with this morning's special guest, Leif Steele." She clicked off the TV and ran a gentle hand over Koi's damp back.

She hoped again that police wouldn't give the film crew her name.

Mabel arrived at The Coffee Cup in dawn's early light—or, at least, the gray light of nine am. John's car already sat in the lot along with several other vehicles, including a 1960s Chevy Impala with winglike tailfins—and an inflatable green alien behind the steering wheel with a skeleton, hopefully resin, wearing a floppy, pink-flowered hat—in the passenger seat. Mabel found a space near John in the far corner.

When she came inside, John had gotten them a booth close to the front. They usually aimed for a back table, but as she thought about it, Mabel realized they'd gotten into this habit because they'd always had sensitive things to discuss. Now, it seemed everyone around her was gabbling about lights and aliens…except for three hunters at the counter, regaling the waitress with their story of spotting a buck up on the ridge, with the face of a bobcat.

The hunters' dueling opinions seemed to be that either a deer had gotten irradiated by radioactive discharge from a spaceship or that the deer was actually an alien, who had somehow shape shifted. "Being an alien, they wouldn't know deer, so they got the face wrong." The waitress expressed her opinion that the boys should lay off the booze before handling firearms.

John's face lit at the sight of Mabel, and she returned his smile. "Good job getting us a table."

"We can look out the window this morning. I already ordered us coffee."

"Thanks."

John always ordered plain coffee, but Mabel didn't want to be a complainer, even though she'd been dreaming of a pumpkin cream latte on the drive over. She picked up a menu and checked the specials.

"Hey, they've got scrapple."

John shuddered.

"You don't like it?" Mabel had assumed any local boy would have been raised on the stuff, though most restaurants didn't carry it.

"Never could abide cornmeal mush contaminated with who-knows-what pork scraps and drenched in maple syrup. Think about it."

Mabel swallowed. She *was* thinking about it and her mouth was watering. "Maybe you need more Pennsylvania Dutch in your DNA to appreciate it."

"No doubt. Bigelow isn't a big name in PA Dutch country like, say, Yoder."

"Well, neither is Browne. But Grandma's side of the family

were Spanglers. She always called it *pannhaas*."

"Far be it from me to disparage your ethnic cuisine. I hope it won't bother you if I gag a little."

Stricken, Mabel laid the menu down. "Are you serious? Will the smell or anything bother you?"

John smiled. "Not a bit—I was kidding. Enjoy."

Oh, she would. Happily, Mabel contemplated sides. When the coffee was delivered, she placed her order for scrapple, thick-cut uncured local bacon—another special—warm applesauce, and scrambled eggs. The waitress didn't even ask John what he wanted. "The usual?"

"Yep. Thanks." Another grim spinach-and-egg white Popeye with whole wheat toast would be coming their way.

While they waited for their food, Mabel listened to the conversation around them. "Everybody's babbling about the mysterious lights in the sky."

John took a folded *Shopper* from the seat next to him and passed it to Mabel. "It's already in the news."

She looked at the front-page article. "Above the fold. It's that rabid newshound Renny Martin. I can't believe it's in the weekly so soon. He must have jumped on the first reports as soon as they happened."

"Fast work." John's voice was dry. He nodded toward the counter. "Speak of the dickens, there he is now, getting the scoop on the bobcat deer from those two hunters."

"Oh, for pity's sake. I guess anything counts as news these days."

For a while, Mabel and John chatted about the election, Mabel's struggles with Acey, and John's preemptive review of the ethics text. "If you want, I can help quiz you on the material," she offered.

"I might take you up on that. But let's wait and see whether I'm actually required to take the course."

Their food had just arrived when Mabel spotted Miss Birdie and Ms. Katherine Ann. She craned her neck to check for an open table but didn't see one anywhere. "Can you believe it? Even those two old ladies are getting squeezed out of a seat. They're the most faithful customers this place has got."

John rose and beckoned, but they didn't appear to notice him. He headed over to escort them. Mabel slid their dishes aside.

"I think we'll all fit," she told them as John slid over and the two ladies took the end seats.

"Thank you, youngsters." Miss Birdie gazed around at the crowd. "This place has turned into a madhouse."

"Look at all these strangers." Ms. Katherine Ann tsked. "It's gotten so the regular clientele's persona non grata."

"Now, Katherine. A restaurant's got to have customers to survive—and people need to eat, whether you and I know who they are or not. You can't blame anybody in this situation."

"Well, I don't have to like it. Places used to take care of their regulars. Once this UFO flap dies down, where do you think this crowd's going to be?"

To Mabel's relief, the waitress appeared and took the ladies' orders. She even leaned down and whispered, "Now, don't tell anybody, but we have some real nice cranberry-orange muffins back there, and I'm going to set a couple aside for you gals to take home. On the house. We all feel so bad you're being inconvenienced right now."

"That's very kind of you, Sally." Miss Birdie smiled and patted her hand.

Ms. Katherine Ann beamed and echoed her thanks. Free food seemed to be a great mood lifter.

The ladies insisted John and Mabel go ahead and eat while their breakfasts were warm. For a while, they all chatted about the latest strange sightings, and Ms. Katherine Ann went on a lengthy reminiscence about her late mother-in-law's method for making scrapple. John caught Mabel's eye, and she nearly burst out laughing. It reminded her of the saying, "You don't want to watch how the sausage is made."

Miss Birdie tactfully, if belatedly, changed the topic. "I hear people are crawling all over Miller's Woods these days. And even the cemetery." She shook her head.

"For a fee," Ms. Katherine Ann sniffed. "That boy over at the 'museum' makes them pay admission to get back there. You and I used to play back in there years ago. Nobody made a fuss over who owned what in those days. People were neighborly. Remember gathering hickory nuts with Mabel?"

Miss Birdie's expression became dreamy. "We used to sit on those big, flat rocks in the clearing and smash them open with stones."

"I haven't had a hickory nut in ages," Ms. Katherine Ann mused with a sigh. "Oh, well. They always did bind me up anyhow."

At this opportune moment, the ladies' food arrived, so Mabel was spared further details of Ms. Katherine Ann's digestive report.

"Look who's here," Mabel muttered as the door opened.

"Arthur Frost," John said.

At Miss Birdie's raised eyebrows, he added, "He's a TV guy—and a professor over at the university. He goes on the UFO and ghost shows to debunk the reports."

"Looks like we're going to get some fireworks." Mabel nodded toward the counter, where the reporter, Renny, had spun around on his stool.

"Mr. Frost."

Frost's neck reddened. "Dr."

"Renny Martin. I'm a reporter. Can I buy you a coffee?"

"From the *New York Times*, I presume? No, thank you. I came to eat breakfast, not chit-chat with the press."

"May I give you my card?"

Frost ignored Martin's outstretched hand as he shoved past. "Visit my website. You'll find contact information for my agent."

A man rose from his seat to block Frost's path. "Don't bother wasting your time, buddy. Frost is never going to sit down with anybody who isn't shelling out cash for the privilege."

The man looked to be in his forties or fifties. He was rather nice-looking, though his hair was receding, and his nose appeared to have been broken at some point, as it had a noticeable bend to the left. From his outfit of jeans and flannel, with a camouflage jacket over the back of his chair and blaze orange vest over it, he might have been one of the hunting crowd.

"He remembers me. Don't you, *Dr.* Frost?"

"Afraid not." Frost attempted to step around the solid-looking obstacle standing in his path. "If you will excuse me."

"We're not on camera now, Frost. *Ghost Diggers*, third season. 'The Cottage at Murky Lake.' Dan Cardamone."

Frost tried to go the other way, only to be blocked again. Renny Martin was now holding up his cell phone, as if to record. Mabel noticed several other customers doing the same.

Frost shoved Cardamone, and Mabel covered her face…leaving a crack open between her fingers, at eye level.

Cardamone's head went down, and he charged, ramming Frost full in the stomach and knocking him off-balance. Frost stumbled and caught himself on the back of a chair, which tipped along with its occupant, a tiny woman who screamed and grabbed for the rim of her table.

John surged to his feet but couldn't straighten up because he was stuck in the booth with Ms. Katherine Ann in the way. After a bit of fumbling about, Ms. Katherine Ann was on her feet, and John was on his way to break up the fight.

"You made a laughingstock out of me on national TV," Cardamone shouted. "I could hardly show my face after that."

John inserted himself between the two sweating combatants, as Cardamone took another swing at the debunker. John feinted aside, but the blow caught him on the shoulder.

"You couldn't show your face because you made an idiot of yourself on that idiot TV show. Don't blame me for your own poor decisions," Frost taunted, shoving at John as if trying to reach Cardamone. "Claiming your cat levitated—pure bunk."

"Stop it, both of you." John's voice cracked like a thunderclap. "Frost, I suggest you sit down. Looks like you're going to get the publicity you crave." He eyed Renny Martin, who was grinning like he'd won the lottery.

"Mr. Cardamone, I suggest you apologize to the lady you shoved Mr. Frost into. This is a place of business."

A spattering of applause echoed through the diner, and people started lowering their cell phones and returning to their meals. Frost was already sitting down with a couple of men Mabel didn't recognize at a corner table she suspected had been reserved for them, and all three were laughing.

The sweaty-faced manager, who had been placating Arthur Frost, appeared at John's elbow. "Thanks, John. That escalated before I could even get out here."

"Sorry," Cardamone mumbled. "It's that phony Doctor Science." He shot Frost a deadly glare. "Everything he does is for show. He's as fake as they come. I told my story the way it happened, and he made a fool of me. He had no call to do that. It's one thing to say you think what happened had a natural explanation. It's another thing to call a man a fraud on national TV. My wife left me after that, and even my kids got made fun of."

"Dan." The manager placed his hand on Cardamone's shoulder. "I've known you at least twenty years. You aren't like this. That's why I'm not going to ask you to leave. But I am going to tell you we can't tolerate this kind of brawling here. This is a family establishment, not some roughneck beer joint."

"I know, Ed." Cardamone pulled some bills from his pocket and put them on the counter. "I'm leaving. Guess he just helped me make a fool of myself again. But if I ever catch that arrogant son of a…good-for-nothing jerk outside, he and I are going to settle that score once and for all."

He looked over to where the woman who'd been nearly knocked out of her chair was watching him. "I *am* sorry, ma'am. My temper got the better of me." He looked at the manager and tipped his head at the money he'd laid down. "There should be plenty there to cover her breakfast."

Not looking right or left, Cardamone pushed his way to the door.

"Your breakfasts are on me, John." Ed the manager released his breath on a gusty sigh. "I guess I came close to picking up Lydia's as well. If I get any more of this 'booming business' from the UFO crowd, I'm going to end up bankrupt."

"You don't have to get ours, Ed."

The manager shook his head. "You defused what could have been a whole lot worse, and I owe you. Don't worry about it."

Ms. Katherine Ann returned from Lydia's table and waited till John had slid back into his seat. "I got video," she cackled as she sat. "That was something, wasn't it?"

Miss Birdie frowned. "Really, Katherine."

"I'm sorry, but the crowd down at the senior center will love it. A couple of TV personalities in a fight, and we were right here for it."

"Looked like other people got pictures too." Mabel nibbled at her bacon. "That was flat-out crazy. If anything like that happens at the book-signing, Nita's going to have her hands full and then some."

"What do you mean by TV personalities, ma'am?" John asked. "I recognized Arthur Frost, but I don't know the other guy at all—except for what he told us a moment ago."

"Oh, I saw that episode," Ms. Katherine Ann said. "He's a local man—lives out on Indian Camp Road, but this concerned his vacation cottage. His cat just floated up off her cushion and hung in the air."

"Oh, Katherine, surely not." Miss Birdie delivered a sidelong glance.

"Well, of course, it was a recreation—not the actual event. It was him talking about it, and then they used actors to portray the whole thing. I suppose even the cat was an actor."

Stunt cat, skilled in the art of levitation.

"Cats don't levitate," Miss Birdie said firmly.

"I guess they don't really, but it doesn't mean that Mr. Cardamone was a fraudster. He might have mistaken something else for his cat floating in the air."

Like a weather balloon.

Mabel forced herself to concentrate on her bacon. Anytime Ms. Katherine Ann got going, it was hard to keep from laughing.

"Well, in any event, we all ended up with a free breakfast." John folded his napkin and laid it on his plate. "I think we should still leave the tip. It was nice of Ed to cover our food, but I didn't want him to do that." He counted out bills and slipped them under his plate.

"Hey, it had to be a huge relief for him to have private security step in right when he needed it. I didn't see anybody else willing to get involved." Mabel spooned up her applesauce, since it looked like the breakfast party was breaking up.

When they stepped outside, Mabel pulled her collar tight against the wind and shivered. The change in temperature, after an hour in the steamy diner, was jolting.

John walked her to her car, holding hands. He drew her into a hug before they parted. "I'll call you tonight and get the plan for tomorrow night at the bookstore."

Dread settled on Mabel's chest the way Barnacle did whenever there was a thunderstorm.

Chapter Nineteen

After witnessing the confrontation at The Coffee Cup the previous morning, Mabel had tried to have a productive day…for a change. It pained her to admit it, but her attention had already been so splintered with the pressures of getting Grandma's house and grounds whipped into shape, that it had become almost impossible to concentrate on writing. Things had gotten even worse since her possible alien encounter. Not to mention being shoved into the cesspool—or should she say, privy?—of Medicine Spring politics.

She'd eventually hammered out a rough-draft account of her foray into the realm of political volunteerism, then cleansed her palate with an hour of dejunking in the spare bedroom. It had once been Grandma's sewing room but as her dementia advanced, it had become a dumping ground for any odds and ends Grandma wasn't sure what to do with.

As always, decluttering had been a depressing job, not at all helped by Koi and Barnacle's discovery of a mouse, which they'd proceeded to chase, clambering over piles of bags and boxes and burrowing underneath and between, until the mouse at last darted into a hole in the baseboard.

In the process, they'd knocked down stacks Mabel had already begun sorting, not to mention ripping holes in trash bags with their claws, sending bobbins and spools of thread unraveling across the floor, along with other mysterious spillage. The latter included a large, stampeding herd of BBs. To Mabel's knowledge, Grandma had never been an aficionado of BB guns, leading her to wonder where on earth they'd come from.

After a full afternoon of this—not to mention searching

online and making notes about how to organize a bridal shower—Mabel knew she couldn't face another day of responsible adulting. In fact, she decided, she was entitled to a whole evening off.

She'd just removed Koi from the coffee table and gotten herself settled with a jigsaw puzzle from Grandma Mabel's stash, when her phone rang.

Jackie.

With little preamble, the sci-fi writer launched into the reason for her call. "I hope you don't mind, but I've been dying to hear about your encounter, if you're up to it. I'm happy to share mine with you. It happened when I was in high school."

Despite her resolution to take the evening off, Mabel couldn't help feeling curious. "Okay."

She listened intently as Jackie described a sighting outside her bedroom window that had wakened her from a sound sleep. The visual details were similar to Mabel's. "Did you hear anything? Or experience any electrical disturbances?"

"No. But of course, my window was closed. It was winter."

Once again, Mabel's sighting was different. The fact made her uneasy. As Mabel recounted what she'd experienced, Jackie squealed. "Oh, Mabel, you've had a remarkable encounter."

Mabel scowled. Not everything remarkable was also desirable.

Next morning, Mabel fixed herself a bowl of instant blueberry oatmeal. She gagged that down with the aid of two mugs of coffee and headed out to pursue her UFO investigation.

At the last minute, Barnacle had flopped on his back in the doorway and refused to budge until she sighed, clipped on his leash, and took him along. She never really minded taking him this time of year when it was cool enough for him to wait in the car. He was a patient passenger and being included in her plans always made him so ridiculously happy.

As she drove, he shoved his head forward and panted for joy. As usual, Mabel talked to him while checking her GPS for Linden Creek Church. "I think it's about two miles out, near the crossroads. According to their website, they should be open by now."

With a couple of phone calls and some internet research, Mabel had learned Pleasant Union Church, though it no longer had an active congregation, was now an occasional worship location for Linden Creek, which had merged with Pleasant Union when the older church dwindled to fewer than a dozen members in the 1960s. All present-day burials at Pleasant Union were now handled through the Linden Creek parish. Mabel hoped Linden Creek had also fallen heir to the older burial records for the Pleasant Union Cemetery.

She'd already dialed the number for the church office when it occurred to her that one could often squeeze out more information by being on the premises, looking the other person in the eye. Sometimes, office workers might try a bit harder to find something for an actual flesh-and-blood person standing in front of them than for a faceless voice on the phone.

The Linden Creek Church sat, as the name indicated, not far from the banks of a winding creek, which flowed under the main road. Mabel crossed the bridge and turned down a crushed-stone driveway. The building was a small, one-story redbrick structure with a little steeple at the center.

All but two spaces in the Linden Creek parking lot—one marked "Pastor" and the other "Secretary"—were unoccupied. Still, Mabel selected a remote spot under a tree in the far corner— not because, like John, she was trying to get a few more steps into her day, but because if Barnacle started barking, he was less likely to scare the pants off someone.

The door off the parking area was locked, so Mabel pushed the doorbell. A garbled voice asked if it could help her, and Mabel replied that she needed help with cemetery records. An unintelligible response crackled at her, and Mabel yelled into the speaker, "I need help with cemetery records."

Whether or not she'd been understood, a buzzer sounded, and the door lock clicked. Mabel slipped inside and followed the arrow to the secretary's office around the corner.

A middle-aged woman with glasses atop her head, pushing back faded brown hair, peered sideways and smiled as Mabel appeared. "I'm sorry. That so-called speaker is more like the thing they use to garble voices when somebody's disguising their identity. Is there something you need help with?"

"I was looking for burial records?"

"Would that be for the cemetery in town? That's where our more recent burials are located."

"No, I was wondering—I understood the records for Pleasant Union Cemetery are housed here."

The woman's smile widened. "Oh, yes. Are you with the investigative team? Someone was already in here yesterday."

Darn. Mabel had hoped to be a bit more subtle, not that it mattered. "No, I'm following something up on my own."

"About our mysterious grave, I imagine."

"A.G.—right."

"You'll need to see Rev. Mathieson. He keeps all that in his office. Let me check if he can see you now."

The secretary dialed a number on her desk phone and explained Mabel's mission. "He'll be happy to talk with you," she said a moment later and pointed. "It's the next door down."

Mabel hesitated outside the office and then decided a tentative knock was in order. "Come on in," a male voice answered.

Rev. Mathieson's office was cramped, but somehow

inviting. Books lined the walls and occupied most of his desk space. An old-fashioned floor lamp with a fringed dark-gold shade stood over his right shoulder. Despite the window behind him, the lamp was on, thanks to the overcast skies.

The minister was an old man to still be working—Mabel guessed nearing eighty, if he hadn't already passed it—short and comfortably round, with a fringe of white hair. He hopped to his feet when Mabel stepped inside and led her to a chair, beaming as he chattered.

"Welcome, welcome. And you are?"

Mabel introduced herself, shaking the warm hand he offered, and explained what she was looking for. Saying out loud to a normal person that she was looking into the history of the mysterious A.G. grave made her mission sound awfully foolish, and she began to regret coming, or at least not better preparing what to say once she got here.

The pastor sank into his desk chair and reclined with the attitude of someone who was looking forward to spending hours chatting. "Yes, the mystery grave. Have you visited it?"

Mabel nodded. "It isn't well maintained." She hadn't meant that to come out like an accusation of neglect but immediately feared that was exactly how it sounded. She wished she had the gift of tact. Words simply had a tendency to form in her head and pop right out of her mouth before her brain had a chance to consider, or at least polish them.

Rev. Mathieson, she was glad to see, appeared unperturbed. He picked up a pipe from an ashtray on his desk and stuck it in his mouth, unlit. Since there was no smell of tobacco in the room at all, Mabel had to wonder if it had ever been lit.

"No, it isn't," he said comfortably around the pipe stem. "I've always felt uneasy about that, but this was never an authorized burial, you see. By the time we became involved with the Pleasant Union Cemetery at our merger, the grave—if that's indeed what it is—had been sitting in the woods for over ten years. One of the old members of that congregation was able to tell me they'd decided just to let it be, as the congregation had been dwindling, and there was no demand for the space.

"Whoever planted that marker back in the trees seemed to have put it there as if to hide it. Cemetery plots have to be purchased, you know. This one never was. There is no deed on file for it at all. That lot still appears on the current cemetery map as open space. For all we know, it's just the stone there, placed for whatever reason we'll never know."

Mabel frowned in thought. "What a strange story. No wonder people started concocting stories to try to explain it."

Rev. Mathieson laughed and shook his head. He tapped his empty pipe on the ashtray, then stuck it back in his mouth. "The human imagination is an amazing thing. Don't you suspect the Lord smiled when He gave us that capacity?"

"Doesn't it concern you at all who might be buried there?" Mabel's brain thrashed with possibilities. "It might even be a murder victim."

The pastor shrugged a shoulder. "Of course, I think of those things from time to time. But we're at least seventy years on at this point. What might it take to even identify the remains, let alone bring anyone—still living—to justice?"

"There are the initials, for starters. Old news reports? And maybe DNA…?"

"Those are questions for the police, who haven't shown any enthusiasm for violating a *possible* grave simply to satisfy their curiosity. I do believe some effort was made to check for reports of missing persons, which turned up nothing."

"The person might not have been local. They might've even gone missing from another state."

He spread his hands. "There are no databases that go back that far. Certainly, no nationwide ones."

It didn't seem right to Mabel, but she could see the problems.

"You have a concerned heart," the minister said. "That is a good thing. At least for the present however, there is no intention to disturb the grave."

"What about the documentary crew?"

He shook his head. "We've already given permission for some noninvasive investigation of the site, but no disinterment. They would need to petition the cemetery board, which consists of two elders and myself."

Good luck with *that*, Mabel thought.

"Who do you think is in there, Pastor—if anyone?" Mabel asked.

"I wouldn't venture a guess. We've speculated many things, but there's no evidence to indicate any is correct. We decided long ago to take a lenient eye, as it might well be a poor soul with nowhere else to go, 'known only unto God' and possibly whomever buried him."

He set his cold pipe down and rubbed his chin. "Even if it turned out to be a dog or cat, we're by no means as fussy as in Edinburgh, where that poor dog Greyfriars Bobby was forced to be separated from his departed master and sleep at the gates. They insisted he not be buried on consecrated ground, so his grave was placed outside the entrance."

Rev. Mathieson sighed. "After all, many dogs demonstrate the fruits of the Spirit better than we do." A sentiment with which Mabel was forced to agree.

"Not," the minister said with a wink, "that we're going to be burying any more of God's non-human creatures."

Chapter Twenty

Mabel and Lisa arrived at the bookstore at five-thirty, two hours before the scheduled signing event. The store had closed early—part of the plan they'd formulated with Nita earlier in the day, since John had suggested it would help keep the innocent "normals" from getting caught up in the chaos of the special event. A notice on the door said the shop would reopen at 7:30.

John was already standing inside the door, dressed in black and looking forbidding.

"Are you ladies here for the book-signing?"

Lisa giggled. "You know we are."

"You're early, but I suppose you can come in."

"Come on back, girls," Nita called. "You can help finish setting up these tables. It's gonna be tight."

Mabel was happy Lisa and Nita had hit it off so well at their last-minute Zoom meeting that afternoon. To her amazement, Lisa currently had Nita's granddaughter, Brooke, in her kindergarten class. Mabel wasn't sure if she'd been more surprised by this coincidence or the idea that Nita was a grandmother.

"Okay, Mabel. Since you were telling me Leif Steele would be the big draw, we put him all the way back here by the nonfiction. I thought first I'd put him right up front, but you know how it is with merchandising—you lead people the long way, so they have a chance to see what else you got. Give 'em a chance for an impulse purchase."

"Okay…" Mabel scanned the set-up. The table was covered by a black tablecloth, and copies of Steele's latest book were arranged to one side, while an empty glass sat to the other, several pens with the bookstore logo next to it. "A lot of authors like to use their own pens, but I always want to provide them with a few of ours, just in case. When we're getting ready to start, we'll pour him some ice water. I hope he's not one of those primadonnas who demand kombucha," she muttered, "…or booze."

Nita gestured toward a corner half-hidden by a used-book shelf. "Our little break room is back there with a fridge and such. That's where the food is right now. That table next to the break room door is where we'll be serving. I'll ask you ladies to set out the goodies as soon as we get all the author tables set up."

When they trailed Nita to the front again, they found John talking to a twentyish couple, one in an *Empty Eyes* sweatshirt, and the other whose Cryptid Bash tee showed under his open jacket. It seemed they were trying to get the jump on the crowd.

"Zac will be handing out numbered tickets at the door, so we don't overcrowd. Once we reach capacity, he'll let people in as others leave." Nita rubbed her forehead. "I hate doing it this way. Hate it. It would be better in the summer when it's not dark—and cold—outside. But we can't let them overrun us."

Subtext: Hope they don't riot.

"I'm sure it'll be okay." Lisa was using her kindergarten teacher voice as she patted Nita's arm.

Nita's ponytailed employee Zac was putting finishing touches on Stanley Koslowski's table. "He may not do a whole lot of business," Zac confided. "His book's been around a long time, and most people in town who want one already have it."

"That's okay. We'll probably get some out-of-towners," Nita predicted. "And sometimes signings bomb out. It wouldn't be the first. He'll still get to chat with people and promote his next title. And the food's free." She waved a hand at another table. "Now, over here's going to be Dr. Arthur Frost."

Mabel cringed. She hadn't realized Koslowski and Frost were going to be in such close proximity. "Um, Nita…"

Zac was already headed to the Frost table. "Would you ladies like to help Zac unbox those last books?" Nita asked. "Or maybe set up the rope lines?"

"I'll unbox," Lisa offered. "Or I can display the books."

"I can set up your rope lines," Mabel said. "But, Nita…those two tables are still awfully close."

Nita shrugged. "Couldn't be helped. Not without knocking out a wall."

It was Nita's business, but Mabel couldn't help thinking she'd be better switching one of the front tables with Leif Steele's in the back of the store. Let Koslowski sit in the back if he'd done other signings here already. He and Frost were the two most likely to kill each other. Steele didn't need to be distanced.

"Well, maybe you…" Mabel cast about for a tactful way of suggesting a major change in Nita's merchandising plan, but tact had never been part of her skill set. "Darn it—you're still asking for trouble. This set-up is crazy. Look, I'm telling you, you're still going to sell Stecle's book like it's the last seat in the lifeboat, no matter where he sits.

"Everybody's here to see him—he's the real celeb. You said yourself, Koslowski's already pretty much tapped out this market. Nobody really likes Frost, except maybe a few real scientists who have an interest in UFOs but aren't inclined to believe in little green men. Put Stanley in back."

Nita shook her head decisively. "Too late. We can't be taking down displays and moving heavy tables through the store so close to opening. There are already people lined up out there. Besides, who's to say Leif Steele and Frost aren't going to get into it…or their fans? Steele must be somewhat open to extraterrestrials. And it sounds like Frost's the guy to blast him on it."

Mabel urged Nita toward the back. "No. I hear you, and it does make sense. But Steele and Frost scratch each other's backs.

It's almost a standing joke."

"I get what you're saying. But the way I have it set up is gonna have to do for now. I just hope I don't have to pull out my fire extinguisher."

By 7:30, the crowd outside had grown restless. People had begun rapping at the door ten minutes earlier, and by the time Nita gave John the signal to open up, noticeable shoving was in progress.

The three authors had come in through the rear entrance earlier, along with Leif Steele's security guys, who looked more like mafia enforcers as they stood flanking the TV star. It seemed it was the sight of Frost and Koslowski taking their seats up front that had activated the impatient crowd, who apparently believed this equaled "go time."

It was a good thing John was up to the task of crowd control, because it soon became clear he'd get no help from Steele's security team unless and until their leader was threatened. The first surge of twenty-five people shoved through the door and John relocked it behind them.

In the interest of customer satisfaction, Nita had asked Mabel and Lisa to pass out flying saucer cookies to the folks waiting outside, but John had nixed the idea. "They'll end up being trampled or something. It's not worth it. So what if you get complaints afterward? It's better than risking any injuries."

By and large, the first "release," as Mabel thought of the initial influx of customers, was pretty peaceful. Lisa manned the refreshment table in back, making sure the punchbowl was filled, that there were plenty of cups, and food was replenished. Nita and Zac circulated, answering questions, breaking up minor squabbles, and tending Leif Steele's ego, between taking turns at the register.

Mabel worked the front. Her primary job seemed to be

straightening out the rope lines, which were constantly being knocked around and tipped over. That changed when the two authors in the front began whining about the customers, most of whom surged past them to get in line for a chance to meet Leif Steele and get his autograph. Steele's line already nearly reached the front door.

Mabel tried to gently steer a few of the last people in Steele's line toward Frost and Koslowski. "Since you have to wait anyway, why not meet one of the other authors?" She lowered her voice, so as not to invite catcalls from the debunker. "Mr. Koslowski has written about his abduction experience, by the way."

"No way," one tattooed young man told her, jerking away from her hand. "Did you see that crowd outside? I can talk to those guys anytime." He hiked a thumb in the other authors' direction.

"Well, just so you're aware, we'll sound a bell after fifteen minutes, and anyone who's already completed his purchase or isn't actively waiting in line will have to exit to allow other customers a chance to come in from the cold."

"I don't plan on getting kicked out before I get to meet Leif Steele."

Mabel met John's sympathetic eye. She heaved a sigh and shrugged. In her opinion, Frost and Koslowski ought to be grateful for the few people who'd stopped to visit their tables, instead of degenerating into whiny brats. Frost was so smug and nasty he was lucky anybody wanted to spend five minutes in his presence. Koslowski was a sweaty bore who didn't seem to know when to stop talking.

Finally, the first bell rang, and Nita and Zac began herding the first batch of customers toward the exit. To Mabel's relief, at least half the group seemed ready to go—or in any event were being good sports about it. Lisa had made sure everyone who wanted refreshments was given the opportunity to take a cup of punch and a bag of snacks with them.

Mabel feared the biggest problem would be keeping the surging crowd from trampling folks trying to leave. John stood planted at the door with his hands on some big guy's shoulders, talking earnestly into his face.

Mabel squinted. The man looked familiar. As he turned to gesture, she recognized Dan Cardamone, the guy with the levitating cat. He was waving his arms and seemed to be yelling. Mabel sighed with relief when John at last convinced him to walk away.

"Never again," Nita muttered. "Never again."

Jackie from the UFO meeting came inside with the second batch of admittees. She smiled and waved at Mabel, who squinted at the scruffy, bearded man who arrived with her. Where had she seen him before? Mabel wondered if they were a couple. The pair disappeared into the back of the store as she puzzled over who he was.

Mabel was about to ask John if he remembered seeing Jackie's companion before. An irritable request from Arthur Frost for more water and a better pen, however, soon distracted Mabel from her reverie.

All remained relatively calm till Jackie and her friend returned to the front, clutching store bags she assumed contained Leif Steele's books. Mabel studied the man closely, but still couldn't quite place him. They stopped to chat with Stanley Koslowski, though neither picked up a copy of *My Lost Hours*. Since Jackie, at least, was a member of the UFO group, she probably knew Stanley well. No one else was in line, so it might have been a mercy stop.

A small group of younger guys from the UFO club soon emerged from the back as well. One called over to Jackie's friend. "Hey, Virgil! Got any eggs? Nobody's at Frost's table right now—you got a clean shot."

The unkempt beard failed to hide the flush on Virgil's face. Jackie grabbed his arm. "Come on. Let's get out of here."

Frost rose and started to come around his table. "Virgil, is it?" His eyes narrowed.

A couple of the boys laughed, but one looked alarmed. "Oops." He stepped in front of Frost. "Hey, man. I was just kidding."

Frost shoved him aside.

"We're out of here." Jackie hustled her friend out the door before Frost could reach him.

Mabel caught John's eye, and he shrugged. So, Jackie's friend Virgil was the guy who'd thrown eggs at Arthur Frost, and now Frost knew who to blame. It had seemed like a minor incident to her when it happened, but from Frost's reaction now, it didn't seem he cared to forgive and forget.

As the evening wore on, Mabel began to feel a sense of relief. There had been a couple minor border skirmishes, but no significant battles had broken out. The line outside had dwindled, as most people had finally managed to get inside or given up. Nita had promised the crowd the store would not close until everyone had had an opportunity to come in—and told those who'd complained bitterly about having to leave after their time was up that they could step to the end of the queue and reenter.

There was even a good chance the event would end in an orderly manner within a half-hour of the scheduled end time. With any luck at all, some of the refreshments would still be left on the table for Nita and her longsuffering helpers.

The trouble started right after the last group had been admitted, including a handful of readmittances. Arthur Frost had taken a break in the back of the store. While there, his resentment over his poor turn-out seemed to boil over. He made a snide remark to Leif Steele, who'd tried to placate him but was rudely rebuffed in return.

As Frost was returning to his table, a middle-aged customer shopping for her nephew made the mistake of squinting at the debunker and asking him whether he was Leif Steele. Frost erupted in the poor woman's face, referring to both her and the nephew as mouth-breathers. This brought Nita steaming from the back, Zac trotting behind her.

"*Mr.* Frost. While in my store, you will treat my customers with the courtesy they are entitled to."

"I did, madam. And it is *Dr.* Frost."

"Whatever. Zac, would you please escort this lady to Mr. Steele's table? I think you'll find a couple more copies of his book still available."

Mabel caught John's eye. He was moving into range but hanging back to let Nita take the lead in her own way.

Nita lowered her voice as she took Frost aside. "I appreciate you coming in tonight and want you to feel welcome here, but you have to realize I'm an independent businesswoman. I rely on keeping my customers happy. If *they* don't feel welcome here, I'm out of business, capiche?"

"My dear woman, I've restrained myself all evening. I can only tolerate this circus so long." Frost turned on his heel and returned to his table, where to Mabel's relief—and undoubtedly Nita's as well—a couple of customers were waiting with copies of his book.

The immediate crisis seemed to be resolved. Mabel's feet hurt, and she found herself using a wad of napkins she'd filched from the refreshment table to mop her forehead. She'd noticed of late that she was getting what she'd reluctantly concluded were hot flashes, particularly when she was stressed. She'd gone through quite a few party napkins this evening.

Steele's line had dwindled to a handful of customers at this point, and most seemed to be repeaters bent on getting a selfie with him or debating something that had happened on one of the *Empty Eyes* episodes. Frost was pontificating to the two fans currently at his table, excoriating the "dimwits who refuse to apply scientific method" to UFO sightings, because they don't want to know the truth.

At least, his two customers seemed on board with Frost's opinions.

Unfortunately, the fragile peace was doomed to explode.

Chapter Twenty-one

A QUIET YOUNG WOMAN, SLENDER AND pale, had sidled up to Stanley Koslowski's table and was talking earnestly with the UFO museum owner. Of course, nobody else was chomping at the bit to take her place, which meant she had relative privacy for what looked like a confidential conversation.

Mabel had been going around straightening books on the non-UFO displays which had been knocked askew. In fact, she'd found more than one book all the way on the floor, including one that had been kicked partway under the shelving with its cover bent. She grimaced, wishing she could catch one of these book abusers in the act.

As she worked, she drifted close enough to hear Koslowski's customer describing an abduction experience, during which she had been whisked away to a planet in another solar system. Koslowski was nodding and patting her hand while his other hand held a copy of his book. Clearly, he was waiting for an opening to shove it at her.

When she paused for a beat, seeming overcome by emotion, Koslowski interjected, placing his book into her hands. His voice fell into the silence more loudly than he might have intended. "What you're describing is strikingly similar to what happened to me. I—"

Laughter drifted from Frost's table, and both Koslowski and the woman flushed.

Frost said something Mabel couldn't entirely catch, but the snatch of conversation she heard contained the words, "mental condition" and "need to create a world view that will explain their deficiencies."

John repositioned himself between the two rope lines.

Koslowski's fists clenched.

Two young men in clothing with graphics marking them as true believers, now stood in line behind the young woman at Koslowski's table. They'd been deep in conversation, but both turned toward Frost and his acolytes.

The skinny guy in an Area 51 tee glowered at Frost.

"Hey, man," the shorter, round-faced guy, who was sporting a Flatwoods Monster hoodie, yelled. "Mind your own beeswax." Frost raised an eyebrow and quirked his mouth. "I don't believe I was speaking to you, fan boy."

"Mind *your* own beeswax," one of Frost's supporters shouted over at Koslowski and his fans. "We're entitled to our opinions."

"This is a UFO event, not a debunker event. You don't even belong here." Area 51 took a step out of Koslowski's line and closer to Frost's table. His buddy followed.

Leif Steele appeared from the back, flanked by his private security guards. "Now, gentlemen. We all share a common interest in unidentified anomalous phenomena. And we have room in the community for many different opinions at this point."

"Nobody asked your opinion either," one of Frost's supporters yelled. "We already know how your 'special investigation' is going to turn out. Your show's been going down the drain for the past two seasons. Time for a big discovery, right?"

Steele flushed, stepping closer. "We never tailor our results, as you ought to know. Both of our last investigations ended in debunking the incident reports."

"So, you're due for a confirmation of this one. Like clockwork. We all know how it works. If all you do is debunk, you lose viewers."

"Now, hold on." Frost put a hand on the man's arm. "Leif is

a colleague and a friend."

"Sorry, sir. I realize sometimes you've agreed with Steele's conclusions of possible alien involvement. But if I look over the past couple seasons, there's a pattern. Check and see if I'm not right."

"Darn right, buddy." Surprisingly, the Koslowski supporter chimed in from across the rope lines. "Look at your guy Frost. He knows if he wants to stay on Steele's good side—not to mention keep the show going—he has to go where the wind blows. Frost talks about following the facts and finding the truth—he's as fake as anybody he ever claimed to expose on TV. Worse, because he's a big, fat hypocrite, and so is Mr. Show Biz Steele."

"Wait a minute." Koslowski started to look a bit panicky. "Let's leave Mr. Steele out of our disagreement." He shot a furrowed glance at the red-faced star.

One of the debunking group advanced on Koslowski. "It's all about money with you too. You're just like Leif Steele. Anything to keep that 'museum' of yours going, sell your book and your souvenir junk…"

Koslowski charged, head down like a bull at the corrida, flanked by his supporters and several men from the Leif Steele camp, one of whom was still carrying a sloshing cup of punch and a stack of pepperoni on a cracker. Frost ducked as the ropes fell to the floor and his stack of unsold books toppled, but his followers charged into the fray and began grappling with the Koslowski group.

Renny Martin popped up out of nowhere, shooting video. One of the combatants turned on him and knocked him onto his rear end, then began grappling for the newshound's cell phone.

John waded in from the front, and Steele's security team finally intervened from the rear. Steele had vanished into the back, accompanied by a gabbling mob of loyal fans, who proclaimed their shock at such rowdy, disrespectful behavior.

"Gentlemen," Nita bellowed. "We're done here."

It took a few minutes for John and the two guards to separate and evict the troublemakers, one of whom managed to wedge his body halfway back through the door as John was attempting to close and lock it. One of the guards ended up with a black eye and the other was bitten by the quiet woman who'd claimed to have been abducted. John managed to escape with a small rip in his shirt.

John looked out at the fight that had resumed under the streetlights. "You better call the police, Nita."

Nita finished setting Frost's table back on its feet. "That tears it. Cops being called. All I needed."

"Martin from the *Shopper's* already out there. It'll be all over next week's paper anyway," Mabel told her.

"Yeah, I'm already dialing," Nita muttered. "I'm just glad they only publish weekly."

Since Leif Steele's show was national, Martin could conceivably be planning to approach some supermarket tabloid. Mabel started to point out that the reporter might intend to sell his video to a bigger outlet but decided to shut her mouth. Nita had had enough for one night.

John stuck around long enough to escort Frost and Koslowski out the rear door, still sputtering at each other. Then, he answered questions from the police and helped clean up the fight scene.

"Looks like only one chair got broken," Mabel said, attempting to strike a note of cheer, "and I'll bet it can be repaired. And there's really very little blood."

Nita leveled a look of disbelief at her. "That's great news. Thanks."

Lisa worked like a trooper, but Mabel knew she had an early day ahead. Mabel hated to leave Nita in the lurch, but when she saw Lisa yawning, she knew it was time to leave.

Nita had noticed too. "Go on. You guys were lifesavers tonight. I shudder to think what would've happened if you weren't here."

Even though she felt ready to crash—and frankly couldn't wait to get out of there—Mabel looked around with regret. "You've still got quite a bit of clean-up."

Nita waved a hand. "Not a big deal. I got my right-hand man, Zac. The worst of this will be done in a jiffy."

Zac emerged from the back, wearing a huge grin. "Wait till you see the sales. None of this mess is gonna matter anymore."

"I doubt that." Nita plopped onto the stool by the register, tilted her head back, and shut her eyes. "I just hope whatever we took in *will* cover the damage."

Zac grinned. He was almost giddy. "You won't believe the total. I want you to check 'cause I'm so tired I'm cross-eyed—but it's good. The Steele book sold out and we got orders for more. We unloaded a bunch of both Frost's books. Even a fair number of *My Lost Hours*…must've been the out-of-towners. Plus, we moved quite a few of the other UFO books and saucer trinkets you stocked."

Nita opened one eye. "I'm not gonna say I'm not thrilled, and tomorrow everything will look better. Listen to what I'm saying though—I am never doing this again."

She sat up and craned to see out the window. "Are they gone? All of them?"

John nodded. "The cops dispersed them."

"Thank the Lord. I never want to see any of that crowd again. What is *wrong* with those people?"

Chapter Twenty-Two

MABEL HAD BEEN READY TO SOAK her feet after the book-signing. Nonetheless, John and Barnacle had convinced her to go for a walk around the big open meadow behind the Medicine Spring Middle School ballfield.

The school sat opposite Pleasant Union Church. Lights flooded the school parking lot, so John parked his low-slung car in a pull-off along the side, facing the field. Barnacle exploded from the car, shook himself, and began romping. With no trees to block the sky, it was surprisingly easy to see where they were going, even after leaving the lights behind.

Mabel pulled up her collar against the chilly wind. She kept the leash on the excited dog, which wasn't all that easy as he darted this way and that, following scents in the dry grass. Although he tended to stick pretty close, she didn't trust him in a new place like this, let alone after dark. All it would take for him to bolt would be a herd of deer coming out to graze at the edge of the field.

"I never thought of bringing him out here, since I have my own little field and some woods. Plus, we're next to the park."

"The streets around you are pretty quiet too," John said. "They also have the advantage of being lit after dark. But I figured we all needed a fresh, open space to clear our heads. Look how happy he is."

"He sure is." Mabel risked letting go of the leash for a moment as Barnacle took a luxurious roll in the grass. As he got up to shake again, she grabbed the hand loop and held on.

They followed the wooded edge of the field, shuffling though fallen leaves and coarse corn stubble. Mabel took deep breaths of the cold night air. John had been right about coming out here under the stars. It was good to take a break and distance themselves from the chaos of the bookstore.

As she walked, she looked up at the sky, scanning for strange lights or movement, as was her new habit. All was blackness, but for the expected bright pinpoints of the stars. John identified the brilliance of Jupiter, riding near the mellow silver disk of the moon.

Mabel was surprised when she realized they hadn't spoken more than a few words since stepping out of the car. The silence was companionable, and she felt herself relaxing.

They'd passed the center point at the far end of the field when she heard something above the rustle of their shuffling feet. Something that sent a chill up her arms. Weird, almost doglike yipping had erupted somewhere nearby.

"Coyotes," John said. "They must hunt in here."

Mabel shortened the leash as Barnacle sniffed the air. She didn't like hearing coyotes she couldn't see, not when she and John were so far from his car.

Though the coyotes seemed to keep pace with Mabel, Barnacle, and John as they circled the wooded edge of the huge field, they remained out of sight. Rather than feeling reassured, Mabel found the disembodied yips of excitement disconcerting.

When or where might a pack of coyotes emerge from the woods and move in to attack? Her head swiveled, but she saw nothing but corn stubble and trees. John seemed to pick up on her anxiety and took her hand.

As Mabel and John circled toward the road again, the high, agitated yipping tapered off. Barnacle ventured a small *wuff.*

Whether Barnacle's commentary was the trigger, Mabel didn't know, but the unearthly howling of multiple coyotes began rising from somewhere very nearby. She felt the hair on her arms rise along with the quavering notes.

Barnacle tipped his head up and joined the call of the wild.

Mabel had only heard him howl a couple times over the years she'd known him, when the Medicine Spring fire siren set off the coyotes in the park behind her house. That generally led to a "community sing," joined by other dogs who lived nearby.

"Come on." She hauled at the leash. "Before they come out of the woods to meet the new tenor."

John laughed. "We're too close the road now for them to venture too near us. Not that they'd do us any harm."

"It's just such an eerie sound, and we're on their turf. Anyhow, I need to get home to Koi. She didn't like our leaving again right away."

The wooded country road beyond them was dark and deserted. John shone his cell phone light so Mabel could cross a soggy spot where the school ballfield met the corner of the parking lot. As she stepped back onto pavement, Mabel caught a brief glimpse of a figure directly across the road from them, lurking in the shadow of the Pleasant Union church.

"John, look." She caught his wrist to point the beam toward the church, but it didn't penetrate that far. Still, there was enough illumination from the schoolyard lights and the moon above to show a human outline.

"Someone must be paying a nighttime visit to the graveyard again," he muttered. "Looks like a woman."

When the figure turned toward the road, the glow from the church's pole light caught it.

"Nanette?" Mabel frowned. "First Pete and now her. I can't imagine what the big attraction is. Let alone at this hour on a cold November night. They have that parking lot chained off to keep spectators away from the cemetery till Steele's crew finishes their investigation."

There was no vehicle in sight. Nanette must have parked out of view somewhere, the way Pete had done the other night, though hers couldn't be in the chained church lot. That, and the furtive way she was skulking around in the bushes, were definitely peculiar.

Mabel tugged at John's hand and started across the road.

As they came closer, Barnacle's head went up at the movement of the figure in the shadows, and he barked. The woman had already taken a few steps down the road. She looked their way, sweeping one arm behind her in a quick motion and back again.

"Nanette?" Mabel called.

Hunched deep in her coat, hood all but obscuring her face, Nanette stopped with clear reluctance. "Hello." A logical question from Nanette would have been, "What brings you out here?" But Nanette didn't ask…possibly because then Mabel would have asked her the same thing.

Nanette cringed back, deeper into the shadows. She didn't seem her usual brisk, unflappable self. Her glance shifted as if to avoid eye contact, and she seemed preoccupied—almost agitated, jiggling her car keys, feet restless.

Mabel didn't know where the conversation might have gone from there, had not something in the sky caught the attention of all three of them at that very moment. A streak of bright white light raced across the sky and buried itself somewhere in the woods the coyotes called home.

Startled, Mabel jerked at the leash. Barnacle looked up and yawned, seeming perplexed by this new signal, when he must have been sure they were headed home for bedtime snacks.

"Did you see that?" she asked. "What was that?"

"I did, but I have no idea." John frowned.

Nanette seemed jarred out of her distracted state. "A shooting star?"

Mabel shook her head. "Much too low in the sky, and the movement wasn't right."

"Surely it wasn't a UFO." Nanette stared toward the spot where the light had disappeared. "I think we all have UFOs on the brain lately. Now, we're starting to have mass hallucinations."

John shook his head. "It wasn't a hallucination. I don't even think I'd call it a UFO—I didn't see an object. Just a streak of light. How about you?"

"No." Mabel and Nanette echoed each other.

John looked at Nanette, who'd started backing away, like a wild animal about to spin around and flee. She appeared smaller and frailer than usual in her bulky coat. "Do you have your car?"

"Yes, and I'd better get going."

"Would you like me to walk you over?"

"No, thank you, I'll be all right."

"I'll be happy to follow you home, and make sure you get there all right."

Nanette shook her head and was already half-trotting away down the side of the road, when she stumbled in the dead grass and weeds and came close to falling. Though Mabel was too far away to do any good, she lurched toward her, but Nanette caught herself. As she did, the coyote choir tuned up again.

Something in that mournful sound seemed to make Nanette shiver. "Thank you. I think I'd appreciate that."

After arriving at their car, John waited with the engine running for a few seconds until they saw Nanette's headlights flare a few yards away. "Don't you wonder what she's up to?" John mused. "Up here all by herself after dark."

"I wish she'd let me know if there was something we could do to help. I can't imagine she has any secret so awful she wouldn't dare let us know."

Nanette's car passed them, headed away from town, and John pulled out behind her.

"Where's she live?" John asked.

"Not this direction." Mabel frowned. "She's headed away

from town and driving like she's lost."

She dialed Nanette's cell phone but got no answer. "It's as well she doesn't have the distraction. Good thing we're following her, though."

Another set of headlights loomed up behind John's car, veered into the left lane, and shot past them. "Death wish," John muttered as they watched the small coupe swerve around Nanette on a curve.

Mabel held her breath, but no sound of a collision followed. By the time they rounded the bend, the strange car was already out of sight.

As they followed Nanette's slow progress down the road, Mabel began to wonder whether they'd be getting home in time for breakfast. The small, grape-colored car kept to a decorous two miles per hour under the posted speed limit and slowed to fifteen for every hill crest and bend in the road.

Nanette hesitated at every intersection, as if trying to read the signs. Finally, to Mabel's relief, the old car made a left on Johnson Farm Road, which she knew arced back toward Medicine Spring.

John was so good to escort Nanette, Mabel told herself. The least she could do was go along with the program.

"What could that light in the sky have been, do you think? Any theories?" At least they could use the longer-than-necessary drive to pick apart the strange event the three of them had witnessed back there at the church.

"Well…" John slowed down even more as a full-size pickup loomed up at their rear bumper, high beams illuminating the backs of their heads. He flashed his lights at Nanette, who could be seen peering into her rearview mirror.

The truck shot around John as they neared the top of a hill, blasted its horn at Nanette, and roared past her as if she were standing still—which she nearly was.

As they began moving again, John said, "It was pretty much what my student described. Almost like a searchlight, but brighter, and only the one quick pass."

"You don't think something came down in the woods? The place where the light vanished, I mean."

"Like I said, I don't think there was any object to come down. Just the light."

Mabel chewed at her lip. She didn't want to sound like one of the kook fringe but… "What about cloaking? Isn't it possible there was a vessel, but we couldn't see it?"

John glanced over and grinned. "What good would cloaking be if you're going to beam a honking big light? Nope. What we saw was no more than a light, and it was very much of this world. I just don't get the point of it."

"It definitely wasn't what I saw up on the ridge," Mabel said.

Barnacle crawled partway over the back of the seat to stick his nose in her ear and whined.

"We'll be home soon, bud. Don't worry. You'll get your snack."

Mabel petted the dog's head and gave him a shove back where he belonged. "Hey, you know what occurred to me? Barnacle didn't pay any attention at all to that light we saw. Everything I've ever read or heard about UAPs suggests they freak animals out—like the animals know they're not part of our normal world. Maybe it's because of electromagnetic fields or something like that, but the critters know."

"He couldn't have been less interested, could he?" John mused.

Mabel looked back at her dog. "I wouldn't want him anywhere near a real UAP. I've seen info on animal mutilations, and it's ghastly."

They were turning onto Nanette's street. The string of small, clear lights around her front window were on, as was the light over her entrance. John waited until she had unlocked the door and waved good night, before turning his car in the driveway across the street.

Nanette was inside now and had lit a lamp in the living room.

John dropped Mabel and Barnacle off in her side driveway then got out to escort them to the door.

"Thank you for everything," she said. "For helping with that free-for-all at the bookstore and taking us for a walk…and being so kind to Nanette."

John gathered Mabel in his arms and kissed her forehead. "I was happy to do it. Maybe now the book signing's over, we'll have a chance to do something fun just for us. Why don't you think about what you'd like to do, okay?"

Mabel snuggled deeper into his arms, thinking how nice it was to have someone want to do things with her—and for her. Even as she had that thought, she remembered Lisa's dreaded shower with a pang of guilt. She'd better plan that event before she started making plans of her own.

John started laughing about the same instant that Mabel felt herself listing to the right. While her mind had been lost elsewhere, Barnacle had been winding his leash around their legs till they were well tied up and about to topple.

"Barnacle, stop." She fumbled with his collar, trying to start him unwinding in the opposite direction. When that system didn't seem to be producing results, she tried turning herself around the other way.

"Mabel, no." John grabbed her shoulders, but it was too late. She felt herself losing her balance, and she was taking John down with her.

As she hit the ground, she began flailing, trying to get off

John. Barnacle had partly unwound himself and seemed to think this was a fine new game, where we all roll around the ground together.

He barked and was frisking and nipping at her hands and feet in fine cattle dog fashion. The nips were standard issue for his breed and didn't hurt. Mabel felt John start to shake and realized he was laughing.

Drool garlands covered his face, and she couldn't help laughing too.

"And a fine time was had by all," John finally managed to say, when they'd all somehow extricated themselves. "I'll give you a call tomorrow."

When he kissed her at the back door, Mabel felt her knees wobble. It might have been love, but in this case, it was Barnacle, who'd started to wrap them up in the leash again.

"Okay, buddy. We get the message," John told him, with an affectionate chuck of the dog's chin. "You are a true knight protecting the lady fair."

Barnacle grinned and almost seemed to wink, though Mabel presumed it was a tic.

Once inside, Mabel reset her alarm and locked the door, as John always reminded her to do. She sighed. He was her true knight too, she thought with a flight of romantic fantasy, before burying her face in her hands. How unbearably corny could she be?

"Koi?" Mabel realized she hadn't seen the cat since she'd come in. Normally, the tortie would have appeared by now— whether to welcome them home, register her complaints, or check for available treats.

While Barnacle dogged her footsteps, crowding her heels lest she forget he was still waiting for his evening strip of jerky, Mabel called out as she checked the hallway and living room. "Here, kitty, kitty."

She found the cat sitting on Grandma Mabel's old tea cart, under the living room window. Koi had her tail neatly wrapped around her feet, and though she flicked an ear, as if to let Mabel know she'd heard her, she didn't turn around.

The cat's intent gaze was fixed on the strip of empty night sky visible above the trees across the road.

Chapter Twenty-Three

NEXT MORNING, MABEL STARTED THE COFFEE and turned on the TV. Since the *Empty Eyes* film crew had arrived in Medicine Spring, she'd developed a habit of leaving the *Country Morning* show on in the background in case something newsworthy had happened.

Today though, she felt depleted. Maybe she didn't want any more UFO-related news. Maybe she'd never figure out what—if anything—had happened to her on the ridge. Yes, she'd gotten to the "if anything" stage in her thinking. So far, she'd learned nothing of any value, except that others had apparently seen something too.

A lot of people "see things." Mabel gave her coffee a sour look as she poured her first cup.

She felt a gentle tap on her leg and looked down to see Koi with one paw resting on her shin. The cat was looking into Mabel's eyes with unusual intensity.

"What? Are you worrying about my mental stability too?"

There did seem to be an awful lot of nuts with a fervent belief in the looniest of theories. Mabel didn't want to head down that road. The fact remained that something she couldn't understand had happened to her, and nobody seemed able to help her. Not TV shows. Not UFO groups.

Maybe she should swallow her distaste and talk to Arthur Frost, since he was right here in town. If the UFO "true believers" couldn't help, maybe somebody who understood the range of logical—earthly—explanations could.

Koi abruptly pushed away and trotted into the living room. The news segment was on now, and Mabel caught the very name she'd just been thinking about.

Barnacle lay sprawled across the couch with Koi sitting up, alert, beside him. He glanced at Mabel and then back at the morning news anchor, Ken Waterman, whose usual rich tones oozed credibility and sincerity. Today, excitement lit Waterman's face, matching the higher pitch of his voice. He swept an absent hand over his forehead, dislodging his careful combover.

Mabel shoved Barnacle off the couch and sat. She had missed the first bit of what the reporter was saying, but the gist was clear at once. "In tragic news this morning, Mr. Frost was found dead in the Pleasant Union Cemetery late last night. Police sources inform us they are not ready to discuss cause of death, pending an autopsy, but request anyone with possible information to contact Medicine Spring Police Department. A press conference with Police Chief Marjorie Dunlap has been scheduled for this afternoon at three. Tune in to WXAT, which will be carrying the conference live."

Dr. Frost. Mabel could almost hear the debunker's irritated correction from the Great Beyond. *Dead.* It didn't seem possible.

Mabel's heart pounded so hard she felt it in her fingertips. Pleasant Union Cemetery. Late last night. Anyone with information.

Did she have any information? She and John had been there—or right across the road. If only she knew when Frost had met his demise.

Barnacle laid a paw on her knee. He'd been there too. And Nanette. And a meteor? Or a searchlight? Was the streak of light somehow connected with Frost's death?

Barnacle whined softly. Mabel patted him, then grabbed her phone as the news program went to a commercial.

She sent a text to John and then another to Lisa, hoping one or both would reply. Mabel glanced at the time. She might catch Lisa before the first of her kindergarten early arrivals landed. John should be up by now and free to talk, but for all she knew, he was in the shower or something.

Think, Mabel. She chewed her lip. What could have happened? Well, she supposed it could have been a heart attack or something. For all his careful self-presentation, Frost hadn't been a young man.

Should she call the police? Not until she had thought this through—where she and John had been and when, what she had seen or heard.

Of course, the one possibly pertinent thing that jumped into her head was Nanette. Nanette, being where she shouldn't have been at the very wrong time. Nanette, acting nervous, jumpy, and totally unlike herself. Nanette, choosing to drive home in the exact wrong direction.

Maybe Nanette hadn't been confused. Maybe she knew that anyone coming from town would see her returning from the direction of Pleasant Union Cemetery—someone like the police.

Country Morning returned with talk about the *Empty Eyes* special investigation and the death of Arthur Frost. Mabel wanted to find out if anything new was developing, but her mind kept skidding off track. Nanette wouldn't—couldn't—have anything to do with Frost's death. Still, the question remained–why had she been out there at that hour?

Even if she had a reasonable explanation for her presence, Mabel realized Nanette wasn't just a potential killer—however unlikely that was, she was also most definitely a potential witness to whatever had happened to Dr. Arthur Frost. Her mind balked. *I can't sic the cops on her.*

Mabel sighed. She was going to have to talk to Nanette, and soon, because Nanette wasn't the only potential witness. So was Mabel.

Not to mention John. Even if Mabel didn't rat Nanette out to the police, John might well feel duty bound to report seeing her. Besides being an upstanding citizen, he had to think about his suspended PI license, which still hung in the balance. Withholding evidence would amount to another black mark on his record.

Mabel had to stop grinding her teeth and do something.

Oh, wait. Here came a remote interview with Leif Steele.

A young reporter, whose long blonde hair tumbled over the shoulders of her belted red coat, stood on the B&B steps, holding a microphone under Leif Steele's aristocratic nose. Steele, for once, wasn't wearing one of his usual poured-on black tees. Maybe in deference to the cold—or respect for the dead—he wore a charcoal quarter-zip sweater, displaying only a tasteful hint of chest hair. The unruly dark forelock, lightly threaded with a hint of gray, tumbled over his brow, suggesting as usual that he'd recently rolled out of bed. He was also wearing black-framed glasses. Possibly, he hadn't yet had time to get his contacts in.

As the reporter asked for comment on Frost's death, the camera panned to a close-up of Steele. The *Empty Eyes* host, caught in profile, frowned over the microphone. "I'm shocked, as I'm sure we all are this morning. Dr. Arthur Frost was an uncompromising icon in the quest for truth regarding so-called UFOs. I, and the *Are Empty Eyes Watching?* family, anxiously await whatever information police are prepared to release at this afternoon's news conference. Our hearts go out to Dr. Frost's loved ones for this tragic loss."

The reporter, looking duly somber, nodded. "Respectfully, Mr. Steele, where does this terrible passing leave the Medicine Spring UFO documentary, which has barely begun filming?"

Steele glared. "Ultimately, I'm confident Dr. Frost would want the investigation and filming to continue—as we would wish to dedicate the documentary to his memory. As you can imagine, we're all still reeling from the news we quite literally woke up to this morning. We are all stunned and grieving at the moment—please respect that and give us space to digest this tragedy before requesting a statement about the future of the investigation."

With that, Steele delivered a curt nod, turned on his heel, and went inside. The B&B's storm door slammed behind him, and the microphone picked up the muffled sound of angry yelling.

Whoa. Whether or not Steele and Frost had been the well-oiled team they appeared to be on-air, it was obvious Frost's death would be a devastating blow to the documentary, as well as the show itself. Quite simply, Frost was—or had been—the most respected scientific debunker in the business. Was there anyone credible who could replace him?

Apart from that huge staffing gap, Mabel now knew from sad prior experience that any continued investigation or filming anywhere in the vicinity of Pleasant Union Cemetery was now at a forcible halt for the immediate future. Police would have created a perimeter around the place the body had been found and locked it down so they could comb for evidence. Had Frost been killed there? Or simply dumped postmortem?

Unfortunately for Leif Steele and his investigation, the immediate proximity of Miller's Woods almost certainly meant the woods were off-limits now too. Which, in turn, meant there was little or nothing for Steele and his crew to investigate till the police removed their tape and any officers standing guard.

Meanwhile, Mabel was pretty sure Steele's production company would be stuck paying tons of overtime to any researchers, grips, and whatever other people had come to town with him. Was any of that equipment rented? If he wanted to keep people and equipment at the ready, he was going to have to keep paying and paying.

What were the implications for Steele's show which, according to Jackie, was already in need of the ratings boost this documentary was supposed to provide? Frost's demise might stimulate more interest in the show, but only initially. Meanwhile, the show would continue to bleed money.

Mabel startled as her phone rang—John hadn't bothered texting.

The moment she picked up, Mabel started talking. "We were there. Maybe even while Frost was being killed. What are we going to do? Should we call the police?"

"Hey, slow down. The first thing is to get down to The Coffee Cup. If there's any scuttlebutt—and I'm guessing there is—that's where we're going to hear it. Not that any of it's true, but you never know what you might pick up. Bet they're really hopping this morning."

Of course—The Coffee Cup. "Meet you there in fifteen."

Chapter Twenty-Four

JOHN'S PREDICTION ABOUT THE SURGE IN The Coffee Cup's popularity proved so true that Mabel had to park down the street a ways. Oh, well, she told herself, the walk was good for her.

True to form, John had managed to wrangle them a couple seats—thanks to Miss Birdie and Ms. Katherine Ann, who'd returned the favor from the other morning by inviting John and Mabel to join them. Ms. Katherine Ann, in fact, was standing and frantically beckoning from John and Mabel's favorite table.

"Oh, my land." Ms. Katherine Ann exploded the moment Mabel got close enough to hear her over the ruckus. "Did you hear that awful man got himself killed?"

"Katherine, please." Miss Birdie tugged at her friend's warm-up jacket. "You're making a scene."

John, seated in the corner of the booth, across from the old ladies, smiled and winked at Mabel as she slid in next to him. He squeezed her hand.

"So, did you hear?" Ms. Katherine Ann repeated, this time from her seat, but still at top volume.

"I did. I was shocked."

"So were we." Miss Birdie cradled her tea mug in both hands. "This flying saucer madness has got to stop. The whole town's been in an uproar ever since that Tuesday night and getting worse. Now this. That poor man." She shook her head.

"He seemed a nasty sort to me." Ms. Katherine Ann shrugged a shoulder.

"But still…"

"Still," Ms. Katherine Ann agreed with a little nod.

"I think it's time we all step back and talk about something other than little green men for a while." Miss Birdie gave her friend a stern look that made Mabel wonder. It seemed like Miss Birdie wanted Ms. Katherine Ann to shut up about something in particular that she was busting to spill.

Frankly, the main reason Mabel had come to the diner was to get the scoop on Frost's death. The last thing she wanted was for her most reliable gossip source to turn off the tap right now.

"I'm so sorry." Their frazzled waitress appeared with her pad at the ready. "It's crazy busy today. Are you ready to order, or do you need a minute?"

Anxious to return to the conversation, Mabel placed her order for the Harvest Special, which had been on the sign out front—pumpkin-pecan griddle cakes with maple syrup and whipped cream and sausage—and added a side of scrambled eggs. Feeling a restless movement from John next to her, she hastily canceled the scrambled eggs. She knew he worried about stuff like her cholesterol.

A wee bit of his concern seemed to be rubbing off on her. Though she suspected he'd more likely have cancelled the Harvest Special than a couple lonely eggs.

When John had placed his order for two poached eggs on whole wheat and a glass of grapefruit juice, Mabel turned back to Ms. Katherine Ann, who was all but squirming in her seat. "Have you heard something?"

Ms. Katherine Ann darted a quick look at Miss Birdie, then leaned over the table and hissed, "I hear they found him in his birthday suit."

Mabel's eyes widened.

"*Naked.*" She seemed to think Mabel required clarification.

"Katherine." Miss Birdie tapped her friend's hand.

"I'm not talking about little green men. Mabel asked what I heard, and I told her."

Miss Birdie sighed, seeming to realize she'd lost any

semblance of control. "He was wearing his boxers, is what I heard. I wouldn't even be repeating *that*," she said with a frown directed at Ms. Katherine Ann, "except to restore at least a shred of the poor man's dignity."

"It went down into the low forties last night." Mabel glanced at John. "Those aren't 'run around the graveyard in your birthday suit' temperatures. If such temperatures exist, which I doubt."

"Well, it's movie people, after all." Ms. Katherine Ann took a bite of her grilled sticky pecan bun, and Mabel's mouth watered.

"We shouldn't stereotype," Miss Birdie scolded. "You will never convince me that gentlemen like Mr. Jimmy Stewart or Mr. Sidney Poitier would have ever gallivanted around like that."

Ms. Katherine Ann sniffed. "Keep up with the times, Birdie. You would not believe the things I read in those magazines down at the beauty parlor." She shook her head.

John cleared his throat. "Well, if the rumors are true, why *would* he be…unclothed…,in the graveyard?" He gave the elderly ladies an apologetic look and blushed a little, which Mabel found tremendously endearing. "It makes no sense."

"Unless…" Mabel said.

"No, Mabel." John shook his head.

"Oh, I'm not serious," Mabel told him. "Not that much anyway."

He rolled his eyes. "She's going to say it."

Mabel rolled her eyes right back at him. "Unless he was abducted by aliens. He wouldn't be the first abductee to land back here without his clothes."

"And there it is," John said.

Miss Birdie stared. "You're not serious, Mabel."

"No, ma'am, not really…. Well, I don't think so. But you've got to admit, some very weird things have been going on, and that explanation isn't so much weirder than anything else."

Ms. Katherine Ann, seemingly encouraged by Mabel's

contribution, added, "That would also explain the marks on the body."

Mabel's eyebrows shot upward. "Marks?"

Ms. Katherine Ann pointed at her own side. "You know. Like the aliens do for their experimentation."

Unfortunately, the ladies had no further details on the nature of the mysterious marks on Frost's body. Miss Birdie, in fact, suggested the rumor mill had ground out far more gossip than the known facts would allow.

"Let's leave that aspect of the story aside for the moment, okay?" John covered Mabel's hand with his, as if to hold her back. "What else have you ladies heard? Have they said yet who found him?"

"Anonymous call, someone here said earlier. Might've been a woman."

Mabel's heart sank. She and John exchanged another look. *Nanette?*

At that moment, their meals arrived. The conversation paused while coffee mugs and hot water carafes were refilled, despite Miss Birdie's belated attempt to cover her carafe.

After the waitress departed, Miss Birdie disappointed Mabel by taking some bills from her fanny pack and giving Ms. Katherine Ann—who was about to dunk her teabag in the replenished hot water—a little shove. "We plan on walking out by Lake Margaret for a change this morning, so we better get on our way."

John's forehead creased. "That's pretty far. Once you get out of town, there's no shoulder. With all this extra traffic, I don't believe that's safe."

Miss Birdie smiled. "Bless you, John. We're not walking the whole way. Katherine is going to drive us up."

From what Mabel had observed of Ms. Katherine Ann's driving, she wasn't at all sure this option was any safer—at least, to those around her. "Be careful anyway," she warned. "There are a lot more cars out than usual…and pedestrians."

They watched the ladies work their way to the front register, with Ms. Katherine Ann talking Miss Birdie's ear off as they went. Once they were out of hearing range, John turned to Mabel. "Well. That was…something."

"You have any thoughts about how the body was found?" Mabel shoveled a big mouthful of pancake and whipped cream into her mouth and sighed.

"Um, the 'alien experimentation?'" He air-quoted. "Assuming, of course, that there's any truth whatsoever in the latest scuttlebutt, which is even loonier than usual."

She wiped her mouth with her napkin. "It kind of makes sense. It's pretty much how Koslowski described his abduction injuries that Frost scoffed at. You think someone might want to use that to make a point?"

John shrugged. "Or frame Koslowski."

Mabel chewed thoughtfully. "I'm worried about Nanette."

"You don't think she's mixed up in Frost's death, do you?" John raised an eyebrow. "I realize she's been acting a bit odd, but murder? It's highly unlikely she ever met him. Not to mention leaving him in the altogether."

"No, maybe not. As you keep pointing out, the rumors may be wrong. Maybe Frost wasn't murdered, wasn't naked, and wasn't marked up in any way—whatever that means."

"Agreed."

"Whether he was, or he wasn't, there's bound to be a big investigation," Mabel said, "This is a high-profile case, and police and reporters are going to be turning over every pebble in sight. I'd hate to see Nanette get sucked into all that."

Her jaw tightened as another thought occurred. "Nanette may not have known Arthur Frost. What if he came upon her, though, when she was doing something at the graveyard?

Something she couldn't let *anyone* know about?"

"So she had to kill him?" John grimaced. "Unlikely, but possible. A sudden impulse maybe and caught him off guard. Even assuming she's innocent, I've been wondering if she might have seen something. You know her better than I do. Do you think she'll come forward if she has any information?"

Mabel took a long pause to think, licking whipped cream off her coffee spoon. "The Nanette I know is a good citizen—a real straight arrow. She'd do the right thing, generally speaking. In this case, I'm not so sure. We know she's covering something up. To come clean with what she knows about last night would mean she'll also have to explain what she was doing out there in the middle of the night."

"Can you talk to her? Maybe she'll feel more comfortable telling you."

"Maybe," Mabel said doubtfully. "Whatever it is, she's been going to a lot of effort to keep it under wraps."

They finished their breakfast, leaving Mabel comfortably full but not stuffed. She was proud of herself for controlling her number of plates. When they stepped outside, however, she realized she and John still hadn't decided whether they needed to go to the police themselves.

"Let's wait," he told her. "We don't, in fact, know very much. Let's see what Chief Dunlap has to say this afternoon. If you do get to talk to Nanette, maybe that will help us decide whether we have anything worth reporting."

Mabel nodded. *If.* She dreaded approaching Nanette about last night.

Chapter Twenty-Five

MABEL AND JOHN PARTED AT HER car. She watched him walk away, but although her engine was running, she continued to sit and think. She couldn't face Nanette—not yet. On the other hand, she couldn't make up her mind what to do about the police until she did.

Nanette was such a gracious and upright person she might well be tying herself in knots over the smallest transgression. All the same—though it seemed preposterous—what if Nanette's secret was really bad?

Mabel threw herself against the headrest with a groan. It was still early, so Lisa wasn't available to talk her through this.

Abruptly, she sat up again. The image of Nanette, caught momentarily in the pole light's illumination, flitted across her mind. In that instant, hadn't Nanette whipped her right arm behind her? Why? Had it been a startle reflex, or had she thrown something into the bushes?

Mabel drummed her fingers on the steering wheel. She remembered right where Nanette had been when they first saw her. More or less.

The area was undoubtedly still crawling with police and techs. If she attempted to get anywhere near the cemetery, they'd be chasing her down the road. She could wait till dark, but nighttime didn't offer ideal search conditions for what might be a small object.

Still, it was a public road. The spot was, or so she thought, out of sight of the church parking lot, due to a high embankment and an immediate bend in the road.

The perfect cover came to her in a flash…an innocent

woman walking her innocent dog along a country road. This could work.

Mabel put her car in gear, and within half an hour, she and Barnacle were getting out at a pull-off not far from where they'd first noticed Nanette last night. Too late, she realized this was likely where Nanette had been parked, and Mabel had backed right over the tire tracks.

After that first guilty gulp, she calmed herself down. The police would either already have taken photos and tire impressions of any potential parking spots of interest or blocked them off by now.

Barnacle leapt from the car as usual and immediately stuck his nose into the frostbitten weeds along the road. Perfect. They'd take their time while she beat the bushes and scanned for evidence as they went.

Pleasant Union Church was not yet visible around the bend, and so far, Mabel didn't see any police. She and John had first spotted Nanette from nearly opposite the church. She could remember about where they'd been standing when the light caught her.

Mabel's challenge, even assuming the cops didn't chase her off right away, would be to make her search through the bushes less obvious. She wasn't sure how to do that.

Well, even if her search came to nothing, at least Barnacle was having a fine time with this impromptu adventure. So far, he'd come up with a crumpled burger wrapper, someone else's used pet waste bag, and some chicken bones. Mabel had been saying "no" a lot and bribing him with treats from her pocket.

As they rounded the curve, she thought she spotted the very place where Nanette had tossed something last night. With one eye on the police cars and uniforms up ahead, Mabel tugged at Barnacle's leash and poked at the overgrown bushes, which had swallowed most of the shoulder. If Nanette had stashed anything very small, Mabel might be right on top of whatever it was and still miss it.

Then, three things happened at once. Barnacle seemed to scent something and dragged Mabel toward a patch of brush. Mabel thought she could see something poking up above the clump of bushes. Then, one of the police officers yelled at her.

"Hey! This is a crime scene. You need to turn around right there."

So close. Mabel dragged at Barnacle's leash and darted a hooded glance at the scrub brush. She didn't want to draw attention to whatever Nanette had stashed in there, at least not yet.

Oh, no. The uniformed officer was coming her way.

Mabel walked toward him with Barnacle, eager to meet a new friend, leading the way.

"I told you to stop. Can't you hear me?"

"Yes, sir." She pulled Barnacle back and asked him to sit, which he did, rear end still squirming with delight.

The cop stood in front of her, arms folded. "Do you live around here?"

"Uh, kind of."

"What brings you up here?"

"Walking my dog, officer."

He was already shaking his head. "See those traffic cones? No foot traffic up ahead. Vehicles only, and everyone's required to stop for the checkpoint."

He pulled out a pad and pencil. "I have a few questions, now that you're here."

This interview was precisely what she and John had decided to postpone till after the news conference this afternoon—and, she'd hoped, after Mabel had talked to Nanette. Mabel handed over her driver's license, feeling as if she'd been pulled over for speeding. Then she had to give her phone number and explain where she'd parked.

"Do you walk here often?"

"No, not really." *Or ever.*

She *could* say "never," since she hadn't ever stood in this spot before. Mabel felt herself flush as she wrestled with her half-truth. She heard Grandma Mabel in her head. *A half-truth's no truth at all, Mabel Josephine.*

"What brings you up here this morning?"

"Oh, just an impulse. It's a nice, quiet country road. Most of the time."

Mabel Josephine.

Grandma had raised her voice in Mabel's head. "Well…I was up around here last night." She waved a hand toward the middle school, where screeching kids were running around the field. "We brought—er, I brought my dog up for a walk over there behind the school."

"You and…?"

She gave John's name and contact information, wondering if they'd be in trouble for trespassing, on top of everything else. The officer looked as if he was prepared to walk her through every single detail of what they'd done and seen and heard last night, and Mabel was kicking herself for coming here this morning. Why hadn't she gone home after breakfast like a good girl?

It seemed inevitable that she'd have to rat out Nanette.

A shout came from the vicinity of the church parking lot. "Hey, MacGregor, you're needed up here."

The cop sighed with apparent frustration and closed his pad. "We'll be in touch."

Mabel's knees went weak as the officer trudged back up the hill. If there had been somewhere to sit, she'd have slumped down onto it. Instead, she leaned on her makeshift walking stick she'd been using to poke at the bushes and drew a deep breath.

Barnacle pulled toward the spot where that taller, sticklike object stuck up out of the brush. Could it be a gun?

Mabel glanced up the hill, but nobody seemed to be paying her any attention at the moment. If she wanted to take a peek, this might be her last chance.

Letting Barnacle lead the way, she turned back toward the mysterious thing in the bushes. She only had a narrow window and didn't want to be caught snooping.

When they drew nearer, Mabel could tell she was looking at a long wooden handle. Barnacle's interest was clearly elsewhere, as his eager snout snuffled through the weeds.

Reflexively, Mabel reached out, then dropped her hand. She didn't dare touch the stick, but she'd be willing to bet Nanette's fingerprints were all over it.

"You're right," she told Barnacle. "So smart. We need to look down there under the weeds and see what that handle's attached to."

With another quick glance up the road, Mabel crouched down and began pulling branches out of the way. Most of the leaves were dead by now, and she worried those thick, dry vines were poison ivy.

Note to self: wash hands ASAP.

There it was—a shovel. A long-handled spade, to be exact. Mabel's heart sank. "Nanette, what on earth have you been up to?" she muttered aloud.

Before they could get caught, she scrambled to stand up again, which required putting one hand down to push herself up with. She grunted as she straightened with a wobble, then scraped the hand down the side of her pantleg to dislodge the grit and pebbles that had pressed into her palm.

Mabel cast another look up the hill and saw another uniformed cop emerging from the parking lot onto the road shoulder. He must be the new checkpoint officer.

Hoping to get away without drawing undue attention to Nanette's discarded garden tool, Mabel began hotfooting down the hill toward her car again.

Slow down, Mabel. Just act normal.

It was hard to slow down. Even harder not to look back and check whether she'd drawn any new attention to herself.

"Mabel Browne."

Mabel froze. She knew that female voice. Sweat beaded on her forehead.

With Barnacle romping in wild excitement at meeting a familiar friend, Mabel turned and faced the church lot entrance. "Hi, Lieutenant."

Detective Lt. Sizemore beckoned, and Mabel plodded uphill, willing herself not to dart a glance at Nanette's protruding shovel handle.

"Good to see you again, Ms. Browne. Are we sightseeing this morning?"

Mabel shook her head. "Just walking my dog."

Sizemore said nothing for a moment, leaving Mabel to sweat a little bit harder. Finally, she commented, "Long way from home. Did you walk all this way?"

Again, Mabel shook her head. She hated Sizemore's intolerable pauses, but then again, her questions were just as bad. "We parked down that way. I—this is a nice, quiet stretch of road. We like a little variety in our walks, you know."

Sizemore's left eyebrow rose.

"Barnacle and I. My dog." Mabel pulled at the jumping canine.

"We've met before." Was that a twitch of a smile on Sizemore's face?

Sizemore motioned her farther off the road as a car approached the checkpoint. "I'm afraid we need to get a little info from you before you run off."

"Oh…" Mabel shifted her feet. "That other officer already asked me some questions and took my contact information.

MacGregor?" She gestured toward the church lot.

"Okay, Ms. Browne. No contact info needed." Sizemore gave her a slow smile. "I know where you live."

Mabel's knees nearly buckled with relief. She returned the smile and started backing away. "Have a good day, Lieutenant."

"And you as well, Ms. Browne."

When they reached the car, Mabel collapsed in her seat. Had her well-intentioned escapade just pointed the police in Nanette's direction? Or her own…and maybe John's?

At least now she knew what she had to do. There would be no putting off a chat with Nanette, no matter how much she'd like to.

She would call and ask Nanette whether she could stop by. It might be easier to get Nanette talking in the security of her own home.

After her call to John went to voicemail, Mabel stared at her phone for a moment. She took a few deep breaths and blew them out. This was so difficult.

Nanette's phone rang ten times, and Mabel was about to give up when voicemail came on. It appeared Nanette hadn't taken the time to set up a personalized message, though Mabel wouldn't be surprised if the voicemail set-up had defeated her.

In any event, a generic recording recited Nanette's phone number and invited Mabel to leave a message at the tone. "Uh, hi, Nanette. This is Mabel. Um, I need to chat. I wondered if I might come over? If there's a time you're free?"

There was a moment of dead air, while Mabel cast about for anything else to say that might help set Nanette at ease, but nothing came to her. "Okay then. I hope you're available. I'll wait to hear from you. On my cell phone. Call any time. Okay? Thanks. 'Bye."

She hung up and groaned. Nanette was polite, so she would call back. Whether she'd be comfortable enough to agree to meet, let alone spill her guts, was questionable.

Mabel looked at the time. Better head home and try to get some work done before the press conference.

Mabel hadn't gotten much writing accomplished before the scheduled news conference. She turned the TV on to WXAT and left it muted while the talking heads gabbed among themselves in front of the backdrop of an empty podium. After a few moments, the police chief and a few others, including Mabel's sometimes nemesis, Detective Lt. Sizemore, filed out to stand behind the lectern.

Mabel scooted closer and turned up the sound in time to have her ears blasted by an extended screech from the Chief's microphone. Barnacle's ears went back, and he looked at her with white rims around his eyes, as if he blamed Mabel for that awful noise. Koi melted under the couch.

"Good afternoon," the Chief said. "We're here this afternoon to answer a few questions regarding the recent death of Dr. Arthur Frost, whose body was discovered in the early hours of this morning at the Pleasant Union Cemetery on Indian Camp Road. We have limited information available for dissemination at this time. Given public interest in Dr. Frost, however, who was in Medicine Spring in connection with the television documentary being filmed in town, we felt it best to address the basic facts, as we now know them. Certain other facts are being withheld in the interest of protecting the integrity of our investigation."

Camera shutters whirred.

"Access to the cemetery and adjacent church is currently closed, as we continue to gather evidence. However, we are actively soliciting input from members of the public, who may have information relevant to this death.

"Although we welcome any pertinent information you feel

you may have, we particularly request you call us if you saw either Dr. Frost or certain vehicles in the vicinity of the church property between ten pm yesterday and ten am this morning or observed any person or persons on or near Indian Camp Road during that same time period. A description of the vehicles of interest will appear at the bottom of your screen, along with our hotline number."

The Chief went on to recite the sketchiest account of the discovery of Frost's body. Not only did it contain nothing new to Mabel, but it didn't mention any of the juicy tidbits Miss Birdie and Ms. Katherine Ann had harvested from the town rumor mill. While listening with half an ear, Mabel scanned the vehicle descriptions.

She recognized Frost's sports car at once. An obvious inclusion. The second description, to her surprise, also looked familiar. She'd been holding her breath, when the Chief mentioned multiple vehicles, afraid Nanette's might be one of them. To her relief, the distinctive purple sedan wasn't there, but police were also looking for a truck.

The description was vague. She recognized that trucks fitting this description were common in the country. Still, she realized this could be the very vehicle that had blown past them on the road last night. Where else had she recently seen a dark, full-size pickup like that?

The conference ended without Mabel's having figured out the answer to that gnawing question.

Chapter Twenty-Six

Following the police news conference, Mabel tried again to focus on her writing but found her mind a perfect blank, at least where her chapter on political volunteering was concerned. All she could think about was Arthur Frost's sudden demise.

The shock of the event alone was enough to keep her thoughts skidding off on that, but she knew there was more. She and John—and Barnacle—had been there, maybe close to the time Frost died. Had the debunker's car been there, maybe hidden behind the church? As well as perhaps a murderer's vehicle?

Was Frost being killed mere yards away, while she and John were walking around, being trailed by coyotes? Actually, she didn't *know* Frost had been murdered, but the police were certainly treating his death as suspicious.

Assuming he had been murdered, might the killer have seen them? Or Nanette? He—or she—might even now be thinking about her and John, or Nanette, and wondering what they'd seen or heard that might put him—or her—in prison. Were they in danger?

It would be hard, she reluctantly concluded, to dodge somebody when you didn't know where the danger was coming from. It wouldn't be the first time a murderer had cornered her in her own house. Mabel jumped up and went to her doors. They were already locked, and the alarm was set.

She sat back down. Maybe she should make a suspect list and then resolve to keep her eye out for all of them.

1. Stanley Koslowski
2. Dan Cardamone
3. The guy who heckled Frost at the UFO group—and threw eggs at him later. He also came to the book signing with Jackie (*

What was his name? Vernon?) She couldn't remember for sure.

There had been plenty of other people at the signing who were mad at Frost, but she didn't know their names and doubted she could identify them again on sight.

Cardamone, though… Mabel considered the man with the allegedly levitating cat. He'd been at the bookstore a few hours before Frost was killed. John had turned him away at the door. It was possible he'd waited somewhere outside—maybe sitting in his car—and watched, then trailed Frost to the cemetery and confronted him there.

Hadn't she heard Cardamone lived somewhere near the cemetery? Perhaps even within walking distance? Mabel tapped her pen on the table. It should've been comparatively easy for him to avoid witnesses out there—and if he did happen to be seen in the vicinity, he was just an innocent man on his way home.

What had drawn Frost to the cemetery in the first place—so late in the evening, and right after that contentious book signing?

Mabel shook her head and moved on. Unwillingly, she added Nanette's name, but then went back and put brackets around it to show she wasn't serious. Then again…. She doodled a clumsy drawing of a shovel sticking out of some scribbles that represented brush.

Shouldn't she add Pete to the list too, if she was going to include Nanette? He might not have been at the graveyard last night, but he *had* been there before, and acting suspicious too.

As she pondered this addition to her suspect list, a sudden image loomed up in her mind. High beams glaring in John's rearview mirror and lighting up the car's interior—headlights of a dark, full-size pickup truck blasting around them on Indian Camp Road last night, heading away from town.

Pete drove a dark, full-size pickup,

Of course, so did a lot of other people, and this truck had been headed away from Medicine Spring. Pete lived right in town.

Then again, so did Nanette, who had also driven the long

way around to get home.

Should she try to talk to Pete? Mabel picked up her phone and put it down again. What on earth would she say to him? *One suspect at a time, Mabel.*

She wiped her forehead with a damp tissue. Was all this sweat due to anxiety? Or a hot flash?

A clatter at her kitchen window made her look up. Sleet hit the glass like a handful of tiny pebbles.

She wondered if Nanette had retrieved her shovel yet…or the police had.

Mabel picked up her phone again, thinking of calling Lisa, who might be free by now. The phone rang in her hand.

She'd hoped it might be Nanette—or even John or Lisa, but it was her sister, Jen.

"Mabel? Did you hear about the murder in Medicine Spring?"

"Hi to you too. Yeah, I saw the news."

"It was the guy from the TV show. What's happening to Medicine Spring these days?"

"I don't know. It's crazy." For once, Jen didn't seem to suspect Mabel of being involved in the latest death in town, and Mabel intended to keep things that way as long as possible.

Anything Jen knew, Mom was sure to find out. Once that happened, Mom would be trying to move Mabel back to her old childhood bedroom in Bartles Corners and feed her home-baked pie till she could no longer waddle. Which, she had to admit, did have its positive aspects.

"Have you heard any rumors?" Jen asked.

"Just all the crazy UFO stuff." Mabel attempted a hearty laugh.

They were still talking when another call came in from a local number. "Oh, hey, it's Lisa. I've got to go."

Mabel fumbled a bit before connecting the other call. "Are you there?"

Lisa giggled. "Yeah. Was I interrupting something?"

"You were getting me off the phone with Jen before I could say anything incriminating that might get back to Mom. Thanks."

"What friends are for? I was checking to see if you heard any news about the murder I might have missed during school."

"Well, they're not calling it a murder, but obviously the police are investigating. Plus, there's going to be an autopsy, but they're not making much info public."

"At least this is one dead body Lt. Sizemore can't pin on you. You don't have any connection with this one."

Mabel hesitated and then hurried to cover up the pause. "No more than anybody else who came in contact with any of those film crew people—or witnessed one of the confrontations folks had with Frost. He seemed to be a lightning rod for that sort of thing, so I'm guessing most of the local population is going to be lined up to report one shouting match or another."

"You're right. The police are going to be drowning in suspects on this one."

Mabel's phone vibrated in her hand. "Oh, here comes another call. I better grab it. I'll call you later."

The number was local and looked familiar, but Mabel couldn't place it. Hoping it was Nanette, she picked up.

"Did you talk to the police yet?"

"Nita?"

"Did you hear from the police yet?"

Mabel swallowed. John's classic car with its unfinished paint job was nothing if not distinctive. If someone had spotted it near the cemetery last night, they might have reported it.

"Me? Why?"

"Oh, that cursed book signing. What else? Somebody told them about that big fight at the end. They want to talk to everyone they can track down. Looks like all that mess happened just a couple hours before Frost bit the dust."

"Oh, Nita, I'm sorry. It was a successful event except for the very end there."

"The food fight? Having to throw customers out of the store? A murder right afterward?"

"Yeah, still…"

"Well, I wanted you to know the cops will be calling."

"Hey, it's better than being a suspect, right?"

Nita growled.

By the time she got off the call with Nita, the sleet had turned to misty drizzle. Mabel grabbed Barnacle's leash, so she could take him out to potty—and get away from her phone. For the next ten minutes, they walked around the field behind her house while Barnacle snuffled through the stubble. Not for the first time, she studied the chronic wet area in the back corner and wondered if she could get it declared a protected wetland, so she could forget about trying to fill it in for no other reason than to make the township happy.

She added it to her mental to-do list: *Check PA criteria for protected wetlands.* As if she'd ever get that far down on her list…

When they came inside again, Koi met them at the door. "Snack time, huh?"

After she'd handed out treats, Mabel checked her phone. *Nothing.* She hadn't really expected Nanette to call back. She might end up having to do the unthinkable and attend a historical society meeting and corner her there.

After Mabel's first attempt at civic-minded volunteerism had ended in murder, she'd tried to back away from the society. But if Nita was right, the police would be coming to call sooner rather than later. Not only had Mabel worked the notorious book signing, but a few hours ago, she'd been stopped by police scant feet away from the Pleasant Union Cemetery and left with her interview still uncompleted.

Mabel couldn't face another interview without knowing what to say about Nanette.

Chapter Twenty-Seven

IT WAS MEETING NIGHT FOR THE Medicine Spring Historical Society. Mabel had gotten no call back from Nanette, which was such a departure from her friend's normal courtesy that it practically shot red emergency flares into the air. Regretfully, Mabel decided she would have to attend the meeting and look for Nanette there.

She was already dressed in her nice black jeans, black long-sleeve tee, and a cranberry velvet blazer Jen had found for her at the thrift store. It wasn't something Mabel would have picked out for herself, but she had to admit it was a bold look for her, and she kind of liked it.

No refreshments, she decided. She had nothing home-baked, and the standards for the historical society refreshment table were way beyond her capabilities anyway.

Koi meowed from atop the Hoosier cupboard. A harsh sound, Mabel could only interpret it as a complaint or a warning.

"What? You've been fed, and I won't be gone long."

Koi stared down at her, slit-eyed.

It felt ridiculous, being stopped in her tracks by a cat's meow. While Mabel didn't necessarily think Koi had extrasensory perception, she knew from experience that her cat had keener discernment than most people she knew.

Mabel hesitated and reviewed her plan for the evening. *Oh, good grief.*

She threw down her slouchy leather bag and started peeling off the blazer. How could she go to a meeting with Cora? And Linnea? She still hadn't resolved the great political sign stand-off. Or even whom she'd be voting for. Without ever confronting

Nanette, this evening had the potential to get ugly—not, to be fair, an unusual situation for the Medicine Spring Historical Society.

Now what? Mabel mouthed a thank-you to Koi and went to put on her pajamas.

Twenty minutes later, she was sitting with her suspect list and a package of not-too-bad store-bought chocolate cookies, trying to think what—if anything—she could do to move things along. She'd try Nanette again tomorrow—maybe even stop by the house. Nanette was too polite to refuse to let her in.

She didn't need to investigate Cardamone or the egg-thrower, she realized. And not even the likeliest suspect, Stanley Koslowski himself. She didn't have to solve the case at all. Let Lt. Sizemore and her merry band of cops get some exercise. All Mabel had to do was try not to get Nanette in trouble unnecessarily. Or Pete, she supposed. Or herself and John.

If Nita was right, the cops would soon be knocking. So, she and John had better get their heads together, and she'd also better figure out the best approach to Nanette and Pete.

When Mabel finally decided to drag herself up to bed early, John called.

"Sorry I couldn't talk earlier. I needed to finish checking papers, so I could get grades posted. What did you think of the Chief's press conference?"

"Not much. I don't mean that to be critical, but I didn't learn anything new. Oh, except one thing. What did you think about that pickup they're looking for?" Mabel propped up her pillows and tucked her cold feet under the covers.

"Probably what you're thinking. It could be the same one that almost blew us off the road last night. It could as easily have been any number of local yahoos who like to drive like maniacs."

"Yeah, but..."

"But what?"

"Remember my friend Pete? We ran into him up there

earlier, acting kind of weird and furtive?"

"That what he drives?"

"Yeah, could've been his, as well as a hundred other people around here. I wouldn't think he'd be driving like that—or in that direction, but—"

"Maybe if he'd just seen a body? Or witnessed a murder?"

Mabel bit her lip. She wouldn't fill in the blank, which was "Or just committed a murder."

"He *was* acting strange when we saw him up there the other night. How well do you know him?"

"Oh, well enough, I guess. He bailed me out of problems more than once when I first rescued Koi."

She wouldn't get into the time he'd come to her rescue when she was stuck in an empty house with a murderer. On that occasion, Pete had pulled out a gun he called his "peacemaker." The police still hadn't announced any cause of death for Frost, either. She couldn't remember hearing a gunshot last night, but that didn't eliminate the possibility there had been one a bit earlier or later.

Telling John how she'd met Pete reminded Mabel that she hadn't known John very long. Every time she realized she'd never told John some huge story from her past, it startled her all over again that she'd only known him a couple of months. "I like Pete," she admitted. "I hate to blow the whistle on him unless I'm forced to."

"Or Nanette."

"Or Nanette," she agreed. "I tried to get hold of her today, but she never returned my call. Nita said the police want to talk to everybody who was at the book signing and witnessed the brawl, so I can't wait forever for her to decide to get back to me. I guess I'll need to run her down tomorrow."

"Hope she decides to come clean with you."

"There's more." Mabel groaned. "Remember how she did

something with her arm in that instant we first saw her?"

"No, I wasn't looking."

"Well, it seemed to me as if she'd shoved or tossed something behind her into the brush. So, I went up there this afternoon—just walking Barnacle up the road—and guess what."

"The police stopped you."

"Well, yeah. But after I got away—"

"You ran from the police?"

"Of course not. They asked me a couple questions, but then the officer got called away, and he said they'd finish talking to me later. Anyway, I had a few seconds before another cop took over, and I found a shovel in the bushes right there."

There was a pause, while John presumably thought. "That doesn't sound like she was up to anything good. Did you get a close look at the shovel?"

"No. Next thing I knew, Lt. Sizemore showed up. After she grilled me a bit, I had to vamoose out of there."

"You didn't notice any…blood?"

"Blood? What?"

"Frost wouldn't be the first person ever killed with a shovel."

Mabel's heart flopped in her chest. *Could* that innocent-looking shovel have been the murder weapon?

For what might have been the first time since she'd known John, Mabel felt worse after they'd hung up.

Chapter Twenty-Eight

MABEL WOKE WITH A SENSE OF dread heavy on her chest, but soon realized at least part of that weight was Koi. She rolled onto her side, tipping the cat off onto the mattress.

Her chest still ached. Mabel remembered her guilty knowledge about Nanette and sighed. How could she call the police on her friend? On the other hand, how could she withhold evidence she'd definitely have reported if she hadn't known and liked the person who'd ditched a suspicious gardening tool in the bushes?

Couldn't John find out if the police had at least a tentative cause of death? Mabel scowled. He still had a couple of contacts in the Medicine Spring PD. Surely, he could find out *something* that could help her make up her mind.

Then again, maybe he didn't want to approach his buddies about Frost's death yet, knowing he'd been out by the cemetery the same night and still hadn't called to let the police know. *Ugh...*

She'd have to try to talk to Nanette, for sure.

What about Pete? That could be even more ticklish.

Seriously, what was with these senior citizens and their nocturnal graveyard prowls? And both skulking around with potentially lethal yardwork implements?

Mabel could think of no possible link either Nanette or Pete might have had with the victim. Their connection seemed to be to the cemetery itself. If either had injured Arthur Frost, it had to have been an accident or self-defense. Or a sudden impulse...maybe he'd surprised one of them, and their carefully guarded secret was threatened with exposure?

She would never believe either of them capable of premeditated murder. She didn't want to, anyway.

Barnacle whined at the door and looked at her. "Okay, wait a sec."

While the dog was on his run-out line and the coffee was brewing, Mabel texted John with a gentle hint that he might work his police connections for some information. Then she poured a cup of coffee and stared outside a while, feeling gloomy about life in general. A hard frost lay thick on the grass this morning, there was a definite thread of cold air blowing in around the window frame, and she hadn't seen Acey in days. Maybe she should go ahead and try to seal her own windows.

Koi pit-patted into the kitchen, yawned at her, and meowed. Rousing herself, Mabel began filling pet dishes.

While Koi ate, Mabel turned on *Country Morning.* The hosts' patter didn't interest her, and she was about to switch the TV off when she heard Barnacle bark. She went to let him in and returned to see the news and weather segment had started.

She plopped down and was joined by Koi, who leapt onto her lap and began kneading Mabel's sweatpants. The weather promised more cold and possible flurries or light snow. Mabel made a face at the weatherman, while visions of scraping her windshield and struggling to pay her utility bills danced in her head.

After a commercial break, which she muted, the morning news anchor came on. Mabel clicked the remote as she saw video of Stanley Koslowski exiting the police station. Was he being arrested? When she finally got the sound back on, it seemed he'd just gone in for an interview.

"I have nothing to hide," he told the field reporter. "I want to bring this killer to justice as much as anyone else does, and I refuse to be targeted because of my abduction experience. In fact, I gave the police their perpetrator, and that is all I'm allowed to say at this time."

Koslowski turned to face the camera. "I'm not some unbalanced, dangerous psycho. My abduction by aliens is a fact—a fact that's come close to destroying my life. You can read about it in my book, *My Lost Hours.* The truth is out there."

Mabel's eyebrows shot up. She was struck by Koslowski's claim he'd identified Frost's killer. At the same time, she was impressed by his bold shot at self-promotion. In the hopefully unlikely event that she was dragged into police headquarters and found herself in front of TV cameras, she'd have to remember to plug her upcoming books. At least, she presumed they would be forthcoming, if she ever got around to writing them.

The news report segued into another topic of interest, as the anchor led into the recent spate of streaking lights in the sky. He brought up jerky cellphone video of the same sort of light display she, John, and Nanette had seen up by the cemetery.

Mabel dislodged Koi, who responded with a flash of claws, and drew close to the TV screen to squint at the video. Naturally, it had ended by the time she got there, being mere seconds long. She could probably find the video on WXAT's website.

The anchorman provided no further information on the sightings, other than to say where reports indicated they'd occurred over the past few days. He offered that "speculation is rampant, and some—including the late Dr. Arthur Frost—have been calling these flashes of light a probable hoax."

Mabel checked her phone—nothing from John. She was too restless to sit down and try to work on her writing. Maybe she should get dressed and try to find Acey. He should be working on lights around the village square by now. Every holiday season, every tree and bush in the small park area, as well as the bandstand, were strung with white lights. Surely, by now, he'd have finished decorating Main Street and hanging the UFO Days banners that were competing with the holidays this year.

She should find out what his intentions were regarding her storm doors and windows. Whether he was going to help get her house winterized or not, she needed to buy the supplies before the hardware shelves got depleted. What she bought depended on whether he or she would be doing the work. If it was going to be up to Mabel, she'd need the plastic sheeting she could—she'd been told—put up with the use of her trusty blow-dryer.

Traffic in town had died down. Mabel wondered briefly whether Arthur Frost's death had put a damper on the festivities. More likely, it was a matter of having to get back to work and school, coupled with the shutdown on the more active parts of the investigation at Miller's Woods and the cemetery.

The biggest crowd she saw, in fact, swarmed around the police station. Several people with huge cameras lurked near the steps, along with a scattering of probable rubberneckers. Mabel could see the WXAT logo on a big video camera, along with others from the Pittsburgh and Johnstown stations. No doubt others represented various newspapers. She recognized Renny Martin from *The Shopper*.

Mabel slowed down in hopes she'd see a suspect emerge from the building, but no such luck. Since there was an angled spot open in front of Gump's Hardware, she pulled in. It appeared decorating had been completed for as much of Main Street as she could see, so she headed for the park.

As soon as she crossed the street, she spotted Acey's familiar, scrawny form up on a stepladder next to the bandstand, wielding a staple gun. Oddly, considering the nip in the air, he was wearing a tee shirt.

Mabel walked up behind him and softly called, "Acey." Heaven forbid she startle him off that ladder.

He whirled around, holding the staple gun like a weapon.

"You scared the bahooeys outta me, little lady."

Mabel saw at once why Acey wasn't wearing a jacket. It would have covered the tee shirt graphics: VOTE FOR PETTIGREW on the back and "Say NO to Coruption—NO to Casselman!" on the front.

What was worst—a political tee shirt on a township job? Libelous content? Misspelling? With an effort, Mabel unclenched her jaw.

"Sorry. How's it coming?"

"Oh, she's coming, all right. Going a bit slow. Hard to work in this cold."

"Yeah, my house is getting cold too. I was wondering if you could tell me when you might be by to do the winterizing."

"Well, now…" He looked around all the trees and bushes, where a few other workers, looking considerably busier, were stringing lights. "Hard to say. Hard to say. I can't hardly walk off this job till she's done."

"Give me a date, okay? We can adjust later if you get done sooner than you expect."

"You still supportin' the crook?"

"I explained that to you, Acey. And stop saying LeRoy Casselman is a crook if you don't have any evidence."

"Be easy enough to get evidence. Just offer him a dollar to push whatever project you want done. He'll snatch it outta your hand so fast you'll land on your keister."

"Are you saying Casselman's offering to take bribes?"

Acey hesitated. "He could be. Cletus says he wouldn't be surprised."

Mabel rolled her eyes. "I'll be waiting for you. You did promise me five hours a week, and you haven't been to the house since."

"I'll be there as soon as I'm done over here. You'll be surprised how fast I can get your little bit of work taken care of."

"I'll be surprised, all right," Mabel mumbled.

Instead of returning to the car, she stopped at another ladder some distance from Acey. "Hi, my name is Mabel. I was hoping to find out when you gentlemen—and lady," she added, noticing a woman loading another staple gun, "think the lighting might be done."

"I am Pablo." The worker smiled. "This job is going well. We should be done with everything in town in the next two days."

Mabel's smile outshone Pablo's. "Thank you. You're doing a beautiful job."

Mabel hiked back to her car, briefly considering lunch at The Coffee Cup, but realized she didn't dare make a bad habit worse. And there was no point in stopping at the hardware store till she was sure Acey was going to return to work. She would give him two days for the lights to get done, another two days for recovery, and then push once more.

She knew she should return home to her writing, but as she approached the police station again, a field reporter with a microphone exited one of the cars. On impulse, she pulled into a spot.

The police station side door opened, and the crowd at the front door stampeded toward the other entrance. "Mr. Cardamone, excuse me, Mr. Cardamone."

The red-faced man with the haunted cottage lowered his head and tried to push through the thicket of cameras but found himself blocked. "No comment. Let me out of here."

"Would you like to make a statement, Mr. Cardamone? Tell your side of the story?"

"What can you tell us about your interview? Do the police consider you a suspect?"

"Do you have any comments on Dr. Frost's death?"

"No comment, no statement." Cardamone began shoving, nearly toppling a videographer. "Frost is dead, and I don't care—

my life's already a wreck, either way. Now, get out of my way."

The crowd moved back a bit as Cardamone continued barging his way toward the parking lot, elbowing, shoving, and kicking as he went. Still, they trailed after him, shooting pictures and questions as they surged along.

Mabel hung back. The whole feeding frenzy felt repugnant. Nor did she particularly want to get shoved, kicked, or trampled.

Cardamone slammed his truck door, and someone screamed. Mabel jumped, sure one of the reporters had gotten their hand crushed. A heartbeat later, she realized the door had only slammed on somebody's cable.

Time to go home…maybe by way of Nanette's. She got into her car and watched as Cardamone drove off—in a dark pickup truck.

Mabel followed him with narrowed eyes. She'd heard Cardamone's place was out beyond Miller's Woods. If he'd been headed home on Indian Camp Road the night of Frost's death, he would have been driving in the same direction as John and Nanette—and the mystery truck.

The swarm of reporters streamed back to the front doors of the station, reminding Mabel of a flock of migratory birds. Though, to her knowledge, vultures didn't migrate.

As she started her engine, a furtive figure in a bulky coat caught the corner of her eye, scuttling from the back of the police lot toward the side entrance. As the woman reached the door, it opened from inside, and she slipped through.

Mabel frowned. *Jackie?*

Chapter Twenty-Nine

MABEL STARED AFTER JACKIE AS THE steel police-station door closed behind her. What on earth could Jackie contribute to the investigation?

She had seen Jackie at the book signing, of course, earlier in the evening. However, maybe she'd also been in the vicinity of the cemetery later. Though what possible reason would she have had to be out there? Surely, being a member of the UFO group, she'd have known the site was closed for the Leif Steele investigation.

She was probably at the station to talk about the bookshop brawl.

Mabel had to get home and do some writing, though her heart wasn't in it. She put her car in gear, trying without success to stifle her curiosity. She wished she could have stayed and maybe caught Jackie on her way out of the station.

Mabel pulled into her driveway a few minutes later, lost in thought. She ought to concentrate on her collection of three-page volunteer stories, but they were much harder to write than she'd anticipated—especially since she had to leave out the most interesting parts, most of which involved murders. She had tried including a murder in one of her stories, but the next thing she knew, her little account of the joys of being a search-and-rescue volunteer was ten pages long and still going. Plus, John had pointed out that discovering bodies didn't reflect a typical volunteer experience.

One good look at her house woke her from her gloomy reverie. The Casselman sign she'd left in her yard had now multiplied to three, one a huge placard on the side of her derelict shed reading, "Proud Member of the Casselman Privy Council." A hand-drawn rendering of a royal-looking crest completed the effect.

Who could have done this? Mabel couldn't imagine Cora scaling a stepladder to tack up the Privy Council sign. Or Nanette, for that matter…not to mention, she seemed to be avoiding Mabel right now.

Mabel's gaze drifted toward the patch of woods at the back of her field, and the glimmer of the house lights beyond, visible through the trees. She gritted her teeth. That left Linnea.

Leaving her bag in the car, Mabel stomped over and tugged the extra sign from the ground. Then, dragging the sign, she marched to the trash can at the side of her shed, planning to rip down the Privy Council sign and dump them both.

When she lifted the can lid, she stared down in horror. Acey's Pettigrew sign, crumpled beyond salvation, had been crammed into the can, where it had also acquired a huge smear of moldy spaghetti sauce. Mabel spun around and stared at the spot where the Pettigrew sign had stood, now marked only by a gaping hole.

This was the last straw. To the sound of Barnacle's barking, she stormed up the street to yank down the original Casselman sign she'd agreed to put up and threw it in the field.

Mabel cast a guilty glance at the Sauer mansion. Cora's car wasn't there, thank goodness, but when she arrived, she'd have to notice the sign was missing.

Mabel hesitated, half-considering sticking the sign back in the field. But no. Acey would burn her house down if he discovered his sign had been trashed, with Casselman's signs still in place.

Mabel panted. She was too out of shape for all this charging around and wrestling signs. Plus, she was hungry.

Defiant, she left the sign where it lay and headed back to the house. It was going to be both candidates or neither. She ripped down as much of the Privy Council sign as she could reach without climbing, then grabbed her purse and went inside to let Barnacle out and find something to eat.

While she enjoyed her lunch of leftover coffeecake with string cheese for protein, Mabel wrote out a list.

Call Linnea—she drew a frowny face next to this.

Call Nanette again

Pete?

Jackie???

The last three were all somehow tied into the mystery surrounding Arthur Frost's death. Logic told her Stanley Koslowski was a more probable suspect than anyone on this list. So was Dan Cardamone—or the nut throwing eggs at Frost, the day Leif Steele arrived in town. Once again, she reminded herself she didn't need to solve this murder—if it was a murder. She just needed to know what Pete's and Nanette's stories were before she told the police something that might implicate them.

Mabel sighed. She might as well call Linnea. and try Nanette again, for what it was worth. She still didn't know how to approach Pete, but she *could* call Jackie, who might be able to tell her what was up with the investigation. Maybe she could ask a writing question and then casually lead into Arthur Frost's death somehow.

She checked the time. She expected she could make the first two calls and still have time to write. If Jackie picked up and was conversational, there was a good chance she'd shoot the rest of her available writing time for the day…tempting, but not advisable.

As it turned out, Mabel had to leave two voicemails, one for Linnea and another for Nanette. The lack of response from

Nanette was becoming worrisome. Mabel promised herself she'd go to the house if she didn't get a call back by tomorrow.

She also called Acey, having realized it would be better to get ahead of the Pettigrew sign debacle than have Acey decide to show up at the house and discover the sign gone. As the call went to voicemail, she realized she hadn't planned quite what to say. Finally, she went with "I was away from home this morning, and the campaign sign you left here for me got damaged in my absence. I'm sorry. Just wanted to let you know."

Good. He couldn't blame her for something that had happened when she wasn't even here, could he?

Mabel managed to shut her mouth at the very moment she was about to automatically say she needed a replacement. The last thing she wanted to be guilty of was asking Acey for any more Pettigrew signs, especially given the risk it would turn out to be one of the "Casselman Is a Crook" variety.

Making a grumpy face, she set her phone down. She would give Jackie time to finish with the police, she decided, while she tried to write a bit.

Weekdays were hard, because both Lisa and John were working, and she had no one to bounce her ideas off. Mabel didn't miss her despised job at the law firm, but more than six months after her firing, she had to admit it wasn't easy being alone all day and feeling like she'd been put out to pasture before her time. Yes, she was a writer. Sort of. But writing didn't feel like much of a job when she rarely did enough to feel productive.

As Mabel opened her laptop on the kitchen table, Barnacle groaned and flopped on his side at her feet. "Give me a break. We'll walk later, okay?"

Koi leapt onto the table and rubbed her arched back along the edge of the computer screen. She seemed much more invested in Mabel's writing career than the dog. Maybe because Koi liked when Mabel sat, while Barnacle wanted to play outside with her.

Mabel shook herself, loosening her tense shoulders. She couldn't simultaneously launch a writing career, satisfy her animals' expectations, get her house and grounds under control, plan bridal showers, campaign for two opposing candidates, navigate a new romance, explain a UFO invasion, and solve a murder.

One thing at a time.

Of course, if she didn't multitask, she'd be in her grave along with the flying saucer crew out at Pleasant Union before she got even half her responsibilities squared away. She couldn't think about all of it right now, or she'd be too paralyzed to write.

For the next forty-five minutes, Mabel worked on her true-crime book about the Sauer ax murders. It had gotten hard to write anything peppy about volunteering, since every time she'd volunteered so far had slid from disaster to disaster. While the true-crime story seemed to limp along, at least she'd have something she could edit later.

When the timer she'd set started buzzing, she sighed with relief. Break time. She stretched, and Barnacle sat up with a hopeful look.

"All right. Quick walk up to the corner and back."

By the time they returned, Mabel had hatched an idea. She passed out treats to Barnacle and Koi, then picked up her phone. No messages.

It was almost lunchtime, and Jackie had to be done at the police station by now. If Mabel invited her to lunch, maybe she could ask for advice about her writing, then ease into the murder investigation. She could multitask and might at least get some answers about her writing, even if Jackie turned out to be close-mouthed about her police interview.

The phone rang till Mabel was sure it was headed to voicemail, but then to her amazement, Jackie picked up. "Hey, hi, Jackie. Mabel here. Uh, Mabel Browne. I've been having some writing issues, and I wondered if maybe I could buy you lunch and pick your brain a bit…? Maybe we could go to Old Tom's, out by Cloud Lake, if you like fish. It's pretty quiet this time of year."

For a moment, the line was silent. Finally, Jackie said, "I don't know what my advice is worth, but I'd be glad to try. I'm off work today." She paused again. "If you don't mind, I'm not very hungry though. Would it be okay if we went for coffee instead? Or, if you'd rather, it's pretty warm this afternoon. We could sit at one of the picnic shelters by the lake to look at your story."

Mabel thought fast. She herself was ravenous, but the picnic shelters would be perfect for a private conversation. "Let's meet at the end of the parking lot near the shelters. Say, in an hour?"

As soon as they hung up, Mabel scurried around and made herself a PBJ sandwich, let Barnacle out again, and distributed more treats. Before leaving, she looked at the clutter and promised herself to clear *something* out when she got home…maybe Grandma's stash of brown paper grocery bags.

She was halfway to her car when she groaned. She'd forgotten her writing.

Back inside, she fiddled with the security system, gathered up her stuff, and reset the alarm. She wasn't even sure what to ask Jackie about her writing issues, but since that's what she'd told Jackie they were doing, she couldn't show up without something she was theoretically working on.

By the time she arrived at Cloud Lake, Mabel could see Jackie encamped at a covered picnic table, facing the water. Sunbeams glanced off the surface, and the reflections of clouds—which she supposed had given the lake its name—rippled in a slight breeze.

Mabel inhaled a deep breath of fresh pine overlaid with the

fishy scent of the lake. When the wind shifted, she also caught a whiff of fried food coming from Old Tom's, which she tried to ignore. That PBJ had been far from satisfying.

Jackie caught her eye and waved as Mabel approached.

"Hi. Thanks for meeting me."

"No problem. I wasn't doing anything."

Mabel couldn't help noticing Jackie had all the animation of a bowl of leftovers. Elbows braced on the table, she was resting her chin on her folded hands as if she might collapse without the extra support.

Should Mabel pretend not to notice her ragged appearance?

With a noticeable effort, Jackie straightened and managed a weak smile. "So, what seems to be the writing problem?"

Mabel shook off her preoccupation with the murder and whatever was eating Jackie. She set her things on the table and pulled out her laptop. "Sorry. I didn't have time to print anything."

"That's okay. What are you working on?"

Can't say nothing.

"Well…I'm doing this series of stories about volunteering. I volunteer someplace and then write about it. I figured when I collected enough of them, I could maybe make a book? And I'm also working on a true-crime."

The election story was at the top of Mabel's recent documents, so she clicked on it. "Here's what I have so far on my latest volunteer thing."

Jackie reached for the laptop, and Mabel found herself clutching it and not letting go.

Jackie's brow furrowed. "Don't you want me to look at it?"

"Um…could I maybe ask you a few questions first?"

"Sure. But I think you'd get more out of a writers' group meeting, where there are people with more experience than I have, since I only write sci-fi."

"Is it okay to work on two books at once? Or which one should I focus on? How do you think I ought to organize this volunteer thing? Should I maybe try to publish some articles in the newspaper or a magazine first? Or do you think—?"

"Whoa. Mabel. That's a lot of questions." A faint smile crossed Jackie's face. "I will say, first of all, that it's perfectly all right to work on two things at once. I do that too—you can give your brain a break from struggling with the same material all the time. But look. If you plan on trying to publish, you can't afford to waste time dithering around and not ever moving forward with either one."

Jackie didn't add the dreaded words "at your age," but Mabel imagined she heard them on the breeze. Mabel cleared her throat. "Uh, could I ask you another wee little non-writing question? I'm sorry, but I'm kind of distracted right now."

Jackie frowned. "Maybe that's part of your problem with your writing. Letting yourself get sidetracked."

No kidding.

"Why don't you set yourself a goal for your writing? Put it down on paper and date it. I like your idea of trying to publish some short pieces first. How about trying *The Shopper* with one of your stories? They're pretty open."

Mabel shifted on the hard bench. That sounded like good advice. She'd never thought about trying to submit something to the weekly, but all this talk about writing was wearing her out.

"Thanks. I might try that. But I—I'm also worried about something, and I need to talk to somebody about this personal thing."

Jackie's eyebrows shot up. Of course, Mabel hardly knew Jackie, so it probably sounded kind of odd that she'd want to bare her soul about something personal.

"I think I might need to talk to the police," Mabel hissed.

Jackie jumped. "What are you talking about?" Her voice had

lost its encouraging tone and now sounded harsh—even accusatory.

Flustered, Mabel began babbling. "The other night, when Arthur Frost died or got killed out at the cemetery, I was there. Or we were there. My, er, friend John and I. And my dog Barnacle. Well, not right there, but we were across the road, and we saw…well, we were—"

Jackie clambered to her feet and took a step back. Her face was no longer friendly. "Exactly why did you ask me out here? Go ahead. What's your problem? And don't say writing."

That had certainly escalated in a hurry. Mabel's mouth felt dry, and her hands shook. "I'm sorry, Jackie. It's just…I saw you—"

Jackie's breath came in short puffs, as if she'd been running. "I can explain." Desperation now laced her voice.

This wasn't going well. "Jackie, I—"

Chapter Thirty

JACKIE'S EYES SCANNED THE EMPTY TABLES and deserted stretch of pebbled beach. Awkwardly, she climbed back over the picnic bench and landed with a thud.

Leaning over the table, she stared into Mabel's eyes.

"I did *not* kill Arthur Frost."

"What?" Mabel was almost too stunned to formulate words. "Jackie, I never thought you did."

"Please let me explain why I was out there. I know it must've looked suspicious, but I only meant to talk to him." Jackie shuddered and covered her eyes. "When I saw him—like that—I just panicked."

"Wait," Mabel said. "You were there—in the cemetery?"

Jackie uncovered her eyes. "You said you saw me."

"I saw you going into the police station today. That's all."

Jackie started laughing then, maniacally, without any trace of humor. "At the police station. Well, I really fell for that one, didn't I?"

As quickly as she'd started laughing, Jackie started to cry. Tears ran down her face, and she started searching her pockets.

Mabel handed her a crumpled tissue. She hoped it was clean. She thought it was.

Jackie took off her glasses and mopped her eyes, but the tears kept coming. She blew her nose.

Mabel dug around her big, slouchy bag, but all she could find was a drugstore receipt. She held it out with what she trusted was a look of apology.

Jackie shook her head. She swiped at her face with her glove.

For a moment, neither spoke. A jogger passed, running the path along the shore. Mabel squinted. It wasn't John, thank goodness.

Sunlight glinted off the water. A heron took off from the shallows with a little splash and a flap of its great wings.

Not for the first time, Mabel wondered how many people had been out in the vicinity of the graveyard two nights ago. For someplace that was supposed to be off limits, it had certainly been a hopping location. Was Jackie about to tell her something that would prove to be the key to everything?

For a moment, Mabel was afraid she would decide to clam up, but then Jackie began talking, looking out over the water as if that were easier than meeting Mabel's eyes. "Twenty-plus years ago, I was Arthur Frost's student. It kills me to admit it now, but I had the worst crush on him back then. So did a lot of other girls. Of course, he was way older than I was, but that just made him seem very sophisticated."

Shocked, Mabel shifted on the bench. If Jackie was going to say he'd taken advantage of her, Mabel wasn't sure she wanted to hear about it. She reached out and covered Jackie's hand with hers.

Jackie gave her a wry sidelong glance. "No, he didn't seduce me. Thank heaven for that, at least. I'd probably have been easy pickings. But I was an awkward nerd—not his type at all. He went for the real babes. I was just so much wallpaper."

Mabel squeezed Jackie's hand. She knew too, what it was like to be plain, awkward, and unnoticed. Till John came along, of course.

"He was an engineering professor, and I was majoring in Spanish, so our paths might never have crossed at all. But my second year, a new general studies class opened up. He was teaching techniques for investigating paranormal events, and it sounded like fun, so I signed up. The first day I walked in, I nearly swooned at the sight of him.

"I guess, looking back, he'd been teaching mostly guys—that's the way engineering still was in those days. I'm sure it gave him a kick, being in a classroom with a bunch of obviously infatuated young women. I was the worst." Jackie buried her flushed face in her hands.

"Every Tuesday night, I planned my outfit. Then Wednesday morning, I put on my makeup and fixed my hair, and I scrambled to get a seat in the first row. If he looked at me, I blushed, and if he talked to me, I giggled and babbled like a fool.

"Well, by some miracle, he seemed attracted to me—or so I thought. Now, I realize he was enjoying my infatuation and feeding off it. He'd look into my eyes and give me a big smile, and he always remembered my name. When he handed me a paper, he'd brush my hand. I was a goner. I was so flattered."

Mabel squirmed. "So, what happened?"

"He started asking me for favors. I picked up his dry-cleaning and did his PowerPoints…that sort of thing. I drove all the way into Pittsburgh to drop something off at CMU for him. At first, I was happy when he gave me big hugs and told me I was amazing. I'd be embarrassed to tell you how long this went on before I woke up and noticed I was no more than his gofer, while he was hitting on everybody else."

"What a creep." Grandma Mabel had always said she shouldn't speak ill of the dead, but dying didn't erase the facts.

Jackie nodded. "Yeah, he was a creep, and I was a naïve fool. But it was all a long time ago, and I'm not naïve anymore. It isn't something I still felt like I had to get back at him for—or kill him." She snorted at the ridiculousness of the idea.

"So…?"

"Well, we knew each other, okay? I was surprised, but when he came to town, he recognized me right away. I was down at the B&B to see if I could catch Leif Steele's arrival, and there was

Arthur. He gave me that same old smile—which I now realize was a smirk—and said, 'Jackie—hi, gorgeous.'"

"Oh, barf. Oops, sorry—I didn't mean… What I meant was—"

Jackie laughed. "I know what you meant. He was a smarmy piece of work."

"So…how did you end up at the cemetery? Didn't you know it was closed off?"

"That's why Arthur suggested it."

Mabel couldn't get used to the casual "Arthur." "He suggested it? You were planning on meeting him? But—"

She mustn't have managed to hide the shock in her voice, because Jackie gave her a wry half-smile. "Yeah. I'd slipped him a note in the B&B door, asking if we could talk."

"But—"

"But, why? Do you remember Virgil? He nearly tackled Arthur at the UFO meeting."

"Was he the same guy who threw eggs at him?"

Jackie nodded. "There's no other way to say it. Virgil's a charter member of the kook fringe. I love him dearly—and I also love my UFOs as much as the next girl—but let's just say he's more invested in alien visitation than is healthy."

"Okay, but I don't get what this guy has to do with your meeting Arthur Frost in a graveyard."

"Once a fool, always a fool." Jackie sighed. "I was trying to protect Virgil. Arthur's a vindictive narcissist. You may have noticed he enjoys humiliating people. Well, it was obvious to me he was going to punish Virgil. The video cameras were rolling the day he threw those eggs at Arthur. That footage was definitely going to show up in the documentary. I heard Arthur ask for a copy."

Jackie turned to Mabel, eyes welling with tears. "Virgil is so sensitive and vulnerable. He was incredibly brave to confront

Arthur the way he did at the meeting, but public humiliation would destroy him. Not to mention it might cost him his job. I couldn't let that happen.

"I realized I still had some leverage over Arthur. He may have managed to cover up most of his escapades from twenty years ago, but here I was, and he couldn't jolly me into keeping quiet if I wanted to make trouble for him. Things are different now, and professorial misconduct is treated seriously."

Mabel stared. "You threatened him?"

"Not in so many words, but in his mind, why else would I be asking to talk? Unless he thought I wanted us to get involved…" She shuddered. "I guess I let him think I could endanger his reputation, so he had no choice but to agree to meet. He said since the cemetery had been locked down, it would be the safest, most private place."

Mabel rolled her eyes. It had turned out to be as private as a Super Bowl game. "What was your plan once you got there?"

"I figured I'd tell him I didn't want to make trouble for him, but he needed to let Virgil alone. We never got that far though, because when I got there, he was already dead on the ground. And I was the girl who'd stupidly sent him a note, asking him to meet me there."

Mabel reflected. "That's pretty bad."

"You think?" Jackie grimaced. "Thanks for your encouragement."

"I'm sorry."

"It is what it is. I called it into 911 before I ran, but I didn't give them my name. I imagine they captured my number, but it didn't make any difference because the police still ended up with my note, which makes me Suspect Number One."

Mabel patted her hand, trying to make up for being her usual insensitive self. "I doubt you're their prime suspect. Not with Stanley Koslowski and Dan Cardamone still in the mix."

"Thanks for trying to cheer me up, but I'm still way up on their 'don't leave town' list."

Mabel chewed her lip. "Um, not to change the subject, but you got a good look at the body, right?"

Jackie stared, no doubt wondering how anybody could be as lacking in sensitivity as Mabel. Still, Mabel wanted to know, and here was an eyewitness, right in front of her. "I was wondering if you could, uh, tell me the condition of the body."

Jackie looked down and swallowed hard. "The back of his head was…I think he'd taken a blow."

"Did you see a possible weapon?"

"There are rocks all around that area. I don't know. It was dark—I didn't notice blood on any of them, but I wasn't exactly in investigative mode."

"Could you tell from looking at the wound whether it looked like something a rock might've done? Or something more like a pipe or a baseball bat? Or…a shovel?"

Jackie shook her head hard. "I tried not to look at the wound. Barely glanced at it."

"Was he…?" Mabel wasn't sure how to phrase what she wanted to know in a delicate manner.

"Was he what?"

"You know," she hinted. "There have been rumors."

Jackie raised her eyebrows.

"Did he have his…?"

When Jackie didn't jump in with an answer, Mabel was forced to bite the bullet. "Was he…naked?"

"Oh, yeah. Pretty much. He was wearing his boxers."

Score one for the rumor mill. "Any sign of his missing clothes at the scene?"

"I didn't see them, but it was dark, and there are acres of woods and brush around there."

"They're saying there were some kind of marks on his body.

Did you see anything like that?"

"I have no idea. That was the last thing on my mind. All I wanted was to get as far away from there as fast as I could." Jackie levered herself off the bench. "Speaking of which, I do need to get going."

Mabel's body screamed at her when she tried to get up and follow Jackie. It was too chilly for someone her age to be sitting on a hard slab of wood this long. Limping a bit, she caught up with Jackie and grasped her arm. "Hey, I'm really sorry you got caught up in this, but try not to worry. I was sort of a murder suspect a while back, and it turned out all right. I'll be praying, okay?"

"Thanks."

Mabel nodded. "Thanks for talking to me. I didn't mean to put you through all that when I called you. I had no idea you were there that night, but I did see someone else in the vicinity, and I wasn't sure whether I should report it or not."

"Report it," Jackie said. "As far as I'm concerned, they can't have too many suspects."

Mabel nodded again but didn't promise. As she waited for feeling to return to her bottom, she watched Jackie go.

She guessed Virgil, at least, was safe now. Nobody would be holding him up to public ridicule. Mabel sincerely hoped that wasn't thanks to Jackie.

Chapter Thirty-One

"YOU GET MY EMAIL?" LISA ASKED.

Mabel had finally fallen asleep on the couch after nearly an hour of fretting over whether Jackie was a murderer—and whether she owed Jackie the benefit of the doubt, even though she barely knew her at this point. Lisa's call had wakened her with a jolt, and the best she could manage was an ambiguous grunt.

"I hope you haven't been stressing too much. Email invitations are okay. I think we both want this shower as casual as possible."

"Um, yeah. I agree." With a twinge of guilt, Mabel wondered how many names were on the promised guest list. She had yet to read the email. The shower had been the furthest thing from her mind. She was a horrible friend to have asked Lisa to create her own guest list in the first place. What kind of maid of honor would do that?

"Bobbi is very crafty, and she loves doing stuff like this. I know you don't enjoy it, so I told her you might be calling on her to help. I hope that's all right."

Mabel felt a rush of gratitude. "No, that's great. I'm out of my depth here, and I don't want to mess up your shower."

"You won't." Lisa's voice was encouraging, but both knew Mabel's pitiful capabilities when it came to organizing anything.

"Did you get my text?" Mabel asked.

"I did. What's up?"

"You remember Jackie from the UFO meeting. She was at the book signing too?"

"Sure. What about her?"

"She told me the wildest story today. About Arthur Frost and the murder."

"Okay, spill." Lisa had shifted from shower plans to murder investigation without missing a beat. "You're sure it was a murder?"

"Well, not a hundred percent. I believe it was, but we don't know for sure. There are a lot of rocks around there. He could've fallen and hit his head or something, for all we know." *After stripping to his boxers in forty-degree temperatures.*

"Anyway, it turns out Jackie knew Frost—like really well. He was her professor for a course she took in college, and apparently, he was a bit of a predator."

"Oh, no. What happened?"

With a caution to Lisa to keep it to herself, Mabel recounted the story, trying to stick to the high points. Lisa punctuated the account with gasps.

"So, now I'm not sure about her," Mabel confessed. "I like her, but I don't know her too well."

"You can't control your emotions. In any case, how you feel doesn't matter, not unless you're worried about whether to report all this to the police."

"No. She already talked to the police, so I guess you're right." *Except I still have Nanette and Pete to worry about, and I don't know whether I should be trying to protect Jackie too. Or trying to find evidence against her to clear my other friends.*

"Anyway, I heard the cemetery's been opened up again, and I'm thinking about trying to go look around before it gets dark."

"Doggone it. I want to go with you, but Tim and I have a premarital counseling session with our minister, and I need to get ready for that. We already had one cancellation, and I can't postpone it again."

Drat. "That's okay. I'll fill you in if I find anything."

They talked a while longer, and just as Barnacle had started pawing at her leg to go out, a second call came in from John. "Got to go, Lisa. I'm getting another call. We'll talk some more later, all right?"

Mabel tucked her phone between her shoulder and ear and led Barnacle to the door. "Hey, John."

"Good afternoon, *ma belle.*"

He had recently started teasing her with the play on her name, and Mabel blushed as if he were in the room with her. "Um, hi."

"I came out of my adjunct faculty meeting and saw you'd called."

Mabel watched as Barnacle sniffed around the back yard, searching for the optimal potty spot. "Yeah. I heard the wildest story today, and I wanted to tell you about it."

"Another UFO sighting?"

"No, it was about Arthur Frost."

"Something to do with his death?"

"Well, about him. Possibly about his death, I guess."

"What was it? You want to go to Eat 'n Park, and we can talk there?"

"Sure." As soon as she spoke, Mabel realized she couldn't tell this story in a public place, no matter how hard they tried to be discreet about it. "I mean, yeah, I'd love to, but I think we should eat at home. This isn't something I ought to spread around."

"Okay, now you've me got me intrigued. You could come over here. I've got leftover chicken cacciatore in the freezer."

"That sounds good. When do you want me?"

"24/7/365, *ma belle.* But let's say an hour. How's that?"

It was near dark by the time Mabel parked in front of John's bungalow. His cat, Billie Jean, sat silhouetted in the front window, watching as she locked the car and came up the walk.

When John let her in, Billie Jean continued to stare, but miraculously, didn't come and attack her. He smiled. "She's getting to know you."

"She's biding her time," Mabel grumbled. "Waiting for me to let my guard down."

"No, I mean it. I think she might be ready to accept you."

Mabel couldn't conceive of a real peace treaty with John's attack cat, but she'd be happy to settle for a ceasefire. Unlikely though that might be.

The house smelled delectable, and once again, John's cooking put hers to shame. While they ate, Mabel told John about Jackie's history with Arthur Frost. Golden eyes glowed in the shadows of the living room entry. Billie Jean was still watching.

She told him about Virgil the egg-thrower Jackie had been trying to protect. "I think she likes—" She used air quotes, "'likes' him."

John grinned at her explanation, which she now realized had sounded as if she were sitting at the seventh-grade lunch table. "Anyway," she continued, "she intended to use her prior relationship and knowledge of Frost's misconduct to pressure him into leaving Virgil alone. So, she sent him a note, asking him to meet her."

John raised an eyebrow. "That was incredibly foolish. She's lucky *she* didn't get killed before she even explained what she wanted."

When Mabel had finished recounting Jackie's story, John gave a low whistle. "To be honest, I didn't see that coming. Do you think she's capable of killing him?"

Mabel chewed her lip. "I want to say no, because I like her, and I really don't think she did it. But I don't know her all that well."

He nodded decisively. "Better not to get locked into a theory too soon. Did she tell you anything about the crime scene? At this point, it's a safe assumption it is one."

Mabel explained the few details Jackie had furnished.

"So, she confirms Ms. Katherine Ann's gossip about the condition of the body," John said. "It gives us a possible cause of death…if Jackie's telling the truth. Getting back to Nanette's shovel, have you had a chance to talk to her yet?"

"No, and I'm getting antsy about it. She's never failed to return a call before. I still hate to go to the police without talking to her first."

"She's your friend, and you know her better than I do, so it's up to you. I still think I'd take the bull by the horns at this point."

Mabel winced. "Go to the police?"

"I was thinking more like go to her house. Give her one more chance to explain." He began clearing the table. "Then, yeah, if you can't get her to respond, my advice is go to the police. You can't help someone who won't talk to you."

Every fiber of Mabel's body rebelled at the thought of ratting out Nanette. She would rather scrub bathroom grout with a toothbrush…and then, brush her teeth with it. She would rather go on a diet. She would rather—

John tapped her hand. "I doubt your friend's guilty of murder—or anything else too serious. If I had to guess, she's carrying a secret that's gotten too heavy for her to carry alone. It might be a relief for her to share it."

Or Nanette might rather share it with Jesus, and have Mabel keep her big nose out of her business. All the same, Mabel couldn't squelch the irritating feeling John was right.

"I guess if I don't hear back from her by tomorrow, I'll try knocking on her door. I don't think she'd refuse to let me in."

John's smile seemed relieved. She knew he hadn't been to the police yet either. Mabel couldn't continue to place John in this position much longer. He'd been holding back to let her deal with her worries over Nanette and Pete. He must be anxious to do his civic duty—not to mention quit risking his reinstatement by withholding information regarding a criminal investigation.

Mabel cleared her throat. She'd postpone thinking about confronting Nanette till tomorrow. "Do you want to check out the cemetery with me?"

He raised his eyebrows. "Now? What do you think we'd see that we haven't seen before?"

"I don't know till we find it, but I heard the police released the site."

"Yeah," he drawled, "they did. But the area's still closed so the documentary crew can get back to filming their investigation."

"Oh, shoot, I forgot about that. It ought to make Leif Steele happy anyway." Mabel rested her chin on her hand and brooded for a moment.

Her mood brightened when John brought out two dishes of warm apple crisp topped with a smidgen of vanilla ice cream. The portions could have been a bit bigger, in her opinion, and the ice cream turned out to be frozen yogurt, but like everything else John cooked, it was delicious. As a bonus, Mabel felt her dessert qualified as health food.

She licked her spoon and wished she could lick the bowl, as well.

"You know," John said, "one thing we could check on is that shovel. Maybe it's still there. Of course, if it's missing, we can't be a hundred percent sure Nanette retrieved it. It might be in the Medicine Spring PD evidence locker by now."

Mabel hopped up, and a hiss came from under the table. She startled, but the hiss, for once, wasn't followed by a flash of claws.

John beamed. "You've about won her over."

"We're practically besties." Mabel looked around her. "Where did you put my jacket?"

"On the back of my desk chair. Why?"

"I thought we were going to look for Nanette's shovel."

John shook his head. "It's barely seven. That road will still be pretty busy, with the Prentice and Heron Creek intersection closed—Indian Camp's the main detour. It isn't safe to poke around in the dark so close to traffic, not to mention we don't know who might be going by and wonder what we're up to."

Mabel groaned. "How long do you want to wait? What are we going to do till then?"

He laughed. "Oh, maybe at least ten or eleven. I figured you could bask in my presence till then."

Mabel felt her face heating up because that didn't sound too painful.

"Come help me clean up these dishes, and then maybe we can find something to watch while we snuggle."

As it turned out, John's choice of viewing was *The Creature from the Black Lagoon.* Mabel didn't know which was worse— his love of vintage horror movies or Lisa's passion for scary suspense—but as usual, she went along with it because it made him so happy, and that made her happy.

After the movie ended, it was followed by *Night of the Lepus,* which he said was a big deal because it didn't air very often. Mabel had been ready to jump up and look for her coat, even though it wasn't quite as late as John had intended to leave. But when the second movie started, with John clearly settled in for the duration, she wandered off to the bathroom and then asked if John wanted a cup of tea.

By the time she returned from the kitchen with their mugs, giant mutant rabbits were running amuck on the screen, and John had slouched down to watch with Billie Jean plumped onto the pillow behind his head. Mabel set their drinks on the coffee table and nestled under John's arm. The cat hissed again but didn't bother attacking.

John smiled at Billie Jean. "Good girl." Mabel reached for her mug, hoping she'd camouflaged her epic eye roll.

It was approaching eleven when the show ended. To her surprise, she'd enjoyed the second movie more than the well-known *Black Lagoon*, mostly because she and John had started pointing out the many goofs. Besides the fun of their friendly competition, the mistakes became increasingly hysterical.

"Okay, you ready to head out?" he asked.

She had been ready since dinner.

"Since we have to drive through town to get out to Indian Camp Road, you want to drop your car at your place on the way and ride with me?"

"I can leave it on Main Street. It'll be quicker, and the meters turn off at five."

Now that they were getting close to searching for that shovel, Mabel felt her stomach tightening. She couldn't help fearing whatever Nanette had gotten herself into.

Chapter Thirty-Two

TOWN WAS DEAD AT THIS LATE hour, as was typical. Mabel, leading the way, glanced up at Lisa's apartment windows, which were dark since she had to get up so early for school. There were plenty of open spots nearby, and she pulled in.

A moment later, they were driving on toward Carteret, where Mabel lived, and the town limits beyond. As they approached the end of Ash Street a few blocks before Carteret, a pickup truck pulled out ahead of them.

John slowed down and nodded toward the truck. "Look familiar?"

Mabel squinted. "You think it's Pete's?"

"I don't know what Pete's truck looks like, but it could be the truck that flew past us the night of Frost's death."

"He lives on Ash."

"Let's hang back a bit and see where he's headed. Don't want to tip him off."

For the next few miles, they followed distant red taillights. Mabel held her breath when the truck disappeared around a bend, but each time, the lights reappeared once again on the straightaways…until they didn't.

Mabel had been leaning forward, peering ahead. "Hey, he's gone."

"No fear." John tilted his head toward the middle school as they drove by. Taillights were rounding the corner of the building. "Looks like he's hiding his vehicle."

"Now what?" They'd already driven past the spot where Mabel had found the shovel. They could hardly park at the middle school if Pete was already there.

"Next pull-off. We'll walk from there."

By the time they'd ditched John's car and made their way back along the road to the Pleasant Union Church and cemetery, Mabel had stepped off the edge of the pavement and come down on the side of her foot. She was now limping a bit and hoped it would work its way out. John was wielding a flashlight, but in the interest of stealth, he was covering most of the beam with his fingers. The wind had kicked up, and Mabel was sure she felt a few snowflakes hitting her cheeks. She shivered, wishing she'd worn a heavier coat.

The church lot looked empty, and so did what she could see of the cemetery from down here. Both sat on a bank a bit higher than the road. "Can you see anything?"

"Nope. Not yet." He stopped abruptly. "Hel-lo. See that?"

Mabel peered around him at the section of fencing he'd spotlighted with the thin flashlight beam. They were still along the Miller's Woods fence, not quite to the cemetery boundary, though the trees and brush extended a bit farther into the cemetery grounds.

Mabel studied the fence corner. "Looks like an animal's been digging its way under there."

"Yeah, and the fencing isn't taut right there. Pete's a smaller guy, isn't he?"

Mabel nodded, then realized John couldn't see her. "He is."

"If I had to guess, he's lifted the wire and squeezed himself underneath."

Mabel's shiver had turned into full-on shaking. She wasn't sure she wanted to take this any further.

"I'll go first and then hold it up for you."

"I won't fit."

"Sure, you will—piece of cake. I'll help you."

No, no, no, no, no.

"Come on, Nancy Drew. Watch me, and then you get down flat on your stomach and commando crawl. Duck your head till I say, 'Clear,' okay?"

Mabel swallowed hard. She wasn't feeling particularly Nancy Drewish, nor could she imagine commando-crawling, let alone in front of John. It already felt like a minor miracle that a handsome PI—even a suspended PI—was attracted to her. Somehow, she didn't think slithering on her belly would increase her allure.

John seemed to assume she was up for the maneuver, since he was already halfway under the fence. Of course, the man lived on a diet that was fifty percent foliage and had the washboard abs to show for it.

A moment later, he was through and holding the fence up for her. "Come on," he hissed. "I think I hear him back in the woods."

Was it worse to make a fool of herself crawling through the brush and getting stuck—or act like a wimp? Great-Grandpa had fought at the Battle of the Bulge. Surely, with that blood in her veins, she could crawl under a fence…with some help. She just hoped she didn't lose any of her ancestral blood in the attempt.

John jiggled the wire fencing.

It was now or never. Mabel flattened herself onto the cold, damp grass.

"Head down, head down." John reached a hand through and smooshed her flat. A weed went up her nose, and she sneezed, then sneezed again.

"Keep wiggling forward."

Mabel tried but didn't move more than a few inches with each push. She was barely scraping under the fence, and twice John had to loosen a snag in her coat.

When he finally whispered, "You're clear," she rolled onto

her back and drew several deep breaths of clean night air. Then, she sneezed again and had to dig through her pocket for a tissue.

John put a finger to his lips and motioned for her to follow him. Mabel scrambled to her feet. She caught the back of his coat and tried to step in his footprints, so she didn't make any more noise than necessary.

There seemed to be some sort of sketchy game trail through the brush—or maybe just the path Pete, or whoever was back in there had broken on his way in. Still, Mabel was glad John led the way, holding the vines and shin-scratchers away for her. Though she was panting—more from anxiety than exertion—at least John was there to protect her if things went bad.

It was weird, not to mention disorienting, being in Miller's Woods in the middle of the night. Moreover, they'd entered way over here, rather than by way of the UFO museum, so Mabel struggled to reclaim her sense of direction. Somewhere deep in the shadows, an owl hooted.

Mabel opened her mouth, about to whisper that she thought they were somewhere near the clearing marking the UFO crash site, but John stopped abruptly and pointed ahead.

She peered around his shoulder and saw a hazy yellow glow through the trees. Someone was moving around. She heard breaking sticks and brush but couldn't see the person.

John crept closer with Mabel clinging to his coattail, till he was able to part the branches for a look. "It's Pete, all right," she breathed, but couldn't tell if John heard her.

Pete had hung up a battery-operated lantern on a low-hanging tree limb, leaving his hands free. There was a flannel shirt draped partway over the light, so it only illuminated the immediate area.

She whispered in John's ear. "What's he doing?"

"Looks like he has a metal detector."

Mabel frowned. Was he trying to get a jump on the film

crew? And why?

Pete drew the bushes apart with one hand as he swept the instrument over the ground. Once, a beeping noise emanated from the detector, and he bent down to poke at the earth with a stick. Then, he tossed whatever small thing he'd found with a sound of disgust.

Her brow furrowed. Did Pete think he was going to find some outer-space metal fragment the United States government had missed?

Just then, Mabel felt something crawl across the back of her neck, and she jumped. It felt like a spider had gone down into her shirt. Wildly, she slapped at it, spinning as if that would help her reach the ticklish spot better.

"Mabel," John hissed, but it was too late.

Pete had frozen. He stared toward their hiding place.

Mabel knew she should hold still, but whatever was in her shirt was still moving around. Visions of spider bites kept her squirming in desperation and slapping at her back.

Pete grabbed his lantern and began crashing through the bushes, away from them, toward the cemetery boundary fence. John gave up trying to calm Mabel down and ran after Pete.

Mabel pulled off her coat and dug inside her collar with one hand while she shook out the shirttail with the other. Whatever had been in there seemed to be gone, but it was hard to relax. *Was it gone?*

Hearing running footsteps brought her to her senses. Grabbing her coat off the ground, she stumbled after John and Pete. Of course, the coat kept snagging on branches and briars, and she wasn't sure she was going the right direction in the dark.

When she heard Pete yell something, Mabel realized he and John had veered left, toward the hole under the fence they'd crawled through on their way in. She'd lost any semblance of a path, so she headed that way, breaking her own trail as best she could. At some point, she'd gotten tangled in a burr patch, and she despaired of getting all the stickers out of her clothing.

The owl called again. A restless wind rustled the tree branches overhead and shifted the clouds enough to let a bit of moonlight wash the landscape.

Mabel caught a glimmer of the road through the woods now and human shapes, which must be John and Pete, standing at the fence. With a wave of relief, she shoved harder at the undergrowth till she was able to stagger up next to them.

Visibility was better here in the open area above the road. Both men turned and stared.

"Mabel?" Pete tilted his head as if he weren't sure what he was seeing.

She reached to sweep her hair back and realized it was now a nest of burrs. "Uh, hi, Pete."

He looked defeated, gasping after the chase through the woods like a hunted animal run to ground. "You got me."

Stricken, Mabel touched his arm. "No, we weren't trying to catch you or anything. It's—we were here to look for something, and…"

"Here I was." He gave her a wry smile. "Oh, shoot, Mabel. I've got to sit down before my legs give out."

"Can you get back under the fence?" John asked. "If I hold it up?"

Pete nodded and passed his metal detector to Mabel.

A few minutes later, they were all across the road and sitting on the bottom bleacher next to the middle school ballfield. Pete slumped with his arms across his knees, looking out over the dark stretch of grass. John straddled the seat facing Pete's profile, with Mabel huddled on the cold metal seat above John, leaning forward so she could see and hear better.

For a few minutes, nobody said anything. When Pete spoke at last, it wasn't what Mabel expected. "Why did you two follow me out here?"

"We?" Mabel sputtered. "We weren't following you. We were coming out here on our own and ended up behind you by chance."

"In the woods?"

"Well…"

John stepped in. "We were driving here when you pulled out in front of us. We were curious, because the night that guy died out here, a truck that looked like yours ran past us on Indian Camp Road."

Pete shot a glance their way and then down.

"The police are looking for a truck fitting your truck's description." Mabel held up a hand as Pete started to bristle. "No, we didn't report seeing it. We haven't talked to the cops at all— yet. But we had to know…"

"You were out here that night?"

Mabel nodded. "Over there, walking my dog. We saw you on our way home."

Pete faced her. "You don't live that direction."

John cleared his throat. "We never said which direction we were going."

"Oh, blast," Pete fumed. "You tricked me."

"It's all right." Mabel stood up and scratched her thigh, where a clump of burrs had been making it prickle. "We aren't accusing you of anything."

"You're gonna report me though, aren't you?"

"Well, we're in kind of a spot," John said. "We need to let the police know we were out here, and they're going to want to know what we saw or heard. We can't keep it all to ourselves. There are laws against that."

"Pete," Mabel said. "Maybe we can help."

He groaned. "I don't think there's a thing you two can do. 'Less you want to go back in there with me and help me dig around some more." Pete gave her a hopeful look.

Mabel scratched her side and shivered. No, she didn't want to go back in there and help him dig around some more. But she was more intrigued by the minute. What could be so compelling that Pete kept making these heroic efforts in the dead of night, to find something locked behind a fence in the middle of all those burrs, briars, and bugs? Yet, he seemed willing to let John and her in on it.

"Let's try this," John said. "Why don't you tell us what you're looking for? I take it it's not related to the death the other night."

"Of course not." Pete bristled. "It's…aw, heck. It's hard talking to anybody about this after all these years." He heaved a deep breath.

"How many years?" Mabel started the miserable task of pulling burrs off her clothing.

"Oh, I don't know. You'd need to do the math. It was the late fifties."

Mabel choked on her spit. "Wait. You mean the night of the big…?" She made a wooing noise and waved her hands in the air to indicate a flying saucer in trouble. She lowered her hands. Good grief. She was getting worse than Ms. Katherine Ann.

"Yep." Pete's hands shook. "I was just a kid, and I did the worst dang-foolish thing. It's been haunting me my whole life. Now it's gonna all come out."

"You can tell us. Like you said, you were a kid. How bad can it be?" John's voice was gentle.

Pete was looking down, and his words were so soft that Mabel strained to hear. "Bad. I'm glad my pop isn't alive to find out."

Mabel and John exchanged a wide-eyed look over Pete's head.

"We used to live right down the road. My pop had an old

twenty-two rifle he let me use to plunk cans out back. I wasn't allowed to hunt or take it out on my own, you understand. Well, that night, my folks were down at the bingo, and I took a notion to go hunt coons back there in the woods."

John frowned. "Okay…"

"I didn't see much of anything but a few deer. Mostly, I blundered around in there and felt like I was pretty grown-up, being out hunting on my own. A plane or something was making noise, coming in kind of low overhead, but I didn't pay much mind to that. I wasn't thinking of nothing but trying to shoot a coon before my folks got home and caught me missing.

"Anyhow, there came a rustle way up in the trees overhead. I had a flashlight, but I couldn't make out what it was. I was anxious to shoot my gun at least once though, so I aimed right at the noise I heard and pulled the trigger."

Mabel had stopped pulling burrs. She realized she'd also stopped breathing. "Did you hit something?"

With an anguished sound, Pete jolted to his feet. "I sure hit *something*. Not whatever animal was up in that tree though. Just like that, I saw all these lights coming down from the sky. Something huge was falling, and I ran.

"I got as far away as I could, hitting at vines and jagger bushes and running into trees. I heard the big crash behind me. I was scared to death."

"Oh, Pete," Mabel breathed.

"I flung that rifle into the brush as far as I could. Way I was running around in the dark, I never could remember afterward quite where. Never did find it again.

"I could see lights flickering back in the trees, and I was afraid the crash set the woods on fire. I didn't know what to do, but when I heard sirens, I figured help was coming. I snuck on home and was laying in bed, pretending to be asleep, when my folks came home."

"When did you find out what happened?" John asked.

"Find out? I saw it happen. Next day, I kept my mouth shut about the whole thing. Everybody was talking about a flying saucer crash in Miller's Woods, and I saw the Army trucks coming through town. My pop never used that old twenty-two, so he didn't notice it was missing till a couple months later. I played dumb and said I must've laid it down someplace and forgot it. After that, I took my punishment for losing the rifle, and that was that."

"So, now you're looking for what?" Mabel asked. "The gun?"

"Try to stick with me, Mabel. Almost right after it happened, a lot of people started saying it wasn't a flying saucer that came down at all. It was some experimental government plane, and that's why the Army came in and scooped everything up and never talked about it.

"Now do you get it? I shot down a military plane." Pete swallowed and his chin came up. "Next thing I knew, I heard they found bodies in the wreckage. I been haunted by that for years.

"Once that stupid film crew gets to barging around the woods, they're liable to find that old rifle—or what's left of it— and trace it to me. But I was twelve years old. I didn't know any better."

Mabel laid a hand on Pete's arm again. "That rifle was what—wood and steel? It's been over sixty years. The most that film crew could ever find would be maybe a tiny glob of rust."

"Besides which…listen to me, Pete." John waited till Pete looked him in the eye. "You did not shoot down a plane. It's a scientific impossibility. Even if it was a plane that crashed, it was no more than a horrible coincidence that you were shooting when it happened."

"You don't know. That thing was coming in low. What if I

shot the pilot?"

"You keep talking about its coming in low," Mabel said. "Sounds to me like it might have been coming down anyway."

John nodded. "The odds of your hitting a plane or a pilot are one in a million. Even a plane that's flying low in the sky is pretty much out of twenty-two range. Then, you have all those trees in the way. Mabel's right—it sounds like it was already coming down. Even if you hit the pilot, which you didn't, the plane wouldn't drop straight down right where you fired the shot. Right?"

In the long silence that followed, Pete's hands shook. "You make sense. But it's hard to let it go after all these years. Guess you think I'm a dang fool."

Mabel smiled and patted his arm. When she withdrew her hand, she saw she'd transferred a huge wad of burrs from her sleeve to his. "Like you say, you were a kid. I can see how an awful experience like that would get burned into your mind."

John stood. "Mabel and I need to get home, and no doubt you do too. Try not to worry."

As they started back to the car, Mabel glanced around. Pete was still sitting on the bleachers. Maybe his legs were still too wobbly to get up.

Pete looked up. "You gonna report me?"

Mabel met John's eyes, and he shook his head. Clearly, he believed Pete's story, and so did she.

Chapter Thirty-Three

OF COURSE, BY THE TIME MABEL and John had reached the foot of the embankment below Pleasant Union Church, Nanette's shovel was gone. Mabel was sure they were looking in the right spot, but to be safe, they'd poked around for some distance to either side. Either Nanette had been able to retrieve it, or the police had found and confiscated it.

The next morning, Mabel sat over her coffee and contemplated her suspect list. She ran a line through Pete's name—not that he'd ever been a serious suspect, but she was relieved to eliminate him.

Her hand hovered over Nanette's name. Still nothing. If she didn't get a callback today, she would have to drive over there and try to talk to her. She and John had decided this was the last day. They couldn't wait any longer to check in with the police and let them know they'd been out by the cemetery that night.

As she considered her list, Mabel realized she'd never added Jackie. While Nanette hadn't committed a homicide—at least, she prayed she hadn't—Mabel had to admit she didn't know Jackie well enough to write her off, no matter how much she might like her. Reluctantly, Mabel wrote Jackie's name at the end of the list.

Her contemplations were interrupted by the realization that Leif Steele had returned to *Country Morning*. Mabel searched frantically till she located the TV remote squashed down between the couch cushions underneath Koi. The sleepy cat blinked at Mabel as she ferreted it out and turned up the volume.

She'd already missed the opening banter. It seemed from the hosts' appropriately gloomy expressions that one must have posed a question about Arthur Frost's death.

Leif, despite what looked like a few new stress lines around his eyes and mouth, still appeared every inch the beefcake paranormal star. This morning, he was poured into a black V-neck sweater that revealed a manly bit of chest hair and highlighted his bicep and shoulder muscles. His tousled forelock covered most of his left eye.

Before answering the question, Leif bent forward and rested his elbows on his knees and his mouth on folded hands. After an awkward moment of dead air, during which Bee and Doug exchanged a glance, and Doug giggled before catching himself and turning it into a cough, Leif raised his eyes. "The loss has been devastating. Of course. Devastating. Dr. Arthur Frost was a giant in our field. A giant."

Already sick of Steele's penchant for repetition, Mabel muttered, "At least in his own mind. His own mind."

"He's irreplaceable, as we all know. But the Medicine Spring project is too important to end this way. Arthur wouldn't have wanted that. So…" Steele allowed his voice to break a bit. "We will carry on in his memory."

"I see." Bee tilted her head like a dog trying to understand human conversation. "Our sincere sympathies to all. But commendably, your show has always included a critical viewpoint. Will you be bringing a new debunker on board to finish the episode?"

Steele's lips tightened. "Perhaps. It's too soon to address that." He rubbed the spot between his eyes. "All of this is still too fresh."

Doug leaned forward. "Has Dr. Frost's passing affected your production schedule?"

To Mabel's shock, Leif snapped. "What do you think? As I mentioned on my previous appearance, we'd planned to open the so-called alien grave on live TV but were unable to secure permission. Naturally, our plans to do scientific analysis of the contents are also off the table."

Doug opened and closed his mouth like a freshly landed

carp.

"Then, Arthur died," Steele continued. "An enormous loss—enormous—and the police locked down the cemetery site for days. To some extent, we were able to move things around. My historical researcher could continue, and so could another interviewer and I. But all the tech stuff's been at a standstill."

Steele paused to hyperventilate. "I've had to keep most of my crew here twiddling their thumbs. Unsurprisingly, none of my people live in Bartle County. And I've had equipment rentals just sitting idle. We're at least two full days behind schedule."

He glowered at Doug. "Now, we're finally allowed to reenter the property, and there's snow in the forecast."

Doug squirmed under Steele's glare. As her co-host was looking like the proverbial deer in the headlights at this point, Bee stepped in. "That must be tremendously difficult for you. We here at *Country Morning* wish you and your entire crew much success as you complete this important project in memory of your beloved colleague."

As that seemed to conclude the segment, Mabel clicked the TV off. So, tensions were running high on the *Empty Eyes* shoot. She paused to give thanks she wasn't working for Leif Steele right now.

With a sigh, she returned to the kitchen and refilled her coffee mug. Back to her suspect list. Glancing at the wall clock, she decided it was late enough to try Nanette again, though she dreaded making that call.

Moments later, she was staring at her list, after having left yet another voicemail. She tapped her pen on the paper and considered Dan Cardamone. There was a man who'd lost about everything he had, thanks to Arthur Frost. A way stronger suspect than Nanette.

Maybe not a stronger suspect than Jackie, a nagging little voice reminded her. How much of what Jackie had confided to her did Mabel owe the police?

With a groan, she moved on to Suspect #1 in her eyes—Stanley Koslowski. His and Frost's mutual animosity was out in the open for anyone to see. She'd not only witnessed it firsthand, but their hostile relationship would live forever on video.

What's more, Koslowski lived right next door to where Frost's body was found. He alone, of all the suspects, could legally walk right up to the cemetery on his own property, and would have been able to stay under cover of the woods the whole time. He didn't even have to worry about where to hide his car, since he owned the entire museum parking lot.

Did Koslowski have a way of slipping into the graveyard from the woods without having to step out onto the road the way she, John, and Pete had last night? Mabel hadn't seen any openings in the fence between the two properties, but Koslowski might well have had some way of passing between them, which only he knew about.

Cardamone too, lived close enough to park on his own property and walk to the graveyard. Therefore, unlikely to have been on the road in his dark pickup, but still a good candidate for murderer. What would have attracted either him or Koslowski to the cemetery in the dead of night, though? Apparently, Jackie's note had brought Frost there—and she and John had now found out what had brought Pete there.

By lunchtime, Mabel had made no progress—not with the murder and not with her life. All she'd done was sit and think and get nowhere. After scrounging up a lunch of leftovers, she checked one more time to make sure she hadn't missed a call from Nanette.

Sadly, she hadn't. After letting Barnacle out for a potty break, she put on shoes and grabbed her coat and purse. But before she could let the dog inside, a fusillade of barking and snarling erupted from outside.

What on earth? Mabel threw her things down and raced outside.

Barnacle was at the end of his tether, throwing himself ferociously at two people at the head of her driveway. The cable appeared in danger of snapping.

Acey's truck was parked halfway up onto her narrow strip of front yard, and Linnea was blocking Mabel's car in the driveway. The two were screaming at each other and swinging campaign signs at each other with wild abandon.

Linnea packed quite a wallop, Mabel had to admit. Besides displaying rather amazing upper body strength, she smoothly dodged most of Acey's blows, all while wearing kitten heels and a tweed pencil skirt.

Mabel grabbed at Barnacle's collar and hauled him inside before approaching the combatants. "Stop it, you two," she yelled, but her voice was drowned in the melee.

As he swung at Linnea and missed, Acey looked toward Mabel "Call her off," he hollered. At the same moment, he caught a whack on the back of the head from Linnea.

He swung again, this time knocking Linnea off balance. She teetered a moment, then caught herself with one hand on the trunk of her car. "Control your help, Mabel," Linnea panted. Her eyes shot fire and a fleck of spittle was sticking to her chin.

"Both of you stop right now," Mabel screamed, wishing she hadn't left her keychain with its mini airhorn inside the house. "What on earth are you two doing?"

Acey and Linnea both answered at once. Mabel sorted the garbled commentary out as best she could over Barnacle's wild, but now muffled, barking.

Linnea had stopped swinging her sign like a baseball bat at Acey, but she rammed it in his direction. "He pulled down all my signs."

Acey stomped his foot. "You lyin', witchy woman. I never touched your durn signs. Mabel said one to a customer, ain't that right, Mabel? I'll bet she took 'em down her own self. I wanna know why you messed up Cletus's sign, which you said I could put up, didn't ya, Mabel?"

Mabel closed her eyes. To her regret, Acey and Linnea were still there when she opened them. It killed her to admit it, but Acey was right. "Yes, Linnea. Each candidate gets one sign. Acey is allowed a sign for Pettigrew, and you are allowed one for Casselman."

Linnea lowered her sign and narrowed her eyes. From inside the house, Barnacle had escalated his barking. "You're clearly part of the dog faction. From the beginning, you've been pretending to support Casselman. All the while, you've been working to have the privy leveled for that filthy dog park."

Mabel shook her head and rolled her eyes with muscular coordination she never knew she had. Could Linnea hear herself?

"No. I am not working against either candidate. And from this moment, I'm not doing anything more to support either candidate. I am officially neutral. I am Switzerland."

Both Linnea and Acey came at her with their signs, jabbering over each other.

Mabel held up one hand, again wishing she had her airhorn. This would be a splendid moment to fire it off. "If your candidates cared about the issue—not to mention the wellbeing of the town—they'd get together and figure out a way to preserve the privy and construct the dog park around it."

Both Acey and Linnea gaped at her before starting to babble once more.

"You sure don't understand beans about politics." Acey spat tobacco juice, narrowly missing Linnea's shoe.

Linnea merely spluttered for a moment before she was able to form a coherent sentence. "Really, Mabel, that tears it. Can you imagine our historic privy with some Saint Bernard squatting in front of it? What can you possibly be thinking?"

"I'm thinking you guys need a referee. Or maybe a third-party candidate who isn't crazy. Please plant your signs—one sign each—precisely where I had them before, and then leave. I have an appointment."

Chapter Thirty-Four

Nanette's little purple car sat in front of her house at the end of Creekside Lane. Mabel parked in the street behind it. Before getting out, she said a prayer and took a deep breath. *Why couldn't you just call me, Nanette?*

Mabel's feet dragged as she followed the steppingstones curving from the street through Nanette's handkerchief-size front garden. Apart from a few hardy shrubs, frost had killed off most of the plantings. Artfully arranged small boulders, an empty vintage birdbath, and a wrought-iron bench still made Mabel feel she was approaching a fairytale cottage.

After another deep breath, she lifted the knocker. She wasn't sure what she'd do if Nanette refused to open the door.

For a moment, she feared that was exactly what was going to happen. She knocked again, and the lock turned.

The door eased open about four inches, and Nanette peered out.

"Hi, Nanette. I was worried about you. May I come in?"

The door closed a bit. "Oh, Mabel, I'm so sorry. I don't feel well. I apologize for not getting back to you sooner."

Or at all.

Mabel wedged her toes into the gap between the door and frame. "I'm so sorry too. Is there anything I can pick up for you?"

Nanette attempted to inch the door closed but struck Mabel's foot. Consternation crossed her face. "No, thank you. So sweet of you to offer, but I just need to rest and drink my tea with honey and lemon." She affected a cough unworthy of a ten-year-old trying to fake his way out of a math test.

"I'd be happy to make you some tea and toast."

"No, no. I wouldn't want you to pick up my bug."

"I'm sure I'm immune. Nanette, we need to talk. There's something wrong, and I know it's not a virus."

To Mabel's horror, Nanette's eyes welled with tears, and she shoved at the door again. "Please don't do this to me, Mabel."

"I don't want to hurt you or cause you any trouble. I want to help."

"There's nothing you can do."

Mabel managed to squeeze a hand through the narrow gap and pat Nanette's shoulder. "I can be your friend."

Nanette dropped her head and drew a shuddering breath. When she looked back up, she sighed and nodded, resignation on her face. The door opened.

Nanette gestured at a chintz-covered wingback chair, shut the door, and turned the lock. Too late, Mabel felt a queasy sensation as she recalled Nanette might be a murderer.

She's not a murderer, dingbat.

Nanette dropped into a matching chair catercorner to Mabel's and picked up a granny square and her crochet hook. Without looking at Mabel, she asked, "What can I do for you?"

Mabel hadn't expected that question. "Um…I guess I just want to know what's wrong. What's the deal with the cemetery? I know you don't think so, but maybe I can help."

She watched in fascination as Nanette's fingers flew, adding row after row of fancy stitches to the square. Mabel guessed Nanette could do this in the dark but was looking at her work to avoid Mabel's eyes. While Mabel waited, Nanette finished the square and dropped it in the basket by her feet. She cast another color of yarn onto her hook and resumed crocheting.

Mabel cleared her throat. "I don't mean to pry. I've been worried about you. You're my friend."

Nanette darted an upward glance. "Yes, I am. It's…I've kept this secret so long, I can't let it go."

Mabel flashed back to Pete's confession behind the middle school. How many other dark mysteries lay buried beneath the cozy, smalltown surface of Medicine Spring?

"You know…" Nanette looked back at her work. "I used to worry I'd get dementia when I was older, and I'd let it slip out. Now, here I am…"

After a long pause, Mabel was about to attempt some comforting assurance, but Nanette spoke first. "It all goes back to that night in 1958. The night that UFO came down in Miller's Woods. It's not my secret, even though I've kept it all these years." She looked up again, her eyes boring into Mabel's. "It might be a relief to tell someone I trust. You must promise me, though, not to tell another soul."

How could she promise when she didn't even know what it was? Mabel shifted in her seat. "Is it a crime?"

"Oh, heavens, no!" Nanette's eyes were wide.

"Well, as long as I don't absolutely need to use the information. Like for instance, if what you tell me might exonerate someone else…"

"I can't imagine how you'd ever need to use it. All it would do is tarnish my poor, dead sister's memory."

Mabel nodded and gently tapped Nanette's knee. "Of course, I won't tell."

Nanette laid her crochet hook and yarn down on the end table between them. "Would you like that tea now?"

Honestly, all Mabel wanted was to hear Nanette's story, but since Nanette was already headed for her kitchen, she nodded. "May I give you a hand?"

Nanette managed a smile. "If you'll set out the cookies, that would be a help."

Tea had never taken so long to brew. Mabel was happy to have a plate of Nanette's homemade raspberry tartlets to stave off her ravenous curiosity.

When they'd settled again, Nanette didn't even touch her tea.

"My sister, Sherry, was out on a date that night. She was sixteen, but I was supposed to be in bed—I was twelve. Mother and Dad were watching the late news, and they were reporting about the UFO. I'd been reading under the covers, and couldn't help hearing the excitement, so I crept to the head of the stairs to listen.

"Sherry came in during the program. She was late for her eleven o'clock curfew, but Mother and Dad were too caught up in the UFO news to make too much fuss—especially after Sherry told them they'd gotten stuck at a police roadblock. As soon as she started upstairs, I scurried to her room so we could talk about the UFO."

Sometimes Mabel nervous-nibbled when she watched something exciting. Nanette's story was having the same effect. Before she knew it, Mabel found herself stuffing most of a raspberry tartlet into her mouth.

Nanette looked off toward her front corner windows, which gave views of a glimmer of creek, the little garden, and Mabel's car. She sighed. "But we never talked. Sherry stayed in the bathroom a very long time. I tried to talk to her through the door, but she didn't answer. When she finally came out, her eyes were red, but her face was like stone.

"Naturally, I asked what was wrong, but she refused to tell me." Nanette gave Mabel a wobbly smile. "She was just enough older that I always looked up to her. To me, she was the epitome of teenage glamor. She was so pretty, and she'd always been so bubbly. Always so patient with me. But all of a sudden and for the longest time, everything changed."

"How do you mean?"

Nanette shrugged. "Every way. She lost her sparkle, her grades dropped, and she kept fighting with Ted—he was her boyfriend—till they broke up. Even her friends didn't seem to know what to do."

Mabel was afraid to ask another question that might cause Nanette to shut down. She took a sip of tea and picked up another cookie.

"I was worried. Since she wouldn't talk to me, my dog Perk and I started spying on her. Once we found her in the church…just sitting. Another time, she was in the bandshell in the park with her best friend, Tammy. We got as close as we could, but they were whispering, and I couldn't make out a thing they said. They both seemed agitated though.

"Finally, one evening we trailed Sherry to the Pleasant Union Cemetery. She was coming out of that overgrown shrubbery at the back. Perk started barking, and I just planted myself in front of her, demanding to know what she was up to." Nanette rubbed her head. "I guess I was a pretty awful brat."

Mabel realized she'd started crushing the raspberry tartlet. She popped it into her mouth and wiped her fingers on her napkin.

"I was surprised when she pulled me over to a bench and started talking. The first thing she did was swear me to secrecy. She was so serious, and I promised I'd die before I leaked a word.

"Then she told me she'd gotten pregnant.

"I was shocked. I didn't know what to say. I think all I did was gape at her, I'm ashamed to admit. But she said she'd had a miscarriage. Ted, of course, was relieved. Since Sherry had been even more worried about the pregnancy than he was, he couldn't understand her emotional turmoil. Or her grief."

The puzzle pieces started clicking into place in Mabel's head. "She buried her baby."

Nanette nodded. "It was a tiny little girl. She named her Amity Grace and buried her in a tea tin, in holy ground at the back of the cemetery where nobody would disturb her. She told me this and then grabbed my shoulders and made me look into her eyes.

'No one must know. Mom and Dad mustn't know. Ever.'

"No one has ever known the truth." Nanette's eyes bored into Mabel's, the same way Sherry's must have looked into Nanette's all those years ago. "Not until now. Sherry died of an aneurysm ten years ago. She'd gotten married eventually and had children and grandchildren. I'm not sure she even told her husband, Rod. I was the only one who knew, besides Ted and Tammy. I never told, and as far as I know, neither did they."

The weight of Nanette's confidence shook Mabel. Pete's secret had been different. John had been able to reassure him. Mabel had no words at all. She wasn't much of a hugger, but somehow, that seemed to be what the situation required.

When Mabel wrapped her arms around her, Nanette seemed to melt into them. Mabel gave her back an awkward pat as the hug went on.

After a moment, Mabel slid down to sit on the arm of Nanette's chair. At this point, the chair tipped. Nanette startled. She giggled and pulled away to wipe her eyes and blow her nose.

"I'm sorry," she told Mabel. "It's as if all those years of sadness needed an outlet."

"I understand." Mabel returned to her own chair. She took a sip of cold tea and, with some relief, picked up the next-to-last tartlet. She needed a sugar boost to counteract the strong emotions of the preceding minutes but didn't want to be rude. Thankfully, with only one tartlet left on the bone china plate, she wouldn't be tempted to exceed her limit.

Nanette lifted her teacup, but the last cookie remained untouched. "We never talked about the baby after that, though I'm sure Sherry put in that grave marker. Every year around the crash anniversary—which of course is also near the anniversary of Amity Grace's birth and death—a few flowers appeared on the spot.

"It was easiest just to go along with the 'alien grave' stories.

After my sister's death, I started going out at night and laid a few flowers down myself. A few times, I nearly got caught, but so far, the flowers just remain part of the local UFO legend."

Well, Mabel thought without satisfaction, I've solved another old mystery. She started to reach toward the cookie plate but then withdrew her hand. She cleared her throat. "So, now you've been worrying about the documentary crew discovering the truth?"

Nanette nodded. "This UFO investigation is stirring things up again. I heard their metal detector has already picked up something metallic under the surface."

"Yeah, I heard that rumor too. The UFO crowd's attributing it to the 'lead-lined box' that's supposed to contain the alien remains."

"How long is that going to satisfy them? I started worrying as soon as they started talking about disinterment and DNA. What if the investigation turns up something that points to the possibility of human remains or even an object as innocent as that tea tin? The decision to bar any digging might still be reversed. The police might even get a court order."

Mabel chewed her lip. If there was potential evidence of a crime, they might, indeed.

Nanette laid her hand on Mabel's. "If they find that baby, you know everybody—including the media—will be off and running. I can't let them sensationalize Amity Grace's story for their horrible documentary. Or have the police start digging into whether a crime's been committed, heaven forbid.

"I've been doing some reading on familial DNA. Did you know they can trace people through their relatives' DNA now?"

"Um…"

Nanette's eyes pleaded for understanding. "After all these years, both Amity Grace and Sherry should be allowed to rest in peace. I can't let them identify them or our family. I can't. What about Sherry's children and their families? To my knowledge, they've never been told."

"Um…" Did Nanette want her advice? Might that be at least part of the reason she'd decided to open up to Mabel?

Tentatively, Mabel asked, "If they don't know about Amity Grace, don't you think maybe they'd want to? Sherry's kids? I mean, she would have been their half-sister. And you won't live forever. Who's going to remember that baby and put flowers on her grave?"

Nanette was silent for a long moment. "Please honor your promise, Mabel. Don't tell."

Chapter Thirty-Five

MABEL DROVE HOME IN AN UNSETTLED mood. Nanette had explained she'd taken it into her head the night of Arthur Frost's death to go try to dig up the grave herself. She'd meant to carry away the baby's remains for reinterment in her own garden.

Mabel thought, uncomfortably, that the child might be better buried with her mother, but that was none of her business. In any event, Nanette's plans had been interrupted by all the activity around the cemetery—and as she'd tried to skulk away, Mabel and John had spotted her.

At least she could tell John she was now convinced Nanette had nothing to do with Arthur Frost's death. She guessed they could notify the police that they'd been in the vicinity of the cemetery that night.

Then what are we going to say, in the probable event we're questioned about what we observed?

Mabel didn't like being responsible for other people's secrets. Not to mention, she reflected sourly, she was still no closer to an answer about what she'd seen up on the ridge when those strange lights had come down from the sky. All her poking around had done was involve her in another murder and make her privy to the skeletons in other people's closets.

Privy. Mabel cringed. She was going to have to excise that word from her vocabulary after this election was over.

While she waited at the last light before her street, her phone pinged. Mabel scanned the text. Lisa's college friend Bobbi was volunteering to help Mabel plan Lisa's bridal shower.

At last, a glimmer of good news. She suspected Lisa, knowing Mabel all too well, had begged Bobbi to salvage the shower. This was embarrassing, but as far as Mabel was concerned, the result was what mattered.

More good news met her eye as she approached her house. Only two campaign signs sat on her property, each in its proper spot, and with no evident bloodstains. Perhaps she would survive these couple of months yet.

It would soon be dark. Since the time change, the sun went down before five pm. Was there still time to walk Barnacle?

She could hear him yelping and flinging himself at the kitchen door. Mabel sighed.

The moment the door opened, the dog launched himself at her with desperate joy…or maybe simple desperation for potty time and dinner. "Hang on."

Mabel kicked off her shoes and slid into her waterproof mocs. She called for Koi and finally spotted the cat looking down from her favorite spot atop the cabinets. "Hey, we'll be right back, okay?"

Koi's eyes narrowed.

Mabel grabbed a flashlight. She was tired of their usual circuits of the field and up to the corner and back. She decided to take the dirt path into Willow Creek Park, which bordered Mabel's property at the dead end. Once part of the farmland owned by Linnea's great-grandparents, the parcel was now township property, the old pastures long ago grown over with woods.

One quick loop, she told herself, to the pond and home again. The pond sat in a grassy, weedy clearing about a quarter mile in, following the old dirt farm road. That would allow Barnacle a good sniff fest and a chance to stretch his legs before dinner, and they should still have a glimmer of daylight for the walk back.

Barnacle frisked as they entered the thicket. The park maps didn't show the farm road or pond, and few people seemed aware this undeveloped section of woods was even part of the public land. Mabel felt almost as if it belonged to Barnacle and her, and she often let him off-leash back here.

As soon as she unclipped him, he trotted happily ahead, snuffling through the leaves on the way to his beloved pond. Belatedly, Mabel hoped Barnacle wouldn't decide to jump in the water.

The sky was turning a smoky blue, but the sun was still sending up golden beams from the footlights below the horizon. Bold washes of coral, gold, and lavender streaked the clouds.

"Barnacle," she called as she approached the clearing, hoping to steer him away from the water.

Though he gave no sign of having heard her, Barnacle seemed to be demonstrating an unusual degree of common sense and sticking around the reedy bank. Maybe after all this time, he'd reached an age where plunges into cold water had become less appealing.

The old dock had caved in a couple years ago, leaving only an old kitchen chair with a frame of rusting metal tubing for Mabel to sit on while she waited for the dog to complete his circuit of the water. Cautiously, she lowered her bottom onto the cracked vinyl seat.

Tilting her chin upward, she scanned the sky. Ever since her UFO encounter, Mabel had found herself looking up. As usual, she saw nothing but sky.

She had been growing sleepy the night of her sighting. By now she was almost ready to believe she'd dozed off behind the wheel and dreamed the whole thing. Was it possible to dream a whole dream in an instant?

The sole evidence—if she could call it that—validating her experience was that other people had reported seeing something that night as well. But their experiences hadn't been strictly like hers. Now, weeks had gone by, and she still had no idea what had happened.

With that thought, a flash of light streaked across the heavens. Mabel jerked so hard, she nearly toppled her rickety seat.

Heart thudding, she gaped at the sun-painted expanse of darkening sky and clouds. She began counting the seconds, waiting for the next flash to indicate she'd seen advertising lights for some store's grand opening.

But the succeeding flash never came. And what she'd seen was too bright for some distant advertising beacon. Still too early to see a shooting star.

This apparition was like what she, Nanette, and John had seen the night of Arthur Frost's murder. Strange, admittedly, but *not* like the event up on the ridge.

What on earth was happening in Medicine Spring?

Mabel stumbled through the leggy grass and weeds and grabbed Barnacle's collar as he was sticking his snout into the scummy-looking water. She didn't want to be alone in the woods anymore. "Time to get home for dinner, bud."

At the word "dinner," Barnacle stopped resisting and produced a doggy grin. A moment later, they were legging it home.

After dinner that evening, Mabel sprawled on her couch, talking on the phone with John. She'd managed earlier to shift most of the shower planning and organizing to Bobbi, a happy and enthusiastic party person—which Mabel was not. In return, Mabel had signed on for most of the grunt work, including mailing invitations, helping Bobbi make centerpieces and favors, handling set-up, and so on.

While she talked with John, Mabel compiled a list of things to buy and do. First on the list was purchasing invitations and stamps. She'd need to count invitees, now including Nita, and see if she needed more than one pack of invitations. It felt good to have a sense of direction at last, thanks to Bobbi. Things now felt under control, and she'd lost her sense of impending catastrophe.

She glossed over her talk with Nanette, hoping John would accept Mabel's assurance that Nanette was innocent of homicide without demanding to know what she'd been up to the night of the murder. Not unexpectedly, John was uneasy with her casual dismissal of Nanette's presence at the cemetery.

"It doesn't matter that I believe you—or that you believe Nanette. What matters is what the police believe. We can literally identify a person who was at or about the crime scene, at or about the time of the murder. I don't think we can continue to withhold that information, May."

Ordinarily, she'd have complained about the nickname, but at the moment, Mabel was too troubled. "I can't tell, John. I just can't. You promised not to squeal on Pete."

John sighed. "That's a different situation. He does admit to being in the vicinity of the cemetery, but we never saw him. We can't even be sure it was his truck we saw. What evidence do we really have?"

He waved aside Mabel's attempt to interject. "Yes, we did see him out there, but *not* on the night of the murder. Besides, he asked us to help him search. I looked into his eyes. It's not that I don't trust your judgment about Nanette, but…it's *your* judgment. You and Nanette haven't given me the opportunity to come to my own decision.

"Why don't you think about it for another day? Or simply tell Nanette I have a responsibility to identify her to police as having been there. You'll be off the hook."

Mabel's heart sank. "Not really. At that point, they'll know I was there and look to me for confirmation."

"All you have to do is say you saw her. You don't have to

reveal anything she told you. That's up to her."

None of this made Mabel feel a whit better. She knew she was being unfair to John but couldn't help feeling cranky after that. Finally, he gave up trying to talk and told her to take one more day to think about it.

When they'd hung up, Mabel sat with her head in her hands, seeking divine guidance. She was in such a pickle.

Koi leapt up next to her and butted Mabel with her head. Mabel tried to ignore her, but the cat rubbed her jaw along Mabel's hand, purring loudly. At last, she poked Mabel's nose with one paw.

Mabel uncovered one eye and gave Koi a dirty look. "Why can't you be more like your brother and mind your own business?"

Barnacle rolled over on her foot, released a loud snore, and jerked awake. He gave Mabel a hurt look, as if to ask why she'd wakened him so rudely.

Mabel got up and stomped into the kitchen. Her animals followed, seemingly unbothered by her surly mood.

She turned and glared at Koi. "Oh, all right. I've got twenty-four hours to solve the murder. Once I've done that, it won't matter about Nanette anymore."

Koi rubbed her body along Mabel's leg and purred.

"Glad you approve. Now, if you have any suggestions for how I'm supposed to accomplish this miracle, maybe you'll let me know."

The cat leapt onto the table, landing atop Mabel's suspect list.

Even I could have figured that much out.

Koi twitched her back end and leapt again, sending the paper fluttering to the floor as she landed on the pull-out shelf of the Hoosier cabinet, then vaulted to its dusty top. Growling, Mabel scooped up the list and plopped herself down at the table.

It wasn't long before Mabel wadded up the paper and tossed it back on the floor. Barnacle ambled over to sniff the list, and Koi jumped down to bat it around till it shot beneath the refrigerator.

Her list of names was worthless. There were still too many people on it. She didn't want to think Jackie could have killed anyone. And how could she even investigate Koslowski or Dan Cardamone?

Sure, somebody else could be guilty—maybe Leif Steele had gotten sick of dealing with his prima donna debunker. Maybe one of the many other people Frost had publicly humiliated had followed him to Medicine Spring. Or perhaps she should be looking at whomever would be taking over the coveted devil's advocate position on *Empty Eyes*. Opening her list up to more people didn't help—it made things worse.

Mabel's gaze fell on an advertising circular lying atop the junk mail in her waste can. The ad was for someone named Miss Dora, who offered palm readings and star charts. "Does your answer lie in the stars?" the flyer asked.

Mabel snorted. She most decidedly did *not* believe the stars foretold destiny. But all this craziness had begun with strange lights in the night sky, and maybe that was where the explanation—somehow—also lay. Perhaps if she focused on that, she could at least get to the bottom of her most pressing mystery—that of her own close encounter. She opened her laptop and typed, "strange lights in the sky."

Results flooded the screen…over 22,000,000, in fact. If she'd thought her short suspect list had been overwhelming, this was way worse. She'd never live long enough to work her way through all the articles.

She tried a few more searches. *Streaks of light. Flashing lights in sky.*

Still way too broad. *Very fast streaks of light moving across the sky.* The top results included meteors and satellites, but Mabel kept shaking her head. She broadened her search to include any strange, moving, or hovering lights in the sky, then narrowed it to western Pennsylvania. A moment later, she narrowed it again to the past month.

These results were more interesting. Mabel scrolled and made notes till she fell asleep with her face on the keyboard. She awoke after midnight with a cheek full of key indentations and Barnacle scratching at her knee.

Groggy, she staggered to her feet and let the dog out. A few minutes later, she crept upstairs with her animals. At least, she had a plan for tomorrow.

Chapter Thirty-Six

MABEL HAD REACHED TWO CONCLUSIONS OVERNIGHT. Medicine Spring, without question, had a long history of UFO sighting reports, stretching back into the 1950s. That said, she hadn't been able to find a lot of reports between 1958 and this year.

Reluctantly, she admitted to herself that despite other witnesses', including Miss Birdie and Ms. Katherine Ann's, having reported incidents the same night as hers, Mabel's encounter had been *different*. For starters, Mabel's had happened miles away from Medicine Spring, and she'd experienced more than weird lights. Hers would be harder to explain.

Medicine Spring sat right in the area surrounding the Chestnut Ridge, where, according to online sources, unexplained happenings were rampant. It appeared ufologists would put Mabel's own encounter well within the "likely inexplicable" category.

Too bad Arthur Frost isn't here to provide the answers.

What about all the other recent sighting reports, like Miss Birdie's and Ms. Katherine Ann's? Leaving aside weather balloons, swamp gas, and other such casual, dismissive explanations that didn't fit the circumstances, what else would a serious debunker like Dr. Arthur Frost be looking at?

Mabel considered the time and decided it was late enough to call Jackie. She hadn't spoken with her since the revelations by the lake, which might make things awkward. Still, Jackie remained her most logical and approachable source of knowledge about UFOs in Medicine Spring.

The phone rang long enough to make her fear she was waking Jackie up…although, she thought, if Mabel was up and about, pretty much any other functional human being also ought to be. Finally, just as she was sure the call was going to voicemail, she heard a voice croak, "Hello?"

"I'm sorry. Did a waken you?"

"Mabel? No. I'm always a bit gravelly in the morning. What's up?"

She'd clearly woken her. "I'm sorry," Mabel repeated. "I had a UFO question."

"Sure. What do you need?"

"I guess it might be more of a local history type question…I've been thinking about UFO incidents in the Medicine Spring area."

"Okay. What do you want to know?"

"The last big event seems to be the Miller's Woods crash in 1958, right? Or has this stuff been going on here for years, and I was oblivious?"

After a momentary pause, Jackie replied. "I believe that's right. There have been a few random accounts of strange objects or lights, but that's all." Her voice carried a question.

"That's what I thought. Now, all of a sudden, it's UFOs all over the place. Why, do you think that is?"

"Well…" Jackie seemed to be thinking. "There do seem to be waves of UFO mania, for want of a better term. Jules Verne stories seemed to trigger one in the 1890s. There was another huge spike in the 1950s, but I'm not sure why."

"What about right now, all these years later? In Medicine Spring, of all places?"

"Hard to say, but just guessing the US government's declassifying all those UFO files might be ramping things up. And why here? I suppose true believers would tell you it's our proximity to the Chestnut Ridge."

Mabel wrinkled her brow. "It sounds like you think people might just be imagining they see UFOs because other events are planting the idea. Then, in the same breath, you're talking like you think we live in a paranormal hot spot."

Jackie laughed. "I guess both or either might be true."

"I know what I saw," Mabel mumbled. "I just don't know what it was."

"So do I. I mean, what *I* saw years ago. We were talking about a sudden, great big spike in sightings, however, not just our own. That could be due to any of several factors, including an alien invasion."

Mabel hoped Jackie was joking about the alien invasion. Nevertheless, she was still left wondering what had triggered the recent UFO surge in Medicine Spring.

Mabel entered the UFO museum later that morning, along with several flying saucer enthusiasts who'd undoubtedly come to town to feed off the UFO fever. Clearly, the documentary filming—and even Arthur Frost's death, particularly with signs of alien abduction—had been helpful to Koslowski's business.

Mabel didn't have a definite idea what she was looking for, but something told her another visit to this place would help her arrange her overnight cogitations into some sort of order. The recent UFO sightings, the '58 crash in Miller's Woods, and the "alien grave" all somehow related to Arthur Frost's untimely demise—and if nothing else, Stanley Koslowski was lord of this particular domain.

Once again, Stanley was manning the place alone, and he seemed somewhat flustered—if cheerful—as he accepted their payments, handed out tickets, and answered questions. He told them they would not be able to enter the woods because of filming, but he would discount their tickets. Mabel decided to save her own queries for later, when presumably things would die down.

She wandered through the exhibits again, pausing at the chalkboard-size UFO timeline. Various significant UFO incidents marched across the section of the wall. Koslowski had been helpful in highlighting events occurring in western Pennsylvania, with Bartle County reports in yet a different color. The clusters were all quite evident. She didn't see anything similar to what she thought of as the current Medicine Spring UFO flap. Even the widespread Kecksburg sightings in 1965 all seemed related to the single purported crash.

No, wait…Koslowski did show a huge wave of Bigfoot and UFO reports, many of which occurred in Westmoreland County around 1973. Had that concentration ever been explained? If so, there was no annotation here that would tell her.

Even given 1973, the abrupt uptick in incidents in Mabel's tiny, immediate area didn't sit well with her. The Westmoreland sightings had covered a much wider area. If she considered the larger region, fifty years had gone by since, with only occasional sightings in the entire area. In fact, if she considered Medicine Spring alone, it had been closer to seventy years. Now all of a sudden, strange lights were being sighted on a daily basis—and a paranormal team had moved into town.

Which had come first? Had the increased UFO activity attracted Leif Steele's production company? Or was the presence of the film crew and investigators stimulating the upsurge of activity?

As if in reply to her question, Mabel's phone rang. She grabbed it and silenced the ringer. *Jackie.*

Surprised, she picked up the call.

"Mabel? Are you sitting down?"

"No, but I could be. Hang on."

The crowd of flying saucer enthusiasts was coming around the corner toward the timeline chart. Mabel ducked into the darkened room where a clip of Stanley's appearance on *Empty*

Eyes ran on continuous loop…minus the brawl with Arthur Frost.

"What's up?" Mabel asked.

"I hear noise. Do you want to turn your TV down?"

"No, that's okay. What have you got?"

"Maybe it's not really a surprise—but guess what. All those lights in the sky lately? The streaks—they're all a big hoax."

"Wow." Mabel plopped onto a folding chair. From the beginning, those streaks of light had been less than convincing. But still… "You mean the quick flashes? Not the full array of hovering lights, like what I and some others saw, right? Do we know who was doing it?"

"Yup. He was caught in the act. It's that gung-ho reporter from *The Shopper*."

"Renny Martin? Whew. He was making a career out of those stories."

"I know, right? I guess there wasn't enough hard news for him here in Bartle County. So, he decided to jump on the UFO wave."

"But even that wasn't enough excitement for him," Mabel muttered.

"Think about it," Jackie said. "He was writing for a weekly. By the time they published, he was always rehashing old stories. So, he started creating breaking UFO news that fit his own schedule, guaranteed to get him on the front page above the fold, every single week."

Mabel shook her head. "It was like he was gunning for a Pulitzer—or at least a move up to a bigger daily. He was getting a lot of buzz too, with the backdrop of the UFO festival in town, the documentary, and all that other stuff going on. He couldn't lose."

"Well, he just did."

After a bit more conversation, Mabel heard the other visitors approaching the theater. "Thanks for letting me know. I'll be in touch."

Mabel slipped out through the back draperies into the quiet alcove where Koslowski displayed his handful of "artifacts." Her brain was shuffling through information faster than she could make sense of it.

Those streaks of light that had set the town abuzz were no longer UFOs—unidentified flying objects—because they were neither objects nor unidentified. They'd been no more than cheap trickery. If she eliminated them from the recent UFO cluster, she was left with only the handful of sightings of dramatic light arrays the same night as her encounter up on the ridge.

Sure, those original few sightings—including Mabel's—had been more sophisticated, but could she be sure they were real? Anyone could see that Renny Martin had had something to gain from the frenzy of public interest aroused by his fake UFO lights. Had somebody else more skilled benefited from those encounters on the first night—enough to have made it worth their while to fake them? Assuming that were possible, of course.

The local merchants had obviously profited. The town itself gained a lot of attention. Yes, Stanley Koslowski had benefited from the publicity…but so had Arthur Frost himself—up till his unfortunate demise, of course—and even Leif Steele.

Mabel eyed a dusty, stuffed two-headed squirrel, allegedly recovered from Miller's Woods the year following the crash. The lighting in here was dim. By design? She imagined she could see a possible seam in the squirrel's neck.

Stanley Koslowski's only visible means of support were museum receipts and the royalties on his book. She doubted anyone could live on what those sources had been bringing in. Plus, he didn't have an ongoing TV gig like Arthur Frost had.

Now, he was riding high on a new wave of UFO mania. He'd gotten his book signing at Nita's store, and she'd said he'd done well. Last time Mabel had been at the museum, she and Lisa had been his lone visitors. Today, she'd had to wait to get her ticket. He must be collecting a hefty fee from the film crew for exclusive access to Miller's Woods.

Yes, she could readily imagine Stanley Koslowski's being involved in staging a few fake UFO incidents in order to generate buzz for his business. She wasn't sure how that might have been accomplished, but he sure had a strong incentive to figure that out. Besides which, he'd been operating a UFO museum for decades. By now, he might well have learned a lot about how to create a phony spaceship.

Mabel smacked her head. *Of course.* Wasn't this what everybody said about Koslowski? That he'd faked his abduction story? If that were true, fakery would be his standard operating procedure, wouldn't it?

The last time she'd been here, she and Lisa had skipped the abduction exhibit. Now, Mabel knew she had to look at it, in light of the possibility it had all been an elaborate hoax.

She turned the corner and found herself staring at gruesome blow-ups of Koslowski's claimed injuries from alien probing. She quickly averted her eyes.

Okay. Not dwelling on that.

Yeah, they could have been self-inflicted. After all, wife murderers had been known to inflict far more serious injuries on themselves—all to make it appear they'd been injured by the same mysterious third-party intruder they claimed had killed their wife. These few small incisions were nothing compared to a self-inflicted stab wound or broken limb.

Mabel studied the timeline, tracing each step of Koslowski's supposed abduction. She had to admit his story fit perfectly with other more famous accounts she'd read about, like Betty and Barney Hill.

Wasn't that in itself a bit suspicious? After all, it would have been a piece of cake to cut and paste all of this from other people's stories. Hadn't someone said a hallmark of authenticity was the inclusion of details that differed from typical reports?

Of course, Koslowski had later been questioned under hypnosis. Even that could have been trumped up in various ways, such as paying a hypnotist to validate his story. In fact, was there evidence anywhere that the supposed hypnotist was real and credentialed?

Approaching voices preceded the rest of the tour group. Mabel slipped out the rear door, where Koslowski had told them they could peer at the woods from behind the fence. She needed a few more minutes alone to think.

The moment she stepped outside, the cold wind struck Mabel with a slushy mix of rain and snow. It melted as it landed, but she didn't want to stay out here long. Though the building hadn't been all that warm, the change was still a slap in the face. She threw her hood over her head and zipped up.

Sounds came from the vicinity of the crash site—presumably the documentary crew. Given the time, she expected they were getting ready to break for lunch…assuming Leif Steele didn't have them working non-stop so he could quit paying equipment rentals.

Mabel tried to think. The obvious motive for killing Arthur Frost, in both Cardamone's and Koslowski's cases, had been fury over the debunker's very personal public humiliation. For Stanley, this might well have been compounded by envy and resentment over Frost's high-profile recurring role on *Empty Eyes.* Couldn't Koslowski have had yet another huge and more immediate motive?

Her heart had begun pounding. If—and she knew it was just a theory at this point—

Stanley had been behind this whole UFO flap, who'd be the person most likely to expose his deception? The most famous debunker in the country—and Stanley's personal nemesis—who had just ridden into town.

Mabel suspected Koslowski's threadbare business wouldn't survive a credible hoaxing scandal, especially if Frost had any direct evidence the sightings had been faked. Nor would Koslowski be securing any more TV guest spots, once he'd been irrefutably outed as a fraud. Leif Steele certainly couldn't afford to provide a platform for a known hoaxer. Mabel bet he'd be furious if he'd already wasted time on interviews of Koslowski, which would now be useless for the documentary.

Mabel wasn't sure what to do with her conjectures. Would the police pay any attention to her amateur analysis? With numb, red fingers, she fumbled out text messages to Lisa and John, asking them to call to discuss her suspicions. Both would be at work right now, but she expected they'd also be taking a lunch break sooner or later.

The museum's back door opened, and the tour group emerged, talking and laughing. A couple of them yelped as the rain and snow mixture hit them, but everyone still crowded along the fence to peer into the famous patch of woods.

Mabel wriggled her way indoors with a sigh of relief at the comparative warmth. Did she want to ask Stanley anything? Definitely not before the other visitors left. She'd noticed a noon-to-one pm break on the sign out front and assumed they'd all be asked to leave after the last person had spent their last dime in Koslowski's gift shop. She glanced at her phone and realized she only needed to hang around for a few more minutes.

A moment later, the back door burst open, followed by the boisterous group of flying saucer fans. As they passed, brushing off wet snow, she heard snatches of lunch plans and speculation about whether or not the gift shop had spaceship model kits, inflatable aliens, or other hot items.

There was a restroom near the exit to the gift shop. Mabel slipped inside. She'd only planned to use the facilities, but after she discovered there was an ancient space heater at work, she happily planted herself on the rickety chair next to it to wait for the other visitors to depart.

The chair creaked ominously as she settled her bottom, but it didn't collapse. Mabel put her damp feet directly in front of the draft of warm air and held her frosty fingers out to thaw as she thought about what to say to Koslowski. She could hardly come out and accuse the man of fraud and murder, based on guesswork.

Maybe she should tell him she was a writer and ask whether he had any books or information on UFO hoaxes for a story she was writing? His reaction should be worth studying. Hopefully, she wouldn't end up being expected to buy a book on the subject.

The warmth made Mabel drowsy, and she jerked upright as she caught herself starting to drift. She looked at her phone.

Oh, no. The museum had been scheduled to close five minutes ago. She hoped she hadn't already been locked in.

Mabel scrambled to her feet. When she opened the door, she heard voices coming from the gift shop in the outer room and breathed a sigh of relief.

She tiptoed to the black curtain closing off the museum from the gift shop and pulled back the heavy cloth far enough to peer through. She startled when she recognized Leif Steele scant feet away to the left, his trademark tousle of dark hair wet from the snow.

Doggone it, she had to admit he was handsome—even if he *was* full of himself.

Steele stood in front of the sales counter, talking to Stanley Koslowski. Mabel could see Stanley's profile and part of his back as he sat on his stool, arms resting on the counter. His posture was relaxed, but from where she stood, she could see the stress lines around his mouth and the little twitches in his shoulder muscles.

"Are you insane, Stanley?"

"Far from it. I'm just a small businessman with a

straightforward proposition I expect to be favorable for both of us."

Steele's broad shoulders strained at the slush-spattered leather of his black jacket as he leaned in, emphasizing the difference in size between him and the shorter, dumpier Koslowski. "Spare me the euphemisms. You're talking about blackmail."

Mabel stifled a gasp. Her fingers tightened on the curtain fabric.

"Don't be dramatic. I'm trying to help you. All I ask for is a little appreciation." Koslowski's voice was level, but his right leg had started to jiggle.

"I don't need your help." Steele pushed away from the counter, as if to storm out.

"Oh, I think you do. And I think you know it."

"Go ahead, then." Steele's face was carved from ice. "Why don't you spell it out?"

After a fractional pause, Koslowski spoke, his voice beginning to reveal a thread of tension. "I saw you. I saw the whole thing."

Chapter Thirty-Seven

Mabel's hands, clutching the ratty black curtains separating the gift shop and UFO displays, felt damp. Her heartbeat thundered in her ears. Between that and her ragged breathing, she wondered fleetingly whether Steele and Koslowski might hear her and rip back the curtains.

But the exchange in the gift shop, a few feet from her hidden observation point, continued—they were as oblivious to her as actors on a screen.

Steele laughed without humor. "If you think you deserve something from me, I want to hear the details. What exactly do you want? Why should I give it to you? What guarantees do I have?"

"You need me to spell out what I know?"

Steele pulled a second stool from the end of the counter and sat. "Absolutely, I do. Because you're bluffing." He folded his arms and waited.

"What do I want? I just told you. You want me to repeat all that too?"

Steele nodded.

"Why? Are you recording me or something?"

Again, Steele laughed. "No, but I don't know why that would concern you. If this really is a business proposition and not anything illegal."

Another pause followed Steele's challenge. Finally, Koslowski seemed to swallow. "Okay. It's simple enough, and good for both of us. I'm not asking for money, so you can see I'm not trying to blackmail anybody. All I want is a recurring spot on *Empty Eyes*."

Steele arched a brow. "Like Frost?" He gave a slow grin. "Doing what, exactly?"

"Yeah, except not debunking, naturally. Just commenting. You know, like the psychic chick you have on there sometimes."

"Are you saying you're psychic?"

"No. That was just an example." Koslowski's breath came in puffs, as if he were trying to talk while climbing uphill. "I think I can contribute a lot to the show and help your ratings."

Again, Steele's right eyebrow raised. "Not that my ratings need a boost from you or anybody else, but I don't know how you think you're going to draw any viewers. We almost never talk about abductions."

"I know about a lot more than abductions." Koslowski waved a hand around the shop. "I've operated this museum for over twenty years. I know UAPs."

A grin twitched at the corner of Mabel's mouth. She suspected Stanley had thrown in the current term for UFOs to demonstrate he was up on the lingo.

"All right. I gather your main qualification for the job—which, I must point out, doesn't exist at the moment—is you think you saw something I did. Pretty odd resume highlight."

"You got me wrong. It's not like that. It's…if we're doing a show together, I…I want to protect your reputation, you know. It's good for both of us, right?"

Steele shot from his seat and made Koslowski jump. "Protect me from what? If you think you know something, say it."

Koslowski's ragged breaths were getting louder, but he pressed on. "I saw you kill Arthur Frost."

Mabel clapped both hands over her mouth in case an involuntary scream decided to pop out. Now unable to see anything in the other room, she eased the curtain open a cautious sliver.

Steele snorted and tossed his head like a defiant horse and returned to his seat. "Baloney. I'll sue you for everything you've got if you dare spread a lie like that."

"It's the truth, and we both know it." Koslowski's voice shook. "I was out in the woods, making a recording. Trying to pick up electronic voice phenomena. Not only can I tell you everything that happened, but I can play the recording."

Steele's eyes narrowed.

"You were meeting Frost because he was trying to blackmail you." Stanley faltered, as if struck by the irony of that statement, coming from him. "It's obvious you two had a deal going for years. One hand washed the other. As long as the big debunker endorsed all *your* investigations, he had access to your platform, right?"

Steele glowered. Mabel had to admit his smoldering countenance didn't detract from his good looks.

Focus, Mabel.

"Whenever either of you had a book coming out, you were all over each other's promos." Bitterness seeped from every word.

"I had you on the show."

"Like twice? And let Frost rip into me."

"That was his function. People expected some flamboyance."

"He destroyed people's lives, and you provided him the stage to do it on. Then the gravy train ran out of steam." Koslowski leaned forward, his long-simmering resentment seeming to make him bolder. "Yeah, your ratings do need a boost—a big boost. So, you got clever, didn't you?"

Steele crossed his legs. For the first time, despite the man's bland sneer, Mabel caught a hint of anxiety.

"Frost didn't start out as a phony," Koslowski said. "I hate to admit it, but he really was an expert—he knew how believable fakes were made. That made him useful for your show, but also someone you couldn't afford as an enemy. That's why you first started hiring him, isn't it?

"Then when your ratings started tanking, you needed more help. This time, you asked him to *create* a hoax for you—one that was going to stir up excitement ahead of your biggest investigation ever. All you needed was a podunk town with a UFO backstory…a place where people weren't too sophisticated. A place like Medicine Spring. And—for whatever you promised him in return—Frost agreed to do it."

"That's a preposterous fabrication. Nobody will believe it."

"Again, I've got the recording, so spare me. Frost created your rash of UFOs, just in time to launch your big investigation. But he soon wanted more, didn't he? He started hinting he could easily debunk your fake sightings if you didn't make him a co-producer and series regular, for a fat salary you couldn't afford.

"Oh, you blustered around—like you're doing with me right now. Threatened to expose him too. All he did was laugh at you—I heard him. He said he'd been careful and could pin everything on you."

"You stupid, two-bit crook." Leif Steele surged to his feet. "You claim I killed someone ten times smarter than you, for doing the same thing you're trying to do. What do you think is going to happen to you?"

Koslowski nearly toppled his stool as he scrambled down. "Take it easy, man. It's not like that."

Mabel drew back. She didn't know who was telling the truth here, but presumably, Koslowski wouldn't have dared confront Steele if he hadn't witnessed something in the graveyard the night Frost was killed. And Steele did look menacing.

Was she about to find herself in the middle of another murder…maybe as one of the victims? She didn't intend to wait around and find out.

On tiptoes, Mabel ran to the rear door and out into the

enclosed yard. The biting wind was ripping down the last of the dead oak leaves and flinging them at her along with the slushy, sideways rain.

She had no way out. The chain link fence was at least six feet high, and the only exit to the parking lot was padlocked.

The women's restroom was her last hope. Desperate, she yanked the back door open again.

Something crashed in the front room, shattering glass and splintering wood. She couldn't hear a word from Steele, but Koslowski seemed to be pleading with him.

Mabel had barely taken a step when Stanley flew backward through the black exit curtains, smashing into the artifact case and onto the floor. Steele flung himself on top of him and grabbed his collar with both hands.

The two thrashing men didn't appear to have seen her, but they were blocking the restroom door, not to mention her escape route through the gift shop to the parking lot. That was unless she could get to the opening in the other set of curtains, at the entrance on the far side of the room, without being spotted.

Mabel scrunched down and began scuttling along behind the displays, headed toward the entrance curtains and wishing bitterly that she was a wispier girl. Steele hauled Koslowski onto his feet as if about to toss him into the artifact case again.

Did he think he could pass a homicide off as a bad tumble? After trashing the gift shop in this free-ranging, one-sided brawl?

She eyed the next—and last—hiding place on her route. The massive papier mache alien who greeted visitors at the exhibit entrance. Mabel darted a backward glance at Steele and Koslowski. Could she make it?

She had no choice. She had to make it.

As Mabel launched into her breathless, terror-driven final sprint, she grabbed her phone from her pocket so she could dial 911 the moment she got out of Steele's earshot, but two things happened at once.

Behind her, Stanley Koslowski dropped like a family-size sack of dog food, apparently in a dead faint. Or—she hoped not—dead.

The *Hot-Blooded* ringtone blared from her phone. John was calling her back.

With an inarticulate bellow, Steele leapt toward Mabel. She picked up the call.

"UFO Museum," she gasped. "It's Steele!"

Though she could hear John saying something, Mabel didn't have time to chat. With a second incredible leap, Steele was upon her, digging at her throat.

She tossed her phone and heard a sickening thunk. She needed both hands to pry at Leif Steele's unrelenting fingers, now clamped around her neck, thumbs probing for her windpipe.

Gulping for air, Mabel struggled to protect her throat. She wasn't strong enough to fight off Mr. Musclebound. Already, he'd managed to cut off much of her air.

What had Miss Birdie and Ms. Katherine Ann told her after their self-defense class at the senior center?

Gouge his eyes?

Even though she wasn't having any success peeling away his fingers, she didn't dare let go of his hands to attempt an eye-gouging.

Stomp on his instep, Miss Birdie had said. Awkwardly, Mabel stomped.

She missed Steele's instep, but landed hard enough on his toes to make him yelp and swear at her.

"Knee him in the groin." She remembered Ms. Katherine Ann delivering that advice with great relish.

It was hard to generate much upward force with her knee while grappling at such close quarters. Mabel gave it her best and was rewarded with a screech. Steele gasped and writhed but didn't let go.

All of a sudden, something moved at her right.

Out of the corner of her eye, she glimpsed Stanley Koslowski staggering to his feet. He caught himself on the edge of the artifact case and seemed to be trying to steady himself.

Leif Steele appeared to have seen the movement too. He now had two problems, both mobile. Distracted, he slackened his grip on Mabel by a hair as he darted a backward glance at Stanley.

As Steele looked away, Mabel stopped shoving at his hands and threw her weight onto him. Caught off balance, Steele let go. He flailed the air as they both went down, crashing together into the ten-foot papier mache alien.

"Nooo…" Koslowski's scream carried equal parts rage and despair.

Steele struggled to free himself from the crumpled depths of their musty-smelling papier mache coffin. Mabel, with the advantage of having landed on top, backed out of the wreckage on hands and knees.

Once free, she turned and plopped down on Steele's legs. For the moment, she felt thankful she wasn't wispier.

That ought to hold him a while. I hope.

Mabel interrupted Koslowski's rant. "Call the cops."

"That lunatic destroyed thousands of dollars of merchandise. My alien was handmade. It was priceless," Koslowski howled.

"Not to mention he tried to kill both of us." Mabel glared.

He gave Mabel a dirty look, as if she were complicit in the destruction. "What are you doing here?"

"Just call the cops, Stanley." She was beginning to rock like a dinghy on rough waters as Steele tried to kick his way free.

At last, Koslowski seemed to notice that they weren't out of the woods yet. Still grumbling, he limped toward the front of the shop.

Steele was still face down, his upper body stuck inside the top half of the alien. Still, Mabel wouldn't be able to keep him down much longer. He was younger, stronger, and adrenaline charged. Steele swore and thrashed like a madman.

"Relax," she told him. "Unless you think you can hop a plane to Mexico before the police arrive, it's game over." He could scarcely take hostages without a weapon.

She hoped.

With a near superhuman thrust, Leif Steele tossed Mabel to the floor and rolled onto his knees, still wearing the upper portion of the alien over his head and shoulders with his arms pinned to his sides. She scrambled to her feet, hesitating between running or trying to subdue him again.

Surely, the police would get here soon. Mabel scanned her surroundings for something to use as a weapon but found nothing more deadly than the ancient flashlight in the artifact case.

In case of emergency, break glass? No, the flashlight was useless.

Steele still hadn't managed to get to his feet. His entire upper body remained jammed inside the alien head and partial torso.

He struggled to stand up without the use of his hands. Helpless, Steele kicked his legs, looking remarkably like an invading Martian in his death throes at the climax of an old B movie. Or maybe an oversize trick-or-treater in a homemade costume, who'd tripped over an uneven sidewalk.

Once again, Mabel plopped herself onto Steele's legs with a grunt and tried to get comfortable. She was getting too old for this.

The Medicine Spring police burst in minutes later, having rolled up without sirens. Uniformed officers led the way, service pistols drawn.

Behind them came Detective Lt. Sizemore. Her eyes went straight to Mabel, and she nodded a greeting.

"Good to see you again, Ms. Browne. I see this time you've bagged an alien." Sizemore tipped her head toward Mabel's captive. "If I'm not mistaken, this is a first for you. Let's chat."

Chapter Thirty-Eight

Two days after Leif Steele's apprehension, the Saturday of the UFO parade and festival events dawned bright and chilly. Since Lisa lived right on Main Street, Mabel and John, along with her fiancé Tim, planned to watch the afternoon parade from her apartment. But by ten-thirty, Mabel was already headed to town. She figured John wouldn't be interested in the festival booths and snacks set up in the old armory, and she wanted to take her time walking around…and snacking…without being rushed.

The festivities had been greatly dampened by the cancellation of the planned documentary after Steele's arrest, followed by a mass exodus of out-of-town tourists. The excess porta-potties around town had disappeared overnight, and once again, residents were able to find seats at The Coffee Cup. From the local merchants' somber expressions, Mabel was surprised they hadn't gone ahead and hung black crepe and covered all the mirrors.

There had been some heated debate on the Board of Supervisors—including impassioned floor speeches from candidate LeRoy Casselman and members of the UFO Days committee—as to whether to cancel the remaining events. Finally, they'd reached the one possible conclusion. It was simply too late to cancel—though the decision had been couched in terms of the continued historical significance of the Miller's Woods crash and the "alien grave."

Still, Mabel thought as she pulled into a spot near Nita's bookstore, the event had lost much of its luster following Frost's death, Steele's arrest, and worst of all, the revelation that all the thrilling recent sightings—the convincing light arrays as well as the quick streaks of brilliant light—had been no more than hoaxes.

All but my own still-unidentified flying object.

She walked the few blocks to the armory with her collar pulled up. The rush of heat when she stepped inside felt wonderful. Mabel suspected it would feel less wonderful after she'd strolled around a bit and still had her heavy coat to contend with.

A surprising number of people milled about the hall, from families with young children to a few seniors with canes or walkers. It appeared the festival wouldn't be a complete bust. Several enthusiasts had even come costumed as little green men or aluminum foil-clad spacemen.

Mabel began her counterclockwise circuit of the room with a stop at the raffle table. Local merchants had donated baskets, though none tempted her enough to drop five dollars on a batch of tickets. To her amazement, the glass jar in front of Stanley Koslowski's basket already held a few tickets. She wondered who was panting for a signed copy of *My Lost Hours*, a bunch of UFO kitsch, and a season pass to the museum.

"Mabel!"

The call made her look up. Nita was presiding over a nearby book table that prominently featured marked-down copies of Steele's, Frost's, and Koslowski's books. Mabel headed over to say hi.

"I pre-ordered all this inventory." Nita groaned. "That was when I was still expecting droves of out-of-towners. I've been slapping fingers when people try to pick up anything but the browsing copies. I'm going to have to send a bunch of them back."

"Don't give up the ship. It's still early. You'll get some lookie-loos who show up just because of the murder and the celebrity scandal."

Nita raised her eyes to heaven. "I hope so. I had to pay my assistant to watch the shop so I could be down here. I can't afford not to make some serious sales."

"Hey, I've got to get going. I'm due at Lisa's to watch the parade later. Did you RSVP to the shower?"

"Sure did. I wouldn't miss it. Getting to know Lisa's been one bright spot in all this mess."

"She feels the same. Don't worry—you're going to unload lots of books. There isn't much else to do in Medicine Spring, so people will come here. Wait and see if I'm not right."

As Mabel continued her circuit of the room, she spotted several familiar faces. There went Pete, wearing a grumpy expression and being dragged around by his lanky wife Viola. Nanette sat at a table offering applications to join the historical society. Mabel waved but kept her distance. Things still felt a bit awkward since Nanette had spilled her long-held secret…not to mention, she didn't want to get sucked into doing a shift at the table herself.

A few folks she recognized from the UFO meeting clustered around a booth selling recording devices, meters for detecting electromagnetic fields, and similar paraphernalia. Mabel squinted. She didn't see Jackie among them.

When she reached the food vendors at the midway point, Mabel finally found Jackie carrying a hot cider and a plate with two cider doughnuts from the Orsino's Orchard booth. "Join me?"

It was after eleven, and Mabel was beginning to feel her energy sag. The doughnut and cider scents pulled her in, and a moment later, she plopped down at Jackie's table to enjoy her snack. The aroma of the cider pulled pork had nearly made her knees buckle, but Mabel realized she had to save room for the food Lisa had spent the morning preparing.

"How are you doing now that Leif Steele's been arrested?"

"I'm still celebrating." Jackie brandished a doughnut. "Thanks for bringing him to justice."

"Well, technically, I can't take any credit for that, but I'm glad if it means you're off the hook."

"I am, and of course, you deserve credit. He'd have killed Stanley if you hadn't been there to bring him down…even if Stanley was asking for it."

Mabel shrugged a shoulder and savored her big bite of doughnut. She figured there was no point in telling the whole story of how she'd merely gotten stuck in the museum when the confrontation erupted, and she had to save her own skin.

Jackie nodded at a woman conducting an interview at a nearby table. "I notice somebody new is here for *The Shopper*. Renny pretty much blew up his career with that stunt—unless he can start over someplace else under an assumed name."

"Yeah, that was colossally stupid." Mabel's glance drifted to the UFO crowd, including Jackie's friend Virgil, who were watching a video of one of the meters measuring electromagnetic fields. "I notice the true believers haven't lost any steam."

"No…" Jackie looked over at her colleagues. "I guess none of us have lost interest in the mysteries of life. Just because a couple of jerks were faking it doesn't mean there aren't still things we can't explain."

Mabel grimaced. She wanted answers.

"Buck up, Mabel. Nobody's refuted what you saw."

"You say that like it's a good thing."

"It's exciting. Maybe somebody will figure it out one day. Maybe it'll turn out to be an experimental plane or something like that. Meanwhile, you've had a unique experience that can't just be dismissed."

"Unless people decide I'm lying or crazy."

Jackie gave her a wry smile. "Sadly, that's the price of the privilege. You got to experience something extraordinary. If people don't believe you, it's because it's outside the realm of what they can understand."

Mabel sighed. "I wish you'd been the lucky one."

John waved from Lisa's street-level apartment door as Mabel skirted the Main Street barricades. "Hi." He planted a kiss on her cheek. "I was just about to ring the bell."

A moment later, Lisa's fiancé Tim opened the door. "Come on up. Lisa's ready to put the food out."

The apartment smelled gloriously of ham barbecue, a huge apple pie baked in a rectangular pan, and hot mulled cider. "Hey, Mabel," Lisa called. "You want to set out the buns and stuff for me, so we can get started eating before the parade?"

While they set up, Mabel told Lisa she'd run into Nita and that she'd be coming to the shower. She squirmed a bit as Lisa thanked her for all her hard work, while they both knew Lisa's college friend Bobbi had taken over most of the planning.

Mabel studied the pumpkin centerpiece, harvest-themed tablecloth, and napkins. She wondered whether she could ever get to the point where she'd feel comfortable inviting anyone over to her cluttered farmhouse—no matter how good a friend they were.

Lisa was so good at this. She made everything look effortless. She'd once told Mabel all the years of teaching had taught her to be organized, but Mabel suspected teaching had merely given Lisa an outlet for her natural talents.

"I have other talents," Mabel silently told herself, then focused on the task at hand before she had to ponder what those might be.

They finally settled around the coffee table to eat. Lisa's one-eyed tomcat, Ulysses, scowled from the hutch cabinet, as if waiting for someone to notice he hadn't been served. Mabel was happy to be sitting buffered between John and Lisa because the former alley cat seemed to particularly despise her. She often wondered what it was about her that had that effect on cats but supposed she ought to be grateful Koi didn't share Ulysses' and Billie Jean's low opinion of her.

"It'll be kind of nice to get things in town back to normal," Lisa said. "I pay for that space in the corner of The Coffee Cup lot, and I kept coming home from work and finding somebody else parked there."

Tim wiped sauce off his chin. "I told you—you should've put out a parking chair."

"I told you I did. It kept getting moved. Finally, somebody with a big SUV just drove right into it, and I had to throw it away."

John shook his head. "Out-of-towners. Never saw a parking chair before."

"I suppose it's a western Pennsylvania thing, but you'd think they'd take a hint." Lisa grimaced.

"Guess Leif Steele made bail," John said. "And it was a big one."

"Stanley's out too." Mabel shook her head. "His attorney's claiming he suffers from PTSD caused by his purported abduction trauma, and they're asking for leniency in return for his testimony. I wonder whether he'll end up doing jail time for any of the stuff he pulled."

John shrugged. "Steele's the bigger fish, and Stanley can help put him away."

"He should be getting a plea deal," Mabel agreed, "but I question whether he can avoid prison time altogether. We're talking withholding material evidence in a homicide, tampering with evidence, abuse of a corpse, attempted blackmail—"

"Whoa, there." Lisa held up her hand like a traffic cop. "You told me about the blackmail. But what's all this other stuff?"

John laughed. "Finish your sandwich, Mabel. It'll get cold by the time you're done explaining."

"No, it's pretty simple." Still, she stole another quick bite before continuing. "All the other stuff was part of the blackmail. Stanley was there in the woods when Steele and Frost had their argument, and Steele whacked Frost on the head with a rock and killed him, right? So, Stanley sees an opportunity.

"The minute Steele hightailed it out of there, Stanley came in and staged the body, so it looked like Frost had been abducted by aliens."

"He really was naked?" Lisa's eyebrows lifted.

"Down to his shorts, anyway, and Koslowski made some small marks on the body, like the ones on people who claim to have been abducted."

"Eww…"

"What was the point of that?" Tim had returned from the kitchen with more pasta salad.

"If you ask me, which I guess you did, I think it was partly his way of humiliating Frost. Stanley never got over Frost's blasting his story about being abducted. It also kind of bolstered Stanley's own abduction claims."

"But it was pretty stupid, since for anybody who doesn't believe in alien abduction—including, I imagine, most of the Medicine Spring PD—it tended to point more suspicion back at Stanley." John forked up the bits of sauce-drenched ham that had dropped from his sandwich.

"Well, in Stanley's defense, he was planning all this on the fly, and probably didn't think that far." Mabel realized she hadn't thought too far ahead, either—she still hadn't finished her first sandwich, but was already wondering whether there would be any meat left in case she wanted seconds after telling her story. Well…there would still be pie, anyway.

Mabel cleared her throat. "Stanley was trying to divert suspicion from Steele too, because keeping him in the clear was his bargaining chip. If he didn't keep *Empty Eyes* on the air, he'd lose his chance to become a co-star."

"All those big ambitions," Lisa said. "Now what's left? Frost is dead, Steele's going to prison…"

"Right. Even if he does get a plea deal, Stanley won't be getting off scot-free either. He'll have to spend some time behind bars," Mabel predicted. "The best he can hope for is a short stay at one of those country club prisons."

"Wait a minute." Tim raised a hand. "Didn't Koslowski announce on TV that he'd identified the killer for the police? I didn't see it, but that's what the paper said."

"Oh, I saw it." Mabel sniffed. "He wasn't going to ID Steele. It was Cardamone—that poor guy. On what evidence, who knows? For all I know, he might have fabricated something to divert suspicion from Steele."

John grimaced. "I've lived here my whole life, and this is hands down the most bizarre episode of Medicine Spring history I've ever seen."

Tim stood at the windows. "Looks like the parade's about to start."

"Pull some chairs over and bring your pie and cider," Lisa said. "There are mugs in the cupboard above the coffee pot, if you want."

"Did Acey get much done on your house yet?" John handed Mabel a mug. "They're predicting twenty-seven degrees one night next week."

"You're kidding, right? He did get started, but now he's in a snit because I refused to walk along the parade route and hand out postcards for Cletus."

John snorted.

"Oh, it gets better. Linnea's fuming too. She wanted me to do the same thing for LeRoy. Even threatened to tattle to Cora. I'm a bit worried about Cora beating me up, but if she drums me out of the historical society, it would be a blessing."

"I still don't understand the big deal about the privy." Lisa cut slices of pie. "They could just fence it off, couldn't they?

Maybe plant some bushes around it."

"Well, according to Linnea, the parcel isn't all that big, and they figure nobody's going to want to trek through a bunch of cavorting dogs to see the privy. Not to mention all the doggie droppings people haven't picked up."

"Honestly." Lisa made a face. "Who's going to want to tour a privy anyway? Fence it off from the dogs and stick a historical marker down by the road."

"I already suggested that, but according to Acey, the dog people insist they need the whole area, since it's not that big to begin with."

"Battle to the death then." Lisa raised her coffee mug, and she and Mabel toasted.

As they carried their coffee and pie over to the windows, John danced around Ulysses, who was rubbing his head on John's pantleg. Mabel shook her head—the cat had just met John, and already Ulysses adored him.

"You know what, Mabel, I've got some time," John said. "I've done weatherstripping and storm windows before. Why don't I come over and do it for you?"

Tim looked up. "I can give you a hand."

Mabel wavered. The temptation to get the job over with, not to mention stop the drafts that were forcing her to wear layers of sweatshirts—and occasionally gloves—inside the house, was hard to resist. "That's a lot of windows. I can't ask you guys to do all that work."

"You didn't," John said.

Tim nodded forcefully. "We offered."

"Wow." Mabel plopped into her chair. "I don't know what to say. Thank you both. Acey's going to have a fit."

Lisa sniffed. "It'll serve him right."

"He's welcome to join us." John grinned.

"I'll feed you," Mabel promised, but noticed the quick look of alarm that passed between the two men. "I'll order in," she clarified.

Both faces brightened. "It's a deal." John shook with her and then with Tim. "We can talk after the parade and pick a day."

The UFO Days parade was nothing if not unique, in Medicine Spring annals. Given the proximity to the traditional Thanksgiving parade, the Bartles Grove-Medicine Spring High School band director had declined to participate, asking how they were expected to find and learn "space music" in the time available.

In their place, the local dance school performed to recordings. Selections included *The Purple People Eater, Rocket Man,* and the old instrumental hit, *Telstar*, which Mabel supposed were the nearest things to outer space music they'd been able to dig up.

"You know, I'm glad that film crew cleared out of town," Lisa said. "I like our hokey little smalltown vibe lots better. All that TV stuff just isn't Medicine Spring."

"Amen." Mabel gave Lisa thumbs up, and the men grunted agreement.

"Isn't that your candidate?" John pointed at a passing Model T. LeRoy Casselman waved from the passenger side and threw candy for the scrambling kids.

Mabel sighed. "One of them."

"And there's the other one." Lisa nodded at the pair of beautiful young women in scanty patriotic costume, carrying a banner that read, VOTE PETTIGREW. Behind them, the candidate himself revved up a huge trike motorcycle, making the women scream and giggle. Mabel hoped they were receiving hazard pay, as Cletus gave every appearance of a first-time rider. As they started forward again, it took him a heart-stopping moment to get headed in the right direction.

"I'm guessing that's either a rental or a loan from a

supporter." Tim frowned. "I hope they made sure he knows where the brakes are."

Boy Scouts and Campfire Girls trooped past in wavering formations. Mayor Huntley beamed from the back of a vintage yellow Thunderbird convertible. Behind the Medicine Spring Volunteer Fire Department ladder truck, kids on bicycles outfitted with streamers rode aimlessly. The bikes veered every time the firetruck blared its horn.

A motley crew of 4-H members marched by with an assortment of livestock. Acey Davis followed, looking grumpy as he trundled a trashcan behind him, scooping up the predictable messes. In between pickups, he dashed to either sideline, distributing campaign postcards. Mabel couldn't resist a snicker.

It was a thin crowd braving the parade route, she noticed. Most people seemed to be bundled for an Arctic expedition, draped in blankets, and clutching takeout cups of coffee or cocoa.

Mabel's snicker erupted into a snort. Here came Linnea, powerwalking along the sidelines and pulling handfuls of what must be LeRoy's campaign literature from a handsome leather tote bag and thrusting it at the spectators. When people waved away the papers, she let them flutter to the pavement and marched on down the street. Linnea wore an expression of righteous fury that made Mabel think of a fast-food manager stuck cleaning bathrooms after the overnight shift had all called off.

"We must be getting near the end." Lisa pointed at the approaching long-bed pickup.

"Ohh." Mabel hopped up for a closer look as Stanley Koslowski rolled by, preening in the truck bed next to the ten-foot papier mache alien from his museum. Stanley wobbled and kept grabbing at the tethered figure to keep his balance. The gray alien's torso was now reattached to its battered legs with silver duct tape. One arm had also been patched together, but backward.

Mabel and Lisa got the giggles and couldn't stop. "That was a spectacular finale." Tim grinned with obvious satisfaction.

After she'd caught her breath, and Lisa and Tim had started tidying up, Mabel looked around and realized John was gone. A moment later, he reappeared from Lisa's bedroom, where they'd stashed their coats.

He handed Mabel a small, somewhat crumpled, brown paper bag. "I wanted you to have a souvenir of Medicine Spring's Martian madness."

Mabel took the bag with amazement. "Where did this come from?"

"The festival, of course."

"I didn't think you'd be interested—I wonder if we were there at the same time."

"We were." John grinned. "I saw you just as I was buying this but didn't want to spoil my surprise. By the time I got my change, you'd disappeared, and I had to grab my car from Eddie's. I'd left it for an oil change and tire rotation, and they were closing for the parade."

"Well, thank you." Mabel opened the bag and peeked inside.

Huge, almond-shaped, black felt eyes peered back at her.

"Oh, I love him." Mabel pulled the little green hand-crocheted alien out of the bag and hugged him. "Nobody ever gave me anything like this."

John looked pleased. "He just jumped up and hollered, 'I belong with Mabel.'"

She swallowed the lump in her throat. "Did you go to the festival just for this?"

"Busted." He grinned and put his arms around her. "I have confidence in the ladies of Medicine Spring. I knew someone would have exactly what I was looking for…for the person who's everything I've been looking for."

"He's perfect." Mabel sighed. "And I hope he's the last little green man I ever run into."

AUTHOR NOTE

I hope you enjoyed Mabel's brush with the world of UFOs—not to mention minor celebrities and long-buried small-town secrets. I had so much fun writing this book, especially when things happened that surprised even me.

Have you ever seen something in the sky that you couldn't explain? I've never had that opportunity, but figure there's still hope—especially since, like Mabel, I have a home in an area near Pennsylvania's Chestnut Ridge, which ufologists consider a UFO hot spot. An interesting book detailing many sighting reports from that area is *Silent Invasion* by Stan Gordon (2010). It's now out of print but may be available through inter-library loan.

UFOs were once treated as little more than B movie fodder. Sightings continued however, and reports came in from reputable sources, including police and military pilots. In 1952, a UFO even buzzed the White House, leading to persistent rumors of a secret meeting between President Eisenhower and alien leaders!

In recent years, the Pentagon and our national intelligence agencies have been working together to try to figure out just what's going on up there. In June of 2021, the U.S. Director of National Intelligence delivered a report to Congress acknowledging they were investigating reported UFO incidents but had not yet arrived at explanations for many of them. A year later, the Pentagon admitted to about 400 sightings by military personnel. Some had been explained to the government's satisfaction at that point, while others still remain unresolved today.

Besides having fun with flying saucers, I've also enjoyed introducing some "western Pennsylvania-isms" in my books, especially in *Mabel & the Little Green Men*. I expect you'll find more of them cropping up in the series, but here are just a few…

"Pittsburghese," also known as Western Pennsylvania English, is our beloved regional dialect. It includes unique words, phrases, and pronunciations, many of which are unintelligible for people in other areas of the country. A frequent label for proud speakers of Pittsburghese is "yinzer." Instead of "all of you," "you guys," "you all," or even "you'uns," the yinzer says, "Yinz." (As in "Yinz wanna come over?")

While true Pittsburghese has become less prevalent nowadays, it can still be heard in the area—and it's lovingly preserved elsewhere by expats who long for the sound of their western Pennsylvania youth. If you're curious, I highly recommend a highly entertaining, as well as informative, video by Carnegie Mellon University linguistics professor Barbara Johnstone, explaining Pittsburghese: youtube/H8ihyTbi2Kw.

In this book, Lisa tried to save her parking spot by setting out a chair to show it was spoken for, but an out-of-towner ran it over. While "parking chairs" are especially common in Pittsburgh and other area communities, a few other cities are also known for the practice, including Boston and Chicago. It's easy to sympathize with people in highly-populated neighborhoods who want to save a space in front of their house or apartment—especially if they've just spent over an hour shoveling several feet of snow to clear a spot!

Finally, we enjoyed some regional favorite foods this time around—scrapple and chipped chopped ham barbecue. Scrapple, Mabel's breakfast mush of cornmeal and pork scraps, is Pennsylvania Dutch cuisine and delicious with maple syrup…but maybe an acquired taste?

Lisa's chipped chopped ham barbecue is a western Pennsylvania staple for everything from graduation celebrations to Superbowl parties. Isaly's dairy and deli chain, once a mid-twentieth-century fixture across western Pennsylvania, first introduced chipped chopped ham, a shaved pressed loaf of ham-based luncheon meat. Just pop it in your roaster or slow-cooker with Isaly's sweet signature barbecue sauce for authenticity, or a blend of Heinz ketchup and your barbecue sauce of choice, and let your guests load their buns. Better provide lots of napkins!

For a nostalgic look at Isaly's, including wonderful historic photos, you may want to check out Brian Butko's *Isaly's Chipped Ham, Klondikes, and Other Tales from Behind the Counter*, or his *Klondikes, Chipped Ham, & Skyscraper Cones: The Story of Isaly's*.